HARLEQUIN OFFICE ROMANCE COLLECTION

Who says you can't mix business with pleasure?
Definitely not these couples…

Office politics can be messy as it is, but mix in
a handsome boss or irresistible coworker and
work life becomes plain messy. And the stakes
have never been higher for these couples.
Not only are their careers on the line,
but so are their hearts.

These men and women may have started out
with opposing agendas, intending to keep
things professional, but once the spark is lit,
they know that life on the job is going to be
anything but business as usual.

Professional rivalry never felt so good…
or so complicated!

Christie Ridgway is a *USA TODAY* bestselling author of more than thirty-five contemporary romances. Known for her stories that make readers laugh and cry, Christie began writing romances in fifth grade, inspired by the Harlequin books she loved to read. Later, after marrying her college sweetheart and having two boys, she left the geeky field of computer programming and returned to what she loved best—telling stories of strong men and determined women finding their happy-ever-afters. Christie lives in California. Visit her on the web at christieridgway.com.

USA TODAY Bestselling Author

Christie Ridgway
and
Jennifer McKenzie

ANYTHING BUT BUSINESS

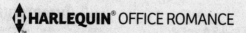

HARLEQUIN® OFFICE ROMANCE

Recycling programs
for this product may
not exist in your area.

ISBN-13: 978-0-373-60127-1

Anything but Business

Copyright © 2015 by Harlequin Books S.A.

The publisher acknowledges the copyright holders
of the individual works as follows:

Bachelor Boss
Copyright © 2008 by Christie Ridgway

That Weekend…
Copyright © 2013 by Jennifer McKenzie

This edition published by arrangement with Harlequin Books S.A.

For questions and comments about the quality of this book,
please contact us at CustomerService@Harlequin.com.

® and TM are trademarks of the publisher. Trademarks indicated with
® are registered in the United States Patent and Trademark Office, the
Canadian Intellectual Property Office and in other countries.

Printed in U.S.A.

www.Harlequin.com

CONTENTS

BACHELOR BOSS

Christie Ridgway

To all the little sisters out there who were never taken as seriously as they should have been— not that I know anything about that!

Chapter 1

Lucy Sutton disliked first days.

Standing before the half-open door leading to her new boss's office, Lucy admitted to herself that in truth she *hated* first days. As family legend had it, she'd hidden at the back of her closet on the first day of kindergarten. While that wasn't clear in her memory, she could recall in vivid detail the first day of high school, the way the tag on her new shirt scratched the back of her neck, how she'd scratched at her nerve-induced hives. The worst, however, was the first day of a new job. Without a mother's hand to hold or a gaggle of girlfriends with whom to get through the hours, that initial eight-to-five at a new place of employment could be excruciating.

Which didn't help explain why Lucy had put herself through quite a few of *those* new days since graduating from college with an accounting degree three years before.

Swallowing to ease her dry mouth, she reminded herself that despite how her employers had liked her and her work, each of those three number-crunching jobs had not been quite right for her. Still, she knew that more than one of her relatives thought it was *Lucy* who wasn't right for successful employment. That was family legend, too, that Lucy, nicknamed "Lucy Goosey" thanks to one of her ultraperfect elder siblings, was just too flighty and too fluffy to take anything seriously— or to be taken seriously by anyone.

Worst of all, though, was how legends like those had an uncomfortable way of becoming fact.

"Not that legend," Lucy murmured to herself, steeling her spine and scratching at a rising bump on her left wrist. "This time I'm going to show every other Sutton that I'm as capable as they are." This job would be different.

Even though it was only temporary secretarial work, she'd stick with it and succeed. Then she'd move on to finding the very best place for herself and her accounting skills. The right position was out there and this was her stepping stone to it.

Her gaze slid over to the nameplate on the wall beside her new boss's office door. Carlo Milano. She had something to prove regarding him, too.

Specifically, that she was over him.

Taking a deep breath, she rapped gently on the grained wood.

"Come in," a man's voice called out.

Lucy found herself hesitating, and instead of moving forward she thought back to the last time she'd seen Carlo. It had been at a big do a couple of years before at her sister, Elise's, home. He'd been making one of his rare appearances, leaning his rangy, six-foot-two body against a wall in a corner of the kitchen, dressed casually in jeans and a button-down shirt. Yet he'd looked anything but casual, his incredible face serious and leaner than ever, as if any soft and approachable thing about him had been pared away.

Pared away by heartaches she knew he wouldn't speak of.

Oh, she'd attempted to lighten his mood that night. Nobody ever said Lucy wasn't one to bring fun to a party. But after trying to get a laugh—she would have settled for a smile!—out of him with an amusing story about an old roommate, Carlo had merely shaken his head.

"Goose," he'd said gently—yes, he'd actually called her *Goose*—"Use your pretty smiles and your charming wiles on someone who'll appreciate them."

Then Carlo had drawn his knuckle down the side of her suddenly heating cheek. In response, and on impulse—another of her weaknesses according to family lore—Lucy had risen to tiptoe and tried one last thing to give Carlo a little jolt of life by brushing her mouth against his.

Seven hundred and thirty-four nights had passed since then, and her lips still burned at the memory.

Her pride still smoldered around the edges, too—because within seconds Carlo had pushed her away and left his corner...never to be seen by her again.

Until now.

"I said 'come in.'" Carlo's almost impatient-sounding voice interrupted her reverie.

Showtime, she thought, and with one last stroke of

right-hand fingernails against her itchy left wrist, Lucy walked into the office.

Her breath caught.

Carlo's massive desk stood in front of her, the leather chair behind it empty, but the wall behind that—ah, that was really something, a whole expanse of glass that revealed a spectacular view of San Diego Bay. It looked like a huge, ten-by-twenty-foot postcard, in which Crayola sky-blue met grayer-blue waters dotted with sailboats and motorboats and yachts. The watercrafts' movement created frothy, egg-white trails across the Pacific's surface and was the only proof they were actually moving and not just part of a lifelike painting titled *Stupendous Southern California.*

It was a multimillion-dollar view that made clear to Lucy that Carlo Milano, longtime family friend and former cop, had struck gold in his high-priced and highly regarded events security business. Obviously he was busy enough to need her to fill in for his secretary for the next three weeks. The man who was her new—albeit temporary—boss had done well for himself.

But where *was* the man who was now her boss?

From the corner of her eye she caught movement at the far end of the room, beyond a spacious seating area that included a love seat, coffee table, two chairs and a built-in bar. A man in a dark jacket was standing there, his back half-turned to Lucy, his attention on a woman in an exquisite powder-blue suit with matching sling backs. Shiny, pin-straight hair fell in a bright chestnut waterfall toward her waist.

The nape of Lucy's neck burned and new hives popped out on her arms. Her hand reached up to finger the ends of her own wheat-colored wavy hair. In her beige heels, khaki skirt and plain white blouse, she'd never felt so, well…washed-out.

And so like a third wheel. The pointy toes of Little Blue Suit's little blue shoes were just inches from the toes of Carlo's cordovan loafers, and the beautiful woman looked one breath away from latching on to his mouth.

What should Lucy do now? Interrupt the moment?

Surely not. Surely it would be better to backpedal out of the office. A woman who wanted—no, needed—to succeed at this job should go back to her desk. A woman who needed—and yes, wanted—to prove to herself she was over her unrequited crush on her boss should do nothing to bar the man from getting lucky.

Or from Carlo getting kissed. She should be happy for him as she snuck away. That's what a grown-up, dignified, over-the-infatuation woman would do.

Grown-up, dignified, over-the-infatuation Lucy heard her throat clear. Not too loudly. But loud enough that her presence couldn't be avoided or ignored.

Argh. How could she have done something so intrusive? Now Carlo wasn't going to be pleased. Now she wasn't feeling the least bit adult and dignified during her first moments on the first day of this new job. And then she heard herself make that attention-demanding, throat-clearing sound again.

Carlo's head turned. He looked her way. "Hey."

Lucy's heart wobbled. There it was, that handsome face she'd never forgotten, those dark eyes taking her in. She couldn't read their expression. Displeasure? Or was that relief?

She wiggled her fingers in return greeting. "Hey." She hoped she looked more together than she felt. Dignified, remember? Adult. But…but…*Carlo about to be kissed by someone else!* Did her weird reaction to that show on her face? "I'm sorry, but you, um, you told me to come in and…"

"No problem." He was moving away from the woman in the teensy suit. Her expression was annoyed, but Carlo didn't appear to be the least affected, let alone angry that Lucy had interrupted his tête-à-tête. If a kiss had been in the offing, he didn't seem worried about the missed opportunity.

Her spirits lifted a little. Maybe this particular first day wasn't going to be too bad, despite her fears. As a matter of fact, Carlo *did* look somewhat pleased as he came toward her. See? It was all good. He didn't appear aware of that little crush she'd once had on him. He may not even recall that impulsive lip-lock she'd laid on him herself two years ago.

Though his nonreaction at the time had only added to her embarrassment, now she was grateful that he seemed to have forgotten it. Yes, in his eyes at this minute she must appear dignified, not to mention all of her twenty-five grown-up years. She took his attitude as an omen for her upcoming job success.

"Damn," he said as he came to a stop in front of her. His long arm reached out to muss her hair the way an uncle would do to a favored young niece. "Long time no see, Goose."

Apparently if she hadn't interrupted a smooch between Carlo and Little Blue Suit, it would have been a kiss-off kind of kiss, anyway. At least that's what he intimated to Lucy—"Please, Carlo, no one calls me Goose anymore," she'd said firmly—when, after ushering his chestnut-haired guest from the office, his first request as her brand-new boss was to ask her to send two dozen roses to the lady who'd just departed. Recipient: a Ms. Tamara Maxwell. Message line: *It wasn't you, it was me.*

He didn't quite meet her eyes when he imparted that interesting nugget, but muttered as he turned back to his office, "Look, we only went out a few times and she didn't get it. I don't do the couple thing."

Lucy got it. She'd always gotten it, though the knowledge had never seemed to cool the particular thing she had for Carlo. Besides the paycheck, putting out that fire for good had been the most pressing reason to accept the job at his company.

When she'd moved back to San Diego, her dad, who was old friends with Carlo's dad, suggested she fill the temporary position at McMillan & Milano before she started a serious search for an accounting position in town. It was supposed to be a favor to Carlo, but it worked for Lucy, too. Moving back to California from Arizona had left her strapped for cash, and acting as his secretary would solve another lingering problem.

The way she figured it, three weeks at McMillan & Milano would finally, for-once-and-for-all, extinguish what she'd always felt for him.

Heck, she decided, watching him walk away from her without a second glance and remembering how easily her humiliatingly juvenile nickname had tripped off his tongue, by quitting time today her libido should finally have heard the message. There was no hope. Carlo would never look at her with the kind of heat a man should hold for a woman.

The idea didn't depress her in the least.

Really.

So she went about her duties, finding this office not so different from any other—including walking into the break room in the late afternoon to find the water cooler drained desert-dry. Stacked on the floor beside it were several full, capped bottles.

"'Water, water, everywhere, but not a drop to drink,'" Lucy murmured, paraphrasing Coleridge to the empty room. She hadn't *just* crunched numbers at school. Shaking her head, she pushed up the cuffs of her sleeves. Even though she wasn't the one who'd tapped the last of the liquid, everyone knew first-day employees couldn't leave the rest of the staff waterless.

No matter that at five foot two and a mere few orders of French fries over her ideal weight, it would be a struggle to replace the bottle. The task was still up to Lucy.

The empty one was a snap to lift away from the top of the water cooler. The blue cap on the closest full bottle took only seconds to peel off. Then, staring down the plastic barrel at her feet as if it were a wrestling opponent, she bent her knees to grasp it around its cool, rotund belly. As she straightened, she staggered on her feet, her heels clattering against the smooth hardwood floor.

Oh, Lord, don't let me drop this.

"Goose, what are you doing?"

Instinct had her swinging toward the voice—Carlo's voice—but that only made her more unsteady on her business-beige heels. Before she could do more than wheeze, there were a man's arms around her—Carlo's arms. Her back was up against his chest, her butt pressed to his—

"Stop," he ordered into her ear.

"I wasn't thinking anything!"

"Obviously not. You're too small to take care of this. I meant 'stop trying to help.' Let go and let me have the bottle."

"Oh." She dropped her hands from the heavy plastic, but that still left her in the circle of Carlo's arms. His warmth was at her spine, his delicious aftershave in her nose, his breath stirring the hair at her temple.

As a wild rash of prickly awareness broke out like more hives over her skin, she dipped under his arm and freed herself from his faux embrace. Without a glance at her, he stepped forward to flip the bottle on top of the cooler.

He turned to find her fanning her face.

"Goo— Lucy..." His voice trailed off as his gaze dropped lower. His eyes widened, then he looked back up. "You, uh, have a couple of buttons that came loose."

She glanced down, gasped. In her struggles with the water bottle, apparently some of the buttons on her all-business blouse had popped free, revealing most of her white lace demibra. Her face burning, she clutched the shirt's edges together with one hand while hastily refastening with the other.

"Relax," Carlo said. "It's just me."

"Yeah. Just you," Lucy repeated.

Just the man she'd dreamed about since she was fifteen years old.

She managed to get decent once more, but was still struggling with the top buttonhole when her new boss made a brotherly noise and moved in as she continued to fumble. "Here. Let me finish it up."

He was wearing an easy, indulgent smile as he pushed her hands away and reached toward her collar. For an instant, his fingertips brushed the hollow at her throat and she jerked in helpless reaction, her pulse pounding against his touch. He froze, his fingertips now only making contact with button and fabric.

Still, his nostrils flared and she could smell her perfume rise around them, the scent surging stronger as her heart continued to hammer in her chest.

He cleared his throat. "Goose," he said. "You smell like a girl."

A nervous bubble of laughter escaped her throat. "Carlo, I *am* a girl."

"Right. Yeah." He made quick work of the stubborn top button, then retreated toward the doorway. There, he shoved his hands in his pockets and cocked his head, studying her. "Actually, you're more than a girl. You're a woman."

"You noticed?" If it hadn't been obvious before, this little comment made it crystal clear that the kitchen-kiss two years before hadn't even rated his attention.

He leaned one shoulder against the jamb and gave her a half smile. "Now I think I'll find it hard to forget."

The deep note in his voice stroked like a brush down Lucy's spine, bumping against each vertebrae. Her tongue swiped at her dry bottom lip and she watched his eyes follow the movement.

Suddenly, her heart sped up again, her pulse fluttering against the place at her throat that still throbbed from his accidental touch. Was…was Carlo looking at her with a masculine kind of interest?

She took in the gleam in his deep-set, dark eyes and then tried to find more clues in the aquiline line of his masculine nose and the sensual curve of his full mouth. He was a beautiful man, every artistic angle of his face a testament to his Italian heritage—but she couldn't read his expression.

She licked her bottom lip again.

Carlo abruptly straightened, his gaze dropping away. "So, uh, Goose—"

"Lucy." And didn't that answer her question? No man would feel the least bit of lust for someone he thought of as "Goose." Disappointment coursed through her, even though she'd taken the job for this—to finally accept there was no mutual heat between her and Carlo.

No heat. No hope.

"So, *Lucy,* I suppose I should get back to work."

With an inward sigh, she followed him with her gaze as he strode down the hall, admiring the way the European cut of his pale blue dress shirt accentuated the muscled leanness of his back and waist. She didn't try to find a word for how she felt about the curve of his tight, masculine behind in the dark slacks.

Three weeks, Lucy. Three weeks to look, but not touch. Three weeks to accept, finally, that's all you'll ever have of him.

A few minutes before five, she was congratulating herself on making it through the could-be-disastrous initial day, when a messenger appeared with a high-priority package for Carlo. Fine, she thought, she'd deliver the slender cardboard envelope and bid him good-night at the same time. Then her first day on the job, and her first day with Carlo, would be behind her.

At her tap on his door, he called her inside. This time he was sitting behind his desk, file folders in front of him, his computer screen angled just so.

He looked up as she entered. "Lucy. Just the person

I've been thinking about all afternoon," he said, leaning back in his chair.

Her fingers squeezed the package. "Me?" The view behind him was still awe-inspiring, but she couldn't drag her gaze away from his face to appreciate it. He'd been thinking about her?

"I realize I don't know what brought you back to San Diego."

"Oh." What to say? Dissatisfaction with the jobs she'd found in the accounting industry she'd spent four years preparing herself for? It made her sound so flighty. So, well…ditzy and goosey, especially when every Sutton sibling had gone straight from graduation to climbing the ladder of success in the corporations they'd joined right after college. "Of course, you know I'm from here, and…"

"Your father mentioned something to mine about disappointments in Phoenix?"

She shifted her weight on her feet. "Well…um…" Her face was heating up again and she didn't know what more to say. While she knew the jobs in Phoenix had not been quite right for her, would Carlo, like her family, only see her as unable to settle down?

"I got to thinking you might have had man trouble."

Lucy blinked. Man trouble? The only man trouble she'd had recently was the trouble she had forgetting about Carlo and the feelings for him she couldn't seem to stamp out. "It's not—"

"I admit that until just a couple of hours ago I was still picturing you at about fourteen years old in my mind. Banged-up knees, a mouthful of braces and all those white-gold curls."

Terrific. While she'd been tossing and turning at

night, wondering what it would be like to be with him, his lingering image of her was something that sounded horribly close to Pippi Longstocking.

Carlo cleared his throat. "But now I see that you're all grown-up. Like I said earlier, a woman."

Hmm. That sounded more interesting. And even more interesting than that was the way he was staring at her mouth again. Could it be…?

Uncertain, Lucy held her breath as the atmosphere in the room seemed to ripple with a new, tingly charge.

He jerked his gaze from her mouth to her eyes. "And I was thinking maybe you're here because someone broke your heart."

"Oh. No. N-not yet." Because so far she hadn't quite accepted she could never have Carlo. And now, with this new shimmer of tension in the room, she was even less sure it could never be.

No, Lucy. No! Don't delude yourself!

Listening to her common sense, she interrupted the drift of the conversation by sliding the priority envelope in front of him. "Anyway, this just came for you. It looks important."

When he picked it up, she turned. "I'll see you tomorrow, Carlo."

"Wait."

She didn't spin back around. "It's after five."

"But we're old friends, and I was thinking that since you're doing me the big favor of filling in—" His voice broke off. *"Damn."*

Curiosity reversed the direction of her feet. "You were thinking…?"

He was staring down at what looked to be a pair of

tickets in his hands. "I was thinking, no, I *know*," he said, grimacing, "that I could use a date for tonight."

Lucy swallowed. "Is there someone you'd like me to get on the phone for you? Tamara, or…?"

"You, Lucy."

"Me?" She was beginning to sound like an echo machine.

Carlo was up and around his desk before she could run for the door. Not that she really wanted to. Not when he came close enough to do up her buttons again…or undo them.

The air was jittering with tension. And heat. Or maybe that was just her. No. *No.* Carlo was standing over her and she saw his nostrils flare as he took in another breath of her perfume. He was looking at her in a manner that surely he wouldn't waste on Pippi Longstocking.

You smell like a girl.

I see that you're all grown up.

A woman.

"So will you go with me to a party tonight?" he asked.

She curled her fingernails into her palms. "Oh, well…"

"I can introduce you around. Maybe find you—"

"The man I've been missing?" Lucy couldn't say what made her utter the words. They came out of nowhere, sounding a little hoarse, a little flirty, a little like she was flirting with *him*.

She felt both appalled and excited. Outside of a few jokes and that one humiliating kiss, she'd never been overt when dealing with him.

Carlo's brow lifted, and a corner of his mouth ticked up, too. One of his fingers reached out to wrap itself around a lock of her hair. He tugged. "Lucy. Is that what you're looking for?"

Her tongue trailed across her bottom lip and she lowered her lashes—again in what seemed a totally unthought-out, yet obviously flirty way—to gaze at him through them. "It depends on how far I'll have to go to find him."

Carlo shook his head, an amused, masculine smile quirking both corners of his mouth. "My, my, my. You *have* grown up."

Enough to know what this was. No mistaking it now. Carlo was looking at her with a new kind of interest, with the sort of heat she'd only fantasized about before. Her blood raced through her body, waking up thousands of nerve endings with the thrilling news.

Carlo's looking at me the way a man looks at a woman!

His knuckle ran down her cheek and she felt it all the way to her toes. "Eight o'clock," he said. "Cocktail attire."

"Yes." *Yes, yes, yes!*

"Where shall I pick you up?"

The racing movement of Lucy's blood stopped, stilling in one fell *swoosh*. That shimmering heat continued between them, but she wondered for just how long.

"Where, Lucy?"

"My sister's. Until I find my own place, I'm staying with Elise."

And then Lucy had her answer. The tension, the temperature, the thread of attraction running between them didn't last even another moment, instead dropping like an anchor from one of the boats traveling through the bay she could see over his shoulder. She leveled her gaze at the pretty sight, even as she noted the unpretty view of Carlo's expression closing down.

His hand dropped, his feet stepped away. "I'll be there at eight."

He didn't renege on the invitation. Former cop, old family friend that he was, he wouldn't be out-and-out rude to her. Even if it meant picking Lucy up at the home of her married sister.

Her sister. The unrequited love of Carlo Milano's life.

Chapter 2

There was a rap on the door of the guest bedroom as Lucy stood before the open closet, frowning. "Come in."

Her sister stuck her head inside the room. "Dad called while you were in the shower. He wanted to know how your first day went."

"I hope you told him I haven't quit," Lucy said. "And I didn't get fired, either," she continued, muttering under her breath. Though not true, she suspected that was what her family had assumed each time she'd changed jobs.

Her grumble caused a frown to mar her sister's perfect face as she stepped into the bedroom and swung the door shut behind her. "Are you okay?"

Lucy avoided a probing gaze by turning back to the closet. "Cocktail attire. For an advance party to hype the Street Beat rock music festival at the end of the month. Don't you think that calls for something a bit less conservative than a little black dress?"

"I don't know," Elise replied, coming to stand beside her. "You're the music lover. Carlo was smart to invite you."

"Yeah. Smart." Lucy figured it was more out of convenience than IQ. Carlo had needed a date for the business thing and she'd been the closest available woman. Those short moments of self-delusion when she'd thought her fantasies had come true…well, self-delusion said it all. "Since I'm working for him, I thought I'd better say yes. Though I'm sure he has a black book full of numbers he could have called."

"He dates. I know that."

Lucy slid a look at her sister. How much *did* Elise know? Was she at all aware of Carlo's feelings for her? Lucy didn't think so. Even though, when Elsie had married her husband, John, six years before, it had been clear to anyone paying close attention that Carlo had lost the girl of his dreams.

Lucy had noticed because he'd been the man of hers, but she doubted that Carlo had ever deliberately shared with others how being best man at Elise's wedding had broken his heart. Lucy might have doubted it herself, except on the big day, wearing her own bridesmaid's tulle, she'd overheard Carlo's sister guess aloud his bitter secret. Lucy's own heart had fractured as he'd reluctantly confirmed the truth. The woman of his dreams was walking down the aisle. Away from him.

But it hadn't changed the way she felt about him, ever. Just as his stiff expression when she'd mentioned her sister made it clear his feelings for Elise were rock solid.

It was why Lucy hadn't made up her mind about what to do tonight. Should she really go? There was still time to claim a migraine or call in an excuse of stomach cramps.

Still uncertain, she reached for a hanger draped with a stretchy garment in sunset colors and sprinkled with sequins. "What do you think about this?" she asked, holding the various straps and scraps of fabric against her terry-cloth robe.

Elise's laugh burst out.

"What?"

Her sister couldn't seem to stop grinning. "Oh, I think you're going to be good for our Carlo."

Her Carlo, Lucy corrected. "I don't understand."

"Let's put it this way. Getting out of police work and into his own successful business didn't lighten up the man."

"Losing a partner to a bullet might account for that," Lucy defended, frowning at her sister. "Patrick McMillan was like a second father to Carlo."

Elise sighed. "It wasn't a criticism."

Crossing to the bed, Lucy tossed the dress down and then grabbed a bottle of lotion from the dresser and started to smooth the cream over her legs. "What did you mean by it, then?"

"You've seen how he's changed over the years," her sister said. "He used to smile more. Heck, he used to laugh. But now he ducks from most of the invitations our group of friends sends out, and when he does say yes, he broods in a corner or brings a date who does all his talking for him."

Like that too-pretty Tamara? Though apparently she was yesterday's news.

"I don't think he knows how to have fun anymore." Elise nodded toward the spangled dress stretched across the bedspread. "Maybe you could make that part of your job description."

Lucy's palm stopped halfway up her shin. "Aren't you afraid I'd botch that up just like I've botched up every other job I've had since graduation?" She knew that's what they all thought, even though leaving her positions in the accounting departments of the law firm, the school district and the insurance company had been completely voluntary. It wasn't that she hadn't done good work...it was that she hadn't *enjoyed* it.

Elise rolled her eyes. "You've been listening to our brothers too much."

"*And* Dad. And then there's Mom, who just keeps giving me these worried glances." Elise wasn't so innocent, either. All of them couldn't fathom why Lucy had yet to find the right job.

"Remember," her sister said, "you're the baby of the family."

"But for pity's sake, I'm not a baby anymore!"

Elise nodded, then leaned over to pluck the almost-nothing dress from off its place on the mattress. "I'm getting that. But maybe it's time you made it clear to everyone else."

Oh, great, Lucy thought. Just another item to put on her list. Don't screw up the temp job, do get over Carlo, do make clear to the public-at-large that Lucy Sutton was no longer in pigtails and braces.

On that last thought, Carlo invaded her mind again. *I see that you're all grown-up.*

A woman.

For a moment she'd actually believed he *did* see that. That he saw *her*. But then she'd mentioned Elise's name and he'd gone distant and cool. No more masculine gleam in his eyes and no more half smile on his mouth. As usual, for Carlo, it was always Elise.

So why should she go through with this "date" tonight? She could comfortably stay home and still torture herself with that particular piece of knowledge.

But no! She capped the lotion with a vehement snap. Elise was right. Lucy should be out there proving she was no longer the Suttons' silly youngest sibling. Tonight didn't have to be about Carlo. Or about Carlo and Elise. Or about Carlo, and never Lucy.

Tonight could be about Lucy alone. If she focused on herself, maybe she could move into the future, leaving him the lone soul left wallowing in what-couldn't-be. Tonight, she should, no, she *would* go to the party as a single, sophisticated woman instead of a goosey love-struck girl.

Her older sister wandered off, leaving Lucy alone to finish prepping for the evening. After putting on makeup and smoothing her hair into straight strands with the flat iron, she wiggled into the stretchy dress she'd selected, adjusting the straps over her braless breasts and criss-crossing them on her bare back in order to tie the ends at her waist. Then she inspected herself in the mirror.

Okay. This was no baby-sister kind of dress. She'd purchased it at a boutique in Phoenix, at a supersale that even then cleaned out her clothing budget. The colors—ranging from palest yellow to the most passionate pink—mimicked a Southwest sunset and brightened her blond hair and fair skin. She paired it with high-heeled pink sandals and a raspberry lip gloss guaranteed to last all night long.

Through kisses and anything else, the product's sexy ad promised.

She didn't let her mind go *there,* though then it did, even without her permission. But why not? Maybe she would meet an attractive man at the party. Maybe he would kiss her.

It could happen.

She heard the doorbell ring, followed by the distant murmur of voices. Her brother-in-law, John's, the deeper rumble of Carlo's.

Her little shiver was merely because the night was turning cooler, of course.

So stifling any second thoughts, she grabbed a gauzy wrap and her evening purse, then headed out of the bedroom and down the hallway. A single, sophisticated woman on the way to a party.

Despite herself, her forward motion stopped just short of the living room. From her place in the shadows, she took in the tableau in front of her.

Her sister and brother-in-law were seated on the couch, Lucy's "date" standing before them. Carlo was dressed in ash-gray slacks and a matching ash-gray silky-looking T-shirt, topped by a black linen sports jacket. He looked relaxed and, well, rich, the shine of his loafers mimicking the gleam of his dark hair. His mouth curved in polite amusement as John related something funny about work. After a moment, Carlo's eyes flickered away from his friend's face to light on Lucy's sister's classic features.

It seemed to her that his smile faded and his eyes turned empty.

Perhaps she made some movement then, giving herself away, because Carlo's gaze suddenly jumped to where Lucy was lurking. Hoping to cover for her staring, she immediately stepped into the living room, her shoulders back, her hips swaying. A sophisticated, single woman on her way to a party.

A sophisticated single woman who watched Carlo's carefully blank expression turn to one of blatant disapproval.

Her first-day nerves returned with a vengeance. Hives felt as if they were rising all over her skin. She would have turned and run, but her sophisticated, single-girl high heels allowed for no fast getaways.

Carlo Milano didn't like parties in general. He didn't like the one he was headed to tonight in particular. In particular, because he was accompanied by five feet and a hundred pounds of potential danger. Five feet and a hundred pounds of potential danger wearing high heels and a flaming-hot dress.

Closing his eyes as he shut the passenger door on her and the view of her bare, slender legs, he allowed himself a groan. If only he hadn't broken things off with Tamara, she would be his date tonight.

Tamara and her palpable hopes for a happily-ever-after life story, with him starring as the male lead.

It was why he'd been forced to end what had been pleasantly pleasant enough. When she'd started making noises about shared vacations and opportunities to meet her parents, he'd felt honor-bound to halt her building expectations. He just didn't think that type of happy ending was written into the Carlo Milano movie script.

Not that he didn't believe in happy endings. He'd seen his sister and many of his friends successfully couple up. Not for a minute did he doubt their commitments to their lovers. He went to each wedding wishing them all the best.

But at one wedding… At one wedding he'd started letting go of the notion of a lifelong romantic partnership for himself.

Then, when he'd lost his police partner to an unfair and untimely murder…he'd been certain he was destined to do the life thing solo.

Not to mention it just seemed simpler that way.

"La Jolla isn't in this direction," piped up the young beauty beside him. "I thought you said the party was in La Jolla."

He kept his focus out the windshield instead of glancing again at the blonde wrapped in salsa that was little Lucy Sutton all grown-up. Curse whatever combination of curiosity and kindness had prompted him to ask her out in the first place.

Kindness.

Right. The truth was, the water-cooler incident in the break room had snapped something inside of him. One moment he'd been remembering her as a bubblegum-popping tweenie, the next he was seeing her as a woman. Desirable. Beddable.

Though not available, of course. Not available to him, anyway. There were several reasons that made that a fact: she was an old family friend and almost like a little sister to him; her brothers were among his best friends and would beat him to a pulp if he and Lucy hooked up and he ended up hurting her; and he'd never forgive himself if—when—that very likelihood came to pass.

Still, aware of all that, he'd opened his big mouth and extended the invitation.

So here he was with Lucy. Desirable. Beddable.
Pure trouble.

His years as a street cop, then as a detective, then
as a security expert had finely honed his instincts, and
his instincts said she was mischief in the making. Lucy
Sutton wearing that dress and looking like that in it was
going to be up to her curvy hips in trouble tonight if he
didn't stay on the ball.

"Carlo?"

He sighed. "We're making a stop before the party."
Thank God. Anything to minimize the amount of time
he'd have to be on guard-dog patrol. "You wouldn't by
any chance dislike loud music and large crowds?"

He caught her grin out of the corner of his eye. "I
love loud music and large crowds."

"Figures," he grumbled.

She laughed. "Why are we going, then, if you dislike the party scene so much?"

"You know. It's a work obligation." His calendar
bulged with them. In a convention town that was also
home to major league sports teams and that hosted big-
name golf tournaments, as well as big-star rock con-
certs, McMillan & Milano's services were in constant
demand. "The company's in charge of security for the
Street Beat festival three weeks from now and I've got
to put in an appearance and do the good ol' grip-and-
grin for at least a few minutes."

Fewer than few, if he could get away with it. If Lucy
Sutton had rattled him, not only a family friend but a
man known as Mr. Keep-It-Light-and-Loose, what effect
might she have on males who were actively prowling?

He shook his head. She was heading for trouble,
all right.

Flipping his car's signal indicator, he turned right into the driveway of a well-maintained two-story, his gaze noting that the landscaping crew was keeping the hedges manicured and the lawns fertilized per his orders. The porch light added a cheery brightness to the entry, complete with a wreath of dried fall foliage on the front door.

"Come in with me," he suggested to Lucy. "You've met Germaine McMillan before, haven't you? I said I'd stop by and take care of a minor repair for her."

Again, he kept his eyes off Lucy's legs as she exited the car. But he couldn't keep her light scent away from his nose as they waited for Germaine to answer the ringing doorbell. The fragrance had caught his attention in the break room at the office, too, and remembering that brought back that quick flash he'd had of her plump, pretty breasts rising from the white lace cups of her bra.

To distract himself from the memory, he ran his hand over the molding around the doorjamb. Good. The paint was tight.

For some damn reason, so the hell were the muscles south of his waistline.

He could have kissed Germaine for choosing that instant to open the door. Actually, he did kiss her, an obligatory peck on her soft cheek that dimpled as he moved away and brought his companion forward.

"Do you remember Lucy Sutton?" he asked his partner's widow. "I'm sure you've met her before, as well as various other members of the Sutton family over the years."

"Of course!" Germaine appeared delighted by the company, which was part of the reason why he'd scheduled the stop. Like the landscaping, he could have hired out the minor repair. But without children or grandchildren of her own, Carlo knew the older woman enjoyed his visits. Just as he'd felt obligated to keep Patrick McMillan's name as part of the security firm the two of them had dreamed up before Pat's death, Carlo felt obligated to be the family Germaine didn't have. "Can I get you two some coffee and dessert?" she asked.

They followed her into the immaculate living room, where fresh vacuum trails showed clearly on the cream carpet. "Nothing for me, thanks," Lucy replied. "We're on our way to a party."

Germaine sat down on the floral couch and Lucy followed suit. "I shouldn't be keeping the pair of you, then."

Carlo waved his hand. "There's no rush. We have plenty of time. The party's bound to be boring, anyway."

And Lucy would be a whole lot easier to watch over among the flower fields that were Germaine's upholstered furniture than she would be at a party filled with rock musicians, businessmen and media types.

"Oh, you," Germaine scolded. "A man your age should enjoy a little nightlife."

Lucy leaned toward her. "We're not even there yet and he's already grumping about the music being too loud. Who knew what a fuddy-duddy he'd turn out to be?"

"Fuddy-duddy?" He frowned at her. *Fuddy-duddy?* For some reason the teasing jab ignited his usually cool temper. "Is that what you think? But coming from someone dressed in nothing more than a scanty pair of handkerchiefs, I'll take that as a compliment."

Lucy's spine straightened. She looked a little bit insulted, too. "Handkerchiefs? I'll have you know this dress is—"

"Outrageous?" *Fuddy-duddy.* He couldn't get the insult out of his mind. "An invitation to pneumonia?"

Her berry-colored mouth fell open and her blue, blue eyes narrowed. "You're—"

"Children, children," Germaine interrupted, her voice verging on laughter. "Maybe we should change the subject."

"You're right." Annoyed by his own out-of-character reaction to Lucy's silly jibes, Carlo shoved his hands in his pockets. "I'll do better than that and in fact change the washers of the dripping faucet like I said I would."

Germaine started to rise, but he shook his head. "I know where I'm going and I know where you keep Pat's tools."

He couldn't exit the living room fast enough. If he didn't already know that Lucy had potential to be a snag in the smooth path of his planned evening, that last exchange would have been proof positive. How the hell had she gotten under his skin so fast?

Fuddy-duddy. Grumping. Good God, he didn't grump. How ridiculous.

But damn, if the descriptions hadn't rankled.

Passing the hall portrait of his late partner on the way to the dripping bathroom faucet, Carlo felt his mood dip even lower. As he tinkered, he thought of Pat's stocky frame and square, capable hands. The man should be here, Carlo thought on a sudden stab of sadness. Pat should be here, working out of his own red toolbox while looking forward to an evening of yet another TV documentary on military history, as well as a slice of his wife's famous mocha cheesecake.

Instead, Carlo's partner was gone.

Gone forever.

Upon completion of the repair, his footsteps were as heavy as his frame of mind as he returned to the living room. Hesitating at the archway, he listened to Germaine's amused voice.

"Then he turned the corner as fast as his old legs could go, wheezing, he said, sure that he'd lost the suspect, only to find the teenager caught on a cyclone fence, hanging upside down by his own oversize trousers."

Carlo remembered the moment as if it were yesterday and he couldn't resist adding to the story. "His own oversize trousers that had fallen down to his ankles, leaving his, uh, assets flapping in the breeze." Coming farther into the room, he couldn't help but grin at the memory. "Pat picked up the fancy cell phone that had fallen out of the boy's pocket and took a picture for posterity, while the dumb kid yammered on and on about police brutality."

He laughed. "Pat told him the only brutal thing about the event was his having to be subjected to a view of the kid's skinny butt." Laughing again, he recalled the expression of insulted outrage on the perp's upside-down face.

"Oh, Carlo."

The odd note in Germaine's voice zeroed his gaze in on her. "What?"

She smiled. "It's good to hear you laugh. It's good that we can remember my Pat with lightness in our hearts. He'd want that."

Carlo felt the smile he was wearing die as yet another pang of sadness sliced through him. All that Pat had wanted was to grow old with his beloved wife. Just a few relaxed and peaceful years of happily-ever-after.

He turned away, embarrassed by his sudden grief and just as determined to hide it. His hand speared through his hair and he cleared his throat. "Anything else I can do for you, Germaine?" His voice still sounded thick.

"No, but, Carlo…" Germaine's own suddenly teary voice filled with a sympathy he couldn't handle, yet couldn't run away from, either. Without looking at her, he sensed her rising and he steeled himself, desperate not to be weakened by any more emotion.

But then Lucy was there first, her hand looping around his arm. "Well, then I think we should be going, Germaine. I have to get the fuddy-duddy to the party before he turns into a pumpkin."

A new jolt of annoyance overrode his other feelings. *Fuddy-duddy* again! *Pumpkin.* He shook his head, frowning down into her bright face and naughty smile.

"Brat," he murmured. Okay, beautiful, but a brat all the same.

Germaine brightened. "Yes, yes. You must go on to your evening out."

Lucy's answer was to tug him toward the door. "Did you hear that, Carlo? Let's get a move on or next thing I know you'll be too busy filling out your AARP membership forms to find your way to a party."

Half-amused by her burst of energy and half-bemused by her second round of insults, he allowed her to pull him through the front door and toward his car. Even without a rock band, she was already dancing along the pavement and chattering away about the stars, the clear sky, how happy she was to be back in San Diego, which always held a hint of ocean in the night air.

When he pulled out of the driveway, he realized he was smiling again. Relaxed. She took a breath and he took advantage of the brief moment of quiet. "Lucy, I'm…"

"Feeling better?"

His head jerked her way. Her gaze was on him, her eyes big. Empathetic.

She knew.

She'd known he was close to losing it back there in Germaine's living room.

It was as embarrassing as hell to realize, but now it was clear that Lucy had intentionally come to his rescue. By stepping in with her sassy attitude and smart remarks, Lucy had given him the time and the distraction necessary to compose himself. Germaine hadn't needed him dumping his sorrow on top of her own.

Lucy had made sure he didn't.

"Lucy…" He was at a loss for words, still embarrassed that she'd read him so easily. Swallowing, he tried again. "You…"

She sent him that bright brat smile and fiddled with the hem of her too-short dress. "Look great in a pair of handkerchiefs, right?"

His gaze fell to her half-naked legs, then jumped back to the impish curve of her bright berry mouth. His blood rushed south and he felt that recognizable tightness at his groin. Of course, it couldn't be because of Lucy and how good she smelled and how delectable she looked in that dress. She was an old family friend, so it wasn't—

Oh, fine. What the hell. Why deny it? He was a man, with all the normal male responses. The truth was, old family friend or not, Lucy Sutton turned him on.

The admission sent his cop instincts hog wild again. This time they had another loud-and-clear message. *Be careful,* they told him. *Be very careful.*

She was still the little sister of some of his best friends, Elise and the sisters' brothers, Jason and Sam.

The Suttons and the Milanos had been connected for years and would continue to be connected for years to come.

So don't risk introducing awkwardness into the mix.

So don't risk getting too close to a woman who'd already shown herself adept at understanding his moods.

He took another breath of her sweet, feminine perfume. *Yeah, Milano, don't risk getting too close.* Because of the two people sitting in the butter leather seats of his Lexus, he had the sudden premonition that the one most likely to get into trouble tonight was him.

Chapter 3

Carlo Milano was wrong about a lot of things, Lucy decided, as they entered the Street Beat party. One, the music *wasn't* too loud, and two, judging by what other women were wearing who were in attendance, there was nothing unusual about her cocktail attire.

"Fuddy-duddy," she muttered to herself.

He leaned closer. "What?"

She glanced up. Okay, he didn't look like a fuddy-duddy, not with those incredible dark lashes surrounding his incredible dark eyes, and not with the way his wide shoulders filled out his casual linen jacket. And she wasn't the only one to have noticed his dearth of duddiness, either. She'd seen it in the eyes of other women they'd passed, and now, good Lord, now there was a tall, statuesque brunette wearing a slinky animal print sliding out of the crowd to close in on them like a leopard scenting a tasty meal.

The feline woman was still two dozen feet away when she called out the name of her prey. "Carlo!"

Lucy couldn't help it, she stepped closer to him. Her hip brushed his groin, and she all at once recalled her plan for the evening. *Not* sticking close to Carlo. *Not* fostering dreams that couldn't be.

Remember? She was a single, sophisticated woman at a party. A single, sophisticated woman who should be looking for other single sophisticates, but of the masculine variety. Clearing her throat, she ignored the approaching woman and started edging away from Carlo's body. "I think I'll go—"

"Stay," he said against her ear. It felt more like a kiss than a command and she froze, making it easy for him to hook two fingers into the waistline at the back of her dress. She felt his knuckles press against her naked skin.

"Carlo—"

"I'll give you a raise if you'll just play along."

There wasn't any more time to protest. The brunette appeared before them on a waft of Chanel No. 5. "Mr. Milano," she said in a scolding voice. "This is beyond fashionably late."

Then the woman moved in for the kill—uh, greeting—and Lucy tried to edge away again. Carlo's fingers curled tighter on her dress, though, plastering her as snugly against him as a "Hi, My Name Is" sticker.

The action forced the other woman to settle for an air kiss in the vicinity of his chin. Then she gave Lucy a cursory glance. "I'm Claudia Cox," she said, holding out her hand even as her gaze returned to Carlo. "So… Who's your little friend?"

Lucy gritted her teeth and gave a little handshake as

Carlo answered. "This is Lucy Sutton. She's just back in town from Phoenix."

Claudia flicked another glance in her direction. "Really? I thought you were seeing Tamara."

His hand slipped out of Lucy's dress to slide around her waist and then press possessively against her hip bone. She tried to look as if her knees were melting—for Claudia's benefit—without standing as if her knees *were* really melting—for Carlo's.

"I'm with Lucy now." He pressed a kiss to the top of her head and her scalp prickled from crown to nape.

"Lucky Lucy," Claudia commented, wearing a thin smile.

Lucy thought it was time to chime in and prove to them all she still had a voice. "That's just what I say to myself every time I hear this man say my name. It's nice to meet you, Claudia." Then she entwined her fingers with those of Carlo's that were wrapped at her hip and tried to subtly peel them off before her dress started to smolder.

His touch made her just that hot.

Carlo allowed their joined hands to fall to her side, but stroked hers with a caressing thumb when Claudia's gaze dropped to their fingers.

"We need to set up a meeting," the other woman told Carlo, her voice a bit sharp, "since it doesn't look as if you're prepared to talk business tonight."

Behind her, Lucy felt Carlo straighten. His thumb stopped its distracting movement. "What's up, Claudia?"

The other woman looked at Lucy. "Do you mind...?"

"Oh, no," she said, taking the hint. "I'll just go over to the bar and leave you two alone—"

"Sweetheart, you know I don't like you out of my sight." Carlo's fingers squeezed hers. Tight.

Lucy swallowed her wince. "Isn't he cute?" she said to Claudia, then looked up at her date. "Darling, I won't go far."

"Baby, I don't think so." His hand gave hers another warning squeeze. "Stay with me."

Baby? That's what she was supposed to be proving she *wasn't* tonight. And she knew he was a boy big enough to handle leopard lady and whatever the heck she wanted to discuss in private.

Lucy beamed Carlo a sickly smile. "Handsome, Claudia wants to talk about business, and you know how little me gets so sleepy when talk turns to numbers and such."

Of course, that was uncomfortably close to the truth. And uncomfortably terrible for someone who'd graduated with honors and an accounting degree to admit.

Claudia shook her head, apparently impatient with them both. "It's not about numbers. I only wanted to let you know that I've okayed a parents group from a local high school to help out with the security."

"Street Beat security?" He sent Lucy a glance, then went on to explain, "Claudia's the festival promoter."

"For the past five years," the older woman added before turning her attention to Carlo again. "The parents are going to use their pay as a fund-raiser for their kids' senior prom. The fairgrounds did something similar last summer. It will be good PR for us."

He frowned. "But parents? I don't know, Claudia. I'll want to talk to the fair security people, and even if they think it went well, I'm not sure—"

"Oh, you should at least consider it," Lucy interjected. "I was part of a community group that raised money in Phoenix last year during the hot air balloon festival weekend. We helped out with security and parking. It worked out great for everyone concerned."

"Yeah?" Carlo lifted an eyebrow.

Even Claudia was looking at Lucy with more interest. "Yes," she confirmed. "We had kids involved, too, because they're always looking for ways to beef up their college applications with community service. If they were over sixteen and accompanied by a parent, they were welcome, too."

"Carlo," Claudia said, looking less leopardlike and more thoughtful. "That sounds even better to me. I think it could increase future ticket sales if more teenagers are exposed to the festival."

"I see your point, but—"

"It's not supplanting your security plans," Claudia insisted. "It's supporting them. The volunteers can do simple things like move barriers and keep order in the food lines."

Carlo switched his gaze to Lucy. "How much do you know about how it worked in Phoenix?"

She shrugged. "It was my baby. I pulled the volunteers together, I worked with the regular balloonfest security people, I spent the weekend slathered in sunscreen and passing out water bottles. It's like Claudia said, we were essentially gofers for the professional security team and we made good money for a local women's shelter."

"Sounds like you made it a success."

"It didn't take a brain trust, just attention to detail and an ability to organize people. I can give you the phone number of a guy in Phoenix—"

"Don't bother," he said. "Any calls that need to be made you can do yourself. This endeavor in San Diego will be your baby, too."

She stared at him. "My baby?"

"Your project. You work for McMillan & Milano."

"Well, yes." And apparently in his rush to deflect predator Claudia's interest he hadn't concerned himself about what the other woman might think about his mixing business with pleasure inside his own office.

"So I'm putting you in charge of the high school volunteers at the Street Beat festival."

"I work for McMillan & Milano answering your phone and bringing you your mail," she protested.

Carlo waved it away. "Because you agreed to help out with that job as a favor, not because it's the position you're suited for. You're the one with experience managing a volunteer activity like this. And even though you say it doesn't take a brain trust, I happen to know you have a sharp mind, as well as a college degree your parents are very proud of. So, I've decided. It's your project, Lucy."

It's my project. Just something else to potentially screw up in the next three weeks because, lucky for her, the music event was scheduled at the end of her time with Carlo's company. Was it now that she told him? Was it now she admitted that in the years since graduation she'd yet to find a position she *was* suited for? Surely, like the Suttons, he'd see it as a major flaw in her character that not one of her accounting jobs had floated her boat. Unlike her forge-straight-ahead family, she'd yet to find her path to success. She opened her mouth.

Claudia beat her to the punch. "Carlo…" The other woman's lips moved into a moue of distress and she lowered her voice as if she considered Lucy deaf, as well as dumb. "Do you really think your little phone answerer is the right person for the job?"

Little.

Little phone answerer.

Lucy's spine snapped straight as she heard in those words and that voice echoes of other words, other voices.

Little Lucy.

Lucy Goosey.

Lucy won't do it right this time, either.

Carlo lifted one dark brow. "Lucy?"

She swallowed. No way could she back down now, not in front of Claudia of the leopard dress and superior attitude, not in front of Carlo, who would likely pass along her balking to her sister and brothers, not in front of *herself* who had so many things to prove.

And now add one more.

"Don't worry, Claudia," she said. "His little phone answerer will be just fine."

Oh, how she wished she'd stuck to her plan and un-stuck herself from Carlo. It was too late, though. There was nothing else to do but accept, and then succeed at this Street Beat assignment. She pushed away her panic at the thought, even though in the past three years she hadn't truly felt successful at much besides finding an-other job after leaving the previous one behind.

Somehow, Lucy had gotten away from him. The lon-ger Carlo didn't see her among the crowd at the Street Beat party, the more anxious he was to get his hands on her—uh, correct that. The more anxious he was to get a bead on where she was. *Hands* off, *Milano*. It was the cop inside him talking again, and his good sense, too. *Hands off.*

Shoving them inside his pockets, he scanned the room, his gaze searching the people either standing in small groups or gyrating to the rock music on the small dance floor. Where the hell was she?

Keeping an eye on her was his obligation, wasn't it? Because he'd invited her tonight, because he was her boss, and most of all, because he'd known her and her family since Lucy still had training wheels on her bicycle.

Before adulthood had given her hips and smooth, curvy legs and that seductive smile that had him heading toward her for the intercept. Blame it on his cop intuition again.

Then Carlo's gaze narrowed and a skitter of irritation shot up his spine. No wonder he was on edge. Take a look at her dance partner! Long shaggy hair, pierced eyebrow, motorcycle boots. He picked up his pace.

Consequently, he was nearby when a wild spin took her into his territory. Carlo caught her in his arms.

Her face flushed, she looked up at him. "Oh."

His hands slid from her shoulders to her hips. He'd held that sweet curve of hers before—and had had trouble keeping his mind focused on Claudia and business.

He squeezed. There was the smallest give to her flesh and his fingers sank into it as he took a deep breath of her tempting, female scent. "You ran away from me," he said.

"Ran away? Carlo, I didn't know you cared," she teased. Her lashes dropped, and she gave him another one of those flirtatious, womanly glances.

Just like that, his male instincts overrode his inner

cop talk, causing his palms to slide up her curves to her waist as he drew her nearer. "Lucy…"

Lucy!

His hands dropped. This was *Lucy,* and she was here as his family friend, his temporary employee, as someone he should be looking after, not looking to touch.

She used her new freedom to sketch him a wave before twirling back onto the dance floor and into the proximity of the grinning possible felon, who then grabbed her by the hand. Irritation spiking again, Carlo elbowed the man standing beside him.

"Excuse me. Do you know that guy over there?"

"Huh?"

"The one with the red lightning bolt crawling up his skinny right arm." The dude was dressed in leather pants, of all things, and a muscle shirt that clung to his scrawny chest.

"That's Wrench."

Good God. He was named after a tool. "Wrench who?"

"Just Wrench. He's the lead singer of Silver Bucket."

Silver Bucket. Before she'd disappeared on him, he'd listened to Lucy discuss with Claudia the musical lineup for the Street Beat festival. That had gotten the older woman's attention away from Carlo and he'd been glad. After a few minutes it was clear Lucy knew her music, impressing Claudia and amusing Carlo.

Until now. She'd professed a deep love for the music of Silver Bucket and here she was boogeying down with Silver Bucket's lead singer. Wrench.

For God's sake, that wasn't funny.

Frowning, he settled back on his heels to watch what happened next. The protective stance and attitude was just what he needed, he decided, to put away those dangerous and recurring moments he'd spent seeing Lucy as a woman.

Of course, she wasn't a little girl any longer, either. No one seeing her in that dress—two hankies, no matter how she denied it—could see her as anything less than an attractive, desirable, adult female.

The lead singer had noticed, that's for sure.

"Wrench," Carlo muttered.

Though loud enough, apparently, for the man standing next to him to hear. He cocked a brow in Carlo's direction. "You do know Silver Bucket, right?"

"Uh…" Great, he was going to be forced to admit that he *was* a fuddy-duddy.

The other man took pity on him. "They're the ones known for their shock-and-awe pyrotechnics show during their signature song, 'Mosh Pit.' It always works the crowd into a frenzy."

Shock-and-awe pyrotechnics. "Mosh Pit."

Frenzy.

Tension grabbed the back of Carlo's neck and he took his eyes off Lucy to seek out Claudia. There wasn't going to be any pyrotechnics, mosh pits or, for that matter, frenzies at the upcoming festival. Not when he was head of security.

With a glimpse of Claudia near the bar and thwarting possible future catastrophe at the forefront of his mind, he cast a last glance at Lucy and then set his jaw and left her unguarded. Surely she wouldn't go far.

Ten minutes later, Claudia's promises had appeased his uneasiness. Five minutes later, it was back again. Lucy was nowhere to be found. And neither was Wrench.

Her voice echoed in his head. *"I just adore that band."*

Carlo's mind abandoned common sense and leaped to a worst-case scenario. If she eloped with Wrench, her family would never forgive him. *He* would never forgive himself.

Lucy was like a…a…almost like a sister to him.

Sister. Right.

Pulse pumping, he strode toward the dessert buffet and the exit doors just beyond. A guy like Wrench would have a limo, wouldn't he? Maybe he and Lucy were in it right now, speeding toward Vegas, and the tool was popping champagne and eyeing her spectacular legs as she stretched out on black leather. Hell.

"Wearing a face like that, you could scare people."

At the sound of Lucy's voice, Carlo spun. Damn it! Preoccupied by the vision in his mind, he'd hurried right past her. She stood on the far side of the dessert tables, half-hidden by a fountain bubbling waterfalls of white chocolate.

"There you are," he said.

Her eyes widened. "Were you looking for me?"

It took concentration, but he managed to relax his shoulders. He hadn't lived in this world for thirty-four years without learning a thing or two. Telling Lucy he'd been looking *out* for her might give a rise to her hackles.

"It's getting late," he said instead. "I was after some dessert before I rounded you up in order to leave." To put truth to his words, he grabbed a plate and started scooping up random items.

She waited for him to finish, then together they wandered out onto a small terrace. It was almost empty of people, but a few small waist-high tables were set up under portable heaters.

He took a breath of the fresh air, then looked over at her. "Having fun?"

She held a white-chocolate-covered strawberry to her parted lips. "Mmm." Nodding, she took a bite out of the juicy thing.

He should look away.

He couldn't look away.

Damn, but there went his common sense again, evaporating under the radiant warmth of the patio heaters—not to mention the radiant warmth that was his libido catching fire.

A drip of pink-tinged juice oozed at the corner of her mouth and she tongued it off. Carlo cleared his throat, tore his gaze away, then couldn't stop it from jerking back.

"There," he muttered, gesturing at her with his fork.

Her eyebrows came together. "There? There where? There what?" She whipped her head around in confusion.

"There on your mouth." Carlo was forced to step closer. "Some of that white chocolate." A dab perched on the rosy pillow of her bottom lip.

Her tongue's next search-and-destroy mission completely missed the spot.

He couldn't stand to watch her send it out again and he couldn't look at the creamy dot for one more second. "Let me," he said impatiently. The edge of his thumb touched down.

And seemed to stick to her bottom lip as if the sugary stuff was superglue.

Her gaze jolted to his. Her breath burned his hand.

Time froze.

Carlo remembered he was a family friend. A former cop who could smell trouble from two blocks away. A man who thought of himself as Mr. Keep-It-Light.

But his blood was hot and heavy, chugging slowly through his veins. Lucy's big blues were looking at him as if she sensed the same thing he did. Attraction in the air. Just like that moment two years ago, a moment he'd thought he'd banished from his memory forever.

Because this was attraction he had no business feeling, not for someone so young, so fresh, so flat-out deserving of all the happily-ever-afters a man like him could never promise. That a man like him didn't want to promise because he couldn't take a chance on all the painful ways ever-after could end instead.

Still, as he stroked his thumb free of her mouth, he couldn't stop himself from thinking he was freeing it for something else….

He leaned closer.

Lucy shifted left, her eyes widening. "Oh! Thanks." She used a little square of napkin to scrub his touch away. "I'm not usually so…so…"

Cowardly? Carlo thought. No, no. He meant smart. Smarter, for sure, than him, because a second ago he'd been close to overriding his brain. His gray matter knew it was crazy to play around with Lucy, even though parts farther south were still registering the fact they considered the idea had some merit.

"So what's with you and Claudia, anyway?" Lucy asked with a shiny smile.

He groaned. "Nothing, and that's just the way I like it."

She nodded. "I figured as much when I was pressed into playing your latest girlfriend."

He looked over his shoulder. "Keep it down, okay? Claudia gets wind it was a ruse and I'm toast."

"Why don't you just tell her you're not interested?"

"Does she strike you as a woman who takes no for an answer? I think the challenge would only cause her to slow long enough to sharpen her claws for the final takedown."

Lucy laughed. "Okay, I clued in on the she-cat resemblance myself, but I have to say that by the time I finished talking to her about Street Beat, I found myself actually liking her."

"She's a hell of a businesswoman, but just not the woman I want in my bed."

At that last phrase, the smile on Lucy's face slid away. Her eyes went wide once more.

And again, the hands of his watch seemed to stop.

His comment begged the question—and all of a sudden it was sizzling in the air between them as if she'd spoken it aloud—who *was* the woman he wanted in his bed?

Lucy.

No matter how wrong the idea was, no matter how many reasons why not, it was suddenly there.

Lucy.

Damn that stinkin', inconvenient, completely un-asked-for sexual chemistry.

Yet despite his condemnation he found himself leaning toward her again. Leaning toward her luscious berry lips.

Halfway there, she blinked, as if sensing danger. Her arm jerked up and she held her fork between them like a weapon. "You…" She swallowed hard, her fluster showing in her new flush. "You have something on your dessert plate I didn't get. That...that pie thing."

"Uh-huh." He didn't give that...that pie thing a glance. He was still preoccupied with the idea of Lucy in his bed—or at the very least of Lucy's kiss against his mouth.

No.

Lucy was a little sister to him...except she wasn't. Lucy was just a kid...except she wasn't anymore. Lucy didn't want him to kiss her...except she was swaying toward him, and her gaze was fixed on his mouth as if she were willing it to come closer to hers.

He found himself moving nearer.

Was he really this weak? Apparently he was. Or the attraction was just that strong.

He couldn't look away from her berry lips and the wet tip of her tongue, which darted out to touch the top one. Now was the last chance to dredge up his common sense, to gather his brain cells together, to do something other than give in.

However, the whiz-bang-pow between them had a mind and will of its own and he found himself unable to alter the course. She swallowed again. "What, uh, what would it take for me to get a bite?"

His laugh was low. "I'm sure we can think of something."

She didn't move as he took the fork out of her unresisting hand and set it on the table. And she didn't blink as he drew her against him. She didn't make a sound as he finally succumbed to temptation and lowered his mouth to taste hers.

Chapter 4

At the last second, Carlo hesitated, his breath mingling with Lucy's. What the hell was he doing? He prided himself on his honesty and he honestly couldn't figure out what impulse was driving him. As that straightforward and truthful man he knew himself to be, he shouldn't start something that he was never, ever going to see through.

But it's just a kiss, the devil on his shoulder whispered. *You're not promising anything more.*

And Lucy was so much more. So much more than the girl who used to amuse him. Now she was a woman with glistening, berry-colored lips and breath that smelled faintly of chocolate.

He wanted just a sample. An experimental caress. A small, not-enough-to-startle-her taste.

And she looked ready to startle. She stood frozen before him, her gaze somewhere south of his, and he cupped her face between his hands to guide her mouth to a better alignment with his own. When she didn't protest, when instead her feathery lashes drifted down, so did Carlo's mouth.

His lips brushed across hers. *Careful, man,* he reminded himself. He reversed directions for another light stroke.

She trembled. *God.* The vibration traveled through him like a jolt of pure energy. He fought against the possessive need to tighten his fingers on her warm skin. When he caressed her mouth again, she gave another shiver, and the honesty of her instant response pierced him once more. It was like holding a butterfly in the gentle cage of his hands.

More energy buzzed through his body, tightening his muscles, but he fought against the tension. Lucy tasted so sweet. Lucy was sweet, so he was determined not to come on too strong.

But he wasn't yet ready to end the experiment. Not quite yet. With his fingers still cupping her from jaw to cheekbones, he brushed over her mouth again, giving her another soft kiss. She shivered again, and he felt another energizing buzz.

Slow, deliberate, he pressed his mouth harder against hers and felt her lips part under the new pressure. Still gentle, still careful not to startle her, he slid his tongue inside to give the tip of hers a tender greeting.

At the warm, wet touch, she made a small sound in the back of her throat and…

She bit him.

A sharp, edges-of-the-teeth erotic nip on the very tongue that he'd been trying so hard to keep gentle and nonthreatening.

He jerked his head back just as all his muscles jerked in hot, sexual reaction.

She was staring up at him, narrow-eyed, with a glint of something—anger?—in her eyes and a flush on her cheekbones.

"I'm…" Carlo started. Sorry? Was she warning him off? But she hadn't moved away, and when he started to lift his hands, she reached up to hold his wrists. Her cheeks felt hot against his palms.

"Do you call that a kiss?" she demanded.

Her voice echoed in his head. *Do you call that a kiss?*

If he was honest—and hadn't he just been thinking of his pride in that?—the restrained caress hadn't been a Carlo Milano kind of kiss. Carlo Milano didn't like fragile women or tentative touches. He was a red-blooded Italian male, and the kind of kisses he liked to give out were designed for grown-up females. Grown-up females like…

Lucy.

Lucy was all grown up, with her berry-pink lips and that damn, tantalizing, two-hankie dress. All. Grown. Up.

She must have read his mind. "I don't want a fuddy-duddy kiss, either."

At the taunt, his fingers tightened on her face and he tilted her sassy mouth higher. Oh, yeah, she was devilish, no doubt about it. Her hands dropped their hold on his wrists and wrapped around his neck to draw him nearer.

"That's right," she whispered, pulling him close. "If you're going to do this, I insist you do it right."

It was all the permission he needed. His lips crashed into hers and they opened immediately for him. She made that sound in her throat again, but it was needy now, womanly, and he thrust his tongue into her mouth to taste her yearning.

Sweet. Hot. Sexy.

Their tongues tangled and he slid his hands from her face down her back to the flare of her hips. He scooped them up against his and then barely suppressed his own groan. She was such a warm, curvy armful. When she trembled, his own muscles shuddered in response.

Her hands tangled in the hair at the back of his neck, and the sensation burned a trail down his spine and then raced to his groin, pulling his skin—and everything else—taut. She had to feel him against her flat belly, but her only response was to slant her head and take the kiss deeper.

Deeper. He'd give his right hand to find himself as deep inside her as he could be. No, no, not his right hand. He needed that, he realized, as it slid between their bodies and then up the delicate ladder of her ribs.

He needed it for *this*.

Her spine bowed as his hand moved between their bodies then cupped her breast. Her hips pressed harder to his as his thumb brushed across the hard bud of her nipple.

The smoke of desire's fire obscured everything but touching more, having more, wanting more, more, more. Behind a hazy screen was his good sense, his cop hunches, his sense of who he was.

There was only this: Lucy in his arms, Carlo alive for the first time in God knew how many years, every part of him tingling with a rush of blood he hadn't experienced in longer than he cared to remember.

Maybe it had never been this good.

Maybe he'd never been this alive.

He slid the hand at her hip lower, cupping the round cheek of her cute behind in one hand while the other continued to play with her breast.

This was heaven.

"Whoops." Stifled laughter broke through the fog in Carlo's head. He opened his eyes without breaking the kiss and saw the interrupting couple disappear back inside the ballroom. Reality crashed like an anvil in a Coyote and Roadrunner cartoon.

This was hell.

They were on a public patio at a public, *professional* event, and he'd been all but ready to go all the way with his paid employee.

He leaped away.

Cleared his throat.

Buttoned his jacket to hide his erection.

Picked up the tepid coffee sitting on the nearby table and downed it in one bitter swallow.

Then there was nothing else to do but look at Lucy.

She was looking right back at him.

"Well." He drew one hand down his face. "I… That…" Taking a breath, he tried thinking of what to say next. What the hell was *wrong* with him? He still couldn't think, not with the smell of Lucy's perfume on his hands and the taste of her still delicious on his tongue.

Clearheaded Carlo Milano, former cop Carlo Milano, successful businessman Carlo Milano, was knocked on his butt by one blue-eyed, blond, family friend.

Oh. That's what was wrong with all this! *Now* he remembered. Lucy Sutton was enmeshed in his life in ways that went beyond the reception area. Though she might be his employee only temporarily, she was for-ever a part of his life—at least through his friendship with her siblings and parents.

He couldn't just play with Lucy, and that's all that he had in him when it came to women. Fun and games.

"Well, I... Well, you..." He gave an inward groan at his bumbling ineptitude. *You kissed the woman, Milano. Now straighten out the mess you've made.*

He cleared his throat, adjusted his jacket, looked at her face, looked away. "You... I..."

"Am going to freeze my buns off if we don't get somewhere warmer soon," she said. "Me, I mean. I can't speak for you, but this dress doesn't cut it against the sudden cold." Then she looked away, as if embarrassed about mentioning the abrupt change in temperature— when they both knew the abrupt change in temperature was because they were no longer in each other's arms.

His thumb tingled at the memory of the small round button that had been her nipple.

Shoving his hand in his pocket, he took a bracing breath. "Let's get you inside, then."

"And maybe out to the car?" she suggested. "It's late and I have that mean boss who'll expect me to be on time tomorrow, I'm sure."

"Yeah." Carlo strode for the door that would take them to the ballroom and pulled it open for her. Then he held his breath as she passed so he could avoid her sweet, beguiling scent.

All the way to the car and on the road to her sister's he stewed about what to say about the kiss that should never have happened. As much as he wanted to beat himself up about it, it didn't make the memories of those minutes any less compelling. How the hell were they going to work together without him thinking of it every damn second? How was he going to explain to her and himself how he'd let that interlude get so out of hand?

"It was just a curiosity queller," he murmured, trying out the sound of it.

"What?"

Oh, damn, he'd been muttering louder than he thought.

But it was the only halfway decent excuse he could think of. "Curiosity. You know."

"Explain, please."

He pretended the road needed all his attention. "We had to get it out of the way, right?"

"The kiss."

"Yeah." He shrugged. "It was there, in the air, you know, and so it was best to get it out of the way. We can forget about it now."

"Forget about it."

The way she was repeating his words in that monotone was annoying. *She* was annoying, he decided. Actually, that was an honest assessment of the whole situation, if you asked him. That dress was annoying, the way her blond hair caught the glow of the streetlights was annoying, the damn position he was in, turned on by the woman who was going to be answering his phones, was *way* beyond annoying.

He pulled into the driveway at her sister and brother-in-law's house.

"Don't tell Elise about this," he heard himself grind out. Because, hell, if Lucy told her bigmouth big sister it would get back to their brothers, who would then turn on Carlo…and what would he do then?

"Tell Elise about what?" Lucy said, her voice without expression.

"About, uh…"

"Us?"

He sighed. "Yeah."

"Why would I do that? There's nothing between us to report, is there?"

She said it so coolly. So matter-of-factly. In just the way he wanted. In just the way he had hoped for.

"Right," he answered. "Nothing to report. All forgotten. Nothing between us at all."

He was still mumbling nonsense phrases as she climbed out of the car. He waited until she'd let herself into the house.

"Nothing between us at all," he repeated to the closing front door. Then he thumped his forehead against the steering wheel. *Bump bump bump.*

With each tap he acknowledged that the man who so prided himself on honesty was now lying through his teeth.

Lucy decided that forgetting about that kiss—okay, series of kisses, and, well, more—on the patio during the Street Beat party was doable, if she wasn't around Carlo. But of course she was around Carlo, her temporary boss, *all the time.*

Even now, when they were on their way to a meeting at concert promoter Claudia Cox's Del Mar offices in northern San Diego County to discuss the volunteer program Lucy had been assigned to oversee. She snuck a look in Carlo's direction, then quickly jerked her glance back to the window. Sometimes she'd find herself staring at his face and remembering the sure thrust of his tongue and the thrilling caress of his lean fingers at her breast.

Oh, great. She felt her face heating up and she squirmed on the leather seat.

"What's the matter?" he asked.

"Nothing." She'd be in hell before she gave away that she was any more affected by what had happened than Carlo "Kiss Me Then Forget Me" Milano. Still, she couldn't help herself from frowning at him. "I could handle this meeting by myself."

"I don't mind coming along."

Well, she minded. He'd given her the job and he should have left her alone to handle it. He probably regretted the assignment. He probably thought she was incompetent, which wouldn't surprise her since the rest of her family did, too.

She yanked on the hem of her suit skirt and ironed out imaginary wrinkles with the flat of her hand. Maybe that was why he'd backed away from her so quickly at the party the other night. He thought she was incompetent when it came to kissing, too.

Hah. She'd prove him wrong. She'd show him she could handle her Street Beat duties just fine.

And she was *never* going to kiss him again.

With those resolves in mind, she strode into the concert promoter's offices with her best all-business attitude, then halted in the reception area to stare around her as if she was a little kid.

While Carlo's company's offices were dominated by those picture-postcard views of the bay, this office was dominated by…colors. Sounds.

Each curved wall delineating the receptionist's space was painted a different shade: cinnamon, goldenrod, turquoise. There was an emerald-green sisal carpet covering most of the blond hardwood floor. The plush chairs were upholstered in fabric that was in a bright Mexican design. On each wall was a flat screen playing music videos, each one at a volume just loud enough to create a cacophony that had Carlo wincing.

Lucy could only think of the three places she used to

work. By some coincidence, in each of them the walls had been painted the same pale cadaver-green of graph paper. By far the most colorful ornamentation in any of the places had to be the freebie calendars the insurance company's national office had distributed each holiday season. Yep, that eleven-by-eleven-inch photograph of the Citizen's Insurance float at the Rose Bowl Parade had provided a much-needed visual punch.

However, there were many, many more ocular knock-outs at the concert promoter's office, only one of which was the receptionist. She wore chartreuse leggings under a floating skirt and a matching blouse, and when she looked up from the phones that were set on a clear Lucite desktop there was a tiny sapphire stud in her nose and the two piercings below her left eyebrow showed off matching jewelry.

"May I—" she started, but then Claudia strode around a corner.

Today, the older woman was dressed in another eye-catching outfit. No animal print this time, but a canary-yellow pants outfit accented with print scarf in Picasso colors.

Carlo pushed Lucy forward with a gentle hand at the small of her back. "You remember Lucy."

As they briefly shook hands, Claudia's eyes ran over her, making Lucy feel dowdy in her gray pinstripes, even though she knew her mother had spent a hefty chunk for it as her post-college graduation "interview" suit. Her palms dampened and she rubbed them together. Great, already her confidence was eroding.

As Claudia gestured them down a hallway painted in more vibrant shades, she slanted Lucy another glance. "Who did you last work for, a mortician?"

A startled laugh escaped Lucy's mouth and she tried hard to swallow it back down, even as she felt her cheeks burn. "As a matter of fact, my older brother once set me up with a job interview at a mortuary." The mortician, thank God, hadn't found her right for the job. "But most places dress a little more corporate than here."

Still, she was beginning to wonder if her family didn't have a point. Maybe Lucy wasn't right for anything.

It made her steps heavy as she followed Claudia's subtle wave of Chanel No. 5 down the hall. With Carlo at her back, Lucy took a quick peek into an office where a young man in dreadlocks was chattering away on a headset. In another, a woman in jeans and a baby tee was shaking her shoulders to something she was listening to through bagel-size headphones.

Claudia glanced over shoulder. "My brother wanted me to be his medical transcriptionist," she said. "And my first husband wanted me to be a double-D cup."

As Lucy digested these interesting tidbits, the older woman paused by an alcove that contained a small refrigerator, a coffeemaker and an espresso machine. "Luckily, the one who got their wish was me."

Without waiting for a response or even asking what they'd like, Claudia reached inside the fridge to hand over slender containers of bottled water. Then she continued heading down the hall.

Lucy slowed so that Carlo came up beside her. "What about her second husband?" she whispered to him.

"Don't ask," he whispered back.

"I heard that." In front of a closed door, Claudia stopped again. "It's no secret. My second husband had me arrested for picking up his dry cleaning and then holding it hostage after I kicked the SOB out."

"Oh." Lucy felt her eyes widen. She *shouldn't* have asked. So far Lucy and her dowdy suit were only racking up negative points. "I'm, uh, sorry."

"Don't be." Claudia's beringed right hand whisked the sentiment away. "Because then I took him *to* the cleaners in the divorce. Now I have all this."

And with that, she swung open the closed door to reveal a conference room decorated in plum tones that held a long table, plush chairs and a small group of middle-aged parent-types who looked a bit overwhelmed by their splashy surroundings. They rose to their feet, and from the way their gazes fixed on Claudia, it looked as if they'd heard every one of her words and weren't sure whether they should run screaming or just plain run.

As if seeking solace, their heads turned toward Carlo, but his dark looks and unsmiling cop face were better suited for intimidation. Their tension seemed to increase until their gazes shifted again and found Lucy.

She almost laughed. Lucy Goosey had never alarmed anyone. Without thinking, she moved forward with a big smile, hoping to put the parents at ease.

"Hi," she said, holding out her hand to each one. "I'm Lucy Sutton and I'm so glad we could meet. I'll be coordinating your volunteer efforts at the Street Beat festival."

The group arranged themselves around the conference table. Claudia, naturally, took the head position, and the parents wore those nervous expressions again. Maybe the concert promoter sensed the situation, because she quickly turned over the discussion to Carlo, who passed it off to his "assistant."

Lucy found all eyes on her once more. Her stomach swooped and her hands were unsteady as she opened the manila folder she'd brought with her. Fanning out the paperwork gave her time to gather her thoughts.

What am I doing?

Why am I in charge?

What if I fail...?

I'd hate to look like a fool in front of Carlo.

My family will never let me hear the end of it.

Lucy Goosey, silly all over again.

Carlo's voice suddenly pierced through her loud fears. "Lucy coordinated a similar effort at last year's hot air balloon festival in Phoenix," he said. "It was a great success according to Arthur McGrath, who co-ordinated the entire event."

Lucy's head lifted. It *had* been a great success. And when had Carlo spoken with Art? She glanced over at him.

He made a little go-ahead gesture with his chin. "A great success," he repeated.

Lucy cleared her throat, then smiled again at the volunteers. "I know we can make this occasion work just as well for all of us and Street Beat."

The older people smiled back. They took out pencils and paper and then looked even happier when Lucy provided sheets that listed what she'd already discussed with Carlo. Outlined were the details about scheduling, what volunteers should wear and a copy of the necessary permission slips they'd need for the teens. They set up an evening meeting at the McMillan & Milano offices, where they would go over with all the volunteers the layout of the festival and what exactly they would be doing.

Then it was over. Everyone was getting to their feet. "Excuse me," Carlo interjected into the casual wrap-up conversation. "Don't forget to hand these out, Lucy." He reached into his jacket pocket and passed over to her a stack of business cards.

She glanced down at them. Stopped. Stared. Lucy Sutton, they read. Security Technician.

Her forefinger ran over the embossed letters. Carlo had had business cards made up. For her.

For Lucy Goosey, his temporary employee.

But Lucy Goosey had handled this meeting with professional aplomb. The volunteers took the cards and tucked them away as they thanked Claudia for the opportunity and then Carlo and Lucy for their time, as well. Finally, the woman who appeared to be their leader held out her hand to Lucy. "We're *very* comfortable working with you."

All the way back to the San Diego security offices, Lucy made notes. Carlo mumbled something about her making herself carsick, but she ignored him to focus on the task at hand. By the time they made it back to McMillan & Milano, she was surprised to find it was way after 5:00 p.m. and that the lights were dimmed.

Carlo passed into his office and was checking his emails by only the glow of his monitor while she put her area to rights before leaving for the night. Her arms got hung up while she was trying to replace phone books on a high shelf, so she had to slip off her constricting suit jacket to reveal her white, lacy sleeveless blouse. "Let me know when you're ready to leave," he called through the open door. "I'll walk you to your car."

She'd expected the offer. Carlo was a thoughtful, considerate man. For example, those business cards…

With quick steps she took herself into his office. "You had cards made for me."

He looked up, obviously puzzled. "Yeah."

"You had them made before today's meeting."

"And this is news because…"

"You…you were willing to lay claim to me as a McMillan & Milano employee even before you saw how I handled the meeting."

He shook his head. "Lucy, you *are* a McMillan & Milano employee, and of course I assumed you'd handle the meeting well. You're a very capable person."

"But…but…"

"Claudia took me aside before we left to say that very thing to me. The words she used, I believe, were that she should know by now not to underestimate anyone, even little blondies like you."

Lucy laughed, unable to work up the least bit of mad at the "little blondie" remark. Yes, it made her sound like a new brand of cookie or some kind of candy, but who cared? The fact was, flush with success and the recognition for that success, she felt like dancing. And so she did. She danced right around the desk, wearing a grin so wide she could see it in the reflection of the window behind Carlo.

After all, she *had* proved she was competent. Capable. Claudia thought so. Carlo said so. Better yet, *Lucy* knew so.

And at that happy thought, she leaned down and gave her temporary boss a great big smack.

On the mouth.

Chapter 5

Uh-oh. The kiss changed on contact. What she'd intended to be a grateful, happy smack, turned downright serious when her lips touched Carlo's. His hands gripped her waist and pulled her down into his lap.

Her head found the hollow of his shoulder as she tilted her chin to give him fuller access. And oh, he accepted the invitation. His tongue slid against hers, dominant and sure. She opened her mouth wider, taking every thrust as her body began to hum from head to toes, more sensitive spots along the way beginning their own heavy throb.

His hand, hot and big, inched upward from her hip and anticipation robbed the last of her breath. *Yes, yes,* she urged him silently, aroused just by the kiss. *Now touch me there. Touch me again there.*

Millimeters short, his wandering fingers froze. His kiss eased. "Goose," he groaned against her mouth, then lifted his head and let his hand drop away.

Without his mouth on hers, Lucy managed to assess the situation. Here they were, both breathing hard, both obviously affected—that was *not* a banana she could feel against the pocket beneath her hip—but one of them was regretting the position they were in. The other only wanted it to go on and on and on.

She swallowed and put off the moment where she'd be forced off his lap simply by pretending she wasn't sitting there. Maybe if she talked about something else, they'd avoid talking about this. She didn't want it once again labeled "forgettable."

"So," she started, as if they were separated by the desk instead of less than five layers of cloth, "you really think I handled the meeting competently? I thought the volunteers looked pleased with me, as well."

Her strategy appeared to work, because while Carlo frowned, he didn't lift her away. "Particularly that guy wearing the Torrey Pines Golf Course shirt. He asked me about you. Whether you were available."

"Really?" Blinking, Lucy drew back to get a better look at Carlo's face and he circled his hands to the small of her back to keep her from falling off his knees. Nice. "I don't remember a man in a Torrey Pines Golf Course shirt," she said.

"He was the one with the gold Rolex and the preoccupation with your breasts."

Just that word out of Carlo's mouth sent a sexual zap up Lucy's spine. She squirmed against his thighs and his hold on her reflexively tightened. "He couldn't see my br— You know," she protested. Not when covered with her mortuary-appropriate suit jacket.

"Maybe he has X-ray vision." As if he might, as well, Carlo's gaze flickered from her face to her chest, and in a rush her nipples contracted inside her bra. Could he tell? The sleeveless blouse she was wearing was of a thin, delicate white cotton with horizontal rows of lace bisected by the placket of tiny pearl buttons.

Lucy swallowed again, feeling a flush rise to her skin. "You…" She had to start again, her throat was so dry. "You told him I was single?"

Carlo's eyes widened. His look seemed to suggest she was insane.

Maybe she was. Because she thought he looked a little possessive, too…and still a lot turned on. One of her hands toyed with the knot of his navy-blue-and-red tie, and she found herself working at loosening it. "By the way, I noticed one of the group giving you the eye, too," she told him, breathless again. The ends of the tie fell loose and she even went so far as to unfasten the button at his collar.

Bad Lucy, she told herself, peeking at him from beneath her lashes. Bad, flirtatious Lucy. But she couldn't seem to halt her daring. "Though I think the woman was more than a little wary of this serious, buttoned-up look of yours."

"Was it the redhead with the large hoop earrings?"

There'd been a redhead with large hoop earrings? "Um, I…" She'd been making the whole thing up. Truth to tell, she'd been too nervous about the meeting itself to absorb those kinds of details about the people in attendance.

"You know," he went on, "the one who wrote her phone number on your business card and passed it over to me."

Lucy's jaw dropped and she sat up straighter. "Some pushy redhead used *my* business card to come on to you?" She flounced and felt her eyebrows lower. "That is so rude."

"She even crossed out your name so I could see hers more clearly."

So incredibly rude!

Carlo made a sound that was suspiciously like a stifled laugh. "Oh, God." He made that sound again. "You should see the expression on your face."

"What?"

He put a hand over his mouth, but nothing smothered the sound of his laughter now. And while Lucy loved seeing this unusual sign of his good humor, it wasn't so great when it was at her expense.

And what was wrong with her expression, anyway? Annoyed as he continued to laugh, she shifted on his lap so that her knees straddled either side of his thighs. Placing her hands on the back of his leather executive chair, she kneeled up to check out her reflection in the window behind him.

Okay, her expression did appear a bit…peeved, but it was all his fault. He'd—

"Oh, Lucy." His laughter had died and he groaned now, his hands clamping around her waist and then sliding toward her breasts. "Lucy, how you tempt me. Every day. Every hour."

His touch, the unwilling need in his voice, tempted her, too. Kneeling up had placed her breasts at the level of his face and she had to wonder if her surprising inner self—that flirtatious, naughty, surprising inner self—had planned it all along. Her heart pounded loud in her ears as his hands inched farther upward, closing gently over her breasts. She could feel his breath, hot, through the thin cotton of her shirt.

"Carlo," she whispered.

"I'm not supposed to want this." His palms gave her a gentle caress.

At the exquisite touch, her lashes drifted down. Through half-closed eyes, she could still see her reflection. As she watched, as he continued to circle and stroke, her nostrils flared and her mouth parted, clearly expressing her excitement. Hunger. Want.

"Carlo," she said again, her hands clutching the chair's black leather. "Please."

His breath blew hot across one nipple, then he latched on to it through her blouse and her bra. Her body shuddered. She'd never, ever felt like this. So quickly. So hot. So needy. "Please don't stop."

He didn't let up the arousing caress, and she wanted to cry at how perfect it was. Then he lifted his head and she moaned in protest.

"Shh, shh," he soothed, as his fingers made short work of her buttons. He brushed the blouse off her shoulders and neither of them minded that it was still caught in the waistband of her skirt. Carlo's hands were as competent with the front clasp of her bra as they were with everything else. Then that garment was gone and he found her neglected breast, running his mouth over every inch of the plump, aching skin—except the inch that needed him most.

Her fingers flexed in the leather, but then she couldn't stand it anymore. Grasping his head between her hands, she placed him right where she wanted him.

He let out a short, satisfied laugh, and then he took her into his mouth. She bowed into the sweet, hot suction and her thighs trembled with each deliberate pull.

His touch wasn't gentle, not like the first kiss at the

Street Beat party. It was strong enough to signal that this was a man who knew how to please her, a man who was making manly demands, and the temperature of her blood rose along with each one of them. His hands roamed over the bare skin of her back, then along her hips and back up again. The hem of her skirt, already hiked up thanks to her kneeling position, caught on his wrists and rode higher as his palms discovered the tops of her thigh-high stockings and the bare skin of her hips.

His head lifted from her breast to peer down at the flesh in his hands. "Hell, Lucy. Hell…"

The rasp of his breath and the dazed look in her eyes let her know he was as affected, as aroused as she. It gave her confidence. Even sass.

"What did you expect?" she asked. "Granny panties?" She backed off the chair to stand on the floor between his splayed thighs, her heart slamming against her chest.

Her flirtatious courage amazed her. Who was this Lucy? This Lucy whose blood was pounding so fast through her system that she felt dizzy with lust? Who was this Lucy who coolly reached behind her to locate the top button of her skirt? This Lucy who let the lined, pin-striped garment drop, taking along with it her blouse. This Lucy who stood before the man she'd been crushing on for what seemed like centuries in a nude-colored thong, nude stockings held up by a wide band of black stretch lace, and wearing black high heels.

This Lucy who loved the poleaxed look on Carlo Milano's face and who had the nerve to take the ends of his tie in one fist and draw him up from the chair. "Wouldn't the couch be more comfortable?"

He followed like a zombie.

Like a besotted lover.

Like a man under a spell that was the same as the one bewitching Lucy. He was the perfect follower, the perfect cobewitchee, until she hesitated by the leather couch. Then he seemed to find his will again, and it caused him to strip off his shirt, then take Lucy in his arms only to drop her onto the couch.

She gasped at the cold against her bare back and bare bottom, but he filled her open mouth with his tongue as he followed her down. He warmed her with the heat of his naked chest. Her heart slammed hard against his, and she opened her thighs to help him settle deeper into the cradle of her pelvis.

At the contact, they both groaned and took the kiss deeper. When she was desperate for breath, he lifted his head and looked down into her eyes as he brushed the hair off her face. The gesture was so tender and made her feel so cherished that this time she felt actual tears sting the corners of her eyes.

Carlo froze. "Oh, Lucy." His lashes swept down and she saw him clench his jaw. "Oh, Goose."

Oh, no.

Don't do this. Please, Carlo, don't stop now.

Desperate to avoid what was coming next, she tried her strategy again. "So," she started, then stopped to steady her voice. "So, you really think I handled that meeting well?"

She scrutinized his face, anxious to see his expression ease from regret to…what? Could she truly hope to turn his thoughts to desire once again?

His lips gave a wry twist. "Not going to work this time, Goose."

Someday, Lucy was going to think of a punishment fitting enough for her oldest sibling, who was responsible for her irritating nickname. The family tried to fob it off, claiming that Jason couldn't say her name clearly and "Goosey" was his mangled form of Lucy. Right. He'd been nine when she was born and was now an eloquent trial attorney. He'd never had trouble talking.

She ran through a series of tortures as Carlo levered himself off the couch and then snagged his dress shirt from the floor. His touch was impersonal as he helped her sit and then pushed her arms into his sleeves.

His gaze focused on the buttons, and he nimbly fastened the shirt.

"You seem to be making a habit of that," she said, sounding truculent yet not giving a damn about it.

He didn't look up. "Buttoning? Unbuttoning? Kissing you? Stopping kissing you?"

"Regretting kissing me." She'd hoped to say it silently, but what the hey.

Carlo's breath came out on a long sigh, and then he sat down beside her on the couch. "Goose—"

"Lucy."

He nodded. "Right, right. *Lucy.* It's just that thinking of you as Goose…it…"

"It makes me sound as if I'm eight years old. And I'm not eight years old, Carlo. I'm a woman."

"I know that."

"A grown woman."

He passed a hand over his face. "Where do you think this crazy sexual chemistry comes from? Obviously I know you're a woman."

"Well, what? What's the problem, then?" she demanded. "You made a date with the redhead and you're afraid you'll be late?"

Unbelievably, Carlo laughed again. Then he took a

look at her face and sobered. "G— Lucy, that's exactly why we can't take this path."

"You actually *do* have a date?"

"No. And there wasn't any redhead, either. But it was so damn fun to tease you about it. I can't mess with that."

She remembered his laughter and how much it had thrilled her to see serious, all-business Carlo amused and letting it show. Still... "I don't like being the butt of your jokes."

"You know you weren't." He gave a brotherly pinch to her chin. "It's just that...that...Lucy, for the past few days you've been the sun around here."

Why didn't that sound promising?

"You're bright and sparkling and you warm this place up. I...I suppose sometimes I need that."

Lucy's heart fluttered. Had he just said he needed her?

"But too close, sweetheart, too close and the sun will burn. I'll burn *you,* Lucy, and I can't have that."

He meant he wouldn't have *her.* Because he didn't do the couple thing, which he'd said from the beginning, which she'd known for years. Another man would have let them be swept out on the tide of lust and to hell with the consequences, but not Carlo.

Damn him.

Okay.

Not damn him.

Didn't you have a crush on a noble, upstanding guy precisely because he *was* so noble?

Carlo picked up her hand and held it in a loose grasp. "Goose, I enjoy having you here. I'm glad there're a couple more weeks that you'll be around the office and we'll be together. But not like this. I need your friendship, long-term, way more than this kind of indulgence."

She opened her mouth to protest. They could indulge, couldn't they? What was wrong with a no-strings fling? She *wanted* to indulge.

But that wasn't a good enough reason, she conceded. Not with all the connections between their families that a casual affair might mess up. There'd be a million future moments that wouldn't be made better with a stilted goodbye between them. Not to mention his long-held feelings for her sister...

And anyway, Lucy had come here to get over her crush!

A woman who read *Cosmo* or who lived vicariously through soap operas or friends' love lives—which sometimes had strikingly eerie parallels—knew you couldn't fling someone out of your system. She had a crush on Carlo and was working here with him in order to crush *it,* not nurture the inconvenient feelings with naked kisses and caresses.

She sighed, then flopped against the back of the couch. "Okay." Withdrawing her fingers from his, she patted the back of his hand. "Okay, you're right."

He looked relieved, and she tried to be fine with that. Maybe it would be best if she resigned from McMillan & Milano, she thought. Put up with the guff she would be sure to get from her nosy family for leaving yet another job. It would be the easiest way to avoid having to be with this beautiful, maddening man—*you're the sun, Lucy*—every day.

But there was that. That, *you're the sun, Lucy.* Despite everything, she liked the idea that she could bring light to Carlo's darkness. He'd lingered in the shadows for far too long.

"Friends, Goose?"

If it kills me.

The hours at McMillan & Milano were going to be the thing that killed Lucy. Not only was there the regular work week, but she had grabbed at the offered overtime and came in on Saturday. Though she could use the extra money, by the afternoon she was exhausted, sick of the same walls around her, and even then she didn't look half as burned out as her temporary boss.

As she brought Carlo the umpteenth cup of coffee, she couldn't help but notice his blank stare at the layout spread across his desk. It was the design of the Street Beat festival venue, with its five stages, food areas, first aid and bathroom facilities. In previous years, Street Beat had been shoehorned into the busy, revitalized downtown area—"a security nightmare," according to Carlo—but it didn't look like the festival's relocation to the parking lot of the football stadium was making the head of security sleep any better.

Without the cramped quarters constraining the ticket sales, the expected attendance—and presumably the nightmare factor—had gone way up.

Lucy set the mug down on the corner of his desk. He didn't even grunt his thanks as he usually did. She wondered for a second if he was asleep with his eyes open.

"Are you even seeing that?"

"Seeing what?" he mumbled, without glancing up.

She was used to that. In the days since their passionate interlude in that very chair, in this very office, Carlo had done his best not to catch her eye. One time he had, his gaze meeting hers as she brought in a stack of reports, and it had all rushed back.

His mouth on her breast.

His hot, rough palms on her naked hips.

The tenderness of his touch.

You're the sun, Lucy.

But since then it had all been business.

How could she warm him, make him smile, if the man who'd had business cards made up for her wouldn't let himself look her in the face?

"Let's get out of here," she said.

"What?" He lifted his gaze to her left shoulder.

She bent her knees so that it was her eyes he was seeing instead. "We've been inside here too long. Let's go to the beach."

"Huh?"

"You know. That place with sand and ocean. The reason so many people choose San Diego to live. You're not getting anything done here. I'm giving myself paper cuts due to claustrophobia."

He blinked, looked concerned. "You've hurt yourself?"

She shook her head. "Lack of fresh air is making you dumb if you can't discern hyperbole when you hear it. But okay, yeah, I've hurt myself and the only cure is you let me take you to the beach."

It surprised the heck out of her when he rose from his chair. "You're right. We both need a break."

But she should have known it wouldn't be that easy. When they reached the parking garage, he peeled off toward his car.

"Carlo!"

"I won't leave until I make sure your car starts."

Lucy rolled her eyes and stomped over to him and grabbed him by the elbow. "This way. My car. Me and you. The beach." His feet dragged against the concrete.

"Goose…"

"You called me that name again. You owe me for that alone." Then they were at her Volkswagen Bug and she was stuffing him into the passenger seat.

"I don't fit in here," he protested as she pushed on his knees to fold them further.

"Stop complaining."

He didn't. Though he wasn't loud about it, he did continue to mutter. He even heaved a sigh as they came to a stop in the parking lot of Belmont Park, the amusement area alongside Mission Beach.

His eagerness to get out of the car wasn't as gratifying as it might have been when he unpretzeled himself from his seat. "Five more minutes and you could serve me with mustard," he said, giving her a squinty glare.

The comment made her feel hungry, not guilty. So their first stop was the ice cream shop, where, as they were waiting in line, she caught him pulling out his cell phone.

"Give me that," she ordered, snatching it away and slipping it into the front pocket of her jeans. "You need a break, you take a break."

He rolled his eyes this time but paid for their cones and then followed her onto the boardwalk. They strolled among others enjoying the beautiful autumn day, dodging skateboards and bicycles, and zigzagging around little kids dragging plastic buckets of shells. Lucy sucked in big lungfuls of air between long licks of her rocky road ice cream.

Tongue out, she caught Carlo studying her over his pralines and cream. She lowered her cone. "What?"

He shrugged. "I was just trying to calculate how long it's been since I've hung out at the beach."

"Too long."

"Yeah." His head turned and he stared out at the water. "My dad used to bring my brothers and sister and me here all the time."

"Brave man." Carlo was the youngest of four brothers; his sister, Francesca, was younger than him.

"We were hellions. Our favorite trick was to convince Franny to catch seagulls."

Lucy had never heard about that. "Catch seagulls? How do you do that?"

"We'd dig a hole big enough for Franny to lie in. Then we'd cover her with a beach towel and cover *that* with corn chips. When the gulls swooped down for the bait, she was supposed to swoop up and trap them inside the towel."

Lucy blinked. "And she would actually do this?"

"For an ice cream cone and the promise that we'd play school with her later."

"Oh, and I bet that happened." Lucy knew all about the promises of elder siblings.

"We did play with her. But we always acted up enough so that Teacher Franny sent us home early." He grinned. "I haven't thought about all that in ages."

They walked a little farther, then turned back toward the amusement area. "My sister and brothers wouldn't play my games," Lucy said. "And included me in theirs only under great duress."

"Even Elise?"

She shot him a sidelong glance. "Perfect Elise wasn't always so perfect, you know."

His neutral expression didn't change. "Who said she was?" As they passed a trash can, he threw away the remains of his cone. "I only thought as the other girl in the family she'd do girly things with you."

"Nope. You should remember that all my sibs were manic about board games. They'd play marathons of word games. Imagine me, Lucy, trying to compete with Jason and Sam and Elise. They're all enough older that they could count better, spell better, and had vocabularies that included *attorney* and *financier* and *actuary*."

Carlo laughed at her bitterness. "Funny, how they then came to choose those professions."

"Yeah, and this when I was at the stage where I wanted to grow up and raise magic ponies." Her brothers and sister still teased her about it. If you opened any old game box at her parents' house, you'd still find the old tallies. Years and years of Lucy coming in last. "So in the game department, Goose always earned the big goose-egg score."

Carlo wrapped his arm around her neck and drew her against his chest in a hug that was all about affection and nothing about seduction. "But you're working your magic now, Luce." He smiled down at her and his teeth were even whiter in contrast to his weekend stubble. "Who else could have enticed me away from my desk and then dragged me to the beach for an ice cream cone and a ride on the roller coaster?"

"Ride on the roller coaster?" Lucy hoped her voice didn't squeak, and she also hoped he couldn't tell she was trying to hang back as he directed the two of them toward the line for the old-time wooden ride, the Big Dipper. "We don't have to do the roller coaster."

His grin only widened and the sunlight was sparkling in his dark eyes. "Make me happy, Luce."

Make him laugh, is what he meant, she thought, recognizing the dare in his eyes. Hadn't she grown up with brothers? Hadn't he just told her about the way he'd get his little sister to let herself be seagull bait?

She slipped out of his hold and stomped to the end of the line. "Don't whine to me if you get a stomachache."

Behind her, his free-and-easy laugh made the flutters in her own belly worthwhile. If she was his sun, then his laughter was the bubbles in her champagne. Being with him like this—Carlo relaxed and funny and comfortable—made *her* happy.

Not happy enough to override her nerves when they were shown their seats in the coaster. Pasting a cheerful smile on her face, she made enough room for him so that she couldn't even take comfort from his warmth. She didn't need it, she told herself.

"This is going to be fantastic fun!" She hoped she wasn't lying.

Carlo glanced down at her and grinned again. The ocean breeze ruffled the edges of his businesslike haircut and made him look ten years younger. Before Elise had broken his heart. Before his partner had died.

"Lucy," he said. "I can't remember the last time I've had such a great afternoon."

Short of expiring from fright, nothing could take away from that perfect moment. Carlo's handsome face. Carlo's *carefree* and handsome face. The smile that he was beaming down at her, and at her alone.

She hung on to that perfection as the car lurched into

motion. Her smile was pinned at both corners by pure determination as they started the climb. With luck, he wouldn't notice her white knuckles clamped around the restraining bar.

They'd almost reached the top. Lucy's eyeballs felt cold and as wide as the pit in her belly. She didn't like heights. She detested fast roller coasters. She hated the sense of falling, so much that she avoided elevators whenever reasonably possible.

But she couldn't ruin Carlo's wild ride.

There was that horrid suspended moment at the top and then they were falling, speeding, rushing. In the car behind them, someone was screaming over and over.

Lucy dug her fingernails into the metal lap bar and kept a determined hold of her rigor mortis grin. Until Carlo reached out and wrapped her shoulders with his arm. He pulled her close. "Wha…?" She looked up, trying to say something over the scary, rushing wind.

His mouth tickled her ear. "I need somebody to hang on to." And then he tucked her closer against his chest and she surrendered to her fears. Burying her face at his throat, she clung to him through the next thirty-seven years of her life.

Later, he told her it was more like thirty-seven seconds. But that was when her feet were on solid ground and she could appreciate that she'd survived. She could also appreciate that glimmering light in his eyes and that smile of his that didn't show a single sign of dimming.

An odd chirping from deep in her pants pocket interrupted her self-congratulation. When she realized it was Carlo's cell phone, she would have liked to have ignored it, but he was already putting out his hand.

So what? she thought, drawing it out. His shoulders were relaxed, his lips were still curved, he still looked happy. And it was all thanks to Lucy.

He flipped it open and held it to his ear.

At a public-safety demonstration, Lucy had once watched a man use a blanket to smother a fire. It was like that now with Carlo's expression. All that was glowing with life was gone in an instant.

It was as though nothing warm had ever existed.

Chapter 6

As he folded his cell phone closed, Carlo grabbed Lucy's hand and tugged her in the direction of the parking lot. It was still bright enough for sunglasses, but he didn't feel the sun's warmth. A little kid ran across their path and the child's vivid red shorts and neon-orange T-shirt hurt his eyes. Teenagers off to the right were laughing and the sound rang too loudly in his ears.

Even the smiles on the people he passed in his hurry to reach the parking lot felt wrong. It seemed as if a dark well had opened up in his gut and sucked down everything good about the day.

"Carlo? Carlo, what is it?" There was an edge to Lucy's voice.

Gritting his teeth, he shortened his stride so he wasn't dragging her behind him. *Keep it together, Milano. You won't help anyone by losing your cool.*

"Carlo?"

"It's Germaine." He schooled his features so they betrayed nothing as he glanced down at Lucy. Their afternoon's adventure had delivered a slight sunburn across her cheeks and a light sprinkle of freckles on her nose. She was so damn pretty. So damn sweet. For a minute he wished he could run away with her, go some place far away where there was no darkness and nothing to worry about besides finding ways to make her eyes sparkle and that rosebud mouth of hers curve in happiness.

"Carlo?"

He shook away the little fantasy. "Germaine had a fall. Or maybe worse. Her neighbor caught sight of her lying on her front walk and called 911, and then called her sister and me."

Lucy's hand tightened on his. "Why didn't you say so right away? Let's go." She picked up her speed, now tugging him. "I know the hospital nearest her house."

He had to go there, of course. He was practically the closest thing she had to family, now that Pat was gone.

Pat. At the thought of his old partner, Carlo's footsteps slowed, but Lucy was having none of it. "Come on," she said, yanking on his hand.

He forced himself forward. *Keep it together, Milano. Keep it cool.* Lucy didn't need to know how this was going to cost him. Lucy wouldn't know, because he'd send her on her way first. Walking into the hospital would set off a rockslide of memories, but he'd be alone with them. Maybe not better equipped to handle their impact, but at least without a witness to their damage.

Lucy didn't prove so easy to shake. At the hospital, she zipped past the hospital entrance and sped toward the parking area without giving even a token tap on the brake pedal when he protested.

"Just drop me off at the front," he told her. "I'll catch a ride home by calling a cab or one of my brothers or something."

Her little Bug whipped into a narrow parking space. "Germaine needs you. You need a friend."

He stared at her and dumbly repeated her words. "I need a friend?"

"Everybody needs a friend," she asserted, and exited the car with brisk movements. "We're buddies, right?"

"Bosom buddies," he muttered, following in her wake. For someone so short she could cover distances in an amazingly brief amount of time. He watched the plate-glass entrance doors automatically whisk open as her running shoes hit the black rubber mat. From his place on the sidewalk, he watched them close behind her. Six steps toward the front desk, he saw her register that he'd remained outside.

She flitted back out the doors. "Are you okay?"

No. Not okay. That pit in his gut had now been filled with boulders and branches and broken pieces of glass that were churning and turning and tearing at his insides.

But that was his private pain. Taking a breath, he started forward. "I'm coming. I was just…thinking."

Thinking too much. Remembering.

Keep it together!

The doors opened again and seemed to draw them inward along with some of the odors of the world outside: warm asphalt, grass newly mowed, the acrid exhaust of a laundry truck. And then the plate glass closed behind them and the outside world and its scents disappeared, leaving Carlo trapped in this other world that smelled of cold equipment, old magazines, desperate hopes.

Lucy was heading off toward the front desk again, but Carlo snagged her arm. "E.R.," he said. "I know how to get there."

She shot him a strange look, which made him guess that he sounded as strangled as he felt. He cleared his throat. "Lucy. Look. You go on home. I've got things covered."

"Sure you do," she answered, but she was walking again, this time in the direction of the emergency room.

He glared at her back in mounting frustration as he followed behind her. "Lucy, go home." Damn it, she was going to make him nuts and he wasn't in any shape to fight it, not when every inhalation of what the hospital called "air" made him think of the night they'd brought in Pat. Even without closing his eyes he could see the stain spreading on his partner's sleeve from beneath his bulletproof vest. Blood bubbling from his mouth and running over the silvery five o'clock shadow on the older man's chin.

Without thinking, Carlo reached out to stroke the back of Lucy's sunny hair. It was the color of butter and felt like that, too, smooth and soft. The picture in his head of Pat receded. "I don't need you, Lucy," he said, even as he twined his fingers in her blond strands. "I don't."

"You won't even know I'm here," she assured him.

Of course, that was a big lie. He'd known exactly where she was for days, ever since she'd showed up to temp at McMillan & Milano. He'd been hyperaware of her every glance, every small sharp intake of breath, every response she'd had to his kisses and to his touch.

Even as hours passed and despite his worry for Germaine and those debilitating memories lurking in the corners of his mind, he was still aware of Lucy. She'd found a chair in the corner of the E.R. waiting room and had drawn up her legs to curl herself into its molded plastic.

Though he tried pretending she wasn't there, her steady gaze kept him from snapping at the E.R. receptionist when she refused to give him any information. It kept his voice calm when he recognized a doctor from his police-department days and asked for news. It was Lucy who nudged him when an older woman entered the waiting area. She'd guessed it was Germaine's sister, Dot, and she was right.

As the late afternoon wore into the evening, then into late evening, they learned that Germaine was stable for the moment, but was being X-rayed for possible fractures. The doctor had yet to rule out a stroke as the cause of her fall. Lucy kept up the supply of coffee and tea for Carlo and Dot, but the caffeine didn't help his mood.

God, all this waiting! Those around them shifted and changed. A baby with a heavy cough was finally seen. A grizzled old man held his arm against his chest at an odd angle but was stoic, his eyes closed, as he waited for his name to be called. Everything took so damn long in a hospital, Carlo thought.

"I wish Pat were here," Dot suddenly said.

Carlo's belly churned. "Yeah." Instead, Germaine was alone.

Carlo was alone.

He didn't remember getting to his feet. He didn't decide to do it. One moment he was staring into the black depths of his coffee, the next he was making strides for the nearest exit.

Can't stand the smell. Can't stand the memories.

Pat on a gurney, his eyes already glazed behind slitted lids. At noon that day, Carlo and his partner had eaten lunch with Germaine in their kitchen. Over the meal, the older couple had talked about their plans following Pat's retirement from the police force. He and Carlo were already well on their way to opening the security firm, but Pat had promised Germaine a cruise before getting too caught up in the new venture. They'd eaten sloppy joes and green salad that Germaine had prepared, and they'd been back at their desks before Pat noticed the sauce stain on his tie.

Pat had shaken his head. "Germaine's gonna kill me. She gave me this tie for my birthday."

Germaine hadn't killed him. That had been the prerogative of a gangbanger with a loose trigger finger. And the sloppy joe stain on Pat's tie had been swallowed by the much larger stain made by Pat's blood.

As he thought of Pat's death, the walls of the hospital hallway squeezed his chest, pressing the air out of Carlo's lungs. Breathless, he was forced to sag against the nearest plaster surface to keep from passing out. Wouldn't that be a pretty sight? Former cop made faint by nothing more than his own bad memories. He was so damn weak, he thought, pushing the heels of his hands against his eyes. Some things made him so damn weak.

"Carlo."

Damn.

Lucy's voice. Lucy.

He dropped his hands and turned toward her, willing his spine to stay straight and hoping like hell the panic was gone from his eyes. When she came nearer, he slapped on a scowl as a preemptive strike. "I told you to go home, didn't I? I wish you'd go home."

I never want you to see me like this.

"Oh, be quiet."

He stared at her, startled by her no-nonsense tone. "What?"

"I have older brothers, you know. And Elise, despite what you think, could be a royal bitch, especially between the years of thirteen to fifteen. So I don't scare off easily."

He hated how she saw through him. Hadn't the same thing happened the night of the Street Beat party? It ticked him off now, it did. His own siblings and father knew when to back off. Why didn't Lucy? "Look. I just want you to go—"

"Away. I get that. Well, we're both going to get your wish, because the doctor just came out and told Dot they're admitting Germaine. They have a room for her on the fourth floor. Dot's staying with her."

"Can I see—"

But Lucy was already shaking her head. "It's just overnight, but they've given Germaine something to help her rest. Nothing's broken and they've stitched up the cut on her head. I think they're only keeping her because of her age and the lateness of the hour. Or maybe your buddy the E.R. doc said something. Anyway, it looks as if it was a simple slip and fall with no major lasting effects."

A simple slip and fall that wouldn't have happened if Pat were still...

He needed to stop thinking about Pat. "All right. Okay. Let's say goodbye to Dot and get out of here."

As he'd hoped, the fresh night air helped. And by the

time Lucy braked in front of his house, he could think of something besides Germaine's fall and Pat's tragic death. Like how he'd been a hell of a lousy companion the past few hours.

With a sigh, he glanced over at Lucy. "I owe you a beer for all you've done today. Will you come inside? Maybe I can scrounge up some food, as well."

She hesitated. "I should probably let you get some rest. It's been a rough day for you and—"

"There's nothing wrong with me!" It came out more defensive than he would have liked, but her solicitude wasn't necessary. "I'm fine. Come in, damn it."

"Well, when you put it so nicely…" With a roll of her eyes, she turned off the car then followed him inside. "I guess I could use a beer."

Once in his kitchen, he kind of shoved a bottle at her, but she took it without comment and pulled out a chair to seat herself at his breakfast table. He turned back to the refrigerator, feeling more of his anxiety fall away as he studied the familiar—meager—contents of the shelves. "We have cold pizza, and cold pizza, and some leftover cold Chinese, not to mention cold—"

The sound of glass breaking spun him around.

"Oh, I'm such a klutz!" Lucy dropped to her knees near a puddle of beer and began picking up shards of the bottle. "This will just take a second," she said, glancing up. "Get me some paper towels, will you?"

He turned away to comply, then turned back. "Here."

She glanced over her shoulder at him as her fingers found another piece of glass. It must have slipped, or been sharper than she expected, because suddenly blood welled from her fingers. A cut, he thought, going cold as he stared at the fresh red. She'd cut herself, and she'd yet to feel it.

From the corners of his mind, anxiety seeped like a dark cloud. His muscles froze though his stomach roiled as drops of shocking red splashed against the tiled floor. Lucy was still looking at him and her eyes widened at whatever expression crossed his face.

She dropped the piece of glass and rose to her feet, lifting that bloody hand to her face to stroke away a piece of hair clinging to her cheek at the same time. The movement left a smear of crimson slashing from the corner of her mouth to the edge of her chin.

The dark smoke billowed, obscuring the line between reality and memory. Lucy's cut. Pat's wound. Lucy. Pat.

"We have to stop the blood," he heard himself saying. "Right away. Gotta stop the blood." He had Lucy's hand now, and was holding the paper towels against the cut, applying pressure to the slice even as he scrubbed at the blood on her face with another towel he ripped from the roll. "Gotta stop the blood."

Dread tightened his chest as he stared down at the paper towels wrapped around the cut. The red stain on them was spreading outward, getting larger by the second. In his mind, the towels morphed into his partner's shirtsleeve, going dark and heavy with the liquid pumping from beneath his vest. The dark blue shirt appeared black.

"So much blood, Pat," he heard himself mutter. "Too much blood."

"Carlo."

From far away, a voice was calling his name. He tried to shake it off—he didn't have time to answer, he had to do something about all this blood or else Pat was going to bleed to death before his eyes—but now there was someone tugging on his sleeve.

"Carlo. Carlo, I'm okay. The bleeding's stopped. It's just a little cut."

Lucy's voice. Lucy's hand. He looked up. Lucy's concerned face. Not Pat. Pat was gone.

His head cleared. The past faded and the dread that had been squeezing Carlo's chest was replaced with heat. The heat of humiliation.

And anger. Anger at himself for not keeping it together. Anger at Lucy—and God, he knew it was unfair, but he was angry at her all the same—for being there to watch him lose it.

She had to think he was nuts. Her free hand stroked his shoulder and there was sympathy in her eyes.

She *did* think he was nuts.

But she didn't run out of the house screaming. Instead, she stroked his arm again. "Maybe…" She licked her lips. "Maybe you should see someone."

"No." Now she was really making him mad. Couldn't she leave well enough alone? This was his little neurosis, and it wasn't hers to comment upon. He didn't want to hear her say he should see a shrink. He didn't want to discuss his crazy little flashbacks.

"Carlo. You could talk—"

"No."

"Talk about—"

She wouldn't shut up. So he did it for her, he shut her up by pulling her close and stopping the conversation by putting his mouth on hers. Hard.

It was punishment, Lucy knew that. Punishment for Carlo being understandably affected by his partner's widow's hospitalization and punishment for Lucy being the one to see that effect.

But she clung to him, offering her kiss and offering comfort, because she understood what today had cost him. And she'd do what she had to—as a friend, okay?—to take that tragedy out of his eyes.

His arm scooped around her hips and brought her closer against his. She felt him harden against her belly as his tongue entered her mouth. At the first thrust, thoughts of comfort evaporated as goose bumps swept across her skin in a hot rush.

Oh.

Her body bowed into his and her friendly intentions were run off by the sensation of his hot hands squeezing her bottom and his mouth moving against hers. She crowded closer to him, and let her tongue tangle with his. Her eyes closed.

Then he broke their kiss, muttering something. Though his hold on her was as strong as before, he merely rested his forehead against hers. Their ragged breathing matched, but she knew the expression in her eyes wasn't anywhere near as sad as his.

Noble Carlo, once again in deep regret.

"I'm sorry," he said a moment later, confirming that she'd pegged his reaction exactly right. "Sorry *again.* Damn it, I keep ending up like this with you when I don't mean to."

At least he hadn't said it wasn't where he *wanted* to be, though she supposed the erection she could still feel pressed against her made that point moot.

He inhaled a long breath. "What *is* it about you?"

His expression twisted her heart. She wished she could do something about that. What had Elise said to her? That Carlo needed to lighten up. That Lucy should make that part of her job description.

He frowned down at her. "Why do you keep getting past my best intentions, Goose?"

So serious. So worried. *I don't think he knows how to have fun.* Lucy replayed her sister's words again. Maybe it was time Lucy reminded him of what that was like. Maybe it was time to bring him a little more sunshine.

"Will you forgive me, Goose?"

"That's the last straw," Lucy said, taking matters in her mental hands as she stepped back from him. "I mean it." She pointed her finger at him. "Strip."

He stared. "What?"

"You heard me. I said strip." She gave him the no-nonsense eye. "I warned you that the next time you called me Goose that you'd owe me, big time, and you agreed."

Had he? It didn't matter. Lucy tapped a toe, signaling impatience. "So now I'm collecting. Take off your clothes."

"What?"

"That wasn't the first time you got me all worked up only to leave me hanging. I'm not taking it anymore. Now I'm demanding. I'm demanding uh…uh… I'm demanding a Carlo sundae." Inspired by her own impulsive words, she moved toward the refrigerator. "Surely you have some chocolate sauce and whipped cream in here."

Though she didn't look at him as she rummaged around in the refrigerator, she hoped like heck that her outrageousness would change the atmosphere in the room. Her fingers closed around a metal canister.

"Is this all you have?" she demanded, spinning back

to face him. "Because I'll make do, but Cheez Whiz is not my first choice."

His arms were folded over his chest. His expression was bemused, a vast improvement over bleak, though there wasn't yet a sparkle of humor. "What the hell are you doing?"

"Complaining about the contents of your refrigerator." She looked back inside and pounced on another item tucked behind a bottle of salad dressing. "Uh-oh. This is chocolate whipped cream."

She slammed the door shut with her hip. "I'm a little miffed about this. Chocolate whipped cream is not a guy thing. It's an item only a woman would buy. Have you been making man sundaes for some other girl?"

He was shaking his head, looking at her as if she was the one who needed a shrink, so she flitted over, can in hand. "Hey, but if it's this or the Cheez Whiz, I guess I'll take the cream."

Toe to toe with him, she arched an eyebrow as she tossed the cap on the counter and shook the can. "Why are your clothes still on?"

He huffed out a breath. "You are not going to get near me with that stuff."

She hadn't grown up the youngest for nothing. She poked his belly with the cold can. "I'm near." Then she nudged his forearm with it. "And look. Near again."

When she reached farther upward he grabbed her hand. "Knock it off," he said, wearing a fierce frown. "What are you doing?"

Didn't anyone ever tease him anymore? She fought to gain back control of the can, but his hold tightened, and then suddenly it sprayed, scattering a flurry of chocolate whipped cream across his beige shirt.

They both stared at the mess. "Whoops," Lucy said, and let loose a little snicker. "Now you really will have to take it off."

"Look what you've done."

"Oh, please, Carlo. Take it off and I'll run cold water over it and it will be as good as new." Maybe.

But at least he didn't look sad anymore as he lifted off the shirt and handed it over. Annoyed was an improvement, in her mind. Still, not what she'd been going for.

And so, well, it was another impulse. As she took the shirt with her left hand, the trigger finger on her right just happened to create a tiny chocolate cloud on the curve of his now-bare pec.

He stared down at it, wearing that thunderstruck expression again. It only deepened when she swiped her finger under the chocolate and brought the daub to her mouth, where she sucked it away.

"Yum."

He looked up. "I can't believe you just did that."

She thought he looked pretty cute, half-naked and all indignant. Carlo was no longer bleak, no longer serious, no longer mired in memories.

"Oh, stop it. You're being a fuddy-duddy again. The stuff's not poisonous. Why, I remember watching you and your brothers filling your mouths with whipped cream when we were all kids."

"Oh, yeah? There's a good idea." A light entered his eyes and he grabbed the can out of her hands. Then he advanced on her.

Lucy shuffled back. Not too far, because she could see he was playing now, too.

"Open up, Goose."

The small of her back smacked the edge of the counter. "Now, Carlo…"

But she couldn't stop the delight bubbling inside of her or the smile breaking over her lips. *He* was teasing now, and truly, she didn't think he'd really go through with it.

"Lucy, open up."

"Oh, fine." But instead she stuck her tongue out at him.

And quick as a snake he coated it with the chocolate cream.

Surprised, she started to laugh, but then it died as he choked out a sound, then swooped down to cover her lips with his.

They both groaned.

Blame it on the chocolate, or on the previous kitchen kisses, or on the days of unacknowledged foreplay that had kept the tension high in the McMillan & Milano offices, but this time it didn't feel like experimentation, temptation or punishment.

This time it felt like pure passion.

"Lucy," he said against her mouth, even as his hands found the bare skin beneath her shirt and slid up her back. *"Lucy."*

"Don't," she said, her voice fierce. "Don't talk anymore. Just kiss me."

Maybe there were some advantages to being the youngest Sutton. Yes, it made her the family's favorite screwup, but it also made her, and she'd admit it, just the tiniest bit spoiled. Sometimes she just wanted what she wanted. Right now.

And right now she wanted Carlo Milano. Damn the consequences.

Chapter 7

Lucy shivered as Carlo's hands slid from her back to cup her breasts. Her nipples tightened and desire darted like white heat down between her thighs. Her heartbeat started pounding in her ears and her skin felt too tight for her bones.

"Lucy, are you sure—"

She ground her mouth against Carlo's to stifle his doubts. *I want it. I want him. Now.*

And if she let him hesitate, she'd be left unsatisfied. Still needy. Lust unrequited.

Spurred by the thought, she grabbed the hem of her shirt and stripped it over her head. He stepped back, his hands at his sides, and she fumbled with the front clasp of her bra on her own.

His nostrils flared as her bra slid down her arms. Looking down, she could see herself, swollen breasts, taut nipples, the way her jittery breaths made her belly tremble.

One of Carlo's tanned hands reached out and his forefinger lightly circled her areola. She gasped, her fingers curling into fists and her eyes closing tight. Carlo's touch teased her again, the circle slow and maddening.

Worrying.

A snail's pace would give him time to think.

Carlo already thought way too much.

She grabbed his hand and pushed it against her breast. His palm felt hard and hot and she stepped closer. "Kiss me," she demanded. "I want your mouth."

His laugh was soft. Deliberate. "So impatient."

She thumbed his hard nipple and leaned in to lick the other with the very tip of her tongue. His fingers closed over her aching breast. She pressed herself into the harder touch and another shiver racked her body.

Carlo's free hand chased the movement down her spine until he slid his fingers beneath the waistband of her jeans at the small of her back. The snap on the front pressed into her belly and Lucy ripped it open.

His breath hissed out as his hand slid lower to heat a cheek left bared by her thong. Her hips crowded closer to his and he pressed his erection against the give of her abdomen. His face lowered to her hair. "Lucy, we should—"

"Take this to the bedroom," she finished for him, closing her eyes at the delicious sensation of his palm caressing her naked bottom. They weren't playing the start-and-stop game, not this time. She opened her eyes and her gaze lifted to his. "And I mean it."

He laughed, that soft, amused laugh, as if her fierceness didn't frighten him. "Else what? You're going to bite me?"

A little smile played across her mouth. "Or else I'm *not* going to bite you." And then she did, she bit him, a tiny nip right into the hard muscle of his chest wall.

Carlo jerked, and then in a blink he had her in his arms and was striding out of the kitchen. Giddy with triumph, she clung to him as her blood sped around her body just like her brothers' slot cars used to careen around their zigzagging track. In a darkened bedroom, she only had the impression of austere space before she found herself dropped to a wide mattress.

Carlo stood beside it, looking down at her.

Her bare torso was pale in the shadows and in the vee of her unfastened jeans was a slice of the brighter white of her thong. Lucy toed off her shoes and socks, then went to work dragging off the clinging denim pants under his scrutinizing gaze.

She marveled at herself all the while. As much as she felt the need for speed, because giving Carlo time for second thoughts meant there'd be no follow-through for them, getting naked for a man wasn't the most natural of Lucy Sutton maneuvers. She'd had a few lovers— three—but at this stage of the process she'd always felt a little fear mixed with the want in the pit of her belly.

A man was so much bigger. So much stronger. So much…other.

But now, with Carlo…

She kicked her pants over the side of the bed and hooked a thumb in each side of her thong. With Carlo she felt only breathless anticipation.

"Stop right there," he ordered.

She froze. Her gaze jumped to his, but his eyes were impenetrable in the dark room. Just more shadows.

The bed dipped as his hip settled on the mattress. His hand cupped the vee between her thighs. "What's your hurry?"

Hot, liquid desire rushed to meet the warmth of his hand. "I…I…" There was a reason, but she couldn't remember right now what it was. "You…you…"

"Am the one who will be setting the pace." He leaned over to deliver an almost-chaste kiss to her mouth, her lips softened by the need his expert fingers were stoking. They rubbed lightly over the satiny fabric of her panties. "I'm the boss."

Her legs edged open and she reached for his shoulders to bring him closer. His chest brushed the tips of her breasts as he let her draw him down. "I've never been the best of employees, Mr. Milano." Her voice sounded strained, but what else could she do? If he wouldn't let her rush, then he had to let her keep it light.

Make it a game.

"So maybe you could outline the rules for me," she added.

"Hmm. All right." He straightened, going business-like. "Take a memo, Ms. Sutton."

Her fingers wandered over his nearest thigh to find his hard length behind his jeans. His hand caught her searching digits before they could curl around his erection.

"Ms. Sutton!" he said in mock shock.

"I'm only looking for a pencil," she protested.

He choked back his laugh, then directed her touch himself so that she located her target. It was gratifyingly thick. Even through denim he felt hot.

"Oh, Mr. Milano. This instrument may be a little larger than I'm used to."

His stern voice hid more laughter. "Are you bucking for a raise?" She heard him suck in a breath as she used the heel of her hand to trace his length. "Never mind then, Ms. Sutton, I'll write the memo myself."

She could have cried as his hand left its aching niche between her thighs, his forefinger drawing a line from the cleft upward, on the way bumping sensitive places that made her squirm against the spread.

"From Carlo Milano," he whispered into the dark around them as his finger made curlicues across her midriff. "To all temporary employees."

"*All* temporary employees?" she questioned.

His hand stilled. "Point taken. Thank you, Ms. Sutton. To all small, blonde, sexy yet temporary secretaries named Lucy. When in bed, there's no rushing the tasks at hand. There's no taking shortcuts. Clothes are optional—" and here he drew her thong down himself "—and screaming in pleasure is completely necessary."

She should have laughed. It was a game after all, a seductive little game that she'd started. He was taking over, coming down on the mattress and between her legs so that they had to widen to accommodate him. He was still wearing his jeans, and the denim abraded the sensitive skin of her inner thighs as he leaned down to suck her nipple.

But the suction of his hot, wet mouth set aside everything in her mind except how right his weight felt, how well he knew to stoke her fire, how the way he blew air over her damp nipple was going to make her mad. "Carlo—"

"Mr. Milano," he corrected, moving over to her other breast.

She gasped as he drew it into his mouth. "Mr. Milano, that…that…oh, keep doing that."

What had she been thinking? She never wanted to hurry this part. And he kept his promise about setting the pace. The slow, slow pace. He left her breasts, left them aching, to move up her neck and explore the hollow behind her ears, the smooth skin at her temples, and to draw a line down her nose with the tip of his tongue.

She leaped like a fish to catch his mouth with hers and she heard him give another of those low laughs as he delivered nipping little kisses on her lips. But that wasn't what she wanted, she wanted more—long kisses, luscious kisses, tongue kisses. Her hands gripped his hair to hold him closer, but he grabbed her wrists and pressed them gently to the mattress.

"Patience, Ms. Sutton," he whispered against her ear, setting off another rush of goose bumps over her skin and liquid heat between her legs.

"Mr. Milano," she panted out, struggling against his hold, which did nothing more than twist their torsos together so that his crisp chest hair teased her aching breasts. "Mr. Milano, I…I think I have some messages I was supposed to deliver to you."

He reared up to look into her face, but again the shadows kept him in the dark. "What kind of messages?"

She raised up to kiss his stubbled chin. Wow. Even the whiskers turned her on. "Personal messages. Might I…I give them to you now?"

His hold loosened on her wrists and she took advantage of the moment to eel out from underneath him. Then she pushed him flat on the bed and leaned in to deliver the kiss she wanted. Long. Wet. Her tongue, she hoped, delivered the communication that she was really, really having a good time here.

His hands caressed her naked hips as she raised her head. She heard him swallow. "Interesting, Ms. Sutton. Are there...are there any others like that?"

"Like that and more." She leaned in to deliver them, even as her hand sneaked down his belly. His stomach muscles twitched and his hand closed more tightly on the curve of her hip as she found the placket of his jeans. Then they were loosened and her hand found the hard heat that was so silky smooth to her touch.

Carlo dispensed with his jeans and his briefs in the speediest move he'd yet to make. Finally he and Lucy were naked next to each other and exchanging all kinds of communiqués: smooth to muscled, hard to yielding, man to woman.

He rolled on a condom. Then her hips tilted to take him in and they both groaned as he slid inside her. The delicious pressure set her to squirming again, and he clamped his hand once more around her hip in an attempt to still her instinctive movements. "Baby..."

"That's *Ms.* Baby," she said, squeezing her eyes shut as he drew out again, the slick friction so sweet and hot that she wanted to beg for more.

"Ms. Baby, this is so damn good. What...what is your critique, if I may ask?"

"Thank you...thank you so much for your interest in my opinion, Mr. Milano. And I, too, think it's very, very good."

Then he started a driving rhythm that made speech, let alone games, impossible. To keep up, Lucy wrapped her thighs around his hips, but he was making her mindless. Release was rushing toward her and she didn't know whether to hold back or run toward its way.

Then Carlo slid his hand between their bodies and stroked the sweetest spot of all. "I think it's time, Ms. Sutton," he said. "I think it's time to scream."

After she did, after he came with an intensity that included a small, stinging bite on her shoulder, Carlo tucked Lucy into the bed beside him. They didn't talk. They didn't do anything to shatter the sated mood.

Sometime in the still-dark hours of the morning, she woke to find him at her breasts again—how quickly he'd learned her weakness! He drew her on top of him this time and she undulated against him, setting the pace, taking what she wanted, giving what he asked for in encouraging whispers.

They slept again.

The next time Lucy woke, the room was filled with pale gray light. Carlo was on the other pillow, studying her face.

She instantly felt a chill at his somber expression. "We shouldn't have—" he started.

"Oh, no," she said, jerking instantly upright. She didn't even bother to hold the sheet against her breasts. "Oh, no, no, no."

"What?"

"Don't you go all fuddy-duddy on me now."

Annoyance replaced the seriousness on his face. "I wish you wouldn't use that term."

"I wish you wouldn't force me to." Now she drew up the sheet, even as she started edging out of the bed. "I'm not going to let you take all the fun out of this."

"The 'fun'?"

"Well, ye-ah." She frowned at him, as fierce as she

could make it. "Have you forgotten the whipped cream? What would you call our little boss-secretary role playing, huh? Huh?"

"Lucy—"

"Look. I've got to get back to Elise's. Then I have this family brunch thing. So listen to me fast and listen to me good. Last night we were both in need of a little fun. So that's what we had. Nothing more and nothing less."

And with luck, she'd have to say nothing else about it. No matter *what* she might want to say. No matter when she figured out what exactly that might be.

Lucy carried a tray of orange juice onto the back patio and stopped before her father. "OJ, Dad?"

He took a glass and she moved on to one of her older brothers, Sam. His nose was buried in the business section of the Sunday paper and she raised her foot to tap the middle with her sandal. "Hey, Mr. Wall Street. Want something to drink?"

He looked up at her as he folded the paper into his lap. "Don't mind if I do. And what's got you all rosy-cheeked this a.m., Goose?"

Rosy cheeks went even redder under his scrutiny, if their heat was any indication. Lucy wasn't going to give him her first guess, though. Telling her brother she was suffering from beard burn was just not going to happen. "What's with the newspaper?" she said, changing the subject as she slid her tray onto a nearby end table. "Don't you get enough financial fodder with your weekday dose of the *Wall Street Journal*?"

He stretched out his long legs and ran a hand over his crisp, short golden hair. "I was poring over the want ads for you, little sister. Someone's got to be concerned about your future."

"For a minute there I thought she could make a mighty fine waitress, but then she neglected to bring *me* a glass of orange juice," Jason, her other brother, complained. "Thanks for nothing, Lucy."

She shook her head, looking between their handsome, supercilious faces. "And to think I moved back to San Diego because I missed you guys." Still, she carried over a juice to Jason, sprawled on a cushioned lounge chair.

"You came back because you were broke," he said, reaching for the glass.

At that, she lifted it higher, letting the liquid slosh over the rim of the glass. "Whoops," she said as juice spilled onto the lenses of his dark glasses. "Look what I just did."

He sprang to his feet as liquid ran toward his chin, whipping off his sunglasses and then lunging for her as she leaped away from him. "Lucy, you'll pay for that."

From her safe position behind her father's chair she grinned at him. "And how am I going to do that when you're so sure I'm broke?"

Her brother gave up and turned toward the hose coiled in a nearby corner. Water gushed out, and he rinsed his glasses and then filled his cupped palm with water to clean his face, too. He glanced over his shoulder, his gaze speculative, but Lucy hadn't moved from behind her father's chair. She laughed.

"Foiled again, Jase," she said, knowing that if he could have gotten a clear shot she'd be drenched by now.

Her mother came out just as he started making another threat for future retaliation. "And here I thought my children were all grown-up," she scolded, though Lucy could tell she was so happy to have them there that they could have started an all-out food fight and Laura Sutton wouldn't have minded. She was slender and as short as Lucy, and it was amazing to think she'd produced two six-foot-tall boys, not to mention Lucy and Elise.

Which reminded her...

"Where's Elise and John, Mom?" Everyone in the family knew about Germaine McMillan's fall, and Lucy had adjusted the timeline a bit to cover her absence from her own bed at her sister's house. As far as the Sutton family members knew, she'd spent all of the night before at the hospital, not just part of it. When she'd made it back to Elise's that morning, her sister and John had already left to run a 10K, but they were expected to arrive for the brunch.

"Your sister and brother-in-law are stuck in traffic." Lucy's mother settled one hip on the arm of Lucy's dad's chair, and he automatically settled his hand on her thigh. "What's going on out here?" she asked.

Sam spoke up. "I was going through the want ads to find Lucy a job."

Lucy's mouth tightened. "I *have* a job."

"Well, and how's that going?" he went on. "You haven't said."

Four pairs of Sutton eyes turned on her. Lucy cleared her throat. "Fine."

"Are you showing up on time? Taking a normal lunch hour?"

Lucy bristled at her brother's interrogation. "Work days start at eleven, right? And lunch goes from twelve-thirty to three?"

"Lucy…" her mother started. "We love you. Your brother is just trying to—"

"Imply I'm lazy? Suggest I don't know how to be an employee?"

"Goose, come on." To his credit, Sam appeared sincere. "You have to admit it's a bit…strange that you couldn't stick with any of those jobs in Phoenix."

"Strange for the Suttons. But a lot of other people find that their first position out of college isn't exactly right."

"Or, in your case, the second, and then the third?" This was from Jason. Leave it to a lawyer to trot out the facts.

"I worked plenty hard at those jobs and the people I worked for liked me." She just hadn't liked what she was doing for them. "I know you guys find that difficult to believe."

"Lucy." Her dad, the quietest of the bunch, entered the conversation. "Nobody's doubting your ability to do a good job."

"Remember all the work she did on her high school's prom?" her mom chimed in. "The principal gave her special recognition at the graduation ceremony. And then there were those very successful fund-raisers she spearheaded for her college sorority's charity."

"Thanks, Mom," Lucy replied. She *had* been damn good at organizing those events, just as she'd done well with things like the balloon festival postcollege. Of course, none of that impressed her siblings, who measured success by climbing rungs on the corporate ladder. "And I'm going to find the right place for me in San Diego. I will."

"Carlo will surely give you a good recommendation," Sam said. "That will help."

Lucy still didn't want to talk about Carlo. She didn't want to think about him, about last night, about how his touch had set her on fire. Thank goodness it was Sunday and she had time away from him to forget that sexy laugh in his voice—would she ever hear "Ms. Sutton" again and not want to quiver?—and the seriously sensual way they'd come together the second time, his palms dragging over her skin and igniting fires in every cell.

"He *will* give you a good recommendation, right, Lucy?"

"What?" she looked around, surprised to find herself out on her parents' patio when she'd been so lost in her memories a second before. "Who?"

Sam rolled his eyes. "What exactly are you doing at McMillan & Milano, anyway? Given the way you're so distracted I hope it's nothing that requires more concentration than opening envelopes."

"Samuel!" her mother scolded. "If that's your way of encouraging your sister…"

He waved off the criticism. "Goose knows I only want the best for her. But I'm concerned, Mom. We're all concerned." He sighed. "Goose, I'm sorry if I seem like I'm coming down hard on you. That's not my intention."

"I know." Lucy sighed, too. This was the curse of being the youngest sibling. Your family remembered you as the five-year-old who couldn't spell, and then it didn't help that you didn't grow up and instantly become a corporate clone of the rest of them. She knew they loved her. She loved their hypersuccessful, hyper-judgmental selves right back.

She only wished they'd trust her to find her own way to her own kind of success. Wherever that was. Whatever that was. She eyed the newspaper her brother had cast aside and then crossed over to pick it up. Accounting positions started on page P-2.

The fine print swam before her eyes and she closed them, picturing herself spending the next thirty years inside the black-and-gray world of a classified ad. Orderly, colorless, one column after another after another after another. Just like accounting. Why had she studied it anyhow? Because her family thought it was a good idea.

Bleh. But she forced her attention to return to the pages. "There's probably a position just made for me in here," she said, her voice bright. "I graduated with honors. I have accounting experience in different types of businesses."

"Good spin, sis. Better than 'I've changed jobs as often as some people change hairstyles.'"

She ignored her attorney brother's latest attack.

"How much longer will you be working for Carlo?" her mom asked.

Oh, that name had to come up again. Lucy left the dreary world of black-and-white and set sail on yet more memories. Swallowing a snicker, she remembered Carlo's surprise when she'd sprayed him with the chocolate whipped cream. Wouldn't that be fun to try again? Next time, she wouldn't use her finger to clean his naked skin of the fluffy stuff. Next time, it would be her tongue, and she could well imagine his little jerk of reaction as she stroked it across his bare pectoral…

But there wouldn't be a next time, right?

Or *could* there be a next time?

Aaargh. In bed that morning, Lucy had been worried about *his* reaction to last night. Now she saw that she should have been worrying about her own, too. What did she want to happen next?

She didn't know what she wanted to happen next. That's why she'd cut off the discussion this morning. She'd insisted to him it was all in fun, but was it a *single* night of fun? Is that what he wanted? Is that what *she* wanted? She couldn't think beyond those memories of his deep kisses and his tender touch.

Ms. Sutton, I think it's time to scream.

"Earth to Goose. Earth to Goose."

Lucy swam free of the latest wave of remembered longing to hear her brother's pestering voice. Lowering the newspaper, she frowned at him. "What now?" She didn't want to come back to earth. Putting her feet on the ground meant coming to terms with the new situation with Carlo.

And she was so confused about that.

She noticed the whole family was staring at her again. "What? *What?*"

Jason looked over at Sam. "I didn't think it was possible, but she's become goosier than ever. I don't think she's heard a word we've been saying."

"About what?" Lucy demanded.

"About what you're doing at McMillan & Milano. Dad got wind that you've taken over some project involving the Street Beat festival. Is that a good idea?"

"What do you mean?"

"I don't know," Jason answered. "But you're trained as an accountant. Should you be involving yourself with a *music* festival? I've heard about Claudia Cox and word has it she's not known for her patience or her generosity. You don't want to screw up the job when it's Carlo who will pay the price."

Lucy's insecurities slithered out of the holes in her psyche like eels from coral-reef caves. She was trained as an accountant and had never loved her duties in that kind of work—even though she was good at it. Why did she presume that her Street Beat responsibilities would go smoothly? She was an accountant. A numbers person.

"Maybe…maybe you're right," she heard herself say. "Carlo…" The festival wasn't something to take lightly. It was his work, his reputation, his business. What if she did screw up? She licked her lips. "Carlo…"

And then it was Carlo's own voice that finished the sentence she was trying to form. "Is very satisfied with everything Lucy's done."

Chapter 8

There was a flurry of greetings as Carlo joined them on the patio. He glanced over at Lucy. "Your mother called a little bit ago and invited me over for brunch," he said, replying to the surprise that was surely written all over her face. "I guess she forgot to tell you. I caught a ride with Elise and John. Maybe you'll give me a lift to my car later?"

"Oh. Um, sure." Of course. They'd left his Lexus yesterday at the office when she'd driven them to the beach. Had that only been yesterday that they'd been at the beach, and then at the hospital, and then in his bed? Her gaze skittered away from his.

Don't make a fool of yourself, Lucy. But it wasn't easy facing him for the first time in front of her family. If her cheeks had been red before, they had to be glowing scarlet now, and she didn't want anyone guessing there was anything romantic going on between the two of them.

Because of course there wasn't.

Last night had just been…

Fun. *She'd* labeled it that, not him, and she refused to make more of it now. And it was *private* fun, so she had to get it together or one of her nosy siblings was bound to figure out something was up and embarrass the heck out of her over it.

Or worse, embarrass Carlo.

She managed to look him in the eye. "Do you know how Germaine is doing this morning?"

"Very well. Dot's already taken her home. I'll visit this afternoon."

"Which means you have plenty of time now to tell us everything, Carlo," Sam called out. "We can't count on Goose to give us the real skinny when it comes to her employment adventures. How's our Ms. Sutton handling her job responsibilities?"

Ms. Sutton.

Lucy's gaze jumped to Carlo again, she couldn't help herself. He was studying his glass of OJ, but as if he felt her looking at him, he lifted his tangle of dark lashes and stared right back.

Ms. Sutton, it's time to scream.

"Carlo?" Sam prodded. "I swear, you're as distracted as Lucy's been all morning. If I didn't know better—"

They were spared the end of that sentence by the arrival of Elise and John, who'd been delayed in the kitchen by a coffee ring they'd brought and had cut into wedges. Now they were ready to pass the pieces around.

"Sweets?" Elise smiled up at Carlo as she offered him a plate. He smiled back down at her and it struck Lucy, for the millionth time in her life, how perfect her sister was with her smooth, Grace Kelly hair, her long legs, her slender figure—she'd already run a 10K that morning! Add to that the fact that she'd recently received yet another big promotion at work.

It wasn't Elise's fault that males had always been drawn to her, despite her unswerving devotion to her husband. Who wouldn't be attracted to such loveliness?

And at the moment, Carlo looked as if he couldn't pull his gaze away from her. Lucy wished it didn't make her feel so stupid and glum. Not to mention short.

A plate of the strudel-y pastry didn't make her lousy mood go away. It just made her feel more dowdy than ever. Neither did her sister's sharp look. "What's the matter, Luce?" she said, keeping her voice below the rest of the conversation on the patio.

Lucy kept her gaze wide-eyed and innocent. "Not a thing. Why do you ask?"

Elise frowned. "You—"

Jason's loud voice drowned out her sister's next remark. "C'mon, Carlo. You've had orange juice, you've had pastry, and Mom's famous egg-and-potato bake is on its way. It's only fair you provide a little entertainment."

"Gee, Jase," he answered. "I left my accordion at home. Maybe you can play us a tune on your harmonica."

"Funny," her brother said. "But I just told you what I'm looking for. Give us the dirt on our Goose. Surely she's done something lately to liven up your days."

Lucy felt her face freeze. *His days...and his nights.*

"Yeah," her other brother chimed in. "We can never figure out why she's played musical desk chairs—"

"Three companies in as many years, Sam," Lucy heard herself protest. "It's not as if..."

But she broke off on a sigh. The way the other Sutton siblings were looking at her she knew that to them, three different jobs in such a short time might as well be thirteen. They just could not comprehend that someone in their family wouldn't land in their dream position after graduation and then succeed beyond everyone's wildest expectations.

"Never mind," she muttered, looking away from them. "You guys won't understand."

Nor would they let up. Maybe if their parents hadn't gone off to the kitchen with Elise's John to put the finishing touches on brunch, her brothers would have abandoned the subject. But they were still looking to have fun at her expense. Hard to believe they were over thirty.

They turned back to her boss. "Tell us how she does it," Sam insisted. "How does she sabotage all her employment opportunities? Does she spill coffee over her keyboard? Take pictures of her naked butt on the copy machine? Sharpen the pens instead of the pencils?"

How many times had she told them she'd never been fired? They never believed her. Lucy jammed her hands in the pockets of her jeans and pretended to ignore their conversation by inspecting a hibiscus bush on the edge of the patio. But the long silence coming from Carlo had her turning to take a peek at him.

He was frowning at her brothers. "You two make me want to call my little sister Franny."

Her male siblings exchanged glances. "Huh?"

"I think I need to drop to my knees for some serious groveling in case I've ever been even half as obnoxious to her as you are to Lucy."

Sam sat straighter in his chair, his expression shocked. "Wait a sec—"

"We're not obnoxious to Goose," her other brother interrupted. "We care about Goose. Who told her that her front tire needed air?"

"I leant her forty bucks two weeks ago."

"Which I paid back to you the next day," Lucy said through her teeth. "The ATM was broken."

If her brothers hadn't looked so honestly bewildered, she might have been angrier at them. If she didn't know they'd take a bullet for her and didn't see how their teasing got so out of hand, she might have given them a dose of their own medicine. As it was, she just wanted to knock their two blockheads together and call it a day.

"Anyway, what does that have to do with shedding light on Lucy and her work habits?" Really, she supposed by definition a lawyer was tenacious, but Jason was the type who never let go of anything. "My bet's on the naked-butt copying."

Carlo shook his head. "There's been *no* naked—" He broke off, cleared his throat, started again. "She's done absolutely nothing like what you're talking about."

"You don't have to cover for her. We love the little screwup just as she is." Sam beamed a smile full of that emotion at her even as she shook her head. Cripes. Nothing like ruining her image around her boss. Apparently they'd known Carlo for too long to even think of that.

Carlo's arms crossed over his chest. "You guys are unbelievable. I'm not covering anything. As a matter of fact, Lucy's an exemplary employee. Besides all the regular secretarial duties she stepped in to perform so ably, she's impressed the hell out of one of my clients and has taken on an additional project of her own for Street Beat. So you two had better lay off Lucy or I'll be forced to remind you what my fist feels like against your faces. We might have been twelve the last time we went a round or two, but I assure you I'm in better shape now."

Sam and Jason stared at Carlo, dumbfounded again and this time completely shaken from their descent into adolescence. Elise murmured, "That's the longest speech I've heard him make in the past six years." Another heartbeat passed, then the three Sutton siblings turned as one to look at Lucy, something that looked dangerously like speculation sparkling in their eyes.

Uh-oh. Though half of her wanted to dissolve in tears and the other half wanted to kiss Carlo silly in gratitude for his support, the suspicion on her brothers' and sister's faces called for something else entirely. There was no way she wanted them to figure out there was anything more than employer-to-employee respect between herself and the dark-haired man on the patio.

So she did what she could to draw them off the scent.

Throwing up her hands, she ran over to her temporary boss and flung herself against his chest. "My hero!" she cried out dramatically. His arms automatically closed around her back, making her want to cry even more.

What a sap she was. But she couldn't, just couldn't, let him or anyone else know how much his defense meant to her. Then they might make assumptions about how much *he* meant to her. So instead, she made a big play of looking over her shoulder at Jason. "Can I borrow that forty again?"

Puzzled, he drew out his wallet. "Sure."

She stuffed the two bills into Carlo's breast pocket. "Like I said, fella, there's more where that came from anytime you can get these two arrogant juvenile idiots off my back." With a big wink, she sashayed out of his embrace.

The Lucy Show seemed to satisfy her brothers—after another moment they laughed at her like she'd hoped they would. Then the conversation moved on to sports and Lucy was able to retreat to her hibiscus bush again.

She blew out a long breath. That had been close. One of the very reasons Carlo had not wanted to give in to their mutual attraction was because it would make events like this awkward. So it definitely would have been a disaster if this morning-after was marred by her family's intrusion into what she and Carlo hadn't figured out yet for themselves.

Fun, Lucy, she reminded herself. *You did figure it out, or at least you told him you did. You told him it was a night of fun and not to make any more of it than that.*

It *wasn't* any more than that.

Still, she wanted to keep the events of the previous night private.

"Lucy!" Her sister hissed her name.

She gave a guilty start and turned to face Elise. "What?" On the other side of the patio, the men were still talking among themselves. "What's the matter?"

"You're the matter," Elise said, her voice almost a whisper. "I know where you were last night."

"I told you. At the hospital, and when I called I also told you that I didn't know if I'd make it home before morning." All true.

"Don't give me that." Elise slid a glance over her shoulder, then pinned Lucy with her gaze. "You were with Carlo."

"Of course. I told you. We were together when the call came about Germaine—"

"You were with Carlo and you and he had sex."

The last word gave Lucy another guilty start. "I don't know why you think—"

"It's written all over your face, and Lucy, he's going to break your heart."

She swallowed. "My heart's not involved. It was just...just...for fun."

Her sister rolled her eyes.

It was just...just...for fun. Had she really said that? Now it sounded stupid to her own ears. Who had sex with a long-time family friend for *fun?*

"Lucy, how could you be so foolish? He's not interested in anything long-term. You're going to have to get that through your head."

Lucy's heart fell like a stone to the pit of her stomach. Her sister was right. Carlo wasn't interested in anything long-term because Elise, the love of his life, was standing right in front of her.

Gazing at her sister's lovely face, she thought of why he'd looked so sadly at Lucy this morning. She'd known how he felt about Elise. And in the light of day, he'd probably regretted waking up in bed with the shorter, bubbly-yet-bumbling version of the woman he'd always pine for.

If Carlo had expected to find the drive from the Sutton family home to the McMillan & Milano offices uncomfortable, he was quickly proved wrong. After squeezing into the passenger seat of Lucy's car, he had to do nothing more than listen while she pattered about some story her father had told them over brunch.

It was natural. Easy. As if everything between them was fine. Unchanged.

He rubbed his palms against his thighs and tried to find a few more inches for his long legs. Wasn't this every single man's dream come true? A spectacular night in the sack without any resulting changes in the status quo.

Yeah. Every single man's dream, and since Lucy herself had proposed it would go like this—that it was nothing more and nothing less than "fun"—then he had no reason to do anything but sit back and breathe through it.

Still, when she paused, he figured it was only fair he do his part in keeping the easy conversation going. "What do you have planned for the rest of your day off?" he asked.

Her sweet mouth turned up at the corners in a little smile. "If you must know, Mr. Milano…"

Mr. Milano. The words fell like the clunk of the other shoe into the middle of the car's sudden quiet.

Mr. Milano. A dozen images bombarded Carlo's brain. Lucy, naked and stretched out before him, the pale curves of her breasts topped by nipples he'd made hard and wet with his mouth. Her slender wrists held gently in one of his hands as she squirmed against his mattress. The perfect, glistening shell-pink flesh he'd discovered between her thighs.

He barely held back his groan. "Lucy…Lucy, about last night—"

"Please. Let's not talk about it."

"Are you blushing?" Believe it or not, a flush was definitely crawling up her neck to her cheeks. He stared.

"Wasn't it you who broke out the chocolate whipped cream?"

She licked her bottom lip. "It was the heat of the moment."

"It was hot, all right."

"It was *fun*."

"Lucy..."

He saw her fingers tighten on the steering wheel. "What's wrong with fun? Where in the male-female relations manual does it say sex has to be performed with a proper level of gravitas?"

"Nowhere." He sighed. But he didn't want her to think that it made what they'd done together meaningless or forgettable. He didn't want to be yet another man in her life, like her brothers Jason and Sam, who didn't take her seriously.

Lucy, for all her sunshiny nature, deserved better. Or maybe *because* of her sunshiny nature, she deserved his best.

She deserved his honesty. Though she'd given him that perfect excuse for ducking from it—"let's not talk about it," she'd just said—he didn't need to go along.

"Lucy, would you mind driving me to the hospital before going to get my car?"

For the first time since they'd climbed into the Volkswagen, she darted a look at him. "I don't know..."

The Suttons were all so damn smart. She could tell he had his own agenda and wasn't sure she wanted to comply. "Please," he said.

She shot him another look, gave a little shrug, then changed lanes and took the appropriate exit. He didn't continue until she'd pulled into a spot in the hospital's visitors' parking lot.

Though the sights and smells of the hospital corridors couldn't reach him here, Carlo's gut was already knotting. He wiped a hand down his face and reminded himself that he owed Lucy an explanation. She'd been there for him last night when he needed someone and there was no reason not to share this with her. He'd stay calm and cool and the whole conversation would soon be over.

Then he would have done the right thing and then they could go forward, because he would have assuaged some of his guilt.

One hand swiped over his face yet again and he finally started, trying to ignore the gruffness in his voice. "I need to tell you about how I was feeling last night. About why we ended up in bed when I was so certain we shouldn't before."

"I know why you've been resisting," Lucy said quickly. She was staring out the windshield and her hands were still on the steering wheel, as if she was planning a quick getaway.

He frowned at her. "You know?"

She spoke the next words with the same speed one ripped a bandage off a wound. "It's because of Elise."

"What?" Astonishment cracked his voice.

Lucy continued staring out the windshield. "I've known about it for years. Since her wedding day. You're in love with Elise."

"Good God." He tilted his head to stare at the Volkswagen's roof. "Where to start? Believe me, Lucy, last night…at no point did any of that concern Elise."

"Okay."

It was not an okay-I-believe-you kind of an okay,

but an okay-I'll-humor-you okay. "Lucy, I'm not in love with Elise!"

Lucy remained silent.

He shook his head. "Do I strike you as the kind of man who would torture myself over the past six years by hanging around with my best friend if I was in love with his wife?"

"You don't hang around so much anymore, not according to my sister."

He grimaced. "Don't tell me Elise thinks I'm in love with her. I don't believe that for a minute."

"She just noted that you're kind of...remote these days. You know, arrive late to social gatherings, leave early...."

"I get it. I'm not the life of the party anymore."

"I thought I understood why," Lucy said quietly. "I thought I understood why you gravitated toward the distant corner. I thought I saw something, heard something at Elise and John's wedding..."

He shook his head. There she went again. Lucy saw things about him that no one else ever knew. "You're wrong about how I feel now. Okay, on Elise and John's wedding day...which was a *long* time ago, I did experience a brief pang. But it was brief and then it was eclipsed by..."

He sighed, even at the hospital it was hard to push out the words. Settling for others, he said, "I was never what you'd call a party animal, Luce—"

"You used to laugh, though. And you used to make up limericks. Not dirty ones, just...funny ones. You had a new one every time I saw you."

He'd forgotten about that. It seemed forever ago, but

the memory made him smile. "You know what? I collected those for you, Lucy."

"Me?"

"You're the only person in the world who knows I
used to have a limerick side."

"So what happened?" Lucy asked. "Where did all
the limericks go?"

Hesitating, he gazed out the side window.

"If it's not Elise, then it's Pat. It's about your partner's death."

His head whipped toward her. "What makes you
think that?" He thought he was so careful to keep its
effect hidden from everyone.

"I was with you at the hospital, remember? And then
that night at Germaine's, too. The night of the Street
Beat party."

The night she'd seen how weak the memories had
made him. The night she'd stepped in and distracted
him from the way they seemed to suck him down.

"Last night…last night you did for me what you did
that other time, Lucy. Sometimes…sometimes remembering gets to be too much."

"Do you want to tell me about what happened?"

Carlo inhaled a breath. It was why he'd come here,
yet still he hesitated.

"He was shot, right?"

Shot. Four letters. One word. It had all happened that
simply and that quickly. "We were heading back from
an interview. Saw a patrol car with a lone cop who'd
pulled over a van full of teenagers in a residential area
of working-class homes."

It had rained earlier. The wipers on their unmarked
detective's vehicle had left a sludge of mud in the cor-

ners of their windshield, and the smell of wet asphalt filled the car when Pat unrolled his window to check if the police officer wanted help with his traffic stop.

Yes, he'd appreciate it. There was a passel of kids who were milling on the sidewalk and they were distracting the officer from his job.

"Pat got out to keep a lid on the kids, but first he strapped into his bulletproof vest. Just a precaution as there had been some gang activity in the area. I drove up the street to find a place to pull over. I put on my own vest, then I was getting out of the car when I heard gunshots."

He'd dived back in the car and grabbed the radio to call for assistance. Then he'd peered over the seat and seen that everyone on the scene, from the patrol cop to the smallest of the teenagers, had gone belly-down. He'd crept out of the car, staying low with his gun in hand, and he'd barked at them, ordering them not to move.

Almost immediately more police appeared on the scene and surrounded the kids. The bullets hadn't come from them, but from someplace across the street, Carlo had figured. When there weren't any further gunshots, the kids started to stir. And that's when Carlo realized Pat wasn't moving at all.

"The bullet pierced him under the armhole of his vest. Unlucky shot, I guess." The end of a life.

Carlo stared out the windshield, remembering Pat's drenched sleeve, the last glimmers of awareness in his eyes, the bewildered look on Germaine's face when Carlo had broken the news. His hands had still been sticky with his partner's blood.

Now he locked down on his memories, refusing to let them run free. His emotions, too, he locked away.

"He was six weeks away from retirement. Germaine couldn't comprehend how it had happened." Carlo had watched, helpless, as she fell apart. "She's stronger now," he said, "but then…but then… I did the best I could. I made the funeral arrangements. I went through his closet and drawers." Even though each time he touched an article of Pat's clothing, Carlo could still see the blood on his hands.

"I'm sorry," Lucy whispered.

"Last night…last night I remembered it all too well."

"Carlo…" He heard her sniff.

He lifted his gaze to her face. "Oh, Lucy." She was crying, the tears flowing down her cheeks. "I didn't tell you this to upset you."

"I know. But I know how you must feel—"

"That's the thing, Luce. That's how I'm different now. I usually don't feel. Not too much."

"What?"

"I work. I work some more. I think about work. I try not to think about anything else or get too caught up in the past or with other people. I like it that way."

"Carlo…"

"It's how I want it, Lucy. It's why I don't do the couple thing, it's why I shouldn't be here right now, raining on all your bright sunshine. I like my distance. I like my darkness. I'm most comfortable without strong connections. It's why I'm better off alone in those distant corners."

She nodded. Drying her cheeks with the backs of her hands, she appeared to understand and accept his explanation. It was all true, anyway, and he should be feeling better for it, except…

Except Carlo suddenly couldn't shake the notion that Lucy's tears would be as hard to forget as the sight of his partner's blood.

Chapter 9

Lucy straightened a small memo pad on the seat of an empty chair and arranged a sharpened pencil at a perpendicular angle beside it. She'd pushed back the partition between the two conference rooms in the Mc-Millan & Milano offices so that all fifty volunteers for the Street Beat festival could be seated during their one and only orientation meeting, scheduled for five-thirty that evening. Checking her watch, she felt her stomach give a nervous twitch, even though she'd checked and double-checked the arrangements.

There was a lot riding on this project. Of course, the high school students and parents needed to walk away from their volunteer experience with positive feelings about Street Beat, as well as McMillan & Milano. But there was more. Her temporary position at the security firm was coming to an end after this weekend—and she needed to walk away from it with something, too.

Sunday brunch at her parents' the weekend before had made clear that she still had a long way to go in proving to her family that Lucy Goosey had grown up. She hoped a successful end to her Street Beat project would shut the traps of her confidence-crushing big brothers. And maybe a successful end to her employment at McMillan & Milano would take that look of concern out of Elise's eyes, too.

For days, her sister had been closely watching, as if expecting that at any minute Lucy would break down and fall apart over Carlo.

Wasn't going to happen. Learning that he didn't love Elise had been a surprise. Okay, a welcome surprise, but discovering how deeply he'd been affected by his partner's death made him as big a mistake for her as ever. Sure, he didn't love her sister, but she was just as sure he didn't want to love any other woman, either.

So she'd rededicated herself to the job and to demonstrating to everyone—maybe most of all herself—that Lucy Sutton was on the path to success in her life. No more job failures, and certainly no more fixations on the completely wrong man.

Tonight's meeting was going to be the harbinger of the new, positive direction in her life.

"Wow," a voice said from the doorway.

Lucy jumped. Carlo. She darted a glance at him and went back to straightening the already-straight materials on the chair in front of her. She hadn't seen him much over the past few days, and she'd been grateful for that. He'd been busy at the Street Beat site and most of their contact had been in brief phone calls and the occasional text message.

"I like the visual aids," he said. At the front of the

combined conference rooms she'd erected an easel. An enlarged map of the festival grounds sat upon it. Along with pads and pencils, she was putting a hand-size version of the same map on each of the seats. "It looks as if you have everything covered."

"Believe it or not," she replied, moving to another chair, "I've been trained to pay attention to details."

"Oh, Ms. Sutton, I know not to underestimate you."

Ms. Sutton. The two words froze her.

They really, really needed to stop slipping those Ms. Suttons and Mr. Milanos into conversation. She supposed he hadn't meant to do it any more than she had, but still, when he used that name…

She darted another glance at him. He was leaning against the doorjamb in shirtsleeves and loosened tie. His hair was mussed, as if he'd been running his hands through it, and stubble darkened the angular line of his jaw.

Ms. Sutton. It echoed in her mind, and in a blink, her attention jumped back to that night in his bed. His beard had been in evidence then, too, and her skin prickled, remembering the burn of those whiskers against her neck and between her bare breasts.

A strangled little moan escaped her tight throat. Her knees buckled and she tried hiding the reaction by sliding into one of the empty chairs, a handful of memo pads clutched against her chest.

"Lucy?" Carlo crossed toward her. "What's wrong?"

She held up a hand, hoping to keep him away. The last thing she needed was him distracting her before she had to face her fifty volunteers. "Nothing, nothing. Just, um, nothing."

Wearing a frown, he crossed to a table she'd set

against one wall and grabbed one of the bottles of water she'd set out. He twisted off the top and handed it to her as he settled into the chair next to hers.

She closed her eyes, but that didn't help much. From here she could smell him, spicy and male, a scent that she remembered from the night in his bed, too. When she'd showered the next morning, that scent had risen off her skin to mingle with the steam.

"What's wrong?" His hand settled on her back.

She jerked away from his touch. "Don't!"

His eyebrows rose. "Lucy—"

"Sorry." She gripped the bottle. "I'm, um… I'm just a little edgy about tonight."

He gazed around the room. "You've crossed all the t's and dotted all the i's, Luce. There's nothing to be edgy about."

"Uh-uh." She jumped up to put more distance between them. "It's going to be fine."

"It had better be," said a new voice from the doorway.

Lucy swallowed her groan as the faint scent of Chanel No. 5 reached her nose. Claudia Cox. She posed in the doorway as if she were in an ad for designer wear: tall, thin and wearing her faintly superior smile.

With a wave of her hand, Lucy acknowledged the other woman. "I didn't expect to see you here."

Claudia strode into the conference room as if it were a fashion runway. "It's not that I don't have complete faith in your abilities but…"

I have no faith in your abilities, Lucy finished for her. Her stomach gave another little twist and she wondered if the office first aid kit included antacid tablets.

It's only fifty volunteers, she reminded herself.

Fifty volunteers.

And McMillan & Milano's reputation.

And pleasing Claudia Cox, the bloodthirsty huntress in charge of the Street Beat festival.

The bloodthirsty huntress was striding toward Lucy at this moment, as if she scented fresh prey. She halted in front of her and looked down from the advantage of her fashion-model-plus-four-inch-heels height. Her gaze traveled the length of Lucy's body and then back up. "She lives," Claudia pronounced.

Despite her nerves, Lucy laughed. Yeah, she wasn't wearing the funereal gear she'd had on the day she visited the concert promoter's offices. Though she watched Elise head off each morning looking elegant and polished in her tailored-to-the-nines suits, Lucy had decided against going that route any longer herself. It just did not suit—no pun intended. Instead she was wearing a silk dress that she'd paired with pumps that picked up the emerald-green in the wild paisley print.

It was bright, sure.

But it would keep the attention focused on her during the meeting.

And it felt like something Lucy Sutton would wear. Not a corporate clone.

Still, the way Claudia was appraising her through narrowed eyes made her slide a jittery hand down the dress. "Is…is everything all right?"

Claudia tapped a glossy nail against her red lips. "Wrench—you remember Wrench?"

"The singer for Silver Bucket. Of course I remember him." At first it had been thrilling to meet the lead of a band she loved, but quickly she'd determined he fit the egotistical, selfish stereotype. Five minutes in his company and she'd known she wasn't the least interested in playing groupie to his hot rocker.

"He mentioned another band to me…the Killer Angels. Do you know them?"

Okay, so he was a hot rocker with good indie-band tastes. Lucy nodded. "I found them through their website and then bought their last CD. All girls, though their lead singer has a bluesy, smoky voice that can go rocker hard or crooner soft. I think they've played some small clubs in L.A."

"I have a last-minute cancellation for the festival, and I'm looking to fill the spot. It's not prime time, but they've got to be able to hold the interest of a big crowd."

Lucy considered. "There's a nice mix on the CD I have. A couple of ballads, as well as some with a dance beat. And the band has a look. Kind of a hard-edged innocence. If I had a vote, they'd have mine."

"If you had a vote…" Claudia murmured, her eyes narrowing again. Then she pulled her cell phone from the slender leather portfolio she carried under her arm. "The Killer Angels it is."

But instead of making her call, she paused and slid a look over at Carlo, still standing on the other side of the room. Her gaze came back to Lucy's face. "Wrench asked about you, by the way."

"Me?"

"Something about maybe getting together with you to party after their gig this weekend."

"I—"

"She's not going to 'party' with that guy," Carlo interjected. He strode over to join them. "I don't know where the hell he'd get the idea that Lucy's interested in him."

Lucy tried again. "I—"

"It's Wrench who's interested in Lucy, obviously," Claudia responded in a cool voice. "And I'm just passing the info along. No need to shoot the messenger, Carlo."

He slid a proprietary hand beneath the hair at Lucy's nape. "You can't blame a man for keeping his eye on the prize, Claudia." His palm caressed the tender skin of Lucy's neck and she locked her knees so they wouldn't betray her by buckling again.

"So that's the way it is? Still?" Claudia asked, one of her perfectly arched brows arching higher. "I thought maybe that had run its course."

Lucy couldn't stop herself from turning her head to raise her own brow in Carlo's direction. He was playing that "I have a girlfriend" game for Claudia, and it didn't seem right that a man who wanted to keep his distance from Lucy would use her to keep his distance from another woman. And maybe she did want to party with Wrench! Well, not really, but it wasn't up to him to decide how the "prize" wanted to conduct her social life.

Perhaps he could read all that on her face.

"Luce…" he said softly.

She let her second brow rise. "What?"

Two of his fingers caressed the side of her neck. "Luce. I don't… You can't…" He huffed out a sigh, followed it up with an "oh, hell," and then startled the breath out of her by lowering his mouth.

And kissing her in front of the huntress, the visual aids and fifty empty chairs.

They might as well have been filled with people,

for all the attention she paid to them. Thoughts flew around her head.

No...

Why...

Why can't I pull away?

She sensed Claudia drawing back, but Lucy's eyes were closed and Carlo's mouth was so gentle yet so hot that a quiver tickled down her spine. She never wanted it to end, no matter who was there to witness it, no matter what else was supposed to be taking place—

Her eyes popped open and she shoved him away.

"My meeting," she said, wiping the back of her hand against her mouth. Thank God for that smudge-proof lipstick. "The volunteers should be here…"

Lucy checked her watch. Something inside her froze and her voice squeezed out in a tight whisper. "The volunteers should have been here twenty minutes ago."

Twenty minutes ago had been the scheduled start of her all-important meeting. The harbinger of her future.

Except there was no one there to attend,

Lucy's sudden, stricken expression yanked at Carlo's heart. "Honey." He moved forward to take her in his arms again, but she backed off.

Right. Okay. He wasn't supposed to be touching her—or, good grief, *kissing* her—anyway. So he shoved his hands in his pockets and pretended he didn't continue to feel the imprint of her mouth on his. Clearing his throat, he took another step back. "I'm sure they'll be here soon."

Lucy's gaze darted back to her watch. "It's 5:52, right?" she whispered, her voice strained. She shifted to give Claudia, still on the phone a few feet away, more of her back. "I don't have the wrong time, do I?"

"Lucy—"

"Check your watch!"

He turned his wrist. "It 5:53."

Her face paled. "That's p.m.? I didn't somehow get the day and night mixed up?"

He shook his head and couldn't help but smile a little. One kiss of hers could turn his world upside-down, too.

"No smiling!" she hissed. "This isn't funny."

To his shock, her eyes started to fill with tears. "Lucy." He reached for her again, remembered he shouldn't and let his hand drop.

"I messed up. Somehow I did something wrong. The wrong day, the wrong time, the wrong directions." She was blinking rapidly to prevent a spillover. "Oh, God, Jason and Sam are right. I *am* a perennial failure."

"Lucy—"

"I *always* get it wrong."

"Don't you think you're overreacting? The volunteers are probably delayed."

But she wasn't listening to a word he said. "I've got to think." Her hands clapped against the sides of her head. "I've got to figure out a way to fix this."

She rushed out of the conference room.

Claudia looked up from her phone call and met Carlo's gaze. *Is she okay?* she mouthed.

"Perfectly fine," Carlo assured the other woman. *Make that perfectly nuts,* he thought. But she was his perfectly nutty responsibility, so he headed after her. What had set her off? Had it…had it been his kiss?

Yeah, right. Though the kiss had affected him, once again obliterating all his good intentions. As he stalked down the hallway in search of Lucy, he made himself the same promise that he'd made before. And before that.

Don't get too close.

But then there she was, huddled in her desk chair, her head in her hands. Now he discovered that it wasn't touching her that could make him break promises. Just looking at her could get him out of his safe, metaphorical corner.

"Lucy. Honey." He hurried forward and lifted her out of her chair to hold her against his chest. Her wavy hair tickled his chin as he tucked his head to press his cheek against hers. "It's going to be okay. No matter what happened, we'll find a way to fix it."

Her body was rigid against his. She wasn't crying, but there was the sound of sobs in her voice. "How are you going to fix *me?*"

She might as well have wrapped her fists around his heart and given it a brutal twist. He gathered her closer. "Lucy. Lucy…"

Over her head, a commotion from the open door to the reception area caught his attention. His tight chest eased. He moved his mouth to her ear.

"There once was a girl with a meeting/who thought that she'd taken a beating/but her boss knew the truth/it was the traffic, forsooth/and her self-doubting should have been fleeting."

Her head turned so their gazes met. "Traffic, forsooth?"

He couldn't help himself from grinning. "I'm out of practice, okay? But it's a limerick, and I never claimed to be good at them." Putting his hands on her shoulders, he turned her in the direction of the reception area. "Put your meeting face on, woman, because your volunteers await."

He could have left it at that. Certainly the way her face had brightened had alleviated his immediate worries. And he should have left it at that, he knew it, but Carlo was a detective after all, and unanswered questions tended to nag at him until he figured them out.

Lucy's behavior today was going to nag at him until he figured *her* out.

So, ninety minutes later, after they ushered the last of the volunteers from the offices, as well as a satisfied Claudia Cox, he handed Lucy her purse, turned off the office lights, then told her, firmly, that they were going out to dinner to celebrate.

He assumed she was dazed by the swing of emotions from failure to success because she was silent as he led her to his car and then to a nearby restaurant. She didn't seem to wake from her meeting afterglow until she'd had a couple of swallows of the martini he'd ordered for her.

Then she blinked, coughed a little and looked around her with the air of someone who'd been somewhere else until that moment. They were seated in an intimate booth, but Carlo had made sure to sit across from her and had angled his long legs so that they wouldn't brush Lucy's.

"Whoa. Wow." Now she peered at the drink and then took another sip. "Nice."

He bit back his smile. Knowing Lucy's habits after the weeks she'd been working for him, he had an idea that she'd gone lunchless again, which meant that martini was going straight from her stomach to her head.

"Have some bread sticks," he suggested.

She ignored him for a nibble at her alcohol-soaked olive. "It went well, don't you think?"

"Told you."

She waved that away with her plastic spear and then dumped it back in her drink before downing another swallow. "Don't be smug."

"That would be Claudia," he replied. "I can't say what's going on with her, but I think she has something up her sleeve. Every time she looks at you she gets this speculative gleam in her eye."

"Probably calculating how many calories I'll cost her when she gobbles me down," Lucy muttered.

He laughed. "Now you understand why I passed you off as my girlfriend that first night."

Her gaze sharpened as she lifted the martini once again toward her mouth. "Okay, I get that. But what was that kiss about tonight? I thought—"

"I get to ask the questions," he interjected, because he'd be damned if he had an answer. "And my first one is why you immediately assumed when the volunteers didn't show that you'd done something wrong?"

She drained the rest of her martini and then their food arrived. Carlo was glad that she looked at her swordfish with some interest, then gave even more to her wineglass once the waiter filled it from the bottle Carlo had ordered.

Lucy was likely to get tipsy.

But that might get him the answers he wanted—and thus the distance from her he needed—that much quicker.

"Luce," he said as she set her wine down. "What happened back there?"

Her gaze slid away from him. "I don't know what you mean."

He topped off her glass and edged it closer to her hand. Okay, he was a bad man, but he'd rustle up some aspirin for her later. "You said Jason and Sam were right. That you're a failure."

A flush crawled up her neck, turning her face a pretty yet embarrassed pink. "Carlo…"

"I got to thinking about brunch after you said that. That morning when your thirtysomething-going-on-thirteen-years-old brothers were razzing you about copying pictures of your naked—"

"I've never done any such thing!" She had her glass in hand again and chugged more of her wine.

"I know. And when they mentioned it, I mostly dismissed it as some run-of-the-mill older-sibling teasing, but now I'm thinking there's more to the story."

She mumbled something into her glass.

"What?"

"I can't keep a job," she muttered, then drained her wine and looked up at him, her gaze defiant. "The first day I was at McMillan & Milano you said you heard I'd had some 'trouble' in Phoenix before coming back to San Diego. It wasn't man trouble like you guessed. It was trouble finding employment that…that I found satisfying."

She said that last as if it was a dirty, dark secret. "So, you didn't like a job," he responded. "So what? I'm not getting it."

Lucy cut her swordfish into bites, not one which made its way to her mouth. "I didn't like any of them. Over the past three years, I worked for a law firm, an elementary school district and at the corporate offices of a large health insurance company."

"Doing what?"

"I was an accountant, you know that. Numbers, columns, reports. Details. And I'm *good* with details."

There was a challenge in that last statement, too, as if she had to convince herself, as well as him. "I know you're good with details, Luce. I have no complaints on that score. None at all."

"Neither did any of my other employers." She was lifting her wineglass again. "But they didn't feel like the right fits. So I left each position hoping the next one would be better."

Her mouth turned down. "But maybe none of them worked out because what I brought to those different jobs each and every time was *me*."

"Lucy." The dejection on her face would have cracked granite, and Carlo discovered with surprise that his heart wasn't nearly that hard. "Lucy, there's absolutely nothing wrong with you."

She was already shaking her head. "Suttons don't flounder. Suttons immediately find their launch pad and then rocket toward success."

"Jason and Sam—"

"Don't forget perfect Elise."

"You're not Elise—"

"Ya think?" Slumping against the back of her seat, Lucy closed her eyes. "Really, did you have to remind me?"

Oh, hell. Carlo couldn't even stand the thought of being a tabletop away from her. In a quick move, he scooted out from his side of the booth and tucked in next to her. She didn't seem to notice. "Lucy..." The back of his fingers stroked the silky skin of her cheek.

Her eyes opened, so wide. So blue. "What if nobody ever wants me?" she whispered.

"Sweetheart—"

There was a vulnerable little slur to her words as she spoke over him. The alcohol had apparently made its way upstream. "Don' tell, but I'm not sendin' out résumés." She spoke as if her tongue had thickened. "I'm 'voiding the want ads. The *A*'s in partcler. *A* is for Accounting, y'know that?"

"Yeah. I know that." He drew his fingers over her cheek again. "But maybe you're right to avoid accounting, Luce. Maybe what was wrong with those jobs wasn't you, but you with accounting."

She was shaking her head, but he was pretty sure she wasn't listening to him. "I'm accountant. I'm *an* accountant. That means I do number stuff. Details."

"Yeah..."

She jabbed herself in the chest with her thumb. "Good with details. I'm good with details."

"Yes. Yes, you are."

Her gaze narrowed. "You mean that?"

"I do, Lucy."

"Nice. Sooo nice." She sighed, then her head dropped to his shoulder. "You wan' me, don't you, Carlo? Tell me you wan' me."

His arm went around her shoulders and he dropped a kiss on the top of her fragrant hair. Oh, hell. "God help me, Lucy, I do. Yes, I do want you."

Chapter 10

Outside the restaurant, as Carlo guided Lucy to his car, he decided against driving her to Elise and John's in her tipsy state. She'd had coffee, but still there remained a little wobble in her walk. Another cup of caffeine was needed, he told himself, and a place to drink it that was more comfortable and less public than the restaurant.

He suggested, she agreed, the car sped to his home.

Still, it surprised the hell out of him to find he was actually parked in his garage and that he was taking her by the hand and helping her out of the Lexus.

This wasn't a thinking man's move.

But the truth was, he wasn't ready to be apart from her just yet. He'd made up the coffee excuse when he was really acting on a whim instead of analyzing the life out of it instead.

When was the last time he'd done that?

When was the last time he'd felt so alive?

You want me, don't you, Carlo?

Those whispered words had acted like a defibrillator, restarting something inside him that had been deathly quiet for the past six years.

The living room felt chilled, so he bent to light the logs set in the fireplace. As they caught, he turned to Lucy, who stood in the center of the room, her arms at her sides, her big blue eyes trained on his face.

Now she didn't look drunk.

Not the tiniest bit tipsy.

You want me, don't you, Carlo?

She held her hand out to him, as if once again she'd seen inside him and heard his thoughts. She kept on doing that, didn't she?

That new living thing in his chest gave a strong jerk. That hand, those slim fingers, were an undeniable invitation. He wanted her; she wanted him. "Lucy…you're sure?"

"Aren't you, Mr. Milano?"

But this was no game, not this time, when the reflection of the flames was licking warmly at her skin just as he intended to. He opened his mouth to tell her, to make clear—what? His brain couldn't come up with a response.

He wasn't thinking again.

God, how he liked that.

His feet ate up the space between them. Then she was in his arms, the fabric of her dress cool against his palms, the body underneath it warm and pliable and so willing to press against him.

He felt a tremor run through her and he shuddered in response. "Lucy," he whispered, running his mouth from her temple to her jaw. "Lucy, Lucy, Lucy." Her head dipped like a flower on a stem so that he could explore the fragrant, smooth flesh of her neck.

He chased goose bumps to the vee over her breasts and felt her heart thudding against his mouth. His body was urging him on and he followed its impulses again, letting his hands roam over her back, her thighs, then up to cover her breasts. Beneath thin silk, her nipples tightened to points that he had to take into his mouth.

Her body arched as he did just that. He ran his tongue over fabric, wetting it, shaping her, then sucking hard, harder, because gentle wasn't alive enough for the man who now held Lucy. His thumb rubbed wet silk as he moved to the other breast and he reveled in the sweet sound of the breathy moans she made as he played with her.

Still, it wasn't enough.

His fingers found the zipper at her back and he drew it down, the sound an erotic hiss that was a counterpoint to their rough, matching breaths. The dress fell to the carpet with a plop, but he couldn't hear it, he couldn't hear anything but the whoosh-whoosh-whoosh of his blood as it galloped through him.

"Lucy," he breathed. Lucy, in a see-through bra, tiny panties, filmy stockings held up at the thighs by lace and a prayer. The high-heeled pumps on her feet only made the picture sexier.

More like a punch to the gut.

"You're so damn beautiful."

Another tremor ran through her body and he saw her sway. He took her in his arms and then bowed to impulse again and took her down to the carpet in front of the fireplace.

In the reflection of the fire, her skin glowed like

the sunshine he'd called her. "You're still dressed," she whispered, her voice husky and low, a tantalizing stroke down his spine.

He shrugged out of his jacket and yanked off his tie, tossing them both away. Then, still in his shirtsleeves and slacks, he made a place for himself between her thighs. "Gotta keep something between us."

She frowned. "Carlo—"

He kissed the protest away. "Or it will be over too fast, baby."

When he lifted his head, her mouth was slack and her eyes were closed. He lowered again to tug on her bottom lip with his teeth, and his blood made another primal whoosh-whoosh-whoosh as she moaned and entwined her legs around his hips.

Clothes couldn't stop him from pressing his erection against the heated notch between her thighs. Nothing could stop him from kissing her again, penetrating her mouth with his tongue while his hips mimicked the action.

Lucy ground up against him, making him dizzy with lust.

He so wanted her.

He told her so, whispering it against her mouth. "You turn me on, so hard, so hot."

Her hips rolled from side to side and he groaned as desire spread a mist over him. "I turn you on." There was a bubble of delight caught in her voice, reminding him of just how bright she made his world. "I like the sound of that."

"It's not a sound, baby," Carlo said, sliding lower on her body. "It's a touch." His cheek brushed against the tops of her breasts, and then he turned his head and stroked against her the other way. Her breath caught, he could tell as the mounds of her breasts rose and held there, swelling sweet and warm against his face. He wanted to bathe in her scent, wash himself in every sweet flavor she had to offer.

His hand was shaking—shaking!—as he worked the front catch of her bra and released her soft flesh. He lowered his head and caressed her new bareness with his cheeks. His chin rubbed against the furled buds of her nipples. Her hands held him there, her fingernails biting into his scalp until he caught her inside his mouth and sucked.

Her arms dropped to the carpet and her body lifted, a sacrifice to his pleasure. He lavished attention on her sensitive flesh, feeling the tension that tightened her muscles and yet left her at the same time boneless.

His tongue took a trip down the center of her, tucking inside her shallow navel and playing there, too, as she gasped for breath. He looked up past her wet nipples gleaming in the firelight to her kiss-swollen mouth and her half-open eyes.

She was desire embodied. Living, breathing lust that tasted like heaven. Carlo felt as if each of his pores was opening in order to take her in.

And now all he wanted to do was take her up, up, up, to give her back all the heat and air and precious feeling of being supremely alive that she gave to him.

"Pretty Lucy," he said, rolling to his side so he had better access to her half-naked body.

Cat-smiling, she turned toward him, but he pushed her flat again with his hand. "Stay where I can touch you."

She pouted, forcing him to lean down and nip at

that pooched-out bottom lip. "Don't you want to feel good, baby?"

"I do feel good. I just don't feel enough of you."

But she let him slide her bra off her arms so that he could study the curves of her breasts and the sleek plane of her flat belly. Under his gaze, her stomach muscles trembled, and he placed his palm over them, insinuating his little finger beneath the elastic band of her panties that ran around her hips. Those muscles trembled again.

"Carlo." She sounded breathless as she tried rolling close again. "Let me."

He pushed her back down with his hand, a gentle touch, but one that allowed his pinkie to slide lower. It tangled in soft hair and he pictured them in his mind— golden curls that did little to hide the amazing folds and layers of her sex. He wanted to see that for real, and he would, but now it was so damn erotic to watch his big tanned hand disappear beneath the scrap of lace.

"Carlo." Lucy wiggled against the carpet. "I need you. Come inside me."

"I'm not done yet." He wasn't done with her. He had to get done with her—the thinking part of him that he'd been smothering all night reminded him of that—and maybe this was the way to do it.

With her, parts of him that had been dead were alive again. But they were unfamiliar parts—maybe even unknown parts—and he wasn't sure it was smart to welcome their rebirth.

Maybe it would be best to bury them in pleasure, drown them in the ecstasy of Lucy's body, let them have this one wild ride, then shut them away before they led him into dangerous territory. He was still a cop at the core and the cop's instincts were sending out flares in warning.

Danger. Danger. Danger.

But now the heat of those flares only added to the burning light flickering against Lucy's skin and the conflagration roaring inside him. It was so damn hot, and he needed the liquid of her body to cool him down and quiet his clamoring heart.

As his fingers found the wet bud at the top of her sex, he stripped off her panties. He heard her swift intake of breath. "You're still dressed," she protested.

It didn't matter. He shifted between her legs and pushed them wide, then bent her knees to open her to him.

"Carlo!" She sounded anxious, maybe even panicky, but he slid his palms down her legs and gripped her ankles. It was *he* who was panicked. It was *he* who had to find a way to chill out and cool down.

He dropped his mouth to the opened petals of her sex. Her body jerked against his hold, but he only tightened his grip and breathed in her spicy, sweet taste. His tongue swiped the wet, private flesh.

She jerked again, made a strangled sound, wrapped her fingers in his hair. "Don't...stop."

Don't stop.

As if he could. As if one taste of her would somehow be the antidote to all this fiery desire. His mouth opened to taste more of her, to have more of her, to take into himself more, more, more.

His hands slid up her silky stockings to reach the even silkier texture of her inner thighs. He pushed against them, widening her to him, opening her so that he could get to everything. He had to have everything this time, satisfying that newly awakened Carlo so that after this he could return to his safe, dark hibernation.

Lucy was whimpering, pleading, moaning, mimicking the sounds that he was too preoccupied to make himself. They both sought release.

Lucy, from his sensual torture.

Him, from the terrible, beautiful light that was Lucy, and that was the thing that she'd awakened inside of him. Beneath his hands, her thigh muscles went rigid. Her hips lifted as she offered herself, gave him more, and he took it, took her firmly in his mouth and hoped that this shaking, quaking orgasm she offered up would be the single sacrifice the beast inside of him needed before going back to sleep.

Early the next morning, leaving Carlo to his apparent state of unconsciousness between his sheets, Lucy called John to pick her up. There were things she had to do that day, and getting to them without first waking the man she'd spent all night with seemed like the best plan.

Gathering her purse and her pumps, in bare feet she eased out onto the porch, prepared to wait for her brother-in-law, whom she'd sworn to secrecy.

But there was to be no waiting.

And no brother-in-law.

Lucy stared as her sister stormed up Carlo's front walk. "You could get a ticket driving that fast."

Elise halted on the step below Lucy, which left their eyes at the same level. Hers held a snap of blue fire. "The one in danger of unwanted trouble right now is not me."

Lucy sighed. "I know you think I'm—"

"I'm not talking about you," Elise said. "I'm talking about *him*." Her gaze transferred to the closed front door, then she made a move to get past Lucy. "And I'm going to talk to him right this minute."

"Whoa." Lucy caught Elise's elbow. "Whoa, whoa, whoa. Where do you think you're going?"

"To tell that…that bounder to keep his mitts off my little sister."

Little sister has a thing for those mitts. Memory Lane beckoned, but Lucy stopped herself from taking that path. "What *is* a bounder, anyway? And why are you insinuating yourself into my business?"

Elise blinked. "I always insinuate myself into your business. It's the natural order of things. And I don't know what a bounder is, either. It just slipped out."

That's what I'm doing here, Lucy thought. *Slipping out.* "Let's go, Elise."

"And have you race off into the shower and then to work? No. If you're not going to let me at Carlo, then *we're* going to have a conversation. Right here. Right now."

The stubborn set of Elise's chin told Lucy all she needed to know. With a sigh, she dropped to the porch steps, tugging her sister down beside her. "You're an obstinate woman, that's what you are. Always have been. I remember when you knocked over Belinda Beall for passing those mean notes about me around elementary school."

Elise sniffed. "You asked for my help then, and admit it, that stringy-haired brat looked better than she ever had sitting on her butt in the dust."

"Yeah, but I didn't need, don't need—"

"Lucy…" Her sister turned her head to pin her with

a laserlike set of blue eyes. "Don't give me that. Why did you move back home?"

"I... Well... Because..."

"You wanted family around to watch your back."

"Okay, maybe I did miss you guys, but I wasn't expecting to be treated as if I were ten."

"Goose—"

Lucy put her palm over her sister's mouth. "My point exactly. And while I'm accustomed to cringing over Jason and Sam using that nickname, I expected better of you."

Elise drew Lucy's hand away, then tucked her Grace Kelly hair behind her ears. "Come on. You'd be the first to kick someone in the ankles who was bothering me."

Sighing, Lucy slung her arm around her sister's shoulders. "That's a crack about my height, I know it is, but you're right. And you're right that I came home to be among family. But as an *equal* among them."

"Jase and Sam—"

"Will get their comeuppance one of these days, please God. It's another reason why I had to be here. To see those two overintelligent, overhandsome, crème de la overconfident big brothers of ours fall flat on their faces."

A little smile played around Elise's mouth. "You might be just in time."

"What?" Lucy goggled. "What are you talking about?"

"I just have one word for you. *Twins.*"

A shiver of delight tracked down Lucy's spine and she squirmed on the step. "No! You've set them up with twins? This is delicious."

"And entirely off topic. I came here to save you from Carlo."

Too late.

"But I see it's too late."

Lucy's gaze jumped to her sister. "Did I say that out loud?"

Elise shook her head. "You didn't need to. I can read it right on your face. You're in love with him."

"That's not true...." Her words trailed off. It was so, so true. Last night, in front of that fireplace, he'd slid into her body and slid straight into her heart. Right then, what had been a little seed—her years-old silly crush—had flowered into something more.

It wasn't just the lovemaking, which had been spectacular and sweet and serious and oh so unforgettable. But that flower had been nurtured time and time again during the past weeks.

His giving her the Street Beat project.

The way he'd stuck up for her in front of her brothers, expressing publicly his confidence in her ability to do a job for him.

His support as she'd come apart at the seams when the volunteers were late.

When you thought about all that, no wonder she was in love with him.

"He doesn't want that from me, though," she whispered to Elise. "He likes his solitude. The way I feel won't fit."

Her sister made a wry face. "It's six-thirty in the morning. You've spent the night at the man's place. There must be some things he likes about you."

She tried to laugh, but it came out as more of a whimper. The night before, after he'd given her a spectacular climax while he was still fully dressed, he'd loosened his clothing, pulled on a condom, and then slid—hard and hot—inside her sated body. Despite the way her bones had been wax-soft, she'd found herself tilting into his thrust, wanting him as deep in her as she could bring him.

Braced on his elbows, he'd cradled her face with his hands. "This isn't going away, Luce, is it?" His thumbs had stroked over her cheekbones. "I want you more than the first time. I think I'll want you more when we're done this time."

She'd managed to shrug, because she'd hated that regret she could see lingering behind the desire. "We're having some more fun. What's so wrong about that?"

His smile had been sad, his kiss soft. "Lucy, you know—"

"I know *you*," she'd said fiercely. "I know what you want and what you don't. I know myself."

"And you're just a girl who wants to have fun?" he'd questioned. "Really?"

She'd dragged down his head and lifted her hips high and let her body and her mouth finish the conversation.

"Luce?" Elise broke into the memory. "What are you going to do now?"

She stared at her bare toes. At her last pedicure, the manicurist had painted the teensiest little butterflies on her big toes. They floated in a sky of pale blue and looked ready to flutter off at any second. She could be like them. She could quit her position at McMillan & Milano. Fly away from Carlo. If she did so, even if she left her Street Beat project in the lurch, he wouldn't say a single word. He'd probably blame himself.

Of course he'd blame himself. Sober, responsible,

noble Carlo Milano would think her defection was all his fault.

It was an easy out.

But hadn't she taken those much too often in the past twenty-five years? Hadn't she let Elise deal with Belinda Beall? Hadn't she let her brothers voice the obvious instead of taking a good look in the mirror? Hadn't the name Lucy Goosey been a too-true reflection of herself at—too many—times?

"Are you going to quit McMillan & Milano?" Elise was reading her mind again.

But the question prodded another memory to life. At the restaurant, under the influence of martinis and too much wine, she'd confessed to Carlo about her nonstarter of a career. And not really paid much attention to what he'd replied.

But maybe you're right to avoid accounting, Luce. Maybe what was wrong with those jobs wasn't you, but you with accounting.

Was that where she'd gone wrong? Was her career a nonstarter because it wasn't the right career path after all?

She glanced over at Elise. "What do you think? I'm wondering if I should get out of accounting."

Her sister's eyes widened. A perplexed frown dug a line between her perfectly arched, golden eyebrows. "What are you talking about? You have a degree in accounting. You're an accountant."

And Elise was an actuary and Sam a banker and Jason an attorney.

Lucy could spell them all now, including accountant, but that didn't make her any better at her siblings' game. Her hand ran down the colorful paisley of her silk dress. It was dang hard to be the wild print in a family of tailored business suits. She'd tried for years to fit in, but then nothing had fit right.

"Lucy?"

The one interrupting her reverie this time wasn't her sister, but Carlo. Her head whipped around, and there he was, standing in his doorway.

Her stomach churned as she mentally cursed her big sister for her bossy ways. They were supposed to be long gone, because this was what she'd hoped to avoid: a confrontation with the man who'd stolen her heart before she'd figured out exactly how she was going to deal with the theft.

And now they had her sister as a witness.

Lucy snuck a glance at Elise, who had half turned toward Carlo, as well, and who even in the early morning looked unruffled and serene. Beautiful. Perfect. But he was ignoring Lucy's sister. His eyes were all for Lucy.

"Luce? What are you doing?"

Good question, huh? Her gaze took him in, from his rumpled short hair to his whiskered chin, to the jeans hanging low on his hips. His naked chest looked sexy and warm and solid.

Like something she could lean on.

Oh, man. How was she going to keep on working with him when she wanted so much more than he was willing to give?

"Carlo…"

At the sound of Elise's voice, Lucy started. In a quick movement, she grabbed her sister's wrist. Squeezed. "Let me," she murmured.

Elise sent her a searching glance. *I've got your back, little sister,* her look said.

But little sister was standing up. Lucy rose to her feet, just to prove it. And it was funny, she could stand up and face Carlo in this awkward moment *because of* Carlo. His confidence in her, the remembrance of his words, "I want you, Lucy," gave her the guts to…to…

What was she going to do? There was still that path of least resistance. That "I'm sorry I can't work with you any longer" excuse that would remove her from further pain.

He frowned at her. "Why were you sneaking away?"

Could she tell the truth? Could she say, "Because I'm in love with you"? But he didn't want to be a couple, and for his benefit she'd painted a picture of herself as a woman who didn't care about something so serious. It wouldn't be fair to him to alter that now.

So she pasted on her best, most upbeat smile and made the hard decision to stick with what she'd started. "Because today's a busy day and I wanted to get a jump on it. See you at the office."

Chapter 11

Germaine slipped her hand through Carlo's arm. "You've changed."

Startled, he stared down at her. "What are you talking about?"

"Something's different about you."

The thought unsettled him. With a frown, he gestured to their surroundings. "I can't imagine why you'd say so. I insisted we make a stop by the Street Beat site on our way back from our once-a-month lunch. You always complain I'm an obsessed workaholic and I've just proved your point."

Germaine's gaze shifted from his face to the immense stadium parking lot that was being turned into a two-million-square-foot festival venue suited to entertaining more than 75,000 ticket-holders over the following two days.

Everywhere you looked, equipment was stacked elephant-high and trucks were bringing in even more. Five stages were already under construction. Workers in hard hats crawled over and around them, while dueling boom boxes belted out each team's musical preference. A far section of the parking lot was cordoned off for the trailers that were now providing temporary headquarters for the concert promoter and Carlo's security people, and for others that would be used as lounge areas for the performers. The big names would have their own trailers towed in, and they'd left room for them in the area along with open spots nearby for the bands' tour buses.

One of his employees strode toward him, wearing a polo shirt with *McMillan & Milano* embroidered on the pocket and a harried expression. Others on his staff were at the venue, as well. "You're here!" Hank said. "Linda was looking for you earlier."

Carlo's eyebrows rose and he peered about, scanning the area for trouble. "Is there a problem?"

Hank shook his head. "No more than to be expected. But the fire marshal is on site and Logistics Linda thought you might want to speak with him."

All thoughts of Linda faded away as Carlo's attention caught on a small, slim figure in a pair of painted-on jeans, tennis shoes and another of the company's shirts, knotted at her waist. Lucy. He could see a slice of the small of her back between the end of the cotton and the beginning of midrise denim. Last night, he'd placed a hot, openmouthed kiss right in that little dip. If he got close enough, would he see proof of his mark on her?

"Carlo?"

He yanked his attention back to Hank. "What?"

The other man sent an odd glance over his shoulder. "What's wrong?"

There once was a woman by my fire....

He cleared his throat. Forget the limerick. Forget the "mark." He hadn't marked Lucy. That sounded way too possessive for a man who kept his distance from other people. "Nothing's wrong. You came to me, remember?"

"Yeah. Linda. Fire marshal. Do you want to meet with him?"

Carlo shook his head. "That's on Linda. She's our go-to public services person. Or does she need me to address something we haven't foreseen?"

Hank's expression was puzzled. "No, as per usual, you've foreseen everything. It's just that...well, you generally want to, uh, have your hands on, uh, everything."

Carlo would *not* look Lucy's way again. "I don't know what you're talking about. I delegate."

"Recently, yes," Hank said. He backed up as if afraid he'd offended the boss. "And I only mean that in a positive way."

Carlo rolled his eyes and waved the other man off. "You'd think I was an ogre," he murmured to Germaine.

"Just a bit controlling," she said sweetly. "But it looks like I'm right. Even your employees have noticed the change."

Carlo didn't want to think about it. He put on his most charming smile. "Maybe I didn't want to interrupt this opportunity to spend time with the most enchanting woman in San Diego."

Germaine's laugh was good to hear. "I haven't seen that magnetic grin of yours in years. I am now curious as can be to know where you found it after all this time."

In Lucy's eyes. On a roller coaster. In front of a

crackling fire. *As I slid into Lucy's sweet body and felt her welcome all the way to my soul.*

Without thinking, his gaze traveled to where he'd last seen her. There she was, chatting like a magpie, her hands moving with the same energy and grace she brought to everything. Her job. Lovemaking.

"I like that smile even better."

Carlo started. He'd forgotten all about Germaine until she'd spoken, but she was right, he could feel the smile curving his mouth.

Germaine touched his arm again. "She sent me a get-well present, you know. Lucy, I mean."

It didn't surprise him. "Chocolate? Flowers?"

"A kitten."

"What?" Germaine had been waiting on her porch when he'd picked her up so he hadn't spotted any new resident at 247 Cavendish Drive. "That's kind of…"

"Exactly what I needed," she finished for him. "And she said that if it didn't appeal she had another good home for the dear thing. But the idea *did* appeal. You see, the night you two dropped by she noticed this framed photo I have of the cat Pat and I had when we were first married. I'd happened to mention how Serpico kept me company at home on the long night shifts, and I suppose…"

"She remembered." Carlo rubbed his palm over his breastbone.

"I think she saw that I need company now, too."

Lucy *would* see that. Lucy saw so much. Her instincts about people were well honed and as far as he was concerned, wasted on ledgers and spreadsheets. Sure, she was good with details, but that didn't mean she had to lock all her light away in shadowy cubicles for the rest of her life, crunching numbers.

That kind of thing suited him far better than it did Lucy.

He preferred being locked away in the shadows.

"I'd like to tell her how the newest member of my family, Kojak, is getting on," Germaine said, starting across the blacktop.

"No," Carlo instantly responded.

Germaine blinked. "No?"

"I mean, she's probably busy." Suddenly he didn't want to get too close to Lucy. The lovemaking had been brain-blowing and he'd been glad when Lucy had dragged her sister away this morning. He'd yet to get his mind around what was happening between them—not to mention how he was going to explain all this to Lucy's sister, and probably, at some point, her brothers, too. He couldn't explain it to himself! He couldn't explain why each time they were together, each time she tried to pass it off as "fun," he was left unsatisfied at some level, even though his body was humming with satisfaction.

A thread of panic iced his blood. What was happening to him? "I'll give you Lucy's cell phone number, Germaine. You can call her later."

"Oh, you're probably right," Germaine replied. "It looks to me as if she's very busy with that young man with the long hair and tattoos."

Carlo's blood ran colder. He swung around, squinting to get a sharper view. Oh, yeah. There was Lucy, animated, smiling, her small hand on the arm of that... that...tool.

"Wrench," he spit out.

Germaine slanted him an inquiring glance.

"Have you ever heard of Silver Bucket?"

"Nooo."

"Me, neither." It was gratifying not to be the only nonfan, though he supposed that did put him squarely in the fuddy-duddy category. "Let's go."

"Go where?"

He was already heading across the blacktop. "I thought you wanted to talk to Luce."

Okay, it looked as if Germaine was swallowing her smile. Damn. "Didn't you?" he pressed.

"Right." Germaine lengthened her stride to keep up with him. "This is all my idea."

Carlo slowed. "Sorry, I walk fast."

"I don't mind. Pat did, too."

Pat. At the mention of the man's name, Carlo's step hitched. What would his old partner think about the company they'd envisioned together? The one that Carlo used to fill his days and nights?

Gotta find some balance, boy. It was as if his mentor was speaking directly into his ear. *All work and no play...*

And he'd been playing with Lucy, hadn't he? Having his fun? But again, that term just didn't sit well with him. Nor did the way that Wrench was slinging his skinny, tattooed arm around Lucy to drag her nearer his concave chest.

It reminded him of what he'd learned at that Street Beat party weeks ago. The band was famous for its pyrotechnics show. Since that had been forbidden during the San Diego festival, perhaps Wrench was looking for a substitute with some fireworks with Lucy. The thought made him want to break something.

Wrench's drumstick-thin forearms would work.

He halted in front of the two, but they were so absorbed in each other it didn't appear they realized he and Germaine had arrived.

It pissed him off. "I'm not paying you to make out with the talent."

She froze, and Wrench's scrawny arm slid away. With a frown between her brows, she turned to him.

A delighted smile broke over her face as her attention shifted to his left. "Germaine! How's Kojak?"

"Wonderful. Thank you so much again."

Lucy leaned in for a quick hug, then introduced the older woman to the lead singer. Next, she gestured toward Carlo with a careless hand. "I don't believe you've met this charmer. My boss, Carlo Milano."

He was forced to shake hands. "Wrench," the man said.

No last name. Figured.

"You should probably let Lucy get back to her work," Carlo said, trying to sound pleasant.

Apparently he didn't pull it off too well because Lucy glared at him. "What? Now you don't trust me to do my job?"

He wanted to groan. Damn it, what was wrong with him? He *was* different. The old Carlo, while not particularly friendly, wasn't bad tempered. The old Carlo could be perfectly civil, even to a rock star named Wrench, no matter what woman he was touching—even his own.

No! Lucy was not his woman.

He tried to make amends. "Sorry, sorry," he said to them both. "This close to the big festival, I get a little edgy."

Wrench nodded. "Lucy, too. I was just persuading

her that tonight, after we wrap up the first evening, that she needs to relax. I'm having a big party at my hotel suite. There's a private whirlpool tub and we'll have music, eats, the whole works. You two are welcome to come."

His gaze included Germaine, which meant that he assumed Lucy was already on board with the plan.

Oh, yeah, Carlo thought. He was different now. Really, really different. Because the idea of Lucy in a private whirlpool tub with the tool-of-the-moment was not something he could accept, even if it meant he was leaving his safe, comfortably dark corner.

"Sorry," he told the singer, grinding his back teeth through a fake smile. "But Lucy and I already have plans for after the festival tonight."

At 2:00 a.m., Lucy was still moving around the spacious McMillan & Milano security trailer, afraid that if she stopped, her legs would freeze up altogether. Gathering half-empty water bottles and disposing of stale baskets of pretzels and crackers gave her mental processes time to unwind after the hours of intense focus.

One night at the Street Beat festival required more of her brain than a week in an accountant's office at tax season. But her mind was downshifting now that the night was concluded, leaving her in a pleasant, zoned-out state of tired satisfaction.

She heard the trailer's door open and close but didn't look up, hoping whoever it was wasn't looking for any intelligible conversation from her. After the last few hours, she couldn't give one more opinion or make one more decision. Unless the new person in the trailer wanted to silently gnaw on some leftover crackers, they were out of luck.

Better yet, maybe they'd be content with taking a dented half-full bottle of water and going away.

"Lucy."

At the sound of that voice, her hand tightened, crackling the plastic in her hand. Carlo. Oh, she was much too tired to figure out how to play him tonight.

Did he want the sympathetic friend? The lighthearted lover? The easy-to-please employee who wouldn't ask for any more than he was willing to give from the distance of his dark corner?

"You don't have to do that cleanup. Let it wait until tomorrow."

Without looking at him, she continued her tidying. "My volunteers are responsible for at least some of this mess."

"Your volunteers did a great job tonight."

Her head lifted and she found the energy to smile. "They did, didn't they?"

He nodded. Though he'd spent more time on the site than she had, the only signs of his long hours were the evidence of dark whiskers on his face and his loosened tie. But his shirt was still a pristine white, and his navy blazer looked as if it had just emerged from a dry cleaner's plastic.

Lucy, on the other hand, felt as wilted as the daisies someone had placed in a glass bowl on the trailer's kitchenette counter. She tossed the bottle in her hand into the trash bag at her feet and then ran her hands along her jeans, as if she could give them a little starch with the touch of her palms.

"You know, you've caused me a big problem," he went on. His expression was serious. Too serious.

Lucy's heart bobbed up and down like a yo-yo. No. She was too tired for this. Their relationship, or nonrelationship, or whatever it was or wasn't, couldn't be a topic of conversation tonight. That little fog of fatigue wasn't lifting in her brain, not at all, and she'd need each one of her faculties to find the right role to act for him.

She licked her lips, wondering how she could put him off. "Carlo..."

"I'm going to have to redo the financials on the Street Beat festival to account for the gigantic bonus check I'm going to write you tomorrow night."

She stared at him.

He smiled, and if she didn't know he didn't have any soft spots inside of him, she'd say the smile looked tender. "Luce, you've got to realize that your volunteers did a bang-up job because *you* did a bang-up job."

Her throat felt tight. "You think so? You really think so?"

"Yeah. I really think so. As do Hank, and Linda, and Fernando and all the other McMillan & Milano staff who worked here tonight. Not to mention Claudia. Apparently a contingent of the parents corralled her and thanked her for your professionalism and dedication."

Lucy's tired legs finally gave up the ghost and she found herself dropping to the trailer's couch. "Well, that was nice of them."

Carlo shook his head. "People don't go out of their way just to be nice. They go out of their way when their experience exceeds their expectations." He paused, then strode over to sit on the coffee table facing her. Their knees nearly touched. "You sure as hell exceeded mine."

Lucy backed farther into the corner of the couch. Oh, what did that mean? That wasn't a segue to a place she didn't want to go, was it? "Um, uh…"

"I didn't think the volunteers would do anything more than get in the way, at best. Instead, you assessed, organized and charmed that clutch of adults and teens into a working crew that made a difference tonight—both for McMillan & Milano and for the concert-goers."

It was maybe the second-longest speech Lucy had heard Carlo make in the past weeks and it was about her job performance. Her excellent job performance.

Lucy sat a little straighter, letting his evaluation join with her own sense of a job well done. Satisfaction heightened into bliss. "I appreciate the compliment. And the confidence you had in me in the first place when you assigned me the project. That meant a lot."

"You can do anything you put your mind to, Luce. You can have anything you really want. I know that. I hope tonight's shown you that."

"Yes." Lucy found herself nodding. Lucy Goosey had finally, for once and for all, flown the coop and left Lucy the capable in her place. "Thanks again for the opportunity to learn that." Her head dropped back to the cushion and she closed her eyes. "But there's still another day of the festival to go."

"Our last day to work together."

That's right, Lucy thought, drifting on the waves of fatigue rolling through her head. Come Monday, Carlo's secretary would be back on the job and Lucy would be back sifting through the want ads. She'd appeased her guilt in the past week by telling herself she was too busy with Street Beat to seek out another position, though on Monday she'd have to start seriously looking.

But I'm not limiting myself to accounting positions, she thought, suddenly certain. *I'm good with details, but I'm good with people, too, and maybe I can find a way to use both those talents.*

"So I told Wrench we had plans tonight," Carlo said, interrupting her reverie. "What would you like to do?"

She cracked one eye open. "Do I look like a woman ready to do anything? I know why you said that to Wrench. Don't worry about actually following through with it."

He frowned. "What do you mean? Why do you think I told Wrench we were doing something?"

She had to open both eyes to roll them, and she managed, despite the fatigue weighing down her lids. "I grew up with Jason and Sam, two of the most overprotective males on the planet. They would have heard the words *party* and *whirlpool tub,* and considering the rock singer source, gone on to tell him anything, up to and including an audience with the president of the United States, to prevent me from hanging out in Wrench's hotel suite. Though for the record, I can handle Wrench just fine. And by the way, he invited my volunteers on stage for his last set tomorrow night. That's pretty great of him, don't you think?"

Carlo's expression blanked. "You…" He took a breath and started again. "You…"

"First things first," she heard him mutter. "Are you saying you think of me like your brothers?"

The tired fog in Lucy's head was making it hard to interpret his tone. "Um, close enough."

He muttered something else. Something possibly obscene. "Hell, Lucy." He rose to his feet, forking a hand through his short hair. His gaze sharpened on her face. "I'm not one of your damn brothers."

"O-kay."

Apparently that wasn't the response he was hoping for because he turned to pace around the room. "I don't feel the least bit brotherly toward you."

"O-kay."

He took another turn around the small space. "Fine. Whatever." It sounded as if he was having an argument with himself. He lifted a hand, let it drop to his side, then he halted in the middle of the room and trained his gaze on her again. "You handling Wrench is not something I find myself keen to think about. At all."

"O-kay." Again.

"As a matter of fact, we're going to have to come to an understanding here, Lucy. About us."

Oh, no.

Now, *that* sounded like what she wanted to avoid. Her brain was spent, her body was all out of energy, there was nothing left inside her right now to deal with this particular person in the particularly right way. "Tomorrow—"

"Now," he bit out. "Right now."

"Carlo—"

"It isn't fun anymore, Lucy. Last night, for your information, was *not fun.*"

She drew back, wishing the couch cushions could absorb her and that she'd simply disappear. Her mind spun, but as it was weighed down by her tiredness, it only gave a couple of drunken revolutions as it tried to find a way that this wasn't a rejection of her.

"We can't keep meeting 'accidentally' in my bed. Not for *fun.* Would you agree with that?"

Lucy couldn't keep up with the words tumbling from his mouth. "I don't know what you mean. What you want…"

"What I want…" He mumbled that under his breath, too. "What I want doesn't seem to matter so much anymore."

Lucy sucked in a breath, trying to focus on what Carlo was saying and how he was acting. Did he want her to be the nonthreatening, nonsexual Goose again? Was that it? Was Ms. Sutton no longer welcome in his life? Between his sheets?

The thought shouldn't feel like a stab to her heart. She'd always known what they had was as temporary as her position at McMillan & Milano. If she now wanted more, it was her own dumb fault. Everybody knew you didn't get over a crush by going to bed with one.

And once you realized it was more than a crush and was really love…

Stupid, Lucy, she thought, staring at the clenched fingers in her lap. Stupid, stupid, stupid.

"Here's the deal, Lucy."

She looked up to see Carlo cross his arms over his chest. "We're going to have to formalize our casual relationship."

"Huh?"

"Everyone's noticing it. Commenting upon it. I've been in a better mood. Easier to work with. Less intense. That's you. That's your influence. I like it."

She couldn't think of what to say.

"And I like you in my bed. I don't want it to be an occasional 'lapse.' You shouldn't want that for yourself, either. So we'll…I don't know…start seeing each other on a more regular basis."

"Starting Monday, I'm not going to be working for you anymore," she pointed out, still trying to keep up with him.

He shrugged. "We'll make time around our schedules. Next week I'm booked pretty solid, but maybe we could meet for a drink on Thursday. Around ten?"

Really, she was so exhausted from the evening and the odd roller coaster ride of the last few minutes that she could hardly form words. "At 10:00 p.m.?"

"You could spend the night with me," he said.

"I could spend the night with you."

A little smile quirked the corners of his mouth. "So I lied. It *was* fun the other night and I want it to be that way again. You told me you're a girl who wants to have fun and I'm more than willing to provide that."

So this is what she'd wrought. With all her twisting and turning to make what happened between them comfortable for Carlo, for all the times she'd worked so hard not to scare him away, she'd contorted herself into the position she found herself in right now.

And all she could think of was that she didn't know how to play the moment.

How to play the moment.

How to *play the moment*.

How to be something she was not.

Like all the years she'd played accountant, taking on a role with Carlo was just as, ultimately, unsatisfying.

Heartbreaking.

He'd given her the confidence to look beyond her training to a new kind of career. Now she'd have to find the courage to tell Carlo Milano what Lucy Sutton really wanted for her life.

"I don't want to formalize our casual relationship,"

she said, her heart beating loud in her ears. "I'm sorry, but I don't want a casual relationship with you at all."

"What?" His eyes narrowed. "You don't want me?"

Funny, he didn't look like he believed that. "No. I don't want you casually at all."

He took a step back. "You know, you know…I don't—"

"Do the couple thing. I do know that."

"Damn it, Lucy, you said…you acted as if…"

"I could be as casual about things as you. As careless—"

"I was *never* careless with you."

"You're right, you're right."

"What happened to the girl who said it wasn't serious?"

For some reason, Lucy thought of the perfect Elise. Despite his denial, was that who he wanted? Would he have wanted to be a couple if Lucy was more like Elise? But she'd been whatever everyone else wanted for too long. The silly younger sister, the sexy temporary secretary. Now it was time to be what Lucy wanted for herself.

"That girl…that girl is really someone who should have been more honest with you and with herself. I want more. I want it all. And, thanks to you and what I've learned through working at McMillan & Milano, I now know I'm good enough, talented enough and, well, *woman* enough to reach for all my dreams."

"Lucy." Carlo ran a hand down his face. "Damn it, Lucy." Now, finally, he sounded as tired as she felt. And as if he truly understood the situation. Understood what she was saying. "I didn't mean to…I didn't see—"

"You didn't do anything wrong, not really." He was

still the star of so many of her sweet dreams. He was still the man who had given her this newfound confidence. She dredged up a smile for him. It wasn't his fault that he couldn't give her any more than that.

"I'm in love with you. But I don't want a casual relationship. I want a man of my own, and someday I hope I'll find him."

Chapter 12

Carlo stalked through the late-night crowds attending the Street Beat festival, the relentless drum rhythm from the nearest stage too close to the throb of a toothache. Less than an hour remained before the festival closed, and it couldn't come quick enough for him. He always grew antsy as an event came to an end, whether it was a charity golf tournament or a holiday parade, but tonight his cop instincts were as palpably on alert as the raised hairs on the back of his neck.

A big hand clapped between his shoulder blades. "There you are."

Startled, Carlo swung around to face the two blond men grinning at him. "What the hell—" Recognizing Lucy's brothers, Jason and Sam, he tried to relax. "I didn't know you guys were coming!"

"With dates." Jason fumbled through the introductions, and it was obvious he wasn't entirely clear on which of the identical women with them was which. "Allie and Jane…or Jane and Allie…this is Carlo Milano."

The twins didn't seem surprised that Jason couldn't keep then straight. "Allie," one said, squeezing his hand with a strong grip. The other gave a shy wave. "Jane."

They were both medium height, with willowy figures and medium-brown hair threaded with auburn. Each wore their hair in a chin-length style that wisped around their heart-shaped faces. Even as a trained observer, and Carlo considered himself a damn good one, if dressed identically these two would even be hard for him to individualize.

"Elise set us up," Sam confided. "This is the first time we've been out together."

"It's nice to meet you both," Carlo said, nearly having to shout as the music grew louder. "Hope you're having a good time."

Sam's mouth moved, but he couldn't hear his reply. "What?"

Leaning closer, Sam spoke directly into his ear. "We're on the lookout for Lucy. Have you seen her?"

Carlo nodded. In his dreams all last night. At least every fifteen minutes all today and this evening. As much as he'd wanted to keep his distance from her, she kept flitting into his consciousness or into his line of sight.

What was it about butterflies that always lifted a man's mood?

"I called her early this morning to tell her we'd be here tonight, but she practically bit my head off," Sam continued, frowning. "Something about not needing a keeper. You know anything about that?"

"I don't know anything about her," Carlo muttered. She'd completely flummoxed him last night in the trailer. After three weeks under the spell of her bright personality, accented by two nights of her silky body in his arms, he'd thought he understood Lucy. He'd thought he understood what Lucy wanted from him. And that she understood exactly how much—how little—he was looking for himself.

And he'd made it clear every step of the way, hadn't he? Up to and including last night in the trailer. *I want to formalize our casual relationship.* Okay, even to himself that made him sound like an ass, but the sentiment was honest.

He'd been honest with her.

An anger he'd been trying to suppress rose from his belly and fired a burn in his chest. There was a name for women who turned the tables on a guy like that. And it wasn't Butterfly.

Man-eater. That was it. He'd thought she was sweet, but boy, was he wrong! His anger ratcheted higher. A woman like Lucy said what she had to, did what she had to, to turn the male of the species upside down and inside out, making him so confused that he was easy prey.

Once he was down, she'd go for all the tasty internal organs. She'd go for the heart.

Too bad for her that Carlo didn't have one.

And lucky for him.

The two couples in front of him were exchanging puzzled glances. "What?" he questioned, raising his voice. *"What?"*

Jason gave him an awkward pat on the shoulder. "You okay, friend? You seem a little, uh, moody."

"If by 'moody' you mean black looks and dark mutters," Sam added. "So we'll leave you to it, if you'll just point our way to Goose."

Goose. That was the damn problem. She'd waltzed into his office three weeks before and he'd remembered her as the sweet, soft, silly little Goose. His memories had left him unprepared for the sharp, sexy, grown-up female who had yanked him out of his dark corner only to tumble him onto his butt.

Yeah, baby, he thought, anger spiking again. *Thanks for that one hell of a trip and fall.*

Jason was staring at him again. "Goose," he prodded. "Remember her?"

"Forget that man-eater?" Carlo ground out. "Never."

Her brothers glanced at each other. Sam mouthed, *Man-eater?* Then their gazes swung Carlo's way again and brightened to matching lasers. "What's going on?" one said. "What have you done to Goose?"

"She's not a goose," Carlo snapped back. "For God's sake, at least get that straight. Your sister is a grown, capable woman, a…a…" *Man-eater.* But hell, he liked his nose just as it was so he wouldn't risk repeating that again.

"She can take care of herself." He faced Sam. "And she doesn't need you undermining that at every opportunity with talk of her photocopying her butt."

Jason lifted a finger. "Oh, I think that was me."

Carlo shook his head. "Never mind. You're idiots, I'm an idiot, and as a matter of fact, if we've got an XY chromosome set, I'm beginning to think we're all doomed to idiocy."

The more assertive twin, Allie, grinned. "I think I like your friend," she said to the brothers.

Carlo huffed out a sigh, then the band on the closest

stage swung into another song with a headache-inducing beat that drummed pain into his brain. Would this night never end? "Let me show you where Lucy is," he shouted over the noise. "She's over by Stage 5. Silver Bucket is performing there."

"Oh," Allie said, nudging her sister with her elbow. "Let's go. We're going to see that hottie, Wrench."

Wrench. Carlo ground his teeth as he led the small group toward the far stage. He supposed Lucy would find her way to the singer's party suite that night. If only to thank him for letting her volunteers up on stage with him for his last set.

Who was he kidding? A man-eater would go after Wrench because she was always hungry for more.

That fire in his chest burned hotter. It was like an ulcer, chewing at his insides with feral teeth. Pushing his way through the concert-goers, he was finally halted by the wall of people gathered around the stage to hear Silver Bucket play. He was fifty yards away, and he was grateful for his height, which allowed him to see over the fans, who were all on their feet and swaying or dancing to the music's beat.

Near the front of the stage, people were packed like sardines and Carlo's cop sense started quivering again, harder. His people were down there, trained security personnel who were built like bar bouncers, and they should be able to keep the excited crowd in order. Still, something didn't feel right, especially when he couldn't see Lucy and her volunteers anywhere. He didn't want them stuck in the middle of an amped-up mob. His fingers found the walkie-talkie clipped to his waist and brought it to his mouth so he could call an extra contingent of security to Stage 5.

As he clicked off, he saw Lucy and a small group of teenagers appear onstage, behind and to the left of the drummer. Relief trickled through his tension.

Okay. There. She wasn't packed in with the gyrating multitude where an errant elbow or knee could bring her slight self down to the blacktop. On the stage, there was nothing more dangerous than a heavy metal rock band and their instruments.

The current song they were playing died out, but they segued immediately into the next. The crowd screamed in an ululating cry of approval. The twin named Allie was close enough that he could hear her yell to Sam and Jason, explaining why the fans were going nuts. "This is their big hit," he heard her yell. "'Mosh Pit.'"

Carlo's stomach knotted as he saw the fans swarm forward, eliminating all the space between their bodies. Wrench yelled something unintelligible into the microphone and the crowd let out another screaming reply.

Carlo didn't wait to see what would happen next. Intending to make it to the stage come hell or high water, he started off.

A hard hand caught his elbow. Jason. "Where's Lucy?"

Carlo could read the other man's lips but couldn't hear a sound over the noise around him.

He pointed on the stage, then his heart froze. She wasn't there.

Where had she gone? His gaze darted around the musicians and their instruments as he tried to locate her.

The fire inside him leaped higher, roasting the place where his heart would be if he'd allow himself to have one. Damn it! Damn it! If she hadn't bewitched him with her infectious laughter, with the way she saw inside him, he wouldn't be feeling this knife edge of panic.

If she wasn't such a temptress—a man-eater—

Oh. Oh, thank God. There she was.

His heart—that heart he wasn't supposed to have—slammed like a knocking fist against his chest wall. *Hello? Hello? Is anyone alive in there?*

And he was alive. More alive than he'd been since Pat's death, he realized. He felt each beat thump inside his chest and felt the muscle work to push his blood through his system. His hot blood. His undetached, undistanced blood rushing through a body that could no longer fool itself about what had happened to him in the past three weeks.

Man-eater. Hah. How could he have even thought such a stupid thing about her for even an instant?

He knew what was eating at him now.

Despite how comfortable he'd been in the shadows, how easy he'd found it before to keep clear of those living and breathing around him, he'd gone ahead and fallen in love with sweet sunshine. With Lucy.

Sam's hand tightened on his arm. Carlo swung his head toward him.

Her brother's mouth moved again. *Lucy?*

Carlo turned back toward the stage, where he'd seen her half-hidden by a tower of speakers. But before he could point her out, explosions erupted from both sides of the stage. Jets of light streamed skyward, while white clouds billowed, obscuring the musicians—and Lucy and her volunteers.

The pyrotechnics. The band known for their light and fire and smoke display had not held to their contractual promise—and instead had unleashed potential disaster.

Carlo didn't remember moving. One minute he was blinking to dispel the after-dazzle in his eyes, and the next he was halfway through the packed crowd. Halfway, but not close enough to Lucy.

The sound of the crowd was so loud they were drowning out the music of the band and there was barely breathing space between each body. Carlo saw his beefy security guys still holding strong at the front of the stage, but the first fifty feet of people standing that near had turned the "Mosh Pit" song into a reality.

As he pushed closer, gaining inches only to be shoved back a foot by the raucous crowd, he saw that Wrench was encouraging the craziness by the way he stood on the stage's edge and sang to the first few rows, his bare-chested body bent at the waist.

A girl popped out of the melee like a jack-in-the-box, trying for a kiss from Wrench. When she didn't make her target, the group threw her up again.

"Damn it," Carlo muttered, pushing through the people around him with new strength. His front-of-stage security couldn't last long without reinforcements, or without Wrench and the rest of Silver Bucket doing something to calm the crowd.

But nothing could calm him, not when he saw Lucy rush toward the lead singer and grab the microphone out of his hand. Positioned at the very edge of the stage, she was saying something to him, then shouting into the microphone, pleading with the crowd, he realized, to quiet down. The whole place was a riot of sound and movement.

Then another explosion sent sparklers of white fire across the stage. The crowd screamed and moved farther forward, arms outstretched, reaching for the band. Panic closed Carlo's throat as he realized his security team couldn't hold out against the wave of rabid fans, their excitement driven high by the forbidden pyrotechnics.

And Lucy was still up there, so close to the edge, now handing the microphone to Wrench, who seemed to have come to his senses. He put his arm around Lucy's waist, as if about to drag her away from the dangerous brink of the stage…

But it was too late.

Time stilled for Carlo, the way it did whenever adrenaline flooded his system. The cacophony around him receded, and it was quiet as death except for the heavy pound of his pulse.

He remembered finding Pat lying on the sidewalk. He remembered the slick and hot feel of the older man's blood between his fingers as he tried to staunch the flow and save his life. He'd lost that battle.

And he'd lose Lucy like he lost Patrick. He could see it all slipping away from him. Her butterfly brightness, her sparkling laughter, their love that could have lit his way for the rest of their lives. He felt it slipping away just as he saw a hand reach up from the pulsing crowd to wrap around her ankle. Just like that, Lucy slipped over the side of the stage and down, down, down, until she was swallowed by the wild throng.

This was why you didn't love people, he thought, pushing forward even as his heart was trampled.

This was why he refused to love. It could hurt so damn bad. It could make you so damn weak.

Someone was inside Lucy's head trying to get her attention by banging both fists on her skull. She squeezed her eyes tighter shut and tried to go back to sleep, but now the someone had a voice besides those insistent knuckles.

The voice sounded like her mother's.

Lucy allowed her eyelids to lift halfway. That was her mother, all right, with a worried frown between her brows. The back of her fingers felt cool against Lucy's cheek. "Honey? How are you feeling?"

"There's a dwarf inside my brain who wants out," she mumbled.

"That's our Goose." It was Sam, sounding a little worried himself. "Other girls fantasize about movie stars, but she dreams of dwarfs."

She turned her head on the pillow to find him with her gaze, and winced at the movement. "Take it easy, honey," her mom said. "Slow and easy."

This time, Lucy moved just her gaze instead of her whole head. Mom, Dad, Sam and Jason. There was a big bouquet of flowers on one of those skinny little hospital tables....

She was in a hospital bed. In a hospital room. Her hand lifted to brush the hair away from her face, but she discovered her arm was too heavy to move.

She frowned at it.

Jason piped up. "We thought you'd like pink."

She was wearing a pink cast on her forearm. Lucy lifted her gaze to her mother's face.

Laura Sutton didn't need more prodding. "Honey," she said. "You broke your wrist and you received a slight concussion when you fell—well, were pulled— from the stage."

Street Beat. Silver Bucket. The pyrotechnics, "Mosh Pit." The real mosh pit in the crowd.

Lucy closed her eyes. She'd brought her volunteers

into the midst of all that. Her stomach contracted as she remembered the acrid smell of the white smoke and the frightened faces of the teenagers who moments before she'd happily ushered onto the stage. Not long after, she'd thought the crowd was about to break through security and leap up to overrun the musicians and everyone else.

"Was…" Her throat was so dry, she had to swallow and start again. "Was anyone else hurt?"

"No." It was her dad who spoke up now, and she knew to trust him. Mom might have tried to soft-pedal the truth, but her father would always give it to her straight. "There were a few squished toes and torn shirts in the crowd from what we understand, but the only one who required a hospital visit was you."

Her chest loosened a little. "And my volunteers? I had a list in the trailer. Are we sure they're all accounted for?"

"Carlo mentioned something about it," her dad affirmed. "He said they were all fine."

Carlo. The dwarf in her head started on her skull again, using hammers *and* fists this time. What flack was McMillan & Milano going to have to take for the debacle? She'd been right there, and with her *volunteers.* Shouldn't she have seen evidence of the fireworks that were about to go off? Shouldn't she have been able to keep her volunteers far from any potential danger?

Carlo was never going to talk to her again, even though he'd likely already sworn never to talk to her again, anyway. The new churning in her stomach made a nauseating counterpoint to the banging in her head.

Someone tapped on the door. A nurse. "You're

awake, Lucy. There's a Claudia Cox out here insisting on seeing you. Do you feel up to it?"

Lucy felt up to finding a hole in the ground, lying down in it and pulling the dirt in after her. But Claudia didn't take no for an answer, which was actually something Lucy really admired about her. "I'll see her," she said.

Jason moved to sit on the end of her bed. The legs of Sam's chair squeaked against the linoleum as he edged closer to her. "Good God, Goose. You're going to talk to her now? She'll rip you to shreds."

"I'd like to see the woman try it," Jason replied, his expression grim. "Lucy might have made herself another mess, but nobody but us has a right to say that. Goose has got backup."

Lucy sighed. Goose had backup, all right, and as she looked at their concerned faces and protectively squared shoulders, she found it hard to resent Jason's comment that "Lucy might have made herself another mess." Because she had.

Chanel No. 5 reached her before Claudia did. Then she was there, ignoring every other person in the room to focus on Lucy. "There she is," she declared, sliding a gold box of Godiva chocolates next to the flowers on that skinny table. "The woman who I—"

"Now, just a minute," said Jason, in his best tight-ass attorney's voice.

Claudia kept on talking. "—am hoping will take a job in my offices starting next week."

"It's not her fault," Jason said, as if Claudia's startling offer had not been voiced. "I know it might look like that, but—"

Claudia's scathing glance would have melted a lesser

man. "It didn't look like her fault at all. Were you even there?"

"Well, um, I was, but we couldn't see anything because of the smoke, and the, um, uh…"

"That's because Silver Bucket broke their contract by bringing in those pyrotechnics. They not only caused all that smoke and confusion, but they also set off the crowd and caused a dangerous situation. A dangerous situation that your sister was instrumental in defusing."

Jason blinked. "Well, um, uh, we couldn't see anything, as I said. There was that smoke, and the, um, uh…"

Lucy took pity on him. "Shut up, Jason. You were saying, Claudia? You might have a position for me in concert promotion?"

"For someone who handles details and people the way you do? For someone who knows music and is quick on her feet? For someone whom I think I can mold into a woman exactly like me?"

At her brothers' identical horrified expressions, Lucy nearly laughed. But not before she wiggled up to a higher position on the pillows. She tried to look as professional as she could wearing a hospital gown and a bright fuchsia plaster cast.

"I accept," she said. "If the salary's right, I'd love to work at your offices." Where, she realized, her hot-pink cast would look right at home. Where, more important, she thought, she'd feel right at home.

Elise and John arrived on the receding wave of Claudia's perfume. With her family gathered around her, Lucy learned more about how the McMillan & Milano security personnel had controlled the crowd shortly after she'd fallen. John had called Carlo on the way to the hospital for all the details. Wrench, the rest of the Silver Bucket and their road crew had been arrested.

"The cops had to pull Carlo off the pyrotechnics guy," John said, sounding smug in that quiet way of his. "If Carlo hadn't been a former cop himself, they would probably have arrested him, too."

Then someone turned on the television and there was Lucy on the news. A video camera had caught her demanding Wrench to stop the show to calm the crowd. After she'd been pulled into the pit—the whole room had winced at the sight—the lead singer *had* cut the instruments with a slash of his hand. As the fans settled down, the camera had taken one last shot—and in it Lucy had seen a dark figure arrowing through the pack toward the place where she'd fallen.

Carlo found me, she thought. He would have been the one to pick her up and find her help. The hospital would be too much for him, she could understand that. But she knew, just knew, it was he who had picked her up from where she'd fallen and delivered her to the medical personnel.

Then he'd gone back to his dark corner, where he liked to observe life alone.

Later, the family left Lucy in her narrow bed. She tried to get out of bed to go with them, but the nursing staff insisted she stay a few more hours, and she was really too tired to argue. Her eyes closed as the dwarf drumming in her head finally put it on mute.

The room held dawn light when she opened her eyes again. Between the tall box of Godiva and the flower arrangement bristling with birds-of-paradise, she spotted Carlo's expressionless face.

"Hey," she murmured. "It's the right order. You come right after candy but before flowering plants."

A frown creased his forehead. "Shall I call a doctor?"

"Even an MD can't make a man better than chocolate."

"Your head injury...I'll come back later." He started to rise.

Blinking, she put out a hand. "You *are* here. I thought I was dreaming again. Last time it was a dwarf."

He settled back in the chair beside her bed, and she pushed at the table to see him more clearly. "It *is* you."

"It *is* me." His hand smoothed the thin blanket where it draped over the side of the mattress. "Are you okay?"

She remembered. "Better than okay. I have a new job! Claudia stopped by last night and made me an offer."

He nodded, as if taking that in. "Life is looking up, then."

"Yes." It was, she supposed. Because last night she'd thought things between her and Carlo were left so awkward that they could never be in a room together again. "You can go now, though," she said.

His gaze jumped to hers. What was that expression in his eyes? "You want me to go?"

"Well, um, whatever you feel like..." Lucy heard herself stepping into that familiar I'll-say-anything-he-wants role. Closing her eyes, she took a breath, then opened them again. "You're welcome to stay. It's nice to see you. But I know that hospitals make you uncomfortable."

"A lot of things make me uncomfortable," he muttered. He smoothed the blanket again, and she noticed the skinned knuckles. So she thought, he really had decked the pyrotechnics guy.

"You're hurt," she said, reaching out to brush his fingers with hers.

He caught her hand, then nodded at her cast. "*You're* hurt. I hate that you're hurt."

"I understand." And she did. It was how he'd changed after Patrick McMillan had died in his arms, under his watch. Carlo didn't want to care that deeply again and so…he didn't.

Carlo rubbed across her fingernails with the pad of his thumb, his gaze trained on their joined hands. "You're giving up too easy again, Lucy. You're willing to take less than you deserve. Less than you want."

Her heart started beating faster in her chest, as if it understood more than her mind. What did he mean? What was he saying?

"Pat's death put me in the shadows, Lucy. You lured me out."

"I'm not a trap." Her whisper was fierce. "I never meant to trap you." And if he didn't want to…to care for her, then she wasn't going to let it ruin her life.

"Still, I couldn't resist all the sticky sweetness."

That had her thinking about sex. About chocolate whipped cream and hot, intimate kisses. "Not fair."

"All right." His voice sounded strained. "But Lucy, just don't tell me that it's too late. Not now that I've stepped into your light."

She looked up. His face was still stone-hard, so expressionless it made her heart ache. "Too late for what?"

"For you to tell me again what you want?"

Oh, talk about traps. Her heart's speed went up another notch, but she still wasn't sure what he was getting at. She only knew she wasn't going to live a life where she did all the giving and the pleasing and the telling.

"So I have to take all the risk, is that it? You want me to jump and then you'll decide if the water's fine?"

He was silent a long minute. Then his gaze met hers. He sighed. "Lucy Sutton, you are one tough woman."

Apparently he couldn't see the untough sting of tears in her eyes, because she had the sudden sense that everything was going to be all right.

Carlo brought her hand to his mouth and kissed each one of her fingers. "Here goes, baby. Don't blink, because I'm about to execute my best dive."

Lucy's heart leaped and beat soft butterfly wings that made it hard to breathe.

"I'm in love with you, Lucy. You don't know—or maybe you do—how much I didn't want to be in this place, because I thought experiencing those feelings would be my worst nightmare. That they'd make me vulnerable to the kind of pain I felt when Pat died, to the kind of pain I've seen on Germaine's face. It seemed so much easier, more comfortable, saner, never to want to do that…"

"Couple thing," she finished for him.

He squeezed her fingers. "But then…but then I saw you fall and my vision of a nightmare changed entirely. Never letting you know what you mean to me, never seeing you smile or laugh or even cry—why, baby, why are you crying?—would be so much, much more terrible."

Leaning across the mattress, he laid a soft kiss on her lips, taking a tear or two away with it. "There's no time to waste, Luce. I get that now. Will you be my light, my love, my hope for happily-ever-after?"

Later, Lucy would make him pay for proposing to her when she had bedhead and was wearing a faded hospital gown. Secretly she would always think it was the most perfect moment in her entire life.

Later, Carlo would apologize profusely when she complained. Loudly, he would always tell her—truthfully—it was the most perfect moment of his entire life.

* * * * *

Jennifer McKenzie lives in Vancouver, Canada, where she enjoys being able to ski and surf in the same day—not that she ever does either of those things. After years of working as a communications professional and spending her days writing for everyone else, she traded in the world of water coolers, cubicles and high heels to write for herself and wear pajamas all day.

THAT WEEKEND...

Jennifer McKenzie

For Clark

Rocking Reporter in Rockdale

Yes, I know the title is lame, but whatevs. Am pumped to be attending Rockdale's film festival again this year! In fact, I will out myself as a child of the '80s and say: I'm so excited. And I just can't hide it.

Rumors, rock-star parties and the ritziest fashions will be everywhere as the Tinseltown glitterati make the place their own for a whole week. I'll be reporting live for Vancouver's *Entertainment News Now,* so tune in every night to get the latest in celeb gossip and the juiciest scoop. Yes, I'll be there covering it all. Bliss!

Shaping up to be the biggest year yet. Attendees already confirmed: Jennifer Lopez (who will surely be decked out in white fur that only La Lopez could pull off), George Clooney (people, I am swooning. Swooning!), plus Matt and Ben, Brangelina, Reese and every celebutante on the planet. And.

…Rob Lowe! Now, I know that some of you are too young to remember him in anything but TV, but let me tell you that Mr. Lowe was the hottest thing happening in movies in the '80s. And I have had a crush on him and his baby blues going on twenty-five years now. (What? I was a precocious seven-year-old.) Suffice to say that if he is here…? There will be much stalking.

Lena is producing the shoot and promises that she will actually squeal out loud if Robert Pattinson talks to her. (I so need to make this happen.) And Brandon is working the camera. (Yep, got-picked-up-by-a-contessa-in-Italy Brandon). Will be posting every second I have a chance, so check this website often to make sure you get the scoop first.

Kiss kiss,
Ava

Chapter 1

Jake Durham was evil.

Okay, so fine. It was Monday morning and Ava Christensen was never at her best until it was past noon and she'd had at least three cups of coffee, but she needed neither caffeine nor sleep to know the truth about the man sitting behind the big fancy desk.

"I hope you understand this was a difficult decision to make."

Ava just stared at him. Jake Durham, *Entertainment News Now* executive producer. Aka: Evil Incarnate. Alias: Beelzebub. Pseudonym: Norman Bates. Seriously, she must have been blind to ever think he was even sorta, kinda, maybe hot.

Well, even the most brilliant reporters made the occasional mistake. And it had only taken her a month to uncover the truth. Probably wouldn't have even taken her that long had she not been on a six-month dry spell. She needed to get out more.

She swallowed and tried not to think about how, even as he was callously and carelessly crushing her dream, she could still find him attractive. "Who is getting the position?"

The position. Said so casually, so free of emotion, as if it was no big deal. Ava swallowed again, wishing she had a coffee to wash away the bitterness coating her mouth. Why hadn't she poured herself a mug before attending this morning's meeting?

And why had she told her mother that she was a shoo-in to be the next cohost at *Entertainment News Now?*

"Tommy." Jake studied her closely. Too closely.

"Tommy?" The little tug of recognition that always twisted her stomach when he looked at her like that was overridden by a sudden roiling. Her fingers curled around the arms of the cheap plastic chair she was sitting in. "Tommy Langtry?"

"Yes."

"No." He couldn't be serious. Could he? But there was no sign of humor in his dark gray eyes.

But Tommy? It didn't make sense. While she'd been a regular reporter on the show for the past three years, Tommy had only been around six months. He wasn't even a regular reporter, but more of a correspondent who was lucky to get a piece to air every couple of weeks. And he'd only gotten the job because his uncle was Harvey Langtry, the station owner.

Her blog on the station's website was incredibly popular. It not only satisfied the appetite for celebrity gossip that couldn't be covered in a thirty-minute program, but it also drove viewers to the show with teasers and tidbits about on-air exclusives. And she was the replacement host when the regulars were sick or on vacation. To date, Tommy's greatest achievements were stuffing Mentos and Coke into his mouth until they exploded in a gush of foam and convincing his uncle to host a holiday party with a top-shelf open bar.

Even for someone who'd been around for only a month, like Mr. Big-Shot Executive Producer, giving her the job was a no-brainer. "You think he's ready?"

Jake clasped his hands on the desk. Long strong hands that Ava had no business remembering the feel of. "We felt he brought something extra to the show. Something that had been missing."

Something that *she'd* been missing? Her spine stiffened. Garbage. Unless they were planning on adding a stupid-human-trick segment to the show that she hadn't heard about, there was nothing in Tommy's repertoire that she didn't do better.

"And we liked the dynamic between him and Danica." Jake's voice softened. "We like you a lot, but we just didn't feel you were the right choice in this situation."

"Oh." To her horror, Ava felt tears prickle behind her eyes. Great. Just great. She blinked rapidly, pretending a speck of dust had lodged in there until she got herself under control. But she knew it was a temporary reprieve. She needed to get out of here before the tears returned and a weepfest ensued. Talk about unprofessional. She started to rise. "Well, thank you for telling me in person."

At least he'd had the courtesy to let her know before the news swept through the station at warp speed. But it was a small consolation when it felt as if he was grinding her career to dust beneath his heel.

"A minute." Jake waved for her to sit back down. Ava was torn between ingrained good manners and the need to get out of there before the tears began rolling down her cheeks. "I'm sure that you're disappointed," Jake said, "but I trust that you understand it was a difficult choice."

Yeah. Or not, considering Tommy was related to the station owner. Yay for nepotism. She clutched the arms of the old chair harder. "Of course."

She hated the warble in her voice. God. She was a trained media professional. She should be able to speak without sounding like a fan meeting one of the *Twilight* kids. For the record, she had and her voice hadn't warbled a bit.

Jake leaned forward. "You were a strong candidate."

Instead of consoling her, the assurance made her feel worse. The prickle behind her eyes became a full-fledged ache. No. The chair arms were going to leave lines in her palm. She didn't care if the hard material sliced right through her skin. She was not going to cry. Not here. Not now. Not in front of him.

"An extremely strong candidate." Jake glanced around his desk and came up with a crumpled napkin from Starbucks.

Ava looked at it, but didn't take it. She didn't want to accept anything from him except his heartfelt apology when he realized what a mess he'd made of things. And he would realize it. She'd make sure of it.

He looked at the napkin when he realized she wasn't going to take it and then slowly folded it into his palm before sinking back into his chair. "You probably just need some time to take it all in."

Anger surged forward, hot and fierce. Some time? As if a good night's sleep or a pint of ice cream was going to make up for losing out on her dream job? Not likely. But she forced her expression to remain neutral, a trick she'd learned during her years of dealing with spoiled celebrities and their publicists. "I'm fine." Because turning into a female version of the Incredible Hulk and upending his desk wouldn't solve her problems. Even if it would feel good. "If there's nothing else, I should get back to work."

Jake balled up the napkin and tossed it in the wastebasket beside his desk. "If you have any further questions, I'll be happy to discuss them with you."

She even managed a cool smile, though it just about killed her. *Phhht.* As if she'd ever discuss anything with him. "I appreciate that."

"Glad to hear it." He smiled back.

She felt it like a punch to the gut.

It was all Jilly's fault. Ava stormed down the hallway toward her best friend's office, the heels of her glorious black shoes clacking like bullets. She never should have gone to that stupid anti–Valentine's Day party Jilly had organized two weeks ago, never should have flirted with Jake Durham while she was there, never should have almost kissed him.

Thank God she'd come to her senses before anything had happened. Heat rose to her cheeks at the memory. The way his hand had rested on her shoulder when they'd gotten shoved together in the corner of the booth, how his breath had tickled the nape of her neck, the feel of his body as he turned into her.

She so needed to get out of here.

She bypassed the door to her own office without glancing at it. So much for that pretty nameplate she'd been hoping to have made. The one that would read Ava Christensen, Cohost, in gold lettering.

But when she arrived at Jilly's office—Jilly insisted everyone at the station call it an office even though as the studio's makeup artist, her space held no desk and was twice as large as any real office in the building—Ava found the door closed. An unanswered knock confirmed that no one was inside.

Well, she wasn't hanging around until Jilly finally turned up, which probably wouldn't be until noon anyway. This was a time for action. Mostly because Ava was afraid if she waited, she'd lose what little composure she still had and would end up saying something she'd regret. Something like, "Jake Durham is a rat bastard and I can't wait until his three-month contract is over and we can get a real producer in here." She didn't even want to consider what her mother would say about that.

She stomped back down the hall. Not only would her mother kill her, but there was a strong possibility that at the end of Jake's contract, Harvey would offer him a long-term permanent placement. And then she'd be stuck forever with a boss she'd called a rat bastard.

Awesome.

She stopped at her non–gold nameplated office only long enough to grab her coat, bag and umbrella—it was late February in Vancouver, which meant cool temperatures and a high likelihood of rain—and left the building. Before she'd even made it partway down the block, she had her BlackBerry out, fingers flying over the tiny keyboard.

Are you up yet, Jilly? Emergency. Meet me for coffee. Now. FYI: This is a Red Alert.

Jilly's response was almost instantaneous.

Did you get it? Of course you got it. Eeeeee! Did you kiss McHot Stuff when he told you? (You know you want to.)

No and no. Devastation being held off momentarily. See you at Bucky's in ten.

"You have got to be kidding." Jilly's face held just the right mix of surprise and disgust. She was a true friend. "Tommy? He picked Tommy?" She huffed in indignation. "Well, one thing is clear. McHot Stuff is a McHot Ass."

"And he's no longer McHot Stuff. He is cut off." Ava sliced a hand through the air. "Plus, he's not really cute." Which was totally true. She'd never thought Jake was cute. He was too dark and rugged to be called cute. And dark and rugged was so not her type.

"Not smart, either," Jilly said. Her hair, currently dyed a bright red that was probably called Spicy Ginger or Fiery Sunset, flashed as she shook her head. "I don't understand it. You're perfect for the job. What has Tommy ever done?"

"You mean besides be born into the Langtry family?" Ava shrugged and took a sip of her latte. "What else did he need?"

Starbucks was warm and steamy with the scent of roasted beans in the air. People were scattered around the room, lounging on chaises and chairs, their chatter blending with the sound of the grinder behind the counter. Jilly had managed to nab a pair of squashy leather chairs in the corner, which was normally Ava's favorite spot, but today she just couldn't feel grateful.

She put the latte down since it was only spreading the bitterness around her mouth. Nothing like the comfort she'd imagined it would be in Jake's office. "You know what really kills me? He didn't even give me a good explanation. Just said that it was a difficult decision and that they thought Tommy brought a new dynamic to the show. Guess they never clued in to the fact that Danica can't stand him."

"Well, to be fair, Danica doesn't really like anyone."

"True." To say Danica was icy was crediting her with warmth that Ava had never seen the tall blonde show. She let her head fall back against the soft chair. The scent of leather blended with the aroma of coffee. She didn't care who Danica liked or didn't like. Not right now. "I flirted with him," she said, closing her eyes. "At that anti–Valentine's Day party. I flirted with him." And almost kissed him.

"Well, he was still McHot Stuff then."

Ava opened her eyes but didn't lift her head. "I flirted with him and I didn't even get the job."

Jilly lifted an eyebrow. "Is that why you flirted with him?"

"Of course not." Ava sat up straight. "But I just feel foolish now."

"Because you flirted with an attractive man."

"I told you." Ava waved her hand again. "He is cut off." Snip. "Like my chance of ever being cohost." Her insides twisted at the words. She picked up her cup again but didn't drink from it. She was too depressed.

"Don't say that." Jilly's green eyes were bright with loyalty. "You'll get it next time. You're too good not to be a host."

Ava stared down at the foamy drink. "What if there is no next time?"

It wasn't something she wanted to think about, but she had to consider what it meant for her if Tommy and Danica made such a great team that they hosted the show for the next thirty years. She'd die if that happened. Die without ever being more than a stand-in.

"That won't happen."

"It could." She wasn't that young anymore. Oh, sure, she still felt about the same age as the girls on MTV's *Teen Mom,* but her driver's license told another story. She, unlike Tommy, was over thirty, and this chance might not come along again until she was considered too old for the job. Her stomach twisted painfully and she took a sip of her latte to try to soothe it. It didn't help.

"It won't happen," Jilly repeated, her hair flickering like an aggravated flame in the watery light that came in through the window. "If you don't get to host here, then you'll get scooped up by some other station that recognizes your greatness."

"Really?" Ava knew she sounded pathetic, but if a person couldn't sound pathetic in front of her best friend after finding out she'd just been denied the promotion of her dreams, then when could she?

"Absolutely." Jilly's tone brooked no argument,

which was good because Ava didn't think she had the energy for it. "And now, your day can only get better, right?" That was Jilly, always looking on the bright side.

"I hope so."

"I know so. Drink your latte."

Ava picked up her drink without sipping. "What am I going to tell my mother?" Normally, she wouldn't have even mentioned that she was applying for a promotion. But she'd been so confident, she hadn't been able to keep the news to herself.

Now she was going to have to listen to that brief pause of disappointment before her mother made a few appropriate noises of concern, which would just be a mask before she could ask how Ava might have done things differently. She'd probably want her to make a list, too.

The very idea made Ava's bones ache with exhaustion. Maybe tonight was too soon. She could call her mother tomorrow instead.

"Maybe she'll forget?"

Ava shot her friend a look.

Jilly sighed. "You're right. Just get it over with quickly and then change the subject." She handed over the chocolate croissant she'd been eating. "Here. You need this more than me."

Ava bit off a huge chunk of the delicate pastry, refusing to even consider the calories. They didn't count today. Everyone knew that when you were depressed, chocolate was a mood lifter and the fat found its way out of your body without making a pit stop on your hips.

The croissant was still warm, the chocolate melting before it even hit her tongue. She reveled in the sweetness for a moment, wanting to lick the chocolate from her fingers, but wiped them on a napkin instead. "I'm so glad to be leaving town on Friday. Rockdale could not have come at a better time."

The Rockdale Film Festival in Rockdale, Idaho, was the little beacon of light at the end of this dark tunnel. She could leave all this—and Jake—behind for a week of fun in the snow with Hollywood's hottest scene makers.

"No kidding." Jilly's eyes lit up. "I know what would get your mind off this. Meet a superhot guy at Rockdale and have a mad passionate week-long affair."

"I could," Ava said, "except for that little thing called work. How many times do I have to tell you it's not a vacation."

"You can squeeze it in. I mean, what do you have to do? Movie premieres, going to parties and hanging out with celebrities? Plenty of time for a love affair with a movie-star hunk."

"Standing out in the freezing cold and begging those celebrities for a minute of their time, avoiding the drunk groupie about to puke on my shoes and never getting more than a couple hours of sleep at a time is not exactly a script for romance."

"Oh, please. You love it."

Ava's mood lifted slightly. She did love it. Even if she had to come home and sleep for three days straight to recover. And the idea of having a short, hot affair made her feel better. Even if it would never happen. "Maybe I'll meet George Clooney and he'll fall madly in love with me and sweep me away to live a life of luxury in his Italian villa."

"He'd be a fool not to."

By the time she returned to her office, Ava was feeling much better. A little chocolate, a little coffee and a lot of knowing that she was about to get seven blissful Jake-free days, which might be even better than having an affair with George, though she wouldn't admit that to Jilly. She hung her coat on the back of her door and woke up her computer. It hummed happily and dinged, letting her know she had email.

To: All Staff [[allstaff@entnewsnow.com>
From: Jake Durham [[jake_durham@entnewsnow.com>
Subject: Lena Wu
I'm sorry to inform you that Lena Wu has decided to leave the station, effective immediately. She's accepted a job as a producer on *Vancouver Tonight*'s six o'clock news program. We wish her the best of luck as she pursues this new endeavor.
Sincerely,
Jake
Jake Durham
Executive Producer, Entertainment News Now

To: Ava Christensen [[ava_christensen@entnewsnow. com>, Brandon Rothschild [[brandon_rothschild@ entnewsnow.com>
From: Jake Durham [[jake_durham@entnewsnow.com>
Subject: Rockdale Film Festival
As I'm sure you both realize, Lena will no longer be attending Rockdale. I will be going in her place. We need to discuss details. Meeting in my office at 1:00 this afternoon.
Jake

To: Jilly Daly [[jilly_daly@entnewsnow.com>
From: Ava Christensen [[ava_christensen@entnewsnow. com>

FW: You will not believe this.
What kind of heinous criminal was I in a former life to deserve this?
Forwarded Message Attached

To: Ava Christensen [[ava_christensen@entnewsnow.com>
From: Jilly Daly [[jilly_daly@entnewsnow.com>
Re: OMG
Seriously, did you used to eat babies?

Chapter 2

Jake glanced at the clock in his office and then back at the doorway, which was empty. Brandon had already come and gone, but there was still no sign of Ava. She was late. Only ten minutes, but that was long enough to have him wondering about the reason for it. Something legit or was this a slap at him because he'd been the bearer of bad news only hours earlier?

He drummed his fingers on his desktop. It had been a lousy morning. First, the deal with the promotion, then Lena telling him that she was leaving and now having to scramble to make sure there would be no hitches with Rockdale.

This wasn't what he'd signed on for.

When he'd accepted this job, it had been with the promise that he'd be a stopgap until someone permanent could be hired. *Oh, no,* Harvey had said, *there shouldn't be anything major happening. It'll just be business as usual.* Except he'd neglected to mention that he wanted Jake to select a cohost to replace the one who had left with the previous executive producer.

If Harvey hadn't been such a close family friend, Jake would have turned around the first day he walked into the station. He didn't need the job and he had another project that demanded his time, one that he wanted to work on. But Harvey and his father had been friends since university, and Jake had promised that he'd help. So he was still here counting the days until his contract was over.

And it was looking to be a long stretch of days. He had to find a replacement for Lena, prepare for what was one of the busiest festivals in the industry and deal with a furious reporter who'd be attending the festival with him.

Oh, hell didn't begin to cover it.

At least he had someone in mind for his position. Although it wasn't Jake's responsibility, he didn't trust that Harvey would start the search on his own.

Hanna Compton was experienced and capable. In fact, Jake had initially asked her if she'd be interested in the position so that he didn't have to take it himself, but she was under contract until the end of April. It was why he'd negotiated his contract to end at the same time.

He and Hanna had gone to university together, finishing one and two in most of their classes. They'd remained close through the years, though she was probably closer to his little sister, Rachel, these days. They were quite the pair, regularly sticking their noses into his business and telling him how to run his life.

While he waited for Ava to make an appearance, Jake took care of some other business. First, he contacted

Harvey's personal assistant to make sure she'd booked
him on the flight and changed the hotel reservations
from Lena's name to his. Then he called some old colleagues scattered throughout the country and left messages about finding someone who'd be a good fit for
the executive producer role, just in case Hanna didn't
accept. The sooner he found someone to take over this
job, the sooner he could get back to focusing on the real
reason for his move across the country.

It wasn't that he hadn't done well in Toronto. He'd
had a good job with a good company. One that had minimal ties to his father's successful production company.
A nice condo, nice girlfriend, nice life. Or, at least, it
had been.

Maybe that was the problem. It had all been too easy,
and he'd become complacent, unable to hone the hard
edge that was necessary when doing business at the
highest levels. So instead of being a player, he'd just
gotten played.

Not anymore.

This time he would be the one in charge. He was
starting his own production company, and keeping it
separate from the one his father owned back East. Alex,
another old friend from his university days, was working on getting the start-up capital, and the money would
come from outside investors.

Alex had put out some feelers and come up with a
list of local businesspeople who might be interested in
backing their project. Some of them Jake vetoed immediately because they knew his father and would be sure
to ask if he was Chuck Durham's son. Though that fact
was much easier to conceal on the West Coast, where
his father's name wasn't quite so well-known, it was

still a concern. At least out here no one had heard about the way his personal life had poked itself into his professional life, entwining the two so tightly that when one went south, the other had no choice but to follow.

Out here, no one knew he had failed.

It was why he'd made those calls to old colleagues now instead of waiting until tomorrow morning when he was more likely to catch them in their offices. Though most of them would try not to show it, Jake could imagine the censure in their tones. Or worse, the pity that he'd been so easily manipulated, that he wasn't such a chip off the old block. It made him want to grind his teeth together and spit out the stumps. Easier to just explain what he was looking for via voice mail and ask that they forward the names of any potential candidates they knew to his new email address.

When he hung up, another twenty minutes had passed and there was still no sign of Ava.

The annoyance buried itself a little deeper in his gut. It wasn't as though she'd been the only possible candidate. Or that he'd brought in an outsider. Not this time. Been there, done that, got the scars to show for it. This had been a pure business decision. One made with his head, which told him to let Tommy have a chance. Not because Tommy was related to the station owner, but because although he was young, he showed promise. Not that Ava seemed to understand that.

To think that only a couple of weeks ago, he'd almost kissed her. He snorted. Hell, he *had* kissed her, though the brushing of their lips had been brief. Didn't matter. Lips had been touching and it had been good, which had surprised him, since he hadn't planned on connecting with anyone during his short stint at the station.

Probably should have remembered that before he'd agreed to go to that anti–Valentine's Day party. But something about it had appealed to his stung emotions. The thought of spending an evening with other people who also thought the forced-romance aspect was a crock and weren't ashamed to be out in the city having a good time without a date, when everyone else seemed to be part of a pair or looking to be one by the end of the night, had been too tempting to pass up. Plus, he hadn't had anything better to do and six solid weeks of entertaining himself by sitting in front of his television while he worked on his production company had long since gotten old.

He'd had a good time, made better by Ava, but it had just been in fun, and when they returned to the office the next morning, it had been business as usual. She hadn't acted any different around the station, no showing up at his office to ask him questions or inserting herself into meetings that she didn't need to attend. In fact, he hadn't really seen much of her at all in the lead-up to his selection of new cohost.

He wondered now if that had been part of her ploy. A teasing warmth followed by the cool, consummate professionalism to make him want her more. It pissed him off that even six months ago, he might have fallen for it.

The phone rang and he grabbed the receiver, intent on chewing a chunk out of Ava's ass if she was calling to cancel. Not that he wasn't reasonable—he was and he understood that things in the entertainment industry had a way of popping up unexpectedly. But that call should have come fifteen minutes ago. At a minimum.

"Jake here."

"It's Alex." Lucky for Ava's ability to sit.

Some of the tension in Jake's shoulders eased. "What's up?"

"I've got good news."

Jake sat up straighter. He could use some of that right about now. "Yeah? What is it?"

"An investor. A big one." He could practically hear Alex drooling. "This group is sitting on some excess cash and looking to put it somewhere now."

Anticipation rolled through Jake's blood. "Talk."

Alex had been busy contacting potential investors. To this point, they'd received little interest, but one was all they needed. "They like the concept."

"Of course they do."

He didn't want to brag, but his idea was brilliant: making a travel show specifically for airlines. Since most shows currently on the market had been created for a television audience sitting at home, they ran according to those prescribed notions of time and need. But times and technology had changed and now was a chance to take advantage of how people had changed with it.

His shows would run no longer than fifteen minutes. Little sneak peeks at restaurants and attractions specific to an area. And nothing that required a serious amount of traveling. On his show, all recommendations would be near the city center or well-known landmarks and easily reached by foot or an inexpensive cab ride.

So people heading to New Orleans would see the cemetery where Marie Laveau was entombed, learn about Café du Monde's special chicory coffee and beignets, and see the best of Bourbon Street. People on their way to San Francisco would check out Pier 39, the Embarcadero and the Buena Vista's Irish coffees. Simple. Straightforward.

"They want to meet you before they commit to giving us the money."

Jake had expected as much. "No prob. When?"

"This Friday."

"This Friday?" Jake closed his eyes. This Friday he was already booked solid with events. Out of the country. Well, hell.

"No, Friday the thirteenth, seven years from now."

"I'm out of town," Jake said.

Alex cursed.

"An appealing offer, but I'll pass."

"Why didn't I know about this? I would have scheduled a different time."

"I only just found out about it this morning." Jake ran a hand through his hair. He didn't want to let this opportunity slip away. Wouldn't let it. "I could do it tomorrow or Thursday."

"They can't do it sooner than Friday. When are you back?"

"Next Thursday, but I can rearrange if we need to." He'd fly back from Rockdale early if necessary.

"No." He could hear Alex typing. "It'll be fine. It's not going to kill them to wait."

Well, that made one of them.

"And we should invite Carly to join us."

Carly Dahl was the cute twentysomething who would be hosting the show. Her bubbly personality and sweet smile made her a natural on camera, and, as Alex had pointed out, she looked hot in a bikini.

"I'll call her." Jake made a note to do that after he finished killing Ava.

"I can call her."

"No," Jake spoke quickly. "I'll do it. I think she likes you."

"I'm hard not to like."

Jake snorted. "Yes, but we'd prefer to keep the host."

"What are you saying?"

"I'm saying that I don't want you breaking her heart. We don't have time to look for someone else."

"You make it sound like you don't think I can control myself." Alex laughed. "But fine. I'll let you know when I reschedule that meeting."

Jake made a couple more notes and was just about to walk over to Ava's office and have the meeting there if he had to, when his phone rang again. "Jake Durham."

His annoyance was turning to anger. Just where the hell was she? This delaying tactic had gone way beyond a slap and was verging on a hard kick in the privates. Well, he didn't take kicks there anymore. Not from anyone. Not even appealing blondes who made him forget that he'd sworn off relationships or even casual dating for a while.

"It's me."

"Oh, hell." It was a snarl, he could admit that, but it was his little sister and Jake thought a world where an older brother couldn't snarl at a little sister wasn't one worth living in.

"Charming as always."

"I'm busy, Rache." Not entirely true. He looked at his door just in case Ava had appeared there in the interim, but the hallway's institutional-green walls were the only thing to stare back.

"Well, excuse me for caring and wanting to check on my brother. Who, I might add, has been avoiding my phone calls during nonwork hours, leaving me no choice but to make a pain of myself at the office." Since Rachel was capable of making a pain of herself at any place or time, Jake wasn't sure her excuse held up.

"You have two minutes. Maybe less." If Ava finally managed to get her butt in here. "What's up?"

"Oh, lots of things." He could hear her smile and picture her settling in for a good long chat. She was just like their mother that way. The two of them often chatted on the phone for a couple of hours at a time, though they only lived fifteen minutes apart and saw each other regularly. Jake had to schedule his own phone calls back home to Toronto, or risk getting a busy signal all afternoon. When he pointed this out to Rachel, she told him that it was their parents' fault for not getting into the new millennium and having call waiting. "But apparently we don't have time for that. What's happening with you?"

"Same old, same old." He blew out a breath, tried not to take his aggravation out on his sister. "Seriously, I'm really busy."

"And I told you I only need a minute. Mom wants to know if you're okay. So if you don't want to tell me, be ready to face a string of ever-increasing worried phone calls, which will end in her insisting that you move back home to pursue the show from there."

Jake thought about that. If he hung up on his sister, he had no doubt that she'd make that scenario come to pass. Hell. "Tell her it's the same as last week. I promised that I'd tell you if there was anything to report."

"I know you will or face my wrath." Some of his irritation eased away in a quiet snicker. Rachel was barely over five feet and the least-likely-looking wrath bringer he'd ever seen. Not that he was going to tell her that. He wasn't a complete idiot. "Mom also says that you sound sad when you call and you're always in a rush to get off the phone."

"That's because I don't like talking on the phone and they won't get Skype."

"Oh, like you'd chat via computer?"

"I might. And I'm not sad, just swamped." Jake glanced at the to-do list he was only half finished writing. "Harvey wasn't clear on exactly how much was happening over here."

"And?"

"And what?"

"That's not what I called to talk about. What's happening with the pilot?"

A small curl of pleasure unfurled in his stomach. Of everyone he knew, the only one who had unabashedly supported his decision to throw away his stable career, move across the country and start fresh was Rachel. "On point for now. Got my host and storyboarded the first show. We just need to hammer out a deal with the investors and then we'll be set."

"That's great. How long before you're in production?" Unlike Jake, Rachel hadn't followed their father into TV and film production. Instead, she'd gone the academic route and was an assistant professor of art history at York University in Toronto, but she'd been raised listening to stories of the industry and still had plenty of opinions on how Jake should run things.

"We're booked to film in about two and a half weeks."

"I'm impressed."

Jake's pleasure grew at the pride in his sister's voice.

He didn't like to think about it too much, but there were times he wondered if maybe he'd been a little overzealous in leaving Toronto so quickly. There had been good things about the city, too.

"Anything else?"

"No time for anything else. I barely have time to shower between juggling the pilot and the station."

"Make time," Rachel said. "I remember how your gym bag used to smell."

"It wasn't that bad."

"Like a sweaty sock had been stewing in it for decades."

"You weren't supposed to come into my room anyway."

"How else was I going to steal your Walkman? You kept that thing locked up like it was a national treasure."

"And yet it didn't stop you."

"It did when you stuck it in your gym bag."

Jake laughed. He'd forgotten that. "Inside one of my socks, as I recall."

"I almost died before I could get out of there. I swear, I still have a lingering cough." She performed one for his benefit. "See? Terrible."

And Jake hadn't been able to use the stupid thing for a week until the plastic aired out enough that he could get close enough to it without gagging. It had been completely worth it. "I hope you learned your lesson."

"Stay away from my brother's nasty socks?"

"Don't steal."

"Oh, yeah. That, too. Okay, enough work chatter. What's happening with the people?" Rachel liked people. She had a large circle of friends and a larger one of acquaintances. "Making any friends?"

"Some."

She sighed. "Could you be a little more tight-lipped? No wonder Mom thought you were depressed."

"Not blathering about inane details of my life doesn't mean that I'm depressed."

"It does to Mom. I have an idea. Why don't you tell me everything because you know I won't judge, and then I can let her know you're okay."

"Nice try. You're just being nosy."

"I'm being a concerned sibling."

"A *nosy* concerned sibling."

"True. Now tell me everything."

For a second he considered telling her about the anti–Valentine's Day party. It might get her—and their mother—off his back about getting out and making friends. But then he thought about that barely there kiss with Ava and decided it was probably best not to bring it up. His sister was like a bloodhound when it came to sniffing out details about his love life, or lack thereof.

"Nothing to tell. I work on the pilot most nights."

"Jake…" She paused and he could sense her gearing up. "You need to get out more. Start getting back into the game. What happened was—"

"Don't say it," he started just as she launched into her "it wasn't you, it was her" lecture. Too late. He felt his pleasure slide away, buffeted on the wind of words and memory.

But there was no stopping Rachel once she started. She was like a five-foot bulldog. "Flat out, Claudia was a bitch."

"I know you never liked her."

"Because I could see that she was a user. She was never worth your time."

"I know," Jake said, and he did. He'd realized that when she'd broken up with him because he'd refused to promote her. But it had still hurt and even though he knew he was better off, he still didn't want to rehash it every time he spoke to his family.

"So don't let her affect you. Get out there. Date. Get lucky."

"Maybe I have."

She choked on her laughter. "No. I know your voice too well. You are tightly wound."

"Because I'm busy."

"Yes, but you'd be more relaxed and happier if you were also having sex."

"No, I wouldn't."

"You only think that because you're not. Trust me."

"Stop," Jake interrupted before she could launch into another sister-knows-best lecture. "I cannot listen to details of your sex life with Rob."

"I wasn't going to go into detail. I was just going to say that it's a healthy part of life. And one that I enjoy with my husband."

Jake could feel the tips of his ears burning. Logically, he knew that his little sister and her husband weren't celibate, but it was one of those things that he couldn't think about and definitely couldn't talk about. "Okay, got it. Please stop bringing it up. Ask me about my depression, or when I'm coming home for a visit or when I'm going to call Mom next. Just no more of that."

Rachel was quiet for a moment. Never a good sign. "Is this because you're jealous?"

"What part of 'stop talking about it' did you miss?"

"We're not talking about me. Do I need to call Alex and have him take you on a double date?"

"Please, no." Alex had already tried and Jake had turned him down. His idea of a good date and Alex's were two very different things. "I've got a handle on that."

Another pause. "Does this mean there is some potential out there?"

"Rache, I didn't come out here for that," he answered quickly, but not before his mind shot to Ava and the shower fantasies he might have indulged in before this morning's promotion debacle and the fact that she'd obviously now decided to hate him. Although, maybe there was some potential in that, too. He could be talked into Hate Sex.

"Too quick to protest," Rachel judged. "Which means there is some potential. Lovely. Who is she? What's she look like? How long before you seal the deal?"

"I am not talking about this with you."

"Why? I give awesome advice and you could use a woman's perspective."

"Nothing wrong with my perspective."

"You think beer and pizza is a good date."

"For a sporting event," Jake clarified. "And only once she's hooked."

"Hooked? Your ego astounds me. She's not a fish to reel in. So tell me about her."

"There is no her."

"Please." Rachel snorted again. "There is so a her."

She waited. Fine. He could outwait her.

"You might think you'll win by playing the strong silent type, but I'll just tell Mom."

He broke. "You would not."

She laughed. "Do you know me at all? Of course I

would. However, I could be convinced to keep it to my-self if you just tell me everything."

He considered it for about a nanosecond before stick-ing to his original decision. He was about to tell his sister to keep her nose out of his business, when he caught sight of Ava coming down the hall. "Oh, gee, baby sister, I would," he lied, knowing it would get Ra-chel's goat, "but my appointment just showed up and I have to go."

"What? No. No."

Jake hung the phone up without responding. Rachel wasn't the only Durham sibling who knew how to push buttons.

Ava stopped just shy of his office. Emotions swirled in his gut as he watched her, and his body tightened, clearly not getting the memo that sex—hate or other-wise—was not in the cards.

It was wrong, but it was hard not to fantasize about her when she looked at him with those big blue eyes, her sunshine-colored hair curling across her shoulders and just a hint of a blush on her creamy white skin. She reminded him of spring. But from the turn of her mouth it looked as if March's lamb was going out like a lion.

Jake felt his own irritation rise to meet hers. He was the one who'd been sitting here waiting for how long? He checked the time again. Thirty minutes. He turned some of that irritation on her where it belonged. "Glad you could make it."

He saw the flash of resentment in her eyes at the sharpness of his tone, but she blinked it away and pasted on one of those phony wide-eyed expressions that was the hallmark of bad actors. "So sorry I'm late. I was busy working."

He didn't respond. Just leaned back and crossed his arms over his chest as she bypassed the plastic chair she'd sat in this morning and instead settled on the ugly brown couch that took up one wall of his office. He'd considered getting rid of it when he'd first taken over the space and then decided that he could live with it for three months. Let the next executive producer decide what they wanted to do with it.

Ava smoothed her skirt, drawing his eyes to her legs and the high heels she wore. "For the record, I did email you to let you know I was running behind." She glared at him while she spoke.

He made a show of checking his email and then felt like a tool when there was indeed an unread message from her. "Oh." If his voice was a little gruffer than usual, she'd just have to deal with it. "Let's get started."

"Sure." She crossed her legs. "Should we wait for Brandon?"

Jake yanked his eyes away from her legs. "Brandon and I have already met." He flipped to a new page on his lined notepad and reminded himself that although he was still irked that she'd been late, getting into an argument with her was no way to kick off their festival. Rockdale was a long, busy week, and a healthy professional relationship with his team was key to making it a success. "Let's start with what you and Lena had planned."

Ava studied him as though she was waiting for him to say something else then nodded. He forced his eyes to remain on her face as she read off a list from the folder in her lap.

Rockdale was an A-list film festival with A-list responsibilities. Juggling the team, dealing with hard-ass publicists, ego-stroking actors, handling the morass of interviews, parties and red carpets, not to mention making sure their stories were well edited and sent back to the station in a timely fashion for air was more than a full-time gig.

Jake felt some of his tension slip away as Ava talked. It was a well-thought-out and clear plan. She and Lena had been prepared, which was good for him. Although Jake had been to festivals before, it had been a while and he was happy to accept any help he could get.

"Do we have some flextime built in?" he asked. There was usually a story or two that didn't turn up until the festival was underway. The good media teams were ready to jump on those at a moment's notice.

She nodded. "Plus, there are a couple of things booked that we could easily cancel." She mentioned a few independent films that only held interest by virtue of their leading actor or director, but weren't expected to create more than a low hum.

"Good." Jake made note of them, as well. "Then we can cut those if we need to. Good work."

"Yes, it is." But she wasn't smiling when she said it. "Anything else or can I go?"

"In a minute." He kept his voice mild. He didn't want to bring up the subject, but the tight twist of her lips told him that this conversation was necessary. "I want to quash these bad feelings between us."

"What bad feelings? I don't have any bad feelings." The fakey-fake smile was back. He would bet she'd perfected it from years of dealing with oversensitive actors who considered themselves *artistes*. He preferred the ones who admitted they were in it for the money.

"Hypothetically, if you did have any problems with

me, I'd like to deal with them now. We can't afford to be at odds in Rockdale." In-fighting was a surefire way to have a terrible festival, both personally and professionally.

"And we won't be." Her smile didn't move a millimeter.

With her sunny coloring and features, she looked like a Kewpie doll come to life. Although the lines around her eyes and mouth reminded him more of Chucky. He bit back the smile that rose to his lips, knowing she wouldn't appreciate his observation. "Then you're not still upset that I chose Tommy as cohost?"

He knew that would rile her, wanted it to, so they could get everything out on the table and get on with their jobs.

"I'm not happy about it." Judging from the rigidity of her back and shoulders, that was an understatement. She shot him a death glare that would have stopped a Brangelunatic in their tracks. "But if you think a guy with less than six months' experience is more capable of handling cohosting duties than me, that's your decision."

"It isn't always about experience." He could see her hands clenching and unclenching as if she was trying to strangle something to death. Probably him. He leaned back in his chair and tried not to sigh. "Look, you're obviously still mad. We leave town on Friday and I'm not taking a pissed-off reporter with me."

Color bloomed in her cheeks. "What are you saying?'

"I'm saying that if you can't handle the fact that I chose Tommy, I'll take someone else to Rockdale. It's not personal." He shrugged. "We just can't afford to be anything but professional once we're there."

"No." Now she really looked ready to go all Chucky on his ass. "The festival is mine."

He eyed her coolly. "So we're fine, then?"

Her lips moved without saying anything. Probably cursing him to hell and back.

Jake didn't care. "Are we fine?" he asked again.

She nodded. "We're fine."

He knew they weren't, but he wasn't completely without feeling. She'd wanted the promotion. Bad. And Rockdale was a consolation prize that he didn't want to take from her unless she absolutely forced his hand.

"All right, then, unless you can think of anything else, that's it." He watched as she rose to go. The sharp movement provided a nice peekaboo view of her thigh, which Jake thoroughly enjoyed.

Even if he couldn't touch.

Chapter 3

Four days after their conversation, Ava was still annoyed with Jake.

The nerve of him, asking if she was going to be able to handle Rockdale, hinting that she was going to be anything less than completely professional while checking out her legs. And *she* was the unprofessional one?

It made her want to spit every time she saw him. But since that wouldn't be professional, she'd settled for avoiding him, which turned out to be a lot more stressful than she'd expected.

Living life in hyperawareness took a lot of energy, always listening and looking, tensed to make a move just in case he turned the corner or popped up in the editing booth. Plus, it made her feel like a bit of a nut job.

And though her plan had worked—she'd only crossed paths with him a few times and always briefly—it hadn't made her any more relaxed. If anything, she'd wound herself up even more, knowing that today it had to come to an end.

Ava tossed another change of underwear and extra socks into her suitcase. Rockdale, Idaho, was nestled at the foot of a mountain and had the snowy ski weather to show for it. Ava had learned the hard way in her first year that it was better to pack too much than get caught without warm undergarments. Although she drew the line at woolen underwear. Really, a person had to have some standards.

She should probably call her mother before she left, but she didn't know if she was up to it. The phone call to tell her mother about the lost promotion had been bad enough. Just as Ava had expected, Barbara Christensen had hemmed and hawed sympathetically for about a minute and then wanted Ava to analyze all the reasons she might not have gotten the job so that she could mitigate them for next time. Her mother, like Jilly, was positive there was going to be a next time. Ava still wasn't so sure. But there was no point in telling her mother that. There was no point in telling her mother anything she didn't want to hear, although that didn't stop Ava from trying.

Dealing with Jake and the drama of having to travel with him were more than enough, thank you very much.

She glanced at the clock as she stuffed her warmest yoga pants around the edges of the bag. She had a few hours before her flight, and her mother would be expecting her to check in, but what was the point? It would just be more of the same: her mother pushing Ava to consider how she could use the festival to advance her career. As if a great festival week was going to make Jake realize that he'd made an epic mistake in choosing Tommy over her.

But that wouldn't matter to Barbara Christensen. No, she'd want to discuss every possibility, from Tommy quitting, which wasn't going to happen, to hiring a third cohost, which was even less likely. And there would be lists to make. There were always lists when her mother was involved.

Ava quit jamming at the yoga pants—they had more than filled the thin tube of space between the suitcase and her jeans—sighed loudly and heavily because she was so hard done by and drained the last of her coffee. It was her third cup of the morning, but she was still tired.

She took the cup to the kitchen, put it and the empty coffeepot in the dishwasher and returned to the bedroom. Her mother would probably say that she wasn't getting enough fiber and was drinking too much caffeine, but Ava knew the truth. She was tired because her dream had slipped away. She was not going to be cohost of *Entertainment News Now.* She wasn't going to be host of anything. Except her own demise, if she didn't finish packing and get herself to the airport.

She folded her favorite pair of jeans, the ones that made her butt look as if she spent daily sessions on the StairMaster, and added them to the suitcase. Then another scarf, a pair of gloves and a hat with a long tail and pom-pom that Jilly swore was adorable and did not make her look like a demented elf. She was debating between more socks or the cutest sweater ever—obviously the sweater, who would see the socks?—when her cell rang. Or sang, since Ava had gone on a kick of personalizing everyone's ringtone a few months ago, Queen's "Bohemian Rhapsody." Her mother.

She should have known.

Ava hummed along with the mama mias, delaying

the inevitable for a few seconds. Of course her mother
would call this morning. Barbara had probably scheduled it in her Day-Timer, between checking her mail
and drinking her second cup of coffee.

Ava sighed, figuring she might as well get it over
with, and answered. "Hello, Mom."

"Ava, you know I don't like it when you do that." Her
mother's brisk tone told Ava that she was right about
the schedule. Ava had probably thrown it out of whack
by not answering in the expected fashion, though she'd
bet Barbara had built in some time for that, too. "I prefer it when you answer the phone like a normal person."

"All right, then. Hello. This is a normal person. Who,
may I ask, is calling?"

A brief—very brief, wouldn't want to bleed all the
extra time in the first minute of the conversation—
pause, followed by, "Very funny, dear."

Ava grinned, knowing it was immature to tease her
mother, but enjoying herself anyway. That or her coffee was finally kicking in. "I like to think so. How are
you this morning?"

"Busy." Barbara was always busy. As an administrator for one of the city's largest hospitals, she worked
long hours and ran an efficient team. She didn't have
time to waste. Ever. "Are you ready for your trip? All
packed?"

"Of course." Ava glanced down at her luggage, which
was mostly packed. Close enough for this conversation.
Besides, she reasoned, if she told her mother that she
wasn't finished it would just bring on a lecture about
the benefits of early preparation. And that would make
her late. "What's up?"

Her mother tsked. "It sounds crass when you use

slang, dear. But your generation's shocking misuse of the English language isn't why I called. I've been thinking."

"Have you?"

"About your job."

Ava's stomach muscles tensed. She so did not need this, but if her mother wanted to talk about this, they'd talk about it. "And what have you been thinking that we haven't already analyzed to death?"

"I know you were disillusioned when you didn't get the promotion, but I feel you should look at this as opportunity." Ah, yes. The old "opportunity is what you make of it" speech. Next came the part where Barbara would ask about Jake. "You said that the producer who made the decision was going on this trip with you?"

Check and mate. "Yes, he is."

Since she didn't really care to hear what her mother might have to say about the man, Ava returned to packing. She added another pair of tight jeans and a sexy top. The festival was always a hotbed of after-hours parties and activities, and while she wasn't sure that she'd attend any of them, it was best to be prepared. She certainly wasn't going to get caught in the bathroom facing a wall of gorgeous celebrities fixing their lipstick looking as if she'd just come from the gym.

"I think this offers you a wonderful opportunity to prove to him how capable you are."

She picked up her toiletry case and put it in the zip-up pocket inside the bag. It was the last thing to pack, but she did a cursory walk through the rest of her apartment to make sure. She didn't want to get to Idaho and discover she'd left something crucial behind. Like her fabulous dress for tonight's red-carpet event.

Her mother droned on. "There won't be other people around demanding his attention, and you'll have to work together. It's a chance to prove to him that you are a valued member of the team."

"I don't have anything to prove to him." The suitcase seemed to be a little fuller than she'd first thought. She had to sit on top of it to get it closed. "Besides, the position has been filled, so it doesn't matter anymore."

"Of course it matters. These things always matter. Don't you want to be first on their list the next time a position becomes available?"

Ava didn't feel like getting into a debate on whether or not any position would ever be up for grabs again. And she really didn't want to be bombarded with other ways she might advance her career, but sometimes it was easier to just go with it. "Sure, Mom. Great idea."

"I don't think you're taking this seriously enough, Ava." Barbara sounded disappointed. Great. Now Ava could add letting down her mother to her list of failures. "Maybe that's why you didn't get the job this time."

Anger flared, quick and hot. The reason she hadn't gotten the job was because her last name wasn't Langtry. She and Jilly had discussed it in detail. Obviously, Harvey had brought down the hammer and insisted that his dopey nephew get the promotion. Not that it excused Jake. He should have been strong enough to stand up and insist on hiring the best person for the position.

"Mom, I explained this already. I didn't get the job because I'm not related to the owner."

"I'm sure that was a factor, dear, but you could have overcome that obstacle if you'd really wanted to. You have to take responsibility for your own life. You are the captain of your own ship."

Since Ava did not want her mother's next words to be something about being the master of your own domain, she unclamped her jaw long enough to respond. "I know, Mom. Maybe next time I'll get it, all right?"

"Exactly. Which is why you need to prepare. Now, the first thing you should do is write a list."

Barbara believed lists were the key to success. Ava despised them. Probably stemming from the fact that her mother had made her start writing them when she was six. *Six.* What six-year-old wanted to write lists about their future? The only future she'd been thinking of then was getting a red banana-seat bike to cruise around the neighborhood.

"First, write down everything you did during the application process," Barbara said in that confident "I know better than you" tone that never failed to make Ava want to jump out of a plane or ride a motorcycle without a helmet. "It should give you a solid basis to determine what worked and what didn't." There was a small pause, which Ava filled by miming bashing her head against the wall before her mother continued. "I always say that it's important to build good relationships with your colleagues. As I recall, you mentioned that this producer is new to the station."

"Yes." Ava forced the response from tight lips.

"So this festival provides an excellent showcase for you to get to know him better. If you can make yourself indispensable, he'll want to reward you." Reward her. As though she was a dog. "Ava, are you writing this down?"

"Every word." She dragged her suitcase off the bed and rolled it down the hall. "Listen, thanks for the advice, but I really can't talk. My plane—"

"Doesn't leave until twelve-thirty and it's only nine."

Ava wondered if her mother had calculated the distance between her apartment and the airport, too. Seemed likely. "That's true, but I still have things to do. Besides getting there early enough to clear customs and security, I need to go to the bank and pop into the station." The last two things were patently false. Ava had gone to the bank yesterday and she had her Black-Berry if anyone from the station needed her, but she didn't feel guilty about fibbing. Call it self-preservation.

"I only have a few more things to say, dear. I'm sure you have time for that."

Ava swallowed a sigh and plunked down on top of her suitcase, resigning herself to the fact that it would take more time and effort to argue than to listen.

As her mother continued advising, Ava mentally went through what she had to do once the team landed in Rockdale. The first night of the festival was always busy. It was the grand opening, which meant a movie premiere and red carpet that would be attended by the biggest names attending the event. She'd requested a fabric steamer for her room so she could erase any wrinkles from her dress, then she'd need a shower and time to fuss with her hair and makeup. She had to study her questions, so that no matter who turned up to walk the carpet, she'd have something to ask besides "Are you excited about the festival?"

Then there was the event itself, which required her to stand in her highest heels in icy temperatures and smile for a solid hour while celebrities and their publicists worked their way down the carpet and into the theater. She didn't have tickets to the showing tonight, which meant once the last star had made their way inside, she could go. But it was still going to be a long, long day.

Ava turned her attention back to what her mother was saying only once it became clear that Barbara's advice had come to a merciful end. "All right, I think that covers it. Have a safe trip, dear. I love you."

"Love you, too," Ava said, feeling a little guilty for not listening but mostly relieved. She knew her mother was only trying to help; it was just that sometimes her help was so aggravating.

She arrived at the flight gate about forty minutes before her scheduled departure and scanned the seats, looking for an empty one. Her mother would tell her to sit with her colleagues, but Ava needed the time for herself. She pressed a hand to her suddenly nervous stomach.

While it had seemed like a really good idea to avoid Jake, she was starting to think that maybe, just maybe, she'd made a mistake. Surely he'd noticed and figured out that something was up. Unless he was a complete moron. And now she was going to have to face him and act as if everything was just peachy and there wasn't any awkwardness between them at all.

Of course, it was his fault, too. If he hadn't been so blatantly checking out her legs, she wouldn't have had to snipe at him. And the fact that he found her—or at least her legs—attractive wasn't flattering one bit. Well, maybe one bit but certainly not two. And not enough to make her forget that he'd chosen Tommy instead of her.

As she scouted the rows of seats, hoping to find a single somewhere in the back corner where she wouldn't be spotted or interrupted, she found Jake instead. Of course she did. Because her luck had been so stellar lately.

Even as she frowned, her heart gave a little treacherous skip of excitement. He looked good. He wore a white button-down shirt with a gray blazer. Very cool business casual. And the jeans. She noticed them the first time he'd worn them. All fitted and sexy and perfectly broken in. Those jeans could undo the most conservative woman.

Ava dragged her eyes away and stomped to the other side of the waiting area. So what if he looked good? Didn't mean anything to her. For all she cared he could be a world-famous Oscar-winning actor who was named *People*'s Sexiest Man Alive for three years running. He was still a jerk.

Which made it even more annoying that she couldn't quite dispel the image of him sitting there, a cup of coffee in one hand, a laptop case in the other and a smile on his lips. Ugh. What was wrong with her?

She peeked over, taking note of Brandon sitting beside him, laughing at some manly joke, no doubt. She didn't care. She was here to work, not to make friends. She tucked her earbuds in her ears and tried to lose herself in one of her favorite glossy magazines, but she couldn't help checking on the pair every couple of minutes to see what else they were doing. Mostly talking and laughing. She sniffed. Brandon was so easily led. Not like her.

She didn't realize she was staring until someone walked in front of her, cutting off her line of vision. She blinked, but before she could tuck herself back into the shadows, Jake spotted her and waved. Her stomach churned when he motioned that she should join them. As if everything between them was fine.

For one short moment, she debated pretending that she hadn't seen his gesture or maybe hadn't understood it, but common sense kicked in. Avoiding him now was sure to make things even worse and she was pretty sure it would be bad enough as it was. Better just get it over with, and text with Jilly later.

"Ava." Brandon's cheerful voice rose above the buzz of travelers as she neared them. "What were you doing over there?"

"I didn't see you," she said, though she could tell by the small lift of Jake's eyebrows that he didn't believe her. Whatever. If he hadn't planted himself in the middle of the waiting area, in front of the check-in gate like some braniac sitting at the front of the class, she might not have seen him. And who sat in those seats anyway unless they needed extra help getting onto the plane? She tucked her magazine into her bag so that she didn't have to look at Jake looking at her.

"Is this festival going to be great or what?" Brandon said. The cameraman was only twenty-three and still excited by the travel and glitz of the film community.

Ava understood. She'd felt the same way when she'd attended her first film festival. The stars, the glamour, the never-ending parties. But that was back when staying up all night on a diet of vodka and Red Bull had no effect on her the following morning. Now after a night of hard partying, she was lucky to make her call time, let alone look presentable on camera. The downfall of turning thirty. "I guess that means you're ready for the festival?"

"Hell, yeah. You coming out with me tonight?" He started to shift to make space for her to sit between him and Jake, but Ava was quicker. She squished herself into the seat on the other side of Brandon, even though there was a large family taking up half of it.

"Depends. What's happening tonight?" She was careful to keep her gaze from straying to Jake. But she could feel him watching her. Probably wondering why she'd practically twisted herself into a pretzel just so she didn't have to sit beside him, when things were supposed to be okay between them.

Brandon's gray eyes sparkled. "I heard about this killer party to launch some new vodka. All on the down low. No invites or advertising. They send a text telling you where and when." He turned to Jake. "You in?"

It was instinctual to look across Brandon at Jake. He looked about as excited as she felt. "I appreciate the invite, Brando." Brando? He'd already given him a nickname? "But I'm a little old for that crowd."

Brandon turned back to Ava. "He sounds like you."

"No, he doesn't," Ava said, wanting to distance herself from anything Jake-like.

Now Brandon was the one raising an eyebrow her way. "Yeah, he does. You always make some lame excuse to bail."

"Wanting to avoid crop circles under my eyes is not lame."

"Isn't that why they have makeup?"

"There is not enough makeup in the world," Ava told him. "And believe me, I've looked for it."

"See?" Brandon shook his head. "Lame."

"It's not lame." She could feel Jake's eyes on her. Embarrassment burned up the back of her neck and made her hairline itch. She refocused on Brandon. "What time does it start? Maybe I'll go if it's not too late."

Brandon laughed. "That's what you always say and then you never show up."

"Only because I'm older and wiser than you."

"Also, less fun."

"I'm plenty of fun. A barrel-of-monkeys worth of fun." She was superfun and she didn't appreciate Brandon making it seem otherwise. Jake was going to think she was some weirdo whose idea of a good time was doing laundry. Not that she cared what he thought.

"Oh, Aves." Brandon slung an arm around her shoulders. "You know I love you, but sometimes you act like a grandma."

"I am not a grandma." Seriously, she was only thirty-two. She hadn't even gotten her first gray hair yet. But the heat crept from the back of her neck to her cheeks. Her gaze darted to Jake. "For the record, I am plenty of fun." She didn't know why she felt the need to assure him of that. Why she needed to assure him of anything.

"I know." A half smile curled his lips, and a different kind of heat joined the burning in her face. She swiped a hand at her cheek, annoyed that any of this was affecting her at all.

"Oh, yeah?" Brandon turned to Jake while Ava unhooked his arm and wished she'd kept her eyes to herself. "Did you get her to go out partying?"

Ava peeked at Jake from beneath her lashes.

"Sure. She was lots of fun at that Valentine's Day party."

Oh, God. Why hadn't she just let Brandon call her lame? "*Anti*-party," Ava corrected even as her face burned more intensely. And why did Jake have to bring that up? It was just some innocent flirting that didn't mean a thing, and had happened before she really knew him.

"Anti-party," Jake agreed, his eyes locked with hers.

Ava broke eye contact and pretended to be busy checking for movement at their departure gate. And okay, so maybe she and Jake had almost kissed during the soiree. But almost didn't count, right?

She should have done what every self-respecting single woman did on Valentine's Day: splurged on a good bottle of wine and shared it with the video version of George Clooney. But no, she'd had to listen to Jilly and go out to prove that she didn't need a boyfriend to have a good time on a Hallmark holiday.

Unaware of her inner turmoil, Brandon was still harping on about going out tonight. "So then come to this party. I promise it will be cooler than your anti-thing."

She shrugged, knowing there was no way on earth she'd be dragging herself to anything that even remotely resembled the anti–Valentine's Day near disaster. Not when Jake was in the vicinity. "I'll think about it."

He looked at Jake. "What about you?"

"If Ava goes, I'll consider it."

Oh, yeah, as if that was going to convince her.

They were both looking at her now. Ava shifted in the chair and wished she'd just stayed in her old seat.

"It might be fun," Jake said.

She doubted that. "I said I'll think about it." Then she tossed her hair, pulled out her magazine and did her best to ignore the sudden pounding of her heart. She was not going to be affected by Jake during this trip.

She hoped.

Chapter 4

The flight to Rockdale, Idaho, was a short one. Thank God, because somehow Ava ended up sitting next to Jake. Fortunately, with her iPod cranked she was able to avoid conversation. But even with the Black Eyed Peas pumping, she couldn't ignore the fact that Jake was right beside her and taking up way more than his fair share of armrest space.

She flipped the page of her magazine and ignored the voice in her head that sounded exactly like her mother, telling her that this was a perfect opportunity to start building a productive relationship. All she wanted to do was get to the hotel and splash some cold water on her face.

She started to feel better once she managed to snag a cab to herself. With all of Brandon's equipment plus luggage for three people, they couldn't all fit in a regular cab and no taxi vans were available. After a hurried discussion, Ava had convinced them to let her take the first cab alone so that Jake could help Brandon lug his cargo. The fact that it gave her some time without worrying about Jake Durham was just a bonus.

Though the official grand opening didn't kick off until tonight, the small town was already hopping. Ava spotted a famous starlet and equally famous little dog, both wearing matching pink coats, drinking coffee on Main Street. Down the block a trio of up-and-coming actors were punching each other on the shoulders and laughing. Everywhere she looked there were famous and semifamous faces.

Plenty of things to think about besides the fact that her executive producer still had the ability to make her shiver.

She unpacked quickly, pleased to discover that her dress for tonight had survived the flight unwrinkled, giving her extra time to decide on which shoes to wear with it. She'd brought three possible pairs. She'd just decided that the nude peep-toes were out—the heel was too high to stand in all night—when her BlackBerry began to sing. Jill Sobule's "Supermodel," best known for being featured in the movie *Clueless* and so Jilly, jangled through the room.

Checking in on my bestie. Have you arrived? Has George asked for your hand in marriage yet? Also, your mother called me.

Ava ignored the surge of irritation at her mother's interference and put the discarded shoe option in the closet.

Just got in. The room is superswank. Don't tell Harvey or he'll send Tommy next year. No George, but give me time. (Unless, of course, Rob Lowe is in town.) Ignore my mother. I do.

Your mom rocks. She's worried about you. (You have a weird fetish for '80s heartthrobs.)

My mother would lecture you for using "rock" to describe her. "I am not an inanimate object, Jillian." And I don't know why she'd be worried. I'm a grown woman. (Eighties heartthrobs? Please, Rob Lowe is still a heartthrob.)

Ava tried not to sigh and failed. Not about the '80s heartthrobs—they were still totally sigh-worthy—but why wouldn't her mother accept that she was fine?

She totally would. Bwahaha. She says she's worried about the cohost promotion. She thinks you're taking it harder than you let on. She wants me to find out if you're okay. Are you? (I will give you that Rob is still utterly doable. But what are your thoughts about Emilio Estevez?)

Ava put the two remaining shoe options side by side. One was a delicate silver sandal, the other a black platform pump. Both coordinated nicely with her dress, which was deep purple.

I'm fine. Or I will be as soon as I get through this festival. (Emilio? After he broke Paula Abdul's heart, I just can't look at him the same way again. Poor, sweet, loopy Paula. I'm forever her girl.)

You're better than fine, which George will surely see because he is beautiful and smart. Although, your hot one-night-stand romance doesn't have to be George. Any Hollywood hunk will do.

The silver sandal looked better. They left her feet practically bare and it was going to be icy tonight, but Ava couldn't resist their glitter against the dark hue of her gown.

Thanks for the update. I'll let the hunk brigade know that I'm available. Hair up or down tonight?

Down. Low ponytail with sleek sides. Easy and polished. Total hunk bait.

Ava didn't know about hunk bait, but she was pleased with the smooth look the hairstylist had achieved. The only problem was that it left her ears exposed and they were currently threatening to freeze and fall off her head to shatter on the cold sidewalk below. Her choice of sandals didn't help, either.

She wished she could put a hat on, but there were still a couple of hours before the start of the movie premiere and she and Brandon were milling around the red carpet waiting for the first arrivals. It was one thing to sport hat head on her own time. Another thing entirely to show it off to their show's entire viewing audience.

Jake had gone to pick up some hot coffee in the hopes it would combat the low temperature. The day, not warm to begin with, had gotten even colder as soon as the sun set, making it feel as if they were inside a freezer. Ava didn't know how people stood it. She'd take a rainy Vancouver winter any day.

"So what's the deal?" Brandon asked, clapping his gloved hands together as they waited on the red carpet. "Are you coming out with me tonight or not?"

"I don't think so." Her dress, though fabulous, was not made for long exposure in winter weather and was currently covered by a heavy wool coat, scarf and leather gloves. She wore yoga pants underneath the gown, but had little hope they would do much to keep her warm. When this was all over, she'd need a hot bath, not a cool party.

"I knew it. You always bail."

"I don't always bail," she said. "I went out with you in Italy." She and Brandon had covered the Venice Film Festival last September and spent one memorable night on a patio drinking enough wine to float themselves back to the hotel. Except she had gone back to the hotel alone. Brandon had gone back to the contessa's villa.

"One time in how many festivals? Three? Four? And how many parties?" He started to count and then shook his head. "It doesn't matter. The point is, I've invited you a lot. And you've only come out once. You're due."

"I'm sure you'll have a good time without me." She patted him on the shoulder.

"I will, but I would have more fun if you came along." His smile made his eyes twinkle, tempting her. "You were a great wingman in Italy."

Ava laughed, remembering that she'd been the one to talk to the contessa first. The woman had been wearing a pair of heels too gorgeous to ignore. "I think you can handle it on your own." Plus, she didn't feel like getting ditched. "Besides, I've got an exciting night planned. Room service and going to bed."

"Seriously?" Brandon rolled his eyes at her obvious lameness. "At least go out for dinner."

"I might," Ava said. She often did at the festivals. She was usually buzzing after filming and it took a while to come down. "I'll decide later."

"You sound exactly like Jake." Brandon ducked to look at his camera and missed the jolt that rolled through her. Good thing, too. She didn't know how she'd explain it. "He gave me the brush-off earlier, said it wasn't really his scene." He fiddled with the lens. "You guys should go somewhere together. You'd probably get a free meal out of it."

There weren't enough words in the world for Ava to explain how that was so not worth it, so she shrugged instead. "I can pay for myself."

That's what she had a per diem for. And unlike Brandon she didn't look for ways to save the money to spend on other things. One of the benefits of being over thirty and financially stable.

"But wouldn't it be more fun to go out for dinner with someone?"

When that person was Jake, Ava was certain that eating alone was highly preferable.

She was saved from having to answer by the flash of a camera. Grateful for the distraction, Ava peered down the line, saw the swish of a long train, the glint of expensive stones, the flutter of feathers. She peeled off her coat and scarf. "We've got something," she said. Something that should keep them busy for the next hour or more and would hopefully make Brandon forget all about his idea that Jake and Ava should go out together.

"On it." Brandon already had the camera on his shoulder and was scanning the crowd for whatever had caused the commotion.

Energy zipped through Ava and warmed her skin. And not just because she felt as though she'd dodged a bullet. This was it. Showtime. She dropped her gloves onto the pile of winter clothing at her feet and saw Jake coming toward her, a tray of coffee in hand. Oh, what she wouldn't give for a quick hit. But then she'd have coffee breath and there was no time to chew gum. "It's starting," she told him, clutching her mic instead.

She felt him watching her as she positioned herself for Brandon's shot, and lifted a cold hand to smooth her hair. He kept watching. Why? "Everything okay?" she asked.

"Fine." He tilted his head, studying her as if she was an exotic flower he'd stumbled upon in the forest. "You look good."

"Thanks." She managed to smile calmly, as though she was used to getting compliments from men all the time, even as she felt herself flush hotter. Then she turned away, slowly, to make sure he got a good view of the way the dress hugged her curves, and focused on doing her job.

By the time the last celebrity had spoken, the last publicist had walked into the theater and the crews had started to pack up, Ava was physically beat. Her feet hurt, her back ached and her cheeks and ears were frozen, but mentally, she felt as if she'd been mainlining caffeine.

She begged off Brandon's party and told him that she

was going to call it a night. But she was too hyped to enjoy a tub and her bed, so after changing into her jeans, a sweater and her favorite heeled boots, she slipped out of the hotel.

It wasn't sneaking out, she told herself as she tucked her chin into her scarf and flipped up the collar of her coat. She just wasn't up for company. She needed a little time to decompress.

She ended up at an Italian restaurant about five blocks away, where she whiled away a good ninety minutes drinking sparkling water and eating a to-die-for mushroom linguine. She was feeling no pain when she left the comfort of the family-run restaurant and headed back to her hotel.

The night was bright. Stars shone more brilliantly out here than in Vancouver, where they had to compete with city lights, and the moon was almost full, spilling out a cool wash of blue. But it was icy cold. The air was sharp when she breathed, and her exposed skin tingled. She tucked her hands into her coat pockets and picked up her pace.

Main Street, which had been bustling on her way to the restaurant, was empty now, the partiers indoors under the protection of the clubs and lounges where the music would be pumping and the martinis plentiful. Brandon was probably having a blast, but Ava was glad she'd skipped it. Now that her on-air adrenaline had run down, all she wanted was a soft pillow and a thick blanket.

She turned down the side street that she thought led to the hotel. She hadn't paid attention to the street names on her walk here, but Rockdale was small, and

Ava knew she was going in the right direction. If she'd chosen wrong, it wouldn't take long to rectify her error.

It was a nice town, all the shops with their ginger-bread molding and roofs dusted with snow, like the North Pole come to life. Not that she'd want to live here—too cold for her coastal blood—but it was a nice break from the norm. She'd just finished looking at a cheerful window display of local art, wondering if she might take a piece back home with her, when she stepped on a stretch of black ice.

She yelped as her heel started to skid, and flung out her hands in a weak attempt to steady herself, but it was too late. She took the brunt of the fall on her left wrist, an awful crunch echoing through the night. Immediately, a wave of pain so intense that she thought she might go blind swamped her. "Oh, my God," she moaned. But there was no one around to hear her.

She managed to roll herself into a sitting position, blinking away the black edges of her vision and praying she wouldn't pass out and end up here all night. She could freeze to death. Tunnel vision averted, she swallowed and forced herself to look at her wrist. Bile rose in the back of her throat. Even with only the limited moonlight, she could see its unnatural angle.

She needed medical attention. But when she tried to stand, her knees buckled and her vision blackened around the edges again, so she sank back onto the icy sidewalk, thinking that staying still for just a moment was probably a good idea.

Maybe for a couple of moments.

Wind whistled down the street. She could hear the thumping beats of nearby clubs and an occasional drunken hoot, so it wasn't as if she was in Siberia, even though the cold seeping into her butt felt like it. But she didn't see anyone.

As the shock started to wear off, the pain expanded, throbbing through her entire body. Everything hurt. Her side, her back, her wrist worst of all.

She tried to stand again, but the wooziness returned and she was afraid she might faint. A few long breaths later, she felt strong enough to dig out her BlackBerry, though even that little movement made her wrist feel as if it was going to explode, and punched in 911.

It rang four times before a recorded voice informed her that all lines were currently busy and asked her to wait for the next available operator. She hung up and called Brandon, hoping that his vodka party hadn't started yet, but she only got his voice mail.

She left a message asking him to call her back immediately. It was a slim hope. Chances were he was already at the party and who knew when he'd listen to the message. Particularly if there were any Italian noblewomen in town.

Ava checked her wrist, noting that at least it didn't have that weird angle anymore. Of course, that was because it was so swollen there were no angles.

She dialed 911 again. Got the same recorded message. Hung up again.

Now what? She couldn't just sit here. Obviously, emergency personnel were overburdened by the flood of visitors to the area and unable to attend to her call, Brandon might never get her message, and she couldn't make it back to the hotel without help.

Her stomach soured. There was only one option left. And she was just desperate enough to take it.

She called Jake.

Chapter 5

It took Jake less than a minute to shove aside his room-service meal and get down to the hotel lobby. Food and whatever game he could find on TV were no longer his primary concerns.

What the hell was Ava doing out wandering the streets alone? What had happened?

In what felt like the first turn of good luck he'd had in the past week, a string of cabs were sitting out front of the hotel, no doubt waiting for the fashionably late to decide that it was time to hit the first party of the evening. He hopped in the one at the head of the line and said, "I need to drive around the area."

"Got a location?" the cabbie asked, looking at him in the rearview mirror as he started the engine.

If only. Ava hadn't known exactly where she was. On a side street a few blocks from the hotel, she thought.

But she wasn't certain which direction. "Nearby," Jake answered.

The cabbie frowned, clearly not thrilled by the lack of details. Jake didn't blame him. He wasn't too thrilled, either.

They pulled away from the curb, the click of the indicator filling the car. "You know," the cabbie said conversationally as he took a left out of the hotel parking lot, "there are clubs for this kind of thing."

Kind of thing? It took Jake a second to twig. "No, I'm looking for a friend."

"Clubs for that, too," the cabbie continued. "I know they do things differently in L.A. than here, and I'm not one to judge, but it might be safer to meet her or him indoors. You Californians don't really understand how cold it gets here. Do you know last year I picked up a couple of girls wearing only skirts and bikini tops?"

"My friend slipped on some ice and fell," Jake told him before the man could get into his lecture on frostbite and how getting it on your privates wasn't a good time for anyone. "We're picking her up and taking her to the hospital."

At least Jake assumed that was the plan. Ava hadn't said how badly she was hurt, but since she'd called for help, he figured it was a safe bet that she'd need a medical evaluation.

"The hospital?" A line appeared between the cabbie's eyebrows. "This isn't an ambulance."

"I'll pay extra."

The line disappeared. "Just so long as she's not bleeding."

"She's not," he said, though he had no idea if that was the case. He hadn't thought to ask.

They drove down a couple of empty streets with no sign of anyone before they turned a corner and hit pay dirt. "There." Jake pointed as the vehicle's headlights lit up Ava's face. It was tight and drawn and her skin looked pasty even in the minimal light. Christ. She looked like hell.

Fear that had nothing to do with finding a replacement for the festival rolled through him. He shoved it back. Right now, she needed his help. He could worry about everything else later.

He was out of the cab before it stopped rolling, eyes searching for signs of injury. There was no blood, but she was cradling her left arm against her chest. And when she tried to smile at him, it was more like a grimace.

"Jake. You came."

Of course he'd come. Did she think he'd leave her hurt on the street in a strange town? He didn't say any of that, though. She was probably shocky and not aware of what she was saying. He crouched down beside her, eyes on her arm. "What happened?"

"It's my wrist."

As he bent closer, a gust of wind whipped past them. Though Jake barely noticed the biting chill, he saw Ava shiver and then turn an ugly shade of green as pain washed over her face.

She pulled up the sleeve of her coat enough for him to see that the joint was already swollen and a blossom of dark bruises was rising on her pale skin. Where it wasn't discolored, the skin appeared tight and sore. In his nonmedical opinion, things did not look good. "Anywhere else?" he asked, keeping his voice neutral.

Ava shook her head. "I don't think so. But it feels like I'm going to faint when I try to get up on my own."

"I'll help you stand," he said. He wanted to carry her over to the cab, but was afraid she might fight him and end up with a more serious injury. It looked bad enough as it was.

He was careful not to touch her arm, but she brushed against him accidentally as she tried to get her feet beneath her. The small touch made her gasp and then exhale sharply through her teeth.

She was clearly hurting. And he was clearly a sick and twisted man because damned if that touch didn't send a jolt of awareness through him. He ignored it and helped her find her balance so that she wouldn't have another date with the concrete. "I think we should go to the hospital."

She nodded and allowed him to lead her toward the cab. Her shoes clicked across the sidewalk as they moved. High-heeled boots that stopped at her knees and clung to the curve of her calf. Black. Leather. Sexy.

"Shouldn't be wearing those boots," he said. Not that he had anything personal against the boots. In fact, he liked the boots a lot.

She glared at him. "There is nothing wrong with my boots. These boots are—" She sucked in a breath when they stepped off the curb.

"You can take that up with the doctor," Jake said and helped her into the cab. She continued to glare at him, but kept her lips clamped shut. He prayed the backseat didn't turn into a splash zone, as he was pretty sure Mr. No Blood in the Cab also had a no-puking policy.

"You okay, lady?" the cabbie asked as Jake closed the door behind them.

"Fine," she said.

"Not fine," Jake corrected, looking at her swollen wrist again. "Where's the nearest hospital?"

The cabbie glanced in his rearview mirror. "She's not bleeding, is she?"

"No blood," Jake said, pulling some money out of his pocket and waving it to convince the cabbie that this wasn't the time for a discussion. "Nearest hospital."

He didn't know whether it was the money or the worry that any delay might turn his cab into a biohazard, but the cabbie shoved the car into gear and sped off as if he was in the Indy 500. No one said a word during the five-minute ride.

A sense of relief began to creep in when he spotted the blinding-white lights of Emergency. They were here. Everything was going to be fine.

He came around to open the door for her, but she only got as far as swinging her legs out of the cab before she stopped, face contorted again.

"You going to make it?" Jake asked, sliding a hand around her back to help her up.

"Just give me a second and I'll be okay." But her gritted teeth and pale complexion said otherwise.

The cabbie stuck his head over the seat. "You sure she's not bleeding back there? Because I have to charge you for that. Costs a lot to get the upholstery professionally cleaned and I can't pick up any other fares if it's not clean."

"She's not bleeding," Jake said, though if the guy didn't quit asking, he might end up with a bloody nose.

Ava still hadn't moved. Jake reached an arm around her, feeling how delicate she was. She closed her eyes and exhaled slowly. "Just give me another second."

He recognized that look on her face. It was one he'd seen at many college beer bashes and generally preceded a lot of hair holding. "Brace your arm against your chest so it doesn't move," he told her, and slid his other arm under her knees. "I'm going to lift you."

He figured it was a testament to how bad she was feeling that she only put up token resistance before resting her head against his shoulder and letting him haul her out. She sucked in a few deep breaths. "I just need some air."

The tires of the cab squealed off, the driver obviously grateful to get away with a backseat that didn't require a bottle of disinfectant, as Jake turned to the front of the building. Ava was still green, so he stopped short of the sliding doors, letting her suck in a few more breaths.

"Better?"

She nodded. "You can put me down now."

"No." He stepped through the doors and into the waiting room. There were about a dozen chairs, only a couple of them filled, and those people didn't look too badly off. Probably friends and family members waiting for loved ones. He got Ava settled and then strode over to the large white desk and the nurse on duty.

It took less than five minutes before another nurse, a woman whose tidy gray curls and tightly laced runners indicated that she didn't put up with any nonsense, arrived pushing a wheelchair. She informed Ava that they weren't going anywhere until she sat in it, and if Ava refused she wouldn't be permitted to see the doctor. Jake hid his smile when he saw the fire light up in Ava's eyes.

"This is ridiculous. I'm perfectly capable of walking to the exam room." The sitting had done her some good.

Besides the fact that she was obviously well enough to argue, the sickly cast to her skin had receded.

The nurse shook her head and pointed at the wheelchair. "No chair, no exam. Standard procedure."

"But—"

The nurse pointed at the chair.

"Fine," Ava grumbled. "But for the record, this is a waste of time and resources." She let Jake help her up and into the wheelchair.

"How long will this take?" Jake asked the nurse. Now that he was sure Ava was in good hands, his stomach was reminding him that he'd never gotten a chance to eat. Didn't most hospitals have a twenty-four-hour cafeteria?

"As soon as a doctor is available."

He looked at Ava. "I'll check back in twenty minutes, okay?"

"You're not coming with me?" Ava stared back at him, wide-eyed.

Oh, hell. He was a sucker for those big blue eyes. Especially when she was looking at him as if he was her lifeline instead of as if she wanted to kill him. "I…" He looked from Ava to the nurse. "Is that allowed?"

The nurse shrugged. "If she wants you there, the doctor won't have a problem with it."

He felt Ava's good hand clamp over his as she turned to face the nurse. "I'd like him to come along."

Jake guessed that meant he was coming along.

They passed through a set of swinging doors and into the treatment area. The bitter scent of medicine filled his nose. A row of beds lined one wall. Some of the curtains were pulled closed, the shadow of bodies visible through the thin material, while others sat open. But the nurse led them beyond the beds to a door marked Exam Room A. The nurse wheeled Ava inside and handed Jake a flat-bottomed pan. "In case she feels sick."

"I'm not going to be sick," Ava said.

The nurse merely nodded, probably having seen this same situation a hundred times already this week, and reached for the door. "The doctor will be with you shortly." Then she closed the door behind her.

Jake looked at the pan and then at Ava. "You sure you don't need this?"

"No." Her jaw was clenched again.

He put the pan on a table near her good arm and took a step back. Just in case she didn't have a strong hold on her gag reflex.

She exhaled slowly and more of her color seemed to return, loosening the knot of concern in his stomach. "Thanks for coming to get me."

"No problem." Jake glanced around the small room. Though tiny, the space was packed. Along one wall was a short counter with a sink and a stack of cupboards above it, no doubt stuffed with gauze and gloves and whatever else the medical staff might need. The examination table filled another wall, and a stool with rolling wheels sat in a corner. Really, with the addition of the wheelchair, there was barely enough room for Ava in here, let alone him.

She had lowered her wrist to her lap. Under the indoor lights, Jake had a better view of her injury. It looked worse than he'd thought.

"How are you feeling?"

"Like Godzilla just stomped my arm." She glanced at it and he recognized the worry in the lines edging her mouth. "Do you think it's broken?"

"Possibly." He was positive that it was. It looked worse than the time Dave Newton had jumped off the swings during recess and shattered his elbow. Dave had sported a full arm cast for weeks and hadn't been able to participate in gym for the rest of the year. But telling her that would only scare her.

"It's my karma." She sighed. "I was clearly a horrible criminal in another life to deserve this."

Despite the death glares he knew she was capable of, at the moment she didn't look capable of taking on a bunny. "Oh, yeah. You were Jack the Ripper."

"What would you know?" She frowned at him.

"All right. Have it your way. You're a former serial killer."

"I didn't say I was a serial killer, you did." Now she looked offended.

Jake tried not to laugh.

"This isn't funny," she told him.

"No, it isn't." He schooled his mouth into a sober expression.

"Stupid ice."

"You should sue it," Jake said. "Though I think a jury might have a hard time sympathizing when they get a look at your footwear."

She looked down, too. "Do you have a problem with my boots?"

Not unless he considered the fact that he'd always had a thing for a woman in sexy boots a problem. But what guy didn't? Surely she'd known that when she bought them. "I should go see where the doctor is," he said, but she talked over him, so he didn't think she heard.

"Because these boots are amazing. Cate Blanchett

once asked me where I got them. Okay, I can tell by your expression you have no idea what a big deal that is."

"I know she's an Oscar-winning actress—"

"Who has incredible style. And she wanted these boots." She raised her eyebrows at him as if that was supposed to mean something.

"So you and Cate agree on boots."

"We do."

"Right." He glanced at the still-closed door. The nurse had said the doctor would be with them shortly. Did that mean ten minutes? Fifteen? Sixty? "I should go and see where the doctor is," he repeated, thinking that the sooner they knew exactly what they were dealing with, the sooner he could figure out his next step.

"Figures. You get bested by me and you run away."

Jake stopped reaching for the doorknob. "I'm not running away." He didn't run away, the move to Vancouver excluded. But that had been more looking for a fresh start, which just wasn't possible in Toronto. And she hadn't bested him.

"That's not what it looks like to me."

Jake frowned. Deciding he didn't like the direction his life was taking and doing something about it was not running away. No matter what it might look like to someone on the outside. But he didn't feel like arguing about it, so he changed the subject. "Afraid to be alone?"

"Of course not. I was just thinking about what would happen if the doctor came and you weren't here."

Though she was doing her best to put on a tough-girl sneer, Jake noticed the fingers of her good hand were clutching the arm of the wheelchair. "You're going to be fine," he told her. "You don't need me here to explain what happened. I wasn't even there."

She didn't look wowed by his logic and her fingers didn't loosen their death grip. "But you spoke to the nurse. Really, we should stick together until the doctor has seen me."

"There's nothing to be nervous about." Jake tried to make his tone calm and soothing.

"I'm not nervous."

"No?"

"No. There's nothing to be nervous about." She parroted his words back to him, but she was still white-knuckling the wheelchair. "And no reason to be afraid of hospitals. My mother works in one."

He didn't know who she was trying to convince, but it wasn't working. "So then you don't care if I stay?"

She blinked and did her best to seem nonchalant. "Do what you want." But he could see her peeking at him from beneath her lashes and there was still that matter of the death grip.

She wanted him to stay. No, she needed him. The thought was oddly pleasing. He couldn't remember the last time someone had relied on him. Not his job title, not his name, not what he could do for them. Just him.

He pulled up the rolling stool and lowered himself onto it. "I'll stay."

The pinched lines around her mouth disappeared and her fingers loosened. "Okay."

During the next round of not talking, Jake discovered that the room was home to three boxes of tissue, one box of latex gloves, a hoard of shiny, pointed instruments and one copy of *Time* from March 2004. Very cutting-edge.

"Jake? Have you ever broken anything?"

He turned toward her, happy to have something to

discuss besides the tension in the room. He and Ava had been at odds but pretending not to be all day. It was weird to feel that sliding away, and he wasn't sure where they were headed next. "Fell off the roof when I was ten and broke my arm. Wrecked my knee playing beach soccer in university, but that was ligament damage."

"I've never broken anything." Ava chewed on her lip. "Do you think I'll need X-rays?"

He glanced at her swollen wrist. "Yes." He saw the fingers on her good hand flinch. Time to change the subject. "So what does your mom do at the hospital?"

"She's an administrator." Ava blew hair out of her eyes. Jake watched the blond strands drift down to frame her heart-shaped face. Seriously, evil glares aside, she was like apple pie and vanilla ice cream in human form. "She wanted me to be a surgeon."

"And?" He pulled his thoughts away from how much he liked the traditional American dessert.

"Ew." She wrinkled her nose. "Blood and guts? No, thanks."

He leaned back against the wall again and braced his feet against the floor to prevent the stool from skidding away. "I thought you said you weren't afraid of hospitals."

"I'm not. I'm afraid of the blood and guts in them."

Jake laughed and was pleased when a small smile drifted across her lips, too. "Makes sense."

"Try explaining that to my mother." She chewed on her lips again. "Do you think I'm going to need surgery?"

He studied her for a second, wondering what she wanted him to say. "You looking for truth or reassurance?"

"I guess that answers that," she said. Her eyes flicked to her wrist, which Jake thought was very likely to find itself under a surgeon's knife. "I've never had surgery before. Have you?"

He nodded, feeling this was safer ground. She might not be freezing him out anymore, but he wasn't really sure how to treat her. Were they coworkers? Acquaintances? Congenial only under penalty of death or a broken bone? "I had surgery on my knee." He tapped the offending area. "It wasn't so bad. The drugs were good."

"Great. So I'll be too doped up to think about the blood and guts."

"Exactly." He smiled and when she smiled back, Jake felt a surge of desire that wasn't congenial in the least.

Chapter 6

Oh, God. Why was she so wishy-washy? Wasn't it only days, no, hours earlier that Ava had been convinced that Jake was the devil incarnate? Or, at least, trouble in blue jeans?

He'd given her job to Tommy, who couldn't host his way out of a paper bag. Who was barely into his mid-twenties. And now, after one kind gesture, she was ready to forgive him?

Brandon was right. She was lame. The minute a man came to her rescue, he was suddenly her white knight.

She tried to work up some righteous anger, maybe figure out a few biting comebacks so they'd be on hand when she needed them. She got nothing.

Ava sniffed. Apparently, she'd left them back on that icy sidewalk along with her dignity.

Jake sat across from her in the private room she'd been checked into post–X-ray. She would have liked to go back to the hotel for the night, but the doctor and nurse had insisted she remain on-site until after her surgery, which was scheduled first thing tomorrow morning. She guessed they were afraid she would oversleep and miss it. As if she was likely to sleep a wink. Her stomach rolled every time she thought about the surgery.

Realistically, she knew there was little to be nervous about. She wasn't even going under general anesthetic, but the idea that a surgeon was going to cut open her skin, exposing the bones and muscle underneath, made her feel sick. So she decided to focus on something else. Like why Jake was still hanging around her private room instead of going back to the comfort of the hotel.

"Seriously, you don't have to stay," she told him for what felt like the bazillionth time. She tried to forget how she'd practically begged him to stay with her earlier. That had been the fear talking, and the astringent smell of the exam room. She was better now. "I'll be okay on my own."

"I don't mind." He smiled at her and went back to typing on his laptop.

That smile. Ava felt heat flash through her system and blamed it on the hospital's furnace. Why was it so hot in here anyway? Did they think she had hypothermia as well as a busted wrist?

"But you have work to do. Obviously." She pointed to the computer on his lap. "And so do I." She had her laptop sitting beside her on the bed, still powered down, but it was only a matter of time.

"I can work here."

That so wasn't the point. The point was that she wasn't sure how to feel about him, and having him in the same room while she tried to figure it out was just impossible.

She watched as he bent his head and returned to his work. When she'd asked if he minded getting her some things from the hotel, she'd expected him to drop off a bag and then beat it out of here. Instead, he'd brought his own laptop along with hers, and parked himself in the large chair that sat in the corner of the room. A chair that could, according to the nurse, be turned into a bed for an overnight stay.

But that wasn't an issue, right? Surely he wasn't going to stay all night?

"I appreciate your concern, but I'm okay. You'll be more comfortable at the hotel. You should go."

"Ava, it's fine." He tilted down the screen of his computer. "It's natural to be nervous before surgery."

"I'm not nervous." A total lie. But she was pretty sure that she'd feel a lot calmer on her own. Not that his presence was the only thing sending her into fits, but it wasn't exactly putting her at ease, either. "I just think you'd be better off back at the hotel."

And not watching her every move with those solemn gray eyes.

He turned them on her now, coupling them with a smile that made her knees quiver. Good thing she was sitting down. "Are you trying to get rid of me?"

"Of course not."

"Then why do you keep going on about it?"

She blinked. "I'm not. I'm just saying that the hotel is a lot nicer than the hospital." She pinned him with a look. "Or are you one of those weirdos who gets off on sick people? What's that called? Baron Munchausen syndrome?"

"I thought that was a movie?"

She rolled her eyes at his pleased-with-himself snicker, but couldn't help the surge of excitement that maybe she'd met another lover of all '80s culture. She refrained from asking, not sure if she wanted to have anything in common with Jake. She had good reason to love the cheesiness of the decade. Those movies with their happy endings and girls who overcame obstacles of unpopularity and bad hair had kept her company during the long hours her mother spent first finishing her degree and then working her way up the ladder at the hospital. But Jake might just be weird. That or he'd think *she* was weird for asking.

"Fine," she told him, busying herself by dragging her laptop over and turning it on. "Stay." If he wanted to hang around all night and wake up with a sore neck and an aching back, it wasn't her problem. And she wasn't giving him any sympathy.

After checking her email and finding nothing that required her immediate attention, she sent a note to Brandon, letting him know that she was fine and to ignore her voice mail. Then she wrote a quick update for her blog. Since she was having surgery in the morning, and would likely be out of commission until the afternoon, she needed to let her readers know that gossip from the festival was coming, it was just going to be slightly delayed.

She should probably call her mother, too. Ava glanced at the clock in the corner of the computer screen. It was only a little past ten, but Barbara would already be in bed. She liked to read for an hour, watch the eleven o'clock news and then go directly to sleep. Ava never called her after ten unless it was an emergency.

She debated with herself and decided this wasn't an emergency. Not really. She was in the hospital and scheduled for surgery. What could her mom do from Vancouver anyway?

Well, besides demand to know the surgeon's name, education, residence program and success rate. And that was before Barbara got into the rehabilitation aspect. Which physiotherapist Ava should see and how much work it was going to be to ensure that there weren't any lasting effects.

Ava sighed. After everything that had already happened today, it would be too exhausting to deal with. And the doctor had told her to try to take it easy and get as much rest as possible. So really, she was just following doctor's orders.

"You okay?"

She blinked and looked up to find Jake watching her again. "You mean, aside from the broken wrist?" Her cheeks felt warm under his gaze. Stupid furnace.

"I can call the nurse."

"No, I'm fine. It's just my mother."

He lowered the laptop screen and focused on her. "Threatening to fly down and feed you her homemade chicken noodle soup?" The edges of his mouth curled up.

Ava found herself smiling back and not just because the idea of Barbara Christensen slaving over a stove when she could buy a perfectly good chicken noodle soup from a restaurant was hilarious. "You have obviously never met my mother. She's more the hands-off type."

Discomfort flashed across his face.

"Oh, no." Ava was quick to correct his misconception. "She's very loving. She's just not the do-it-yourself type." Barbara ordered food in, sent laundry out and had a weekly maid to handle the household chores. "She doesn't cook, but she'll probably have my physio scheduled and therapist booked before we even get back."

"I guess she's got some connections."

"A few." Which got Ava thinking—no, make that panicking—about tomorrow again. How was she going to sleep at all?

"Hey…" His voice curled around her even from across the room. "It's going to be fine. You're going to be fine."

"Easy for you to say." He wasn't the one who was going to be wheeled into the O.R. at some ungodly hour of the morning. And though she might try to fool herself into thinking otherwise, Ava knew that the surgery wouldn't be pain free, nor would there be puppies and rainbows. "I don't like pain," she told him.

She'd been the kid who used to scream when the neighborhood bullies cut earthworms in half. Funny that her mother had ever thought she might have a shot at making it in the medical field.

But she didn't want to talk about that or anything health related. "What about your mom? Is she the homemade-chicken-noodle-soup type?"

Jake nodded. Ava wondered if he knew his eyes softened when he thought about his mom. It was sweet. "Definitely. She has a huge vegetable garden. When I was growing up, she tried to stick zucchini in everything." He frowned at the memory. "I still don't like zucchini."

Some of the nerves tightening her chest eased. "More a beer-and-pizza guy?"

"Is there any comparison?"

"Wine and cheese."

He shook his head. "Only if you're trying to impress someone."

She raised an eyebrow at him. "So you're telling me you're against wine and cheese? I don't think we can be friends, then."

"I'm not against them. You need cheese for the pizza."

She smiled, felt the temperature in the room ratchet up when he smiled back. Seriously, were the hospital staff cannibals in disguise and trying to roast her like chicken? She took a sip from the water glass on her bedside table. "I know I said it earlier, but thanks for being so great about all this. I realize it's a hassle."

"It's not a hassle. Accidents happen."

He was watching her with that little half smile that should probably be outlawed. "Well, I wasn't very gracious about the whole promotion thing." That might go down as the understatement of the century. She barreled on, not wanting to delve into her rude behavior. "I wouldn't have blamed you if you'd decided not to pick up my call tonight."

"I wouldn't have done that."

"Well..." She trailed off. She should probably look somewhere else. Check out the hem of the hospital blanket or study her nail beds, but she couldn't pull her eyes from his.

"Are we okay?" he asked.

If the fantasies running through her head were any indication, they were more than okay, but Ava only shrugged. "I think so."

He smiled. "Good."

She swallowed. This would be the point where her mother would mention something about her future at the station. What she could do to ensure she was next in line for a promotion. If he had any suggestions for how she could improve. But Ava wasn't her mother and she didn't feel like upsetting this friendly balance they'd found, so she smiled back and said, "I should try to do some work."

"Me, too."

But it was a few more seconds before Ava looked away. And even once she did, she could still feel Jake watching her. She picked up her BlackBerry and started typing.

It might be too late to call her mother, but Jilly probably wouldn't even leave her apartment until midnight. It worked for Jilly, but the past few years Ava had found herself choosing a quiet night in over a night on the town most weekends.

I'm broken, Jillsy. Literally broken. As in I slipped on some black ice and broke my wrist. Not the festival start I was looking for.

Oh, my God. Are you okay? Do you have to leave the festival? Are you sure it's not just a bad sprain?

Ava wished it were only a bad sprain.

Like Shakira's hips, X-rays don't lie. I have to go in for surgery tomorrow. Minor, according to the doctor, which just means that they aren't knocking me out. Ugh.

I almost think I'd rather sleep through the whole thing. Jake had to come and rescue me. Can you believe it?

Ooooh…Jake rescued you? Details, please.

Ava reminded herself that there was nothing going on with Jake and no reason for anyone to act like an excitable teenager. Especially her.

Whatever you're thinking, it wasn't like that. He got me to the hospital and is staying with me to make sure I'm okay. That's all.

Has he been upgraded back to McHot Stuff?

Ava fanned her face and hoped Jake wouldn't notice.

I don't know why you started calling him that anyway.

Uh…because you so clearly have the hots for him.

She fanned a little faster.

No, I don't. But I may have to rethink the whole evil thing. He's been really great. He even stuck around because he knew I was nervous.

He hung around in the waiting room for you? Awww. That is so sweet. I definitely think he needs to be upgraded.

Ava snuck a peek at the man in question, but he was simply typing away on his laptop, unaware of the conversation he was currently featuring in.

No upgrading! He's probably just hanging around to make sure I don't bolt presurgery. I have a private room.

Wait...what? He's there with you now? Oh, yeah. You are so into him again. *bamp-chicka-bamp-bam*

Ava dragged her eyes away from Jake before he sensed her staring and caught her in the act.

Uh, hello? This is not a porno and I don't like him that way. I just think I might have been wrong about him. (I know, I know. Pigs are flying.) I'm willing to admit that maybe I judged him a bit harshly. He's a good guy.

You want to marry him and have his babies.

She rolled her eyes.

What are you, twelve? Can't I just say that he's a nice guy?

No. Admit your love for him.

Not for the most beautiful shoes on the planet.

You're a nut.

A nut who knows the truth. You want him to be your lov-ah.

Some days, there was just no stopping Jilly.

No, I don't. Gah. I just think...oh, I don't know.

"I just think...oh, I don't know." He is totally upgraded. You're crushing on him! McHot Stuff rides again!

Ava tried to muffle her snicker. She stole another peek at Jake and wondered what he would think about Jilly's nickname for him.

Am not crushing.

It'll be much easier if you'd just admit it. Hey, maybe your hot festival love affair can be with him!

Ava heard the rustle of clothing as Jake shifted and knew the exact moment his eyes fell on her.

I admit nothing, and quit making me laugh. I think he's on to me. He's watching me now.

He's staring at you? Right this second? *mrawr*

She didn't dare check, but the tingle beneath her skin made her certain.

No mrawring. And yes.

There is so mrawring. More important, do you like it? (When he looks at you, not the mrawring.)

Ava wasn't sure if she liked it or not. The tingling was unsettling, but in a good way. Probably just a sign that she'd been out of the dating game for too long. Maybe she should start going out with Jilly on the weekend more often.

Of course not. I mean, I don't really care. He can stare at whoever or whatever he wants.

You can't even lie via email.

Busted.

Believe whatever you want. I'm not lying.

You know…your lying is only going to hurt you and your future lov-ah.

Ava thought she did a pretty good job of stifling her laugh, but the new email alert on her BlackBerry said otherwise. It was from Jake. She darted a glance over at him, but he appeared to have returned to typing away on his laptop.

To: Ava Christensen [[ava_christensen@entnewsnow. com>
From: Jake Durham [[jake_durham@entnewsnow.com>
Subject: What's happening over there?
Funny website?

To: Jake Durham [[jake_durham@entnewsnow.com>
From: Ava Christensen [[ava_christensen@entnewsnow. com>
Re: Nothing exciting
I think I might be giddy from the meds.

She scrolled back to her text conversation with Jilly.

Ack! He's on to me. He's emailing me now. I had to blame the medication.

I heart him. First he saves you, now he's writing you love letters? *swoon* He's the bestest boyfriend ever! P.S. That old "Oh, it's just the medication" line never works.

Ava almost choked trying to contain her laughter.

Seriously now. Quit making me laugh! (And he's not my boyfriend.)

Yes, he is.

Ava's chest was starting to hurt from trying to maintain her silence.

No, he isn't. Oh…just forget it. I know you and you'll just keep writing back that he is until you wear me down.

Too true. (You know me so well.) Don't you feel better for admitting it? Now, you have a good night and you can fill me in on the rest of your hot hospital romance tomorrow.

To: Ava Christensen [[ava_christensen@entnewsnow. com>
From: Jake Durham [[jake_durham@entnewsnow.com>
Re: Just wondering
Was that a snort?

To: Jake Durham [[jake_durham@entnewsnow.com>
From: Ava Christensen [[ava_christensen@entnewsnow.com>
Re: FYI
Ladies do not snort.

To: Ava Christensen [[ava_christensen@entnewsnow.com>
From: Jake Durham [[jake_durham@entnewsnow.com>
Re: You sure?
It sounded like a snort.

To: Jake Durham [[jake_durham@entnewsnow.com>
From: Ava Christensen [[ava_christensen@entnewsnow.com>
Re: Surer than sure
It was probably your chair.

To: Ava Christensen [[ava_christensen@entnewsnow.com>
From: Jake Durham [[jake_durham@entnewsnow.com>
Re: The chair is innocent
Nope. I just moved in it and nothing. I think it was a snort.

To: Jake Durham [[jake_durham@entnewsnow.com>
From: Ava Christensen [[ava_christensen@entnewsnow.com>
Re: It was not a snort
I should probably go to sleep. I have a big day tomorrow.

To: Ava Christensen [[ava_christensen@entnewsnow.com>
From: Jake Durham [[jake_durham@entnewsnow.com>
Re: For the record
You blush when you lie.

To: Jake Durham [[jake_durham@entnewsnow.com>
From: Ava Christensen [[ava_christensen@entnewsnow.com>
Re: It was still not a snort
Good night.

Chapter 7

Jake stepped out of the cab and hurried into the hospital. His neck hurt like hell, not that he was going to tell Ava. He could already picture her smug smile when she told him so. It made him grin even as he rubbed the offending area. In truth, he wasn't sure he could blame the chair. He often woke up with a stiff neck when he was stressed and he was definitely feeling pressure today.

He'd stuck around at the hospital long enough to see Ava safely wheeled into surgery, then hustled back to the hotel for a quick shower, a quicker breakfast and to make a few very important phone calls.

After reassuring Brandon that Ava was really okay and he didn't need to feel guilty about not answering his phone last night, Jake had sent the young cameraman off to cover a panel since it was something that didn't require Ava's presence. Brandon was fully capable of linking up his mics for sound and filming the whole thing on his own. Jake would view the footage with him later this afternoon to see if there was anything interesting they could turn into a piece. At worst, they'd get a sound bite or two. Maybe not enough to make a whole story, but something good for the cuts to and from commercials.

He'd also called the station and had his assistant email him a schedule for the other reporters to see who was available to fly out at a moment's notice. Although the doctor had said it was unlikely that Ava would need to miss any work, Jake wasn't taking chances. If the surgery was harder on her than expected, he needed someone in town by tomorrow morning. He'd had his assistant call to see if there were still seats available on tonight's flight. There were, but Jake really hoped he wouldn't need to use one.

The waiting room near discharge was empty. Jake found a seat in the corner and killed some time flipping through an old *Reader's Digest*. Ava was being discharged now. He wasn't meeting Brandon until one, but he had a lot to do before then. Including getting Ava settled in her hotel room with anything she might need for the rest of the day.

He stood when she was finally wheeled into the room, surprised by the little spark that flashed through him when she smiled in his general direction. Her arm was fully casted in black, but the color in her cheeks told him that she was feeling a lot better.

"You look good," he told her.

She rolled her eyes at him. "I'm not that drugged up," she said. "I only had a local anesthetic, so I'm well aware that my hair is a rat's nest."

It was pulled back into a tidy ponytail and didn't

seem ratty to him at all. She looked sporty and cute, but he kept that to himself. He wasn't entirely sure where they stood after yesterday, but it seemed prudent to let her set the tone. "Ready to go?" He glanced at the nurse, who nodded.

"More than ready," Ava said. Jake fell into step beside her, watching as she fidgeted in the chair as though wanting to leap out of it. The nurse pushed faster, probably used to difficult patients who attempted to thwart hospital procedure.

"How did everything go?" he asked, partially because he wanted her opinion on how she was feeling—the doctor had said that Ava would be the best judge of whether she was ready to return to work—and partly because he thought it would keep her from making a run for the exit. He didn't know if there was some sort of paperwork for a breakaway patient, but he didn't want to find out.

Distracting her seemed to work or, at least, settled her into the chair as they wheeled down the hallway. "It was gross." She shot him a look. "You didn't tell me that part."

He shrugged. "I didn't think it was gross."

"Yes, well, you probably think the greatness of a movie depends on how many helicopters are in it."

"That's just fact."

She snorted. "Clearly, you can't be trusted."

"Are you trying to tell me that *Die Hard* isn't a classic?"

She craned her neck to look at the nurse. "See what I have to deal with?"

The nurse nodded. "My husband makes me watch it every year at Christmas. His version of a holiday film."

"Don't give him any ideas," Ava said. Jake noticed that she seemed happy to give the nurse the impression they were a couple. He probably shouldn't like that so much. "Anyway, I was awake for the whole thing, so I could hear it and it was nothing like they show on TV. Well, maybe it was like what they show on those real-life operation shows, but I don't watch those. I can barely watch hospital dramas."

She sighed heavily, looking so adorable that Jake had to bite back his grin. He didn't think she'd appreciate it.

"What do you think of the cast?"

He eyed the dark weight covering her arm. "Very black."

She nodded. "It goes with my outfits."

"Then it's very stylish."

"You're learning." She sighed again. "But it's going to be a huge pain." She looked at the nurse again. "Can you recommend a good hair salon?"

Huh? Now Jake was confused. What did a hair salon have to do with her cast?

"I can't get it wet," she said in response to his questioning look. "Also, no picking at it or jamming hangers inside it."

"Is it itchy?"

"Not yet, but I'm prepared."

The nurse rattled off a few salon names as she pushed them toward the pneumatic doors where Jake had paid a taxi to wait for them. Ava shivered when the blast of cold air hit her, but tried to give back his coat when he slipped it around her shoulders.

He shook his head. "Easterner, remember? You need it more than me." Besides, he liked the way she looked all bundled up in it.

She looked as if she was debating arguing with him for a second, until another cold gust blew past them. She shivered again and tugged the coat more tightly to her with her lone good arm. "Thanks."

"Doing okay?" he asked once they were both safely in the cab and on their way back to the hotel.

"Not bad. Not great, but not bad."

"How not bad?" Jake needed to know. He'd managed to get DVDs of a couple of the movies being screened today. Since she was out of commission, she couldn't attend them personally, but he hoped that she'd be up to watching them later. Tomorrow was the interview circuit, where media and movies collided in a frenzy of questions and promotion. If she couldn't do it, he was going to have to watch them himself and spend the night prepping for the reporter he'd have to fly in.

The cab took a sharp turn, pressing her up against his side. She stayed there after the vehicle straightened out. "I'm okay. I don't feel one hundred percent, but I guess that's expected."

He liked the way her body felt against his, even with his coat in the way. "Well enough to do a bit of work?" He told her about the films he'd charmed out of the festival's media department. "I thought we could watch them together later."

"Oh?" She lifted her eyebrows at him, but didn't shift away. A definite improvement.

"I had to miss the screenings, too," he pointed out. "We'll order in some room service and hunker down." He kept plan B to himself.

"We could," she mused. "Or you could have the night off since you didn't get one last night and I could handle the movies alone."

Despite the ache in his neck, Jake didn't regret spending the night when she'd needed him. "I'd like to watch them, too." And while he could give her the movies to watch this afternoon, watching them alone this evening with nothing but food and drink for company didn't hold the same appeal. "So, my room or yours?"

She tilted her head to look at him. "You don't have to babysit me again. I feel bad enough about everything that's happened and how great you've been. Let me do this for you."

"Ava." Her name felt like a whisper in his mouth. "I'd like to watch the movies, too."

"Why? Don't think I can come up with some searing questions on my own? Because I can." She shook her head, setting her ponytail bobbing. "Also, how am I supposed to express my appreciation for last night if you insist on doing my job for me?"

He could think of a much better way. Might have even vocalized it six months ago. Before things had changed. Before he'd changed. Now he only smiled. "You just had surgery. I don't want you to push yourself."

"Sitting around and watching movies is hardly pushing myself."

It was his turn to shake his head. "What if you're wrong? I need to be able to step in and run the interviews."

"No." She held up her good hand. "That will not happen. It just can't." He could read the fear and assurance as they took turns sliding across her face. "I'm fine, totally fine. And I'm doing the circuit tomorrow. So I'll handle the viewings and you can have that relaxing evening you missed out on last night. I'll even order for you."

That she'd remembered touched him, and if tomorrow was simply about willpower, he'd agree that they had nothing to worry about. But the body didn't always respond to willpower. Not when there was surgery and actual physical damage involved. It could wake you up in the morning and knock you on your ass. "Let's table that discussion for now. We'll see how you're feeling later."

"Table the discussion?" She frowned at him. "You've spent way too much time in the boardroom. Table the discussion. Were you watching *Wall Street* last night?"

"I was with you last night." He felt a little thump in his chest when he said it. Rachel would probably tell him it was a sign that he needed to get back in the game. But he'd had a lot of years ignoring his little sister's advice and he saw no reason to change that now. "After Brandon and I are done editing today, I'll swing by your room with the movies. Probably around five."

That would be early enough to see if he needed to fly out another reporter. Jake wondered if maybe he should just fly someone out anyway.

"Hold on a minute." Ava's eyebrows came together. "What are you and Brandon editing?"

He told her about the morning's panel, which Brandon should still be at. "I'm hoping we'll get enough for a story. Shouldn't take more than a couple of hours in the editing suite."

She smirked. "When's the last time you wrote copy?"

Jake might have felt insulted if he hadn't seen the spark of professional pride in her expression. "A few years." Once he'd moved into a position that was more about managing and delegating, he'd stopped doing the detail work himself. He'd never been that great at it to begin with.

"And Brandon's bringing the footage by when?"

Jake glanced at his watch. "About an hour from now."

"There's no way you'll be done by five. Even if you two manage to view all the film at warp speed, you still have to put it into a story, write the voice-over and re-cord it." She frowned. "Speaking of, who's doing the voice-over?"

"Me."

"So you're going to do everything by five? No way. Not even if you were used to writing copy. I'll swing by. What time do you think you'll finish with the footage?"

"Ava. Come on." Even if she hadn't been right about his ability to write copy, he would have objected. "You need to take it easy today."

"I will be. Normally, I'd be in the suite for the viewing, too."

"I can handle it for today. I'd rather you rest so that you can work tomorrow."

"I can do both." She raised her chin, a little jut to it now. "The doctor said if I felt up to it, I'm allowed to take on some light duties. Since my entire job is light duties, I can be back in action in a few hours."

He debated his options. He could tell her that she wasn't welcome in the editing suite and insist that she stay in bed. Good luck with getting her to obey that order, though. He could try to convince her that she didn't want to come out today, but the quick refusal with which she'd already greeted that made him real-ize it would be futile to bring it up a second time. Or he could trust that she was an adult and knew her own limits. If she thought she could do it, he had to believe that she was right.

"Jake?" She sounded irritated now. "What time should I be there?"

He studied her. "You're sure I can't convince you to take it easy today?"

"No."

"Okay, but you have to promise me that if you feel even the slightest bit tired or unwell, you won't come. I mean it, Ava." He pinned her with a look. "I need you to be ready for tomorrow, and insisting on doing a little work tonight only to miss a lot of work tomorrow is a problem for everyone."

"I promise I'll be fine."

"Then be there by four."

Her smile was one of pure pleasure that had him glad he'd already given her his coat so he didn't have to shrug it off.

"And we watch the movies together tonight," he added.

"You didn't say that was part of the deal. I thought I'd watch them this afternoon."

"No." His refusal was succinct. "You're taking a nap this afternoon or the deal is off." She was by far his best reporter. Having her around and healthy, even semi-healthy, was his best option to make sure that Rockdale went smoothly.

"Deal." She pouted. "Slave driver."

"You know it." He grinned, pleased that she'd given in without a fight. Though last night hadn't exactly been relaxing, Jake had still enjoyed being with her. He hadn't been to a festival in years and he'd forgotten that immediate camaraderie that developed between good teams. He was looking forward to spending more time with her. Hopefully not in the E.R.

They pulled up to the hotel and he helped her out of the cab, keeping one hand on the small of her back until he'd safely delivered her to her room.

By quarter to four, Ava had updated her blog, changed into something that didn't reek of hospital and managed to squeeze in a visit to the hotel's salon for a quick blowout. Her hair now fell in soft waves around her face, a massive improvement over this morning's ponytail.

It wasn't that she was trying to impress Jake with her looks. She wasn't attractive enough for that, not in the land of the long-legged, slim-bodied, glossy-haired Hollywood star. But she was representing her station at one of Hollywood's biggest film festivals, so she needed to look her best. Really, it had nothing to do with Jake. Nothing at all.

As she got into a cab, Ava was feeling pretty good. Her wrist didn't hurt too much, the painkillers prescribed by the doctor seemed to be keeping most of the discomfort at bay, the afternoon was crisp and clear, and she was ready to get back to work.

It was time to show Mr. Durham just how good she was at her job.

The building that housed the suites was busy. Though most doors were closed, it was clear the rooms were occupied. Lights glowed from beneath and the low rumble of voices, occasionally pierced by a delighted laugh or annoyed shout, indicated they weren't the only team on-site pulling together a story. The smell of fried food permeated the air, a staple of the long days and longer nights when grabbing a meal was second to getting a scoop.

She hoped to eat something nicer tonight. Besides being unable to handle the late-night parties that left her face looking ravaged, she found that fast food made her skin oily and prone to breakouts. God, was she getting too old for this? She shook off the thought before it dared to take root. In a business where youth was king, as evidenced by the fact that seemingly every actor—no matter how young or famous—had undergone touch-ups to look a little fresher, even thinking old was a death blow.

Her boot heels clicked down the hall as she made her way to the suite number Jake had texted her. She'd thought about wearing sneakers, but her boots were warmer. Plus, weren't you supposed to get back on the horse when you got bucked off? And they made her legs look really long, quite a feat since she was only five foot two.

The room was deep in the building, but that was good. They'd be less likely to be interrupted by other media outlets, many of whom she was familiar with from covering festivals for the past few years.

It was quiet behind the door and she figured Jake and Brandon were in the middle of watching something or writing. Not wanting to disrupt the creative process, she opened the door as silently as possible and slipped inside.

The monitors were on, running a shot of a panel with a few famous faces. Ava glanced around the room. Brandon wasn't even there.

"Hey." Jake looked up from the desk where he was

scribbling on a piece of paper and smiled. "How are you feeling?"

"Fine. Great, even." She slipped out of her coat and hung it in the closet, checking the shadows just in case Brandon was tucked away in one of them. But there was no sign of the young cameraman. "Where's Brandon?"

"I sent him off for the night." Jake smiled at her again, which sent her already bouncing nerves on another trip. "He said he had a line on a great party."

"Of course he did." Ava took a seat near Jake and reminded herself that she was just here to do some voice-over work. Not a big deal and something she'd done a million times before. No reason for butterflies. Even if Jake was wearing those jeans.

"How's your arm? You feeling okay?" He crossed the room to grab a bottle of water from a small collection sitting on a table. "You want one?"

"No, I'm fine." She tried not to notice the jeans. Damn those jeans. Was she going to have to steal them and burn them? "The arm is good." She waved it to show that it wasn't just talk.

"Great, then let's get started." He gestured for her to take a seat in front of the screen. She did, swallowing hard when he stood behind her.

He pushed a couple of buttons, turning the monitor dark before it started again. This time the footage had a clear story arc, though it was a rough cut. They watched it through once and then Jake handed her the script he'd written. Normally, she preferred to write her own patter, but this wasn't a normal situation. She read it over, running the footage through her brain as she did. It wasn't perfect, but it would do. Still, she made a few notes, changed some things around to make the copy flow better and then asked him to run the cut footage again. This time she tightened the commentary even more and did a complete rewrite of the introduction before she handed it back to him.

Not that she'd needed to. He'd been standing over her shoulder reading the whole thing. But that was fine. She could show him what she was made of, and it was sterner stuff than his preamble about the picturesque town nestled at the foot of a majestic mountain range. It was the same meaningless intro that would be used in all the second-rate broadcasts and more than half of the first.

He read it over. "I like this. It's better than mine."

She couldn't help the small flush of pleasure. "It is what I do for a living."

His mouth twisted at the corner in that way she found so sexy. Stupid sexy smile. "Point taken."

The recording took a while, taping and retaping, eliminating phrases that didn't work and adding different ones when a better bridge from shot to shot was required. Ava exhaled when they finished, pleased that when they started to dub in her taped words, her voice didn't sound shaky or quivery or anything at all like she was feeling inside.

Look at her. Professional Career Woman Kicking Butt and Taking Names. Her mother would be so proud.

"Nice. Let's call it a wrap," Jake said with a smile that was clearly designed to knock a woman's socks off, and she felt her toes tingle. Great. Just great.

She hooked her bag over her good shoulder and then positioned it directly in front of her. Nothing like using her purse as protection or, at least, to get in the way, should she decide to throw herself at him.

Which, of course, would never happen, but still, it didn't hurt to be prepared.

While Jake collected his belongings, Ava turned her BlackBerry back on and scrolled through the menu. Two missed calls. Both from her mother.

She'd tried to call her mom earlier this afternoon to tell her about the accident, but had gotten no answer. No doubt Barbara was at a meeting or some other business-type event. So Ava had simply left a message to call back.

And now she had. Ava considered her options. She could wait until she got to the hotel to call, but that would just be postponing things. And taking a moment to speak to her mother now might cool some of the ardor she was beginning to feel. Nothing like talking to a mother to kill a person's sex drive.

She excused herself to Jake and went into the hallway. It was cooler out here and she rested her forehead against the wall while she dialed her mom.

"Barbara Christensen." Her mother always answered like that even though she should know it was Ava by the ringtone. Ava had downloaded the Black Eyed Peas' "Hey Mama" onto her mother's phone as her signature ringtone and she knew it was still on there because just last week Barbara had asked how to get it off.

"Hi, Mom."

"Hello, dear. How are you? How is the festival?"

"Fine."

"Good. How are things going with your new producer? Have you given any thought to how to show him that you're ready for more responsibility? I feel strongly that a list could help in this instance."

"Mom." Ava cut her mother off before she could really get going. "I have something to tell you, but I don't want you to worry."

There was a short pause. "Well, really, Ava. I don't know how you can expect me not to worry with a statement like that. What's wrong?"

"It's very minor and it's all been taken care of. But I slipped on some ice and broke my wrist." She plowed through her mother's sharp intake of breath. "I needed surgery, but it went well and everything is fine." Well, everything except that her little crush on Jake was coming back into play. "In fact, I'm working right now, so there is nothing for you to worry about."

But, of course, her reassurances seemed to fall on deaf ears. "What kind of break? Are you sure the surgery was done correctly? Who was the doctor?" And on and on until Ava felt as if she was being interrogated for being a klutz.

She answered her mother's questions to the best of her ability. Was still answering them when Jake came out a few minutes later. He grinned at her, apparently enjoying her predicament. She rolled her eyes at him. Oh, sure. It was easy for him to laugh. He wasn't the one under formal investigation.

She turned her attention back to her mother, who was still cross-examining away. "No, Mom, it wasn't the shoes." She'd have crossed her fingers, but the cast made that impossible. She settled for crossing her legs. "It was just one of those things." Jake's snort filled the hallway. She ignored him.

"You were wearing those heeled boots you love, weren't you?" Her mother sighed heavily. "I don't know why you insist on wearing those heels. They cause knee and back problems, can shorten your calf muscles, can give you bunions—"

"I said I wasn't wearing the boots." Because she sure wasn't going to admit to it now. She swatted at Jake when he pointed to her feet, which made him laugh.

"Who is that laughing?"

"No one," Ava said and turned her back on the human hyena. "Just someone who thinks he's way funnier than he actually is."

"Is that your producer?"

"Yes. I'm at work, Mom."

"Why is he laughing?"

"He's a funny guy." Ava made a slashing motion with her cast, but Jake continued to snicker.

"Ava. I sense that you're trying to evade my questions. Why?"

"I'm not trying to evade anything." She would have hung up, but knew her mother would only call back. Endlessly.

"I can tell when you're trying to hide something from me."

"What are you, psychic?"

"You know I don't believe in that," Barbara answered. "So what are you hiding?"

"I've told you everything." She really wanted to get off the phone. *Argh.* Why hadn't she waited and called her mother once she was in the privacy of her hotel room? "Look, I need to go. I still have work to do tonight." Which wasn't a lie. "Can you just schedule an appointment with one of your experts and I'll see him when I'm back home?"

"It's a her and I've already noted that. Have you spoken to your producer about your injury? Is he aware of the severity of a fracture that requires surgery and how it needs to be treated?"

"Since he's standing right here and can see my cast, I'd say he's aware of it." Ava declined to tell her mother that Jake had spent the night in the private hospital room with her.

"Because you both need to know that a fracture, any fracture, can have serious consequences both short- and long-term. You shouldn't be pushing yourself too hard, Ava. You might end up doing more harm."

"I won't push, okay?"

"I just want you to be healthy, dear." Ava knew that was true, but it didn't make her any less irritable. "You promise that you'll take good care of yourself?"

"Yes."

"And you won't wear those high-heeled boots again if it's icy?"

Ava didn't know why she even tried. "I'll be careful." She listened for another minute, promised once more that she'd be careful and then finally hung up.

Jake was leaning against the wall, arms crossed over his chest, grinning at her.

"What?" She scowled. She wouldn't have laughed if his mother had been harassing him. Not very much, at least.

"The boots?" Jake pointed at the offending footwear.

Ava lifted her chin. "I like them. They stay." He smiled, but didn't laugh, which was good or Ava might have had to kick him.

They started down the hall. Most of the previously closed doors were now open; they were one of the last teams to leave. "Guess your mom was worried about you," he said.

"One of the things she does best." Ava tried not to be annoyed by it because she knew she was lucky. Her mother loved her and showed her that in every way, but sometimes it was hard to remember when she was being lectured—*advised* was the term her mother preferred—to death. About everything.

"I know the feeling." Jake sighed. "Since I moved, I have a scheduled phone call every week."

"Really?" Ava was intrigued. "And what happens if you miss it?"

"I'm afraid to find out."

They both laughed. "I have a biweekly dinner with my mom," Ava told him. "Every other Sunday."

"At least you get fed."

"I'm not sure it's worth the trouble." She smiled when Jake raised an eyebrow. "She likes to try to run my life. No matter how many times I tell her that I have it under control, she's sure she can help."

"Sounds familiar."

"You, too?" Her heart thumped hard when he grinned and nodded. "And do you get the lecture about how you need to apply yourself to get ahead in your career?"

"Not lately."

There was an uncomfortable tightening around his mouth. "Because you moved?" Ava ventured a guess.

"Partially." He shook his head. "It's really not that exciting a story."

Ava would have liked to be the judge of that, but she didn't push. "Well, it's my mother's favorite topic."

"She doesn't like what you do now?"

"She's dissatisfied. After the whole doctor thing didn't work out, she wanted me to be an accountant."

"So you decided to major in drama at university?"

Ava laughed. "No, I majored in economics just as she wanted, but I didn't like it much. And I liked the job I got after graduation even less."

"So how did you get into reporting?"

"Luck and circumstance. I've always loved movies. Jilly was working at the station." At the time, Jilly had been dating the best friend of Ava's boyfriend, and while neither romantic relationship had worked out, their friendship had. Ava and Jilly had often joked that they'd kissed frogs to find each other. "I'd mentioned that I was looking to make a career move and she told me about the opening for a junior reporter at the station. Even though I didn't have on-camera experience, she convinced me to apply. Harvey liked me and decided to give me a chance." Ava left out the part about her mother's massive disappointment, how'd she'd had to listen to a doomsday-scenario lecture for six months every time she had dinner with her mother before Barbara had finally accepted that she was happy.

"But your mother still wants you to be an accountant."

Ava liked that he didn't ask but made a statement. Who said that all men were bad listeners?

"She wouldn't be upset if I went back to it, but it's not happening." It was one of the reasons she'd wanted the promotion so much. She'd thought it would somehow prove to her mother that she'd made the right choice.

"I'm glad you stayed," Jake said, making Ava's insides go all mushy.

They turned down the main hall, heading toward the front door. It was dark out now and Ava knew it would be freezing. She shivered in anticipation of the cold and not because Jake was walking so close to her that their arms kept accidentally brushing.

"Have you given any thought to dinner?" Jake asked.

"What about it?"

"Where? When? What you want?"

What she wanted was to get a handle on her hormones. But that wasn't appropriate professional banter. She dropped back a half step, wondering if it was wrong that she was enjoying the view so much. "Why don't you go out with Brandon tonight. I feel fine, so I can handle the movies on my own."

"Ava." The little curl that tugged at her every time he said her name was back. He stopped, waited for her to catch up to him. "Stop trying to brush me off."

"I'm not." She hitched her bag in front of her again. "I just thought you might want to go out tonight. Have some fun." And she could go back to the austerity of a bland hotel room and pretend that she wasn't attracted to Jake at all.

He leaned against the wall. There was no sign of anyone, save them. The hall lights had been turned down low to save energy and gave a decidedly romantic feel to the encounter.

She shoved that idea away, determined to keep things professional. "Look, you've had a really long day and the festival is just going to get busier tomorrow. Having some downtime would be good for you. Plus, the movies probably won't be that exciting. I can assure you there won't be any helicopters." She was rewarded with a broad smile that made her pulse jump. "Also, I don't think I'll be very good company. I'm tired. I might even fall asleep." Was the editing suite having the same furnace problem as the hospital? What was it with this town?

He reached out to brush a lock of hair off her cheek. Her pulse jumped higher at the brief contact of skin on skin. Oh, no. This was bad.

"Then I'm definitely coming over." He smiled at her. "You'll need me around to poke you awake."

Poking? There would be no poking. Ava yanked her mind out of the gutter. "Wouldn't you rather have the night to yourself?"

He shrugged. "No." He was good, but she saw the way his eyes flicked down her body and back up.

Her breath caught in her throat then and she had to look away before she did something crazy like lean forward and kiss him.

"Ava."

Again with her name. She could smell the mint of his toothpaste. If she leaned back now, she would be sending a clear message. Hands off. No entrance. Keep your distance.

"You okay?"

No, she was not okay. So, *so* not okay. She let her purse fall to the floor and leaned forward.

Chapter 8

Jake knew he had no business kissing Ava, but it didn't stop him from burying his fingers in her hair and sinking into the heat of her mouth. He barely heard the *thunk* of her bag as it hit the floor, wouldn't have cared if she'd dropped it on his foot once their lips met.

She sighed into his mouth, sending a flash of need through his body. His hold on her tightened and he felt her soften, melt into him. Oh, yeah. Hell, yeah. He spun them so she was backed up against the wall, safe and sound where he could press his body into hers, anchoring them together. And he thought maybe he could stay just like this forever. Or at least an hour or two.

So, of course, she had other ideas.

"Wait." She pulled her mouth away from his, breathing hard. Their bodies were still in full contact and her good arm remained wrapped around his waist. Jake wondered if she realized that even now her body was straining against his. "I can't do this."

He swallowed the growl that rose to his throat, but didn't move. "What's wrong?"

She stared up at him for a moment and bit at her soft lower lip. Jake wanted to suggest that he could do that biting for her, but held back.

She looked away, tilted her head down. Oh, no. He didn't think so. He ran a finger down her cheek and under her chin, pressing until she was forced to look up at him. She blinked, her eyes wide and sky-blue, her lips pinker than usual. She looked so delicious that for a second he considered saying to hell with it and kissing her anyway.

Instead, he shored up the good-guy part of his personality and slapped his hands on the wall, knowing that if he kept touching her it was going to be impossible to stop. The plaster was cold against his palms, but did little to cool him down. He took a slow breath in and out. "You going to tell me what the problem is?"

"It's just…" Ava trailed off and shrugged, her clear eyes watching him. For a moment, he had a sharp hope that maybe she'd say to hell with it and yank him back where he belonged, but then she blinked and the moment fluttered away. She smoothed a hand over her hair. "You know."

Actually, he did know. But he also knew that she felt amazing against him and anything that felt that good couldn't be wrong. It was a struggle to take a step back, give them both a little breathing room. But because he was pragmatic and not one to let opportunity slip away, Jake made sure that she was still within reach. Just in case she came to her senses and decided that she needed to touch him again.

She didn't. Instead, she studied him with those wide blue eyes. He didn't need to be a psychic to see the confusion swirling in them.

"Sorry." He took another step back. "I shouldn't have kissed you without asking." He ground out the words, only because they seemed like the right thing to say. He didn't mean them. Not even a little.

"No." Her sigh whispered over him, made him think of long nights between cool sheets. "The kissing wasn't the problem. Well, not the way you're thinking. I liked the kissing just fine."

The primal part of him reared its head. Jake punched it in the throat.

"It's just that we work together, and as recently as yesterday, I hated your guts." She shook her head, the blond strands waving around her face. "Well, maybe not hate, but I was mad at you about the promotion. And..." She squeezed her eyes shut. She was still breathing hard. He could see the way her chest rose and fell.

"And?"

When she looked at him this time, she seemed to have come to some sort of decision. "And I'm not mad anymore." She looked up at him with that sweet, fresh-faced smile. Now it felt as if someone had punched him in the throat. "But we still work together."

She was right. He could see that, reminded himself that this was exactly the sort of entanglement he'd sworn to avoid. And yeah, he wouldn't be working with Ava for that much longer, but the fact remained that he didn't really have time in his life to prioritize a relationship. No matter what Rachel might think.

"Jake?" She looked at him, her eyes soft and liquid. He forced himself not to get caught up in them, clenched his hands so he didn't drag his fingers through her hair and pull her back against him.

"You're right," he said and widened the space between them even more. He willed his muscles to relax, to give up this harsh need to kiss her until she stopped talking and started feeling.

She was still breathing hard and a part of him liked to see it. Proof that she'd been affected as much as he had. She straightened her coat, brushed a finger across her lips. "I'm supposed to be showing you what a good reporter I am." Jake wondered if she realized she was stroking her thumb back and forth across the delicate skin. "Not this."

"Oh, yeah?" Some of the tension in his bones eased.

She nodded and a furrow appeared between her eyebrows. "You aren't going to think less of me for this, are you?"

Jake wasn't sure he was going to be able to think at all if she kept touching her lip like that. He managed a shake of his head.

"I mean, professionally." The furrow deepened. "I'm a good reporter. Really good."

"I know." He wanted to soothe the wrinkle away. With his words, his finger, his mouth.

"But that wasn't professional." She closed her eyes for a moment, those long thick lashes standing out against her rosy cheeks. When she looked at him again, they were full of worry. "I don't want you to think I'm that kind of person. I've never kissed a colleague before."

It pleased Jake to think that he was the first. She was

so unlike Claudia. His ex would have been trying to claw his clothes off right now. Though Jake could honestly say that Ava doing the same would rate high on his list of fantasies, he appreciated her concerns. And that, also unlike Claudia, she wasn't looking to use him to get ahead. "How about we just pretend it never happened?" he suggested.

The frown she shot him was unexpected, proving that his sister was right when she said he really didn't understand women. "Are you... Seriously? You can forget about it just like that?" She snapped her fingers.

Now he was confused. Isn't that what she wanted? To return to their friendly professionalism? What the...?

"I thought—"

"Thought that I'm a terrible kisser." She tossed her hair with a sniff.

The fact that he was ready to pin her against the wall and kiss her until her lips were bruised and she was gasping for breath spoke to just how wrong she was. "No, it's not that."

"Are you sure?" She had her hand on her hip now. "Because telling me that you can so easily pretend it didn't happen isn't exactly good for my ego."

"And telling me that you hate me is good for mine?"

"But I don't hate you anymore," she pointed out.

It was the kind of logic that Jake knew he had no chance of refuting, and trying to do so would only give him a headache. Not to mention if they kept talking about it, he was going to feel obligated to prove just how much he *did* want to kiss her. "Ava."

"No." She held up a hand. "I don't even know why I'm arguing with you about this. I don't want to kiss you, either. Bad for my career and all that."

He waited, watching as she took a deep breath and then seemed to let it fizzle out of her.

"And maybe not officially, but it is possible that I might be overreacting just a smidge. I blame the medication. But—" her gaze locked on his "—for the record, I am an amazing kisser."

It took all Jake's willpower not to ask her to prove it.

By the time they climbed into the cab he'd called, all their talk had turned to normal festival-type things. The setup for tomorrow's circuit, who was scheduled to attend, other events booked for later in the week, but Jake's mind wasn't really focused on any of that. Instead, he kept noticing that her hair smelled like coconut, her skin like sunshine.

Ava was like a tiny hit of summer in this snow-covered landscape. He wanted to breathe her in deep, wrap his hands in that hair, stroke every inch of that skin, but settled for letting it brush against him whenever the cab took a tight corner.

It was for the best, letting things swing safely back into the Colleague Zone. Better for him to spend his free time focusing on work; with the pilot and the station he certainly had enough of it. But try telling that to his body, which kept nudging its way across the backseat of the cab to get closer to Ava.

Ava didn't say anything as he escorted her to her hotel room. But Jake could sense her stealing looks at him when she thought he wasn't looking. It made him think she wasn't as sure about this "no nooky with the colleagues" thing as she wanted to be.

Neither was he.

She tried to talk him out of watching the movies with

her again, but he cut off her suggestion. Even if they hadn't just shared a kiss that would make any grown man weep, he still intended to spend the rest of the evening with her.

He told himself he was just looking after her. She was a valuable commodity and one he needed to keep healthy until the festival was over, but that wasn't the entire truth. He enjoyed her company. Despite the ache still nagging the back of his neck, last night had been the most fun he'd had in ages.

How sad was that anyway? A night spent in the hospital was considered hot times in the city. Maybe Rachel was right about him needing to get out more.

He was on his way back from a nearby convenience store, his bags filled with candy, popcorn and soda—all required goodies for a long night of movie watching—when his phone rang. He fumbled for it, juggling the bags in the frosty air.

"Hello?"

One of the bags slid dangerously low on his wrist, threatening to spill its contents onto the sidewalk. He swung it back up, wondering if he might have overdone it a bit. Probably. But to Jake, a movie just wasn't a movie without the treats. It was a habit that stemmed from his mother, who'd made an event out of every made-for-TV movie his father had ever produced. And there had been a lot. Although he didn't do it every time—it wasn't appropriate at theater premieres and his ex had never wanted the extra calories—when the time and company were right, Jake indulged himself.

"It's Alex."

"Hey." Jake rebalanced his treats bags and continued

to the hotel, keeping one eye on the sidewalk in case there was any more stray ice around. They didn't need a second trip to the hospital. "What's up?"

"Rescheduled the meeting with the investors to this Friday. Dinner. Some good food, good wine and you can wow them with your charm. Oh, no, wait, that's me."

Jake snorted. Friday was tight. He wouldn't get home until Thursday afternoon, but he was confident that he'd be ready. He'd spent every free moment in the past six weeks making sure he was ready. "What time?"

"Eight. I've emailed you the details, and I tried calling Carly. I know you said I shouldn't, but we're pressed for time and I think she should be there. Makes things look more stable." Which made investors much more likely to hand over their money. "Also, never hurts to have a pretty face around."

"I thought we agreed that I would be the contact for Carly." Since Alex wasn't involved in the filming part of the show, it made more sense for Jake to liaise with the on-camera talent. Plus, he was concerned that pretty, bubbly Carly had developed a bit of a crush on Alex's golden-boy good looks.

"You're out of town."

"Yes, but you need to keep your distance."

"Why? Are you questioning my ability to charm her?"

"No, I'm just saying that your old love-'em-and-leave-'em technique isn't going to fly in this instance."

"Hey, I've perfected that technique to a fine art."

"And you aren't using it on Carly. I don't have time to look for another host if you piss her off." It had taken three rounds of auditions to find Carly.

"Don't get your panties in a wad. She's not answering her phone anyway," Alex said.

Jake reached the front of the hotel and nodded at the doorman. "Good. Maybe that means she was smart enough to avoid your calls. Anyway, just leave it and I'll call her."

"You don't give me enough credit."

"That's because I know you." Jake grinned. Even in university, Alex had always had a knack with women. Jake could remember a trio of them coming to his dorm one Friday night, each one sure they were his date for the evening. Alex had somehow not only managed to avoid a fight, but convinced them that they could each be his date at the same time. As far as Jake knew, a good time had been had by all. The only person who had been bothered was Hanna, who felt that Alex hadn't shown the women any respect and had taken it upon herself to spread the word to the rest of the females on campus. "I need to go. I'm flying home Thursday. Don't worry about Carly, I'll get in touch with her. See you in a few days."

Ten minutes later, after a quick shower and some fresh clothes, he was clean and clearheaded and knocking on Ava's door. She pulled it open and after perusing him closely, frowned. "You washed your hair."

He shrugged, suddenly feeling as if maybe he had been primping for her. It was a little embarrassing to get caught.

"I have to make an appointment with the hotel's salon to get my hair washed. It's not fair that you can wash yours any old time you want."

"So you'd prefer I stay dirty?" He held out the treats, still in the plastic bags. "I brought snacks."

"Good thing I like snacks." She plucked one bag from his hand. "I'll accept these as a peace offering."

He laughed, pleased that there seemed to be no lingering awkwardness between them. If she could act as though nothing had changed, so could he. Well, except for the tingle he felt whenever he looked at her.

Jake moved into the room and sat at the desk chair, unloading the second bag of snacks and reminding himself that he hadn't moved all the way to the West Coast, a three-hour time difference from friends and family, not to make a success of his life. It wasn't just about leaving Claudia and her duplicity behind. It was proving to his father and himself that he could do it.

He could still picture the disappointment in his father's eyes when he'd heard about what had happened with his ex. Jake shook the uncomfortable memory away and focused on the snacks.

Just as his father had taken a risk by producing a little independent movie—somehow convincing a pair of national television stations to enter into a bidding war for the broadcast rights—which had become one of the most watched made-for-TV movies in the country, Jake wanted his travel show to be a massive hit.

"What did you bring?" Ava hovered over his shoulder, her scent filling his head.

"Just a few things." A comment that completely belied the bursting seams of the bags. "I didn't know what you liked, so I bought a little of everything."

They were friends, just friends. And he was okay with that. He turned to smile at her. "You want the Red Hots or the Junior Mints?"

Boo to Ice

Seriously, tooling around town in a cast is not for the weak-willed. I have to be on constant alert for more ice (because it clearly cannot be trusted), try to make my cast look less "casty" and do everything one-handed!

Jake, my producer, assures me that he and Brandon, who has been sans contessa this trip, will help out whenever they can, and I plan to take full advantage. I've earned it.

After all, I did not weep like a baby during surgery, though I desperately wanted to. (I mean, I can't even watch *Grey's Anatomy!*) So, although I'll be working the rest of the festival as damaged goods, I won't be missing out on anything juicy. Such as…

…the adorable Ashley Tisdale (if you don't like *High School Musical,* we can't be friends) and her equally adorable dog wearing coordinated outfits.

…Bieber. (Yes, I know I am old enough to be his mother. Don't judge.)

…Rob Lowe! Still just as dreamy as he was in *St. Elmo's Fire.* (My first babysitter lurved her some Brat Packers, though she preferred bad boy Judd Nelson. She used to make me watch the movies every time they were on TV, which was always. Once I was old enough to stay home alone,

I kept up the tradition. Come on. How can you not love John Hughes movies no matter what year you were born?) And he said hello! Really, this is truly shaping up to be the best festival ever—even with my broken wrist.

Kiss kiss,

Ava

Chapter 9

Ava watched through her keyhole as Jake walked down the hall to the elevator. She was glad that he'd finally left. Maybe now her racing heartbeat could return to normal.

It didn't even make sense. She didn't want to kiss him, didn't want him to kiss her. Okay, that was a lie. But it was a bad, bad idea. They worked together. They had to maintain a professional relationship no matter what happened. And she did not think she was up to the drama that would ensue if they didn't.

Still, he hadn't even tried.

She tossed the last of the Junior Mints into her mouth and chewed.

After four more days of covering the festival and attending star-studded events, Ava had to admit that whatever was happening between her and Jake wasn't going away.

She pulled out her BlackBerry and crossed her fingers that Jilly was available.

Is Dr. Jillian in the house? Advice needed.

For you? The doctor is always in. What's up?

Ava took a deep breath and typed quickly, as if that would make it easier.

Jake kissed me.

WHAT!? When? Where? How? (I figure the who and what are covered.)

Ava could practically hear Jilly's excited shriek.

A few days ago. Saturday night, to be exact. I'd like to blame it on the surgery meds making me loopy, but I was only on ibuprofen and aspirin. Hardly a drugging combo.

How could you keep this from me for the last *checking calendar*...FOUR DAYS! I thought we were friends.

Because Ava had spent the past four days trying to convince herself that the kiss was no big deal.

We are friends, which is why I'm telling you now. I'd been hoping that I could just move past it. Forget about it. But that's not happening.

Oh, wow. Tell me exactly what happened. How he swept you off your feet and dipped you like one of those hot Russians on *Dancing With the Stars*, then made your head spin with his luscious lips.

Ava smiled despite her roiling emotions.

No dipping, but he pinned me to a wall and there was definitely some head-spinning. So, of course, I told him not to do it again. And now I can't stop thinking about it. About him. Gah. I'm pathetic.

Not pathetic. You like him. What's wrong with that?

She didn't even know where to begin.

We work together, meaning the complications could be astronomical. And I don't want to like him. But he makes it hard. Did I tell you that he always gets my coffee order right without my having to remind him?

He's a prince. Back to the good stuff, what do you intend to do about it?

Wasn't that what she'd texted Jilly for?

Le sigh. Stupidly, I'm hoping when we leave here that it will just go away. Maybe it's the whole forbidden-fruit thing. I only want him because I can't have him.

Maybe. But what about while you're there? (I notice you didn't mention that you have another night before you come home. Anything could happen...)

The thought made her hands shake.

Do you think if we kissed again, it would all go away?

Ha! I think you're looking for a good reason to kiss him.

No, she wasn't. She was looking for a good reason *not* to kiss him.

You brought it up.

I'm sorry. Recheck the conversation. Nowhere do I say that you should kiss him again. (Though I totally think you should.)

Ava scrolled through the texts and saw that Jilly was right. But that wasn't important.

I could except for the small (and embarrassing) fact that when I told him we shouldn't do that, he agreed. He even said that we should pretend nothing had happened. How rude.

Well, what did you expect him to do?

Wasn't it obvious?

Pledge his undying love and throw himself at my feet. What else?

Then kiss him.

If only it were so easy.

Have you forgotten that we work together? And worse, that he's my boss?

First off, he's not exactly your boss. Second, don't you watch *Grey's Anatomy*?

Ava had tried a few times because so many people had talked about what a great show it was, but she just couldn't get past the blood. It was too much for her weak stomach.

Do you even read my blog? You know I can't watch it. All that blood and ick.

Let me fill you in: Meredith (the main character...in fact the Grey in *Grey's Anatomy*) slept with Derek when he was her sort-of boss.

Ava wasn't sure what this had to do with her situation.

Yay for them. And it was probably superweird and awkward, right?

Only for a little while. Now they're married. Do you think McHot Stuff>McDreamy?

Ava didn't know what Jilly was talking about or who McDreamy was, but this was not helping.

My life is not a TV show. I'm not marrying Jake. And besides, they're not real people.

You asked for my opinion, I gave it. If you don't want to kiss him and he agrees, why are you upset?

And there was the million-dollar question.

I didn't say it made sense.

Then I think you should let nature take its course. Forget Clooney, McHot Stuff can be your festival love affair. Just for tonight. Tomorrow you can go back to being your normal, proper self. P.S. I expect all the details when you consummate the relationship.

Ava's hands started shaking again.

Excuse me. I didn't say I was going to consummate anything.

You didn't have to.

Ava put her BlackBerry down and decided that her time was better spent getting ready for tonight's wrap-up party than letting Jilly convince her to do something she wasn't sure was a good idea. That was just Jilly being Jilly. Supportive, impulsive and more than a bit reckless. Which Ava was not.

It had been a busy few days. Ava had run the interview circuit with panache and gotten a humorous story out of Brad Pitt. She'd bumped into Kate Hudson in the bathroom and given her the extra lip gloss she always carried in her purse for emergencies, which resulted in a charming and funny interview later that day. Not to mention all the hours she'd spent with Jake in the editing suite as they raced to get their stories finished in time for the show's evening broadcast. Even her mother would be impressed.

And now they were leaving. Their flight was at noon tomorrow, so this was their last night to whoop it up in town before they returned to the status quo. A part of Ava was looking forward to getting back into the station, where she could keep Jake at arm's length and get over this silly crush, while another part was loath to leave Idaho and the opening it offered. Once they were back in Vancouver, the chance to kiss Jake would be gone. And try as she might to remind herself that it was the professional thing to do, she couldn't quite convince herself it was really what she wanted.

The wrap-up party wasn't so much an organized send-off as a crashing of an already planned party. There were plenty of media teams sticking around until the end of the festival, which wouldn't officially end for another week, but there were many others who, like them, showed up for the premieres, stayed a few days to get enough footage for a couple of weeks' worth of stories and then jetted home.

Ava was blotting her lipstick when a knock sounded at her door. Even though she knew it was only Brandon—she'd asked him to stop by for her on his way out—her heart still picked up speed at the thought of seeing Jake in just a few minutes.

"Hey," she said as she swung the door open. "I just need to put on my boots and then we can... Oh." She stopped talking when she saw Jake standing in the hallway.

She didn't need the mirror to know that her eyes had widened and her mouth had fallen open. Great. Just how she wanted to start the evening, looking like Horror Movie Victim #2.

But she recovered quickly. Interviewing celebrities had taught her to be prepared to launch into cool professionalism at any moment. "I was expecting Brandon. Come in. I just need to put on my boots and coat and we can go."

"Brandon's still primping," Jake said. "Something about how this is his last night in town."

"And he wants to get lucky," Ava finished. She laughed and the odd thumping in her chest eased. "He'll probably ditch us later."

"I'll try not to be offended."

She felt his eyes on her and tried not to think about it. It wasn't the kind of staring that meant anything; he was just looking at her because it was natural to look at the person you were speaking to. "So, where are we going for dinner?"

"The concierge told me about a little Italian place a few blocks away. I managed to get us a reservation. Supposed to have amazing mushroom linguine."

Ava's hand stilled on the zipper of her boot. "Italian?"

"You don't like Italian?"

"I love it." But she couldn't believe that out of all the restaurants in town, Jake had chosen the one that had brought them together. The back of her neck tingled and she rubbed at it. "Are we walking there?"

"It's not far."

"I know. I was coming back from there when I fell." She glanced down. "Maybe I should skip the boots."

He put a hand on her shoulder when she bent to start unzipping them. "Leave the boots."

"Oh, really?" She glanced up at him. "You like the boots now? You've come to see the truth of their awesomeness?"

He smiled, that quirky half smile that made her stomach tighten. "I always liked the boots, Ava."

Her heart was thrumming that odd tattoo again. She shifted, dislodging his hand, and lowered her head, glad that she'd left her hair down so it could veil her hot cheeks. She would not throw herself at him. Well, not unless he specifically asked for it.

"But if you're worried, I promise not to let you fall." He held out a hand to help her up. "I'll even hold your hand the whole way." His fingers squeezed hers and for a second, Ava considered leaving them there.

But she tugged lightly and told herself she wasn't disappointed when he let go without a fight.

Dinner was a riot of laughter and pasta, and by the time the server came around to clear their plates, Ava was feeling very relaxed. When he asked if they'd like any dessert, she nodded emphatically.

"Ooh, yes. Something gooey and chocolaty." She liked having something sweet after a meal, though she didn't often treat herself. Too short to carry any extra weight and too worried about how she looked on camera. But tonight was special.

"Not for me." Brandon checked his phone.

"Not for me, either," Jake said.

Ava frowned at them. "Excuse me, but it's rude to make me be the only one to order dessert and feel like a pig. You're ordering something."

Brandon laughed. "Can't. I gots to get to the party."

He waggled his phone at them. "My presence is requested."

Ava looked at the waiter. "Well, I want dessert. Bring me the most decadent thing on the menu." She cut her eye to Jake. "You're staying and having some."

He raised an eyebrow at her. "What about Brandon? He doesn't have to stay?"

"He's young and horny."

"And I'm not?"

"I wouldn't know." She felt her cheeks flush despite her attempt to be cool. Stupid fair coloring.

"He's a dude," Brandon said. "He's horny. Goes without saying."

Ava didn't dare look at Jake lest she embarrass herself by asking him if Brandon was right.

Brandon headed off, leaving the two of them at the table alone.

Neither of them said anything.

Ava swallowed. One more second and this would go way past awkward and then who knew what might come out of her mouth? She'd done a fine job of keeping things professional since their talk that weekend, but she hadn't been thinking about the fact that as soon as they got back home this closeness was very likely to end.

She tried to steer her thoughts down a safer path. "So what made you decide to take a job in Vancouver?" she asked. She knew Jilly would call her a chicken, but Jilly wasn't here. "Family? Friends? Weather?"

"What is the obsession you people have with weather?"

"Us people?" She raised her good hand to her chest as though shocked. "You mean the amazing residents who call Vancouver home? Of whom you are now one?"

"Yes."

"Don't be angry just because we don't have to shovel snow all winter."

"You also don't get sunshine all winter. What did we have, twenty-nine days of rain last month?"

"Small price to pay." There, this was much better than asking about his libido.

"Actually, I'd have to agree. I shoveled the driveway for my parents when I was home for Christmas and I thought my back might never straighten again."

She doubted that. "So you don't like manual labor."

"I don't mind it. I like doing things with my hands."

Oh, she was so leaving that comment alone. "And the move came about because?"

"I needed a change. I like Vancouver."

She could tell he was leaving something out. Years of interviewing celebrities had honed her instincts in that regard. "You like Vancouver and you needed a change. That's it?"

"That's it."

"I don't believe you." She studied him. Usually a big life change like moving three thousand miles away was prompted by a personal crisis. Maybe a girlfriend who'd broken his heart? Or maybe he'd been the heart-breaker. And the ex-girlfriend had turned all crazed and started stalking him and he'd had to move away before she boiled his pet bunny. "What aren't you telling me?"

"Nothing." He didn't look as if he'd lost his bunny, but he wasn't meeting her gaze, either. "Sometimes a cigar is just a cigar."

Ava was saved from analyzing whether or not his slip had been Freudian—really? He was throwing out a cigar analogy? Or was she just way too aware of sex thoughts?—by the arrival of her dessert. Three cannolis oozing cream filling and drizzled with dark chocolate.

And just like that the sex thoughts were back. She filled her mouth with the sumptuous dessert and tried not to think about it.

It proved impossible. Especially when he was watching her with that dark gaze. "Was it hard to move?" she asked, thinking that chatter of boxes and packing would do what the dessert couldn't.

"Some. I've never lived anywhere but Toronto."

"Is your family all still there?"

He nodded and scooped up a bite of dessert. "My parents and my sister and her husband." He smiled when he said it.

"You like them." It was obvious from his expression.

"Usually. Sometimes my sister drives me insane. She tells me it's just part of being a younger sibling, but I think she's making it up. My mom we've already discussed. She's great. Even when she's trying to feed me zucchini."

Ava couldn't help but notice that he hadn't mentioned his father, though he'd clearly said *parents* earlier. "What about your dad?"

The corners of his mouth hardened, though his smile didn't drop. "We have an understanding."

When he didn't elaborate, Ava pushed. "Meaning what?"

"Meaning we're different." Jake shrugged. "He's a very successful man. He owns a large production company that mainly works on made-for-TV movies. In Toronto, everyone knows his name."

Ava could appreciate the feeling, though at least she

wasn't in the same industry as her mother. "Must be hard to live with sometimes."

Jake looked at her, really looked at her. She could feel his eyes bore right into her, and swallowed, feeling shy all of a sudden. "It is. Most people don't understand that."

"That's because they've never lived with it."

His mouth was soft now, as were his fingers when he reached out to brush a lock of hair from her cheek. "Exactly."

Ava felt something click deep inside. Not like the last puzzle piece falling into place or a cog catching on a wheel. More like a crack as everything she knew or thought she knew began to tumble into shards around her feet.

Chapter 10

Jake wasn't sure why he'd trusted Ava with that little nugget from his life. Maybe because she understood. He'd gotten that feeling when she'd talked about her mother that night in the hospital. Maybe because she'd asked. Maybe because he trusted her.

He liked knowing that she wouldn't use the information against him. There was no reason for him to feel so strongly that this was the case, but he did. Something about the way she looked at him when he talked, as though she was really listening. Not to score points or get the dirt, but because she was interested in what he had to say.

He glanced down at her as he helped her with her coat. Her blond hair got caught under the collar and he reached inside to free it, letting his fingers slide along the back of her neck. She shivered, the delicate movement sending a similar response through his body. Her words might say that she wanted to keep things professional, but her body told a very different story.

When they stepped out into the cold night, Jake wrapped his hand around hers and held tight. This time, she didn't pull away.

He could hear the music from the nightclub long before they reached the front door, a deep, rumbling bass that he could feel through the soles of his shoes. Though he knew the responsible thing would be to go back to the hotel early and prepare for the meeting with the investors that was only two days away, Jake found he was looking forward to the party, looking forward to spending some nonwork-related time with Ava.

Even if it was also with a few hundred other people.

He nodded to the bouncer and slipped him a bill. The crowd outside the club was large and Jake figured it was money well spent.

Inside, the crowd was even larger. They pressed their way into the mass of moving bodies. Jake stepped in front of Ava to prevent anyone from jarring her wrist. He found an empty corner and led her toward it.

"Here?" She looked around. "But I can't see any of the action."

"You have a broken bone."

"Which is protected by a cast." She showed it to him and almost whacked him on the nose with it when a glassy-eyed man plowed into her, mumbled an apology and kept moving. "Okay, you might have a point."

It was only natural for Jake to put his arm around her to shield her from any further contact. And if he left it there a little longer than necessary, it was only because he wanted to make sure she had her balance. He wasn't about to let her leave Rockdale with two broken wrists.

Her blue eyes were bright with excitement as she scanned the room. "I can't see, is Brandon anywhere?"

Jake forced himself to look around. Aside from an actor who was regularly papped on the party scene, and his infamous posse, he didn't see anyone he recognized. "I don't think so."

"How much you want to bet he's already gone?" Ava shouted over the thumping beat.

Jake leaned down to speak into her ear, felt his belly tighten when her scent wafted over him. "Is he that good?"

She nodded. Her hair tickled his nose. "Definitely."

He needed to put some space between them. Before his body overrode his brain and he kissed her again. "Sounds like my friend Alex. Want something to drink?"

"Just water," she shouted back. "I'll go look for seats." She grinned at him and, before he could protest that she shouldn't be fighting through this crowd on her own, she disappeared into the swirling mass of bodies.

Jake let the objection die on his lips. She was an adult. She could make her own decisions, and what right did he have to tell her what to do? Plus, it gave him the opportunity to watch her work it in those boots.

As Jake threaded his way toward the bar, he saw a famous actress standing on a table, flailing her arms to the music and kicking her storklike legs at odd intervals. She had less rhythm than he did, though it didn't seem to bother the circle of men standing around her. In the corner, there was a TV star kissing his model girlfriend. His hand was up her skirt, but no one around them seemed to notice or care.

It took him five minutes to get the bartender's attention and three more before he found Ava again. She was sitting in a round corner booth, laughing with the group that surrounded her.

There was a young blond man seated beside her with his hand on her shoulder. Jake's fingers tightened around the plastic bottle. He strode up, placing the water in front of Ava with more force than required, and stared the kid down.

The kid was a typical pretty boy who frequented film festivals. The "mactors," struggling model/actors, who were in town looking for their big break. His blond hair was perfectly mussed as if he'd just gotten up, but was more likely from ten pounds of product and a carefully choreographed blow dry. His jeans were strategically torn and his leather jacket had scuff marks that were probably made by the manufacturer. Little punk. He had the gall to look down Ava's shirt when she leaned forward to introduce him. Jake would have poured his own water over the kid's head except that would be a waste of a valuable natural resource.

"Hey, man." The kid made no move to make room for Jake or leave Ava's side.

"Hey." Jake stood his ground, not looking away, not sliding around to sit on the opposite side of the large booth, and waited. It was an obvious ploy, but it worked.

The kid chugged what was left of his beer under Jake's steady gaze and wiped his mouth with the back of his hand. "I'm dry." He looked at Ava. "You want anything from the bar, dude?"

Ava lifted her water. "I think I'm okay right now."

He pushed himself up, forced to meet Jake's eyes head-on since Jake wasn't moving. "What about you, man? You need anything?"

"I'm fine." Or he would be as soon as the kid vacated his seat.

"Cool." He looked around the table. "Anyone else need anything from the bar?"

There was a chorus of orders and the kid rose to leave, adjusting his step so as not to bump into Jake. Jake couldn't help feeling a little smug as he sat in the vacated space. If the kid could be so easily intimidated, then he wasn't much of a catch. Ava should thank him.

She didn't.

"What was that about?" She leaned toward him so he could hear her over the noise.

Was she annoyed with him? Too bad. Jake didn't feel even the slightest twinge of guilt about chasing the kid off. "You don't want to hook up with him."

"Who said anything about hooking up?"

"He wasn't your type."

She rolled her eyes. "How would you know?"

"He called you *dude*."

A smile flickered at the corner of her lips. "He surfs. He's from California."

"Via Iowa." Jake put his water on the table, staking his place.

"Gee, Jake. If I didn't know better, I'd think you were jealous."

He didn't answer that, but just smiled. Usually, he preferred a sports bar with oversize TV screens and chicken wings by the dozen, but Ava was clearly having a good time and he was swayed by her enthusiasm. She even convinced him to join her on the dance floor and didn't complain when he stomped on her toes with his two left feet.

The kid was out there, too, in a dance sandwich with a pair of brunettes who looked as if they could be twins.

Ava followed his gaze and then tossed her hair at him. Jake couldn't help his smug grin. She tossed her hair again. "You don't have to look so pleased with yourself. You hardly had to be a psychic to know his type."

"Then why were you letting him manhandle you?" He danced, or shuffled, since that was more his speed, toward her. There was a tiny woman directly behind him who kept throwing her arms wide because she "loved this song so much," who'd already hit him in the ribs three times.

"He wasn't manhandling." A group of hooting girls piled onto the floor beside them, forcing them even closer together. "He was sitting beside me."

"He had his hand on your shoulder." Jake had to bend his head so that she could hear him over the shrieking group next to them.

"Right." She lifted an eyebrow at him. "And that's clearly a prelude to sex."

He put his hand on her shoulder.

She laughed and shrugged it off. "Aren't you the funny one."

"I can be." He put both hands on her shoulders. "So what's this a prelude to?"

Their eyes caught and held. Attraction sizzled between them. But then she shook her head, shattering the moment. "Nothing." She placed her hands on his waist and began stepping side to side in a rhythm that even Jake could tell was offbeat. "This just means that your dancing hasn't evolved beyond an elementary school level."

He chuckled and tugged her up against his side. She let her body mold to his. Jake knew they were playing with fire. He was certainly burning up inside. But before he could take that next step, the one from which there would be no turning back, raised voices on the other side of the bar caught his attention.

When he saw the first fist fly, he stepped in front of Ava, pulled her good arm around his waist and started moving for the exit. "Stay behind me," he told her as they pushed forward though the suddenly violent crowd.

Angry shouts carried above the music, and he could see the bouncers converging from all corners. He'd spent enough time in bars in his errant youth to recognize the signs of a brawl. The booth was empty when they got there, everyone else recognizing that the party was over, too. Jake snatched up their coats. "Do you have a bag?"

"No." She shook her head. The color had drained from her face.

"Let's go."

The buzz of the room had grown louder as excitement and fury warred with one another. Jake could hear the sound of flesh hitting flesh. He used one arm as a blocker, steering people out of his path, and kept the other on Ava. She'd locked both arms around his waist now. He shouldn't have noticed how good it felt.

"You okay?" he asked once they'd popped out the front door and into the cold Idaho night. He led her away from the front of the club and the people spilling out onto the sidewalk.

Her skin was still paler than normal, but she wasn't wincing or holding her casted arm. "What happened?" She was shivering, probably from a combination of the temperature and the fight.

"Stupid people who had too much to drink and decided to show off."

"Stupid *men,*" she said. "Woman don't usually throw punches."

Jake smiled. "Not usually. Though I recall someone telling me to warn the masses, because with her fancy new cast she was going to kick ass and take names."

"I never said take names. Or kick ass. But I totally could." She waved her arm around. She still didn't look tough. "Or not."

He helped her into her coat. But even once she was buttoned up, her lips continued to quiver, so he put his arm around her as they turned away from the club and headed back to the hotel. He told himself that he was just doing what any good friend would do. She was rattled from the fight and needed some support.

And, by the way, he also owned a bridge in Brooklyn that was for sale.

"You don't think Brandon was in there, do you?" They were almost back to the hotel when she asked.

Jake considered it. "I didn't see him." He was pretty sure they would have stumbled across him at some point if he'd still been around.

"Yeah." But her eyebrows were making a worried V shape. "We should call him to make sure." The wind whistled around their legs as she punched in the number. After a minute, she glanced up at him. "He's not answering."

"I'm sure he's fine. Probably holed up in a warm hotel room. I suggest we do the same." He tugged her forward, getting a move on. He tried to feel happy about the abrupt end to their evening. It had surely halted any less-than-professional impulses. And it was still early enough that he could do a bit of work on the pilot.

"Brandon?" Ava was talking into her phone now.

"Oh, God. You're not answering. I hope that's because you met someone. There was a fight at the club. This is why I don't like to go out with you. If Jake hadn't rescued me…" She glanced at him. "Anyway, call me when you get this. Or Jake. Let us know you're okay or if we have to bail you out of prison."

"He was likely gone before we even got there," Jake said when she put the phone away.

"You're probably right." She tucked her chin into her coat. Her hair bounced in the wind and brushed the back of his hand. He pretended not to notice.

When they finally reached her room, she turned to look at him. "I really wish Brandon would call back." Her mouth turned down. "You're sure he's okay?"

"Brandon can take care of himself. I'm sure he's fine." Jake told himself not to be suckered in by the sweet tilt of her lips.

"Yeah." She chewed on her lower lip. "But I'm still worried. You want to come in for a nightcap and worry with me? I don't feel like being alone right now."

How was he supposed to say no to that?

They found a movie to watch on TV and settled in to wait. Jake claimed the desk chair, while Ava sprawled on the bed. Finally, Brandon called and assured them that he was all right and didn't need them to bail him out. He'd left the club before any of the excitement started. Jake figured that was the end of the evening. "Well, I guess I'll head off." He started to push himself out of the chair.

"You might as well watch the end of the movie," Ava said. She glanced over to the hard plastic seat he'd taken. "You sure you wouldn't rather sit on the bed? That thing does not look comfortable."

It wasn't, but Jake didn't trust himself on the bed with her. "I'm good." He stood up anyway. "You can tell me how it ends tomorrow."

"Sure." Disappointment flashed in her eyes before she covered it with a friendly smile. She walked him over to the door. "See you tomorrow."

Jake battled his own flash of disappointment as the door clicked shut behind him. Then he pushed it aside and headed for his room.

Realizing he'd never turned his phone back on after dinner, Jake powered it up as he walked. It buzzed with new messages. Probably Rachel again. Did his annoying, high-energy sister never sleep?

He slipped his key into the door and scrolled through his call list. Six calls total. Two from Rachel during dinner. He gave himself a mental pat on the back for avoiding those. One from Carly when they'd been at the club, and three from Alex, all in the past hour.

A cold shiver trickled down the back of Jake's neck. He hadn't been able to get hold of Carly all week. And why would Alex be calling after midnight on a random Wednesday? He called Alex first. "What's going on?" he asked as soon as his friend picked up.

Alex was equally direct. "You talk to Carly recently?"

"No, I've been trying to reach her since Saturday, but I keep getting her voice mail." Jake tossed his wallet on the small desk in the corner of the room and hung his jacket over the back of the chair. "Why?"

"She quit."

The cold shiver intensified, sending a sharp spasm down his back. Jake sank onto the bed. "What do you mean quit?"

"She got another job. She's not doing the pilot."

"Alex, did you—"

"Of course not. She called me this evening after she couldn't reach you, said she was sorry to do this, but she had another offer."

No. Hell, no. Jake closed his eyes and squeezed the bridge of his nose. "With who? When does she start?"

"I didn't ask for the details."

"Well, you should have. We're supposed to start shooting in two weeks." Not nearly enough time to hire a new host. And without a host, there was no way they were going to be able to keep on schedule. Jake squeezed his nose harder.

"I was kind of caught off guard," Alex said. "I'll call her back. Damn. I might have sworn at her."

"No, leave it. I'll call her." His mind was already ticking on fast-forward, all thoughts of the flirtation that wasn't a flirtation with Ava gone.

If he was lucky, he might be able to convince Carly to shoot the pilot anyway. After all, it was only a single weekend of work. And then he could worry about doing another round of auditions. He hoped that the same batch who'd shown up the previous times weren't the only applicants. His stomach soured at the thought that Rachel would no doubt ask next time they spoke, and he'd have to tell her and word would get back to his father. Maybe if he worked fast he could fix the problem before then.

"We're still meeting the investors on Friday, right?"

"Yes."

"And they won't back off if we don't have a host, right?"

"As long as we don't tell them."

"Then we won't." Jake rose and sat in the small desk chair that was only slightly more comfortable than the one in Ava's room. He started scribbling notes on the hotel pad. "We won't mention it at all unless they ask. And if they do, we tell them that we have a couple of options to choose from and should they be interested in investing, they can help."

"You are good," Alex said. He paused. "You know what kills me about this?"

Jake was still making notes. Book a room for auditions, send out a casting call, go over his notes from the first set of auditions as there were sure to be some repeats. "What? That your perfect record of only backing winners might fail?"

"Hell, no. I still have every faith that our show is going to be a big hit." Jake was glad one of them was. "But I regret that I didn't sleep with her."

Jake snorted. "Like you had a chance."

"I did. She called me a few times, but I always pretended that I was busy because you told me that she was off-limits. I wonder if I could work something out before she leaves."

"You swore at her," Jake reminded him.

"That just tells her I'm passionate."

"Don't call her until I've talked to her," he warned his friend. "I might still be able to salvage this."

"And if not?"

"Then feel free to make your move."

Carly answered after one ring when he called. "Jake, hi. Have you talked to Alex? You have, I can tell. I feel terrible about this. I was really looking forward to working with you, but I just couldn't turn this down.

It's a two-year contract with a soap and if I'm good..."
She trailed off.

"It's fine, Carly," Jake assured her. What else was
he going to say? "Listen, I know you aren't available
to be the permanent host, but I'm hoping you can still
shoot the pilot for us."

"Oh?"

He needed her to say yes. If she agreed, everything
would be okay. He could figure out the next steps later
when he had time. But there was no time to get another
host for the pilot. "It's only one weekend and we've got
everything set up."

"But I'm leaving town tomorrow. I start the show
next week."

"We aren't filming for another two weeks. What's
your schedule like then?" His mind was working
quickly, running through everything he knew about
television production and trying to find a way to make
this happen. Since television tended to film Monday to
Friday, like office jobs except that they could be working day or night, the cast and crew generally had their
weekends free. "We could fly you in Friday night and
make sure you're back by Monday's call time."

"Oh, Jake." He could tell by her tone that he wasn't
going to like her answer. "I would. I totally would, but
my agent has me booked solid doing promotions and
interviews around L.A. for the entire month. I have to
be there."

"Could we work around them? Could you take even
one day off?"

"I'm really sorry, but I can't." She did sound sorry.
"Maybe I could ask a friend or see if my agent knows
someone?"

Probably someone who'd already been in to see him. Someone he'd already turned down as not having that something special he wanted for his show. He couldn't and wouldn't trust his production to just anyone. The pilot was the big pitch; if it wasn't great, he might as well not even bother.

"No, that's okay, Carly." His hope deflated as quickly as it had risen. "Don't worry about it." This wasn't her problem to solve. It was his.

He hung up and then hurled his phone across the room, where it bounced off the bed and landed on the floor. It didn't make him feel any better. Nothing was going to make him feel better.

The overwhelming fear that he was going to fail again filled him. He beat it back. Rachel told him that he hadn't failed, that things not working out the way he'd hoped was just life. But that was easy for her to say. Her life had pretty much gone according to plan.

She hadn't dealt with snarky whispers about getting her job because of who her father was. He doubted any of Rachel's professorial peers had even seen any of their dad's productions. She hadn't had to work longer and harder than her colleagues to get only half the recognition. And she'd never had to wonder that maybe they were right.

To hell with that. He shook off the old questions about his success being based on name and not merit. He hadn't moved all this way just to let those demons get the better of him. They were wrong. He was going to prove that once and for all.

Just as soon as he found a new host for his show.

Chapter 11

"Wait, you want me to host this pilot?" Ava stared at Jake.

He nodded and reached across the scarred pine table for her hand. "I wouldn't ask, but I'm desperate."

The excitement that had flowed through her body at his words eased considerably. She tugged her hand free. "Gee, don't flatter me or anything."

"Ava." He reached out and caught her hand again, squeezed lightly. "I meant that you'd be saving my ass. And for the record, I wouldn't ask if I didn't think you'd be great."

"That's a little better." She looked up from their joined hands. Was it wrong that she was enjoying his touch as much as his request? "Wouldn't hurt if you wanted to go on for a while about how great I am, though."

A small smile began to curl his lips. "Does this mean you'll do it?"

"Maybe." Her heart was beating a little too fast, the thump in her ears drowning out his voice. She pulled her hand free and let it drop to her lap before he could capture it again.

"*Maybe* doesn't sound like *yes*."

"I haven't said no, either. Tell me more about it."

When Jake had shown up at her room this morning and informed her that he'd changed their flights home, she'd been surprised. It wasn't standard procedure to extend an assignment unless there was a world-altering story driving it. But when she'd asked, he'd simply said that he wanted to talk to her about something and he didn't want the pressures of home to intrude.

He'd taken her to a restaurant on the side of a mountain, one that required a sleigh to get to. His thigh had pressed against hers the entire way. And when they'd finally arrived at the adorable log cabin, he'd kept his hand on her back until they were seated. She wondered now if those had just been ploys to butter her up.

Jake leaned forward. "I'm not asking you to do it free."

"Okay." Ava didn't care about the money. It wouldn't be enough to pay off her mortgage or change her life in any drastic way, but she didn't say that. It was nice to know that he was prepared to offer her fair compensation.

"It would mean a lot to me."

She thought about it. "How long will it take? A week? Two?" He'd only said they were filming a pilot, not whether it was broken up into a long shoot around their normal work hours or a quick one jammed into a few short days.

"Just one weekend."

"Filming both days? Morning through night?"

"Filming both days. Afternoon and evening the first day, morning and afternoon the second."

"When?"

"Two weeks from now. Saturday and Sunday." His eyes twinkled as he relaxed. "This is starting to sound like a yes."

She picked up her water glass and sipped. Jake had explained that his original host had quit and that he didn't have time to audition another host before filming. But that didn't explain why he'd settled on her. She wasn't the only choice in town. She wasn't even the only choice at the station. "What about Tommy?"

"What about Tommy?" Jake sat back, his surprise evident.

"Did you consider him?" Because if he had—if she was second choice again—then she didn't owe him anything.

"No." His hand snaked out across the table, peeling her hand off the glass before she could react. "I didn't." He tightened his grip when she would have pulled free.

"What about Danica?"

He looked surprised. "No. You're the only person I've asked. The only person I trust with this."

That helped.

"I didn't know the promotion was still bothering you." He let his fingers go slack, allowing her to remove her hand if she wanted to. She didn't. "I'll understand if you say no."

"I didn't say no and it's not still bothering me." Okay, it was, but only a little. "I understand your reasons. It was just disappointing. I'd worked really hard and I felt I'd earned it."

"I know." His thumb kneaded her palm. "If it helps, you earned this."

Ava looked away, afraid that if she didn't she'd agree without even considering the ramifications. Except, as she gazed around the restaurant, taking in the large floor-to-ceiling fireplace, the small stage and dance area, where a band played country tunes and locals two-stepped to their hearts' content, she couldn't think of any.

Beneath the music, there was the clang of pots and pans from the kitchen. The scent of roast beef filled the air. The rubbing motion of Jake's hand against hers soothed her remaining hurt feelings. She turned back to him. "Okay, this is an official yes."

His smile spread across his face. He leaned forward, tugged on her hand, so she had to move as well or be bisected by the table, and kissed her. "Thank you."

Her heart thumped wildly, but she managed a semi-professional smile as she settled back in her seat. "You're welcome."

She took another sip of her water and told her nerves to calm down. It was just a friendly kiss, the kind she'd planted on plenty of people in her life. It didn't mean anything more and she resolved not to think about it further.

They celebrated their agreement with dessert. This time, Ava didn't have to tell him he was helping her eat it. When she pointed out that it seemed he was capable of being trained, he laughed.

"I'm a dog?"

She swirled a forkful of apple pie through the melting ice cream. "I believe I have heard men referred to that way once or twice."

"I hope not by you."

"Hope away." She popped the pie into her mouth.

He gave her that crooked grin of his, the one that made her forget she wasn't supposed to be thinking about kissing him. She stuffed in another bite.

When they'd finally finished their meal and made their way outside, they were the only ones there. Most of the customers had left earlier and those that were still hanging around were busy kicking up their heels on the dance floor. That, or they were waiting for the sleigh indoors where it wasn't freezing.

Ava tucked her hands into her pockets. They probably had about ten minutes before the sleigh would arrive to take them back down the mountain. She didn't mind the wait. The fireplace in the lodge had been kicking out enough heat for an entire country, and the winter air felt good on her face.

Jake was standing close to her, really close. She shivered.

"Cold?" He reached out to slip an arm around her. She shifted away.

"I'm fine." Or would be as soon as her heart returned to its normal rhythm.

They waited in silence. The occasional hoot of an owl and whisper of pine needles as the wind gusted through their branches were the only sounds until his phone rang. That annoying old-fashioned rotary phone ringtone. The one that had been cute when it first came out, but was now just annoying. "You need to change that ringtone," she told him.

"What's wrong with it?"

"It's impersonal. And, to be honest, a little lame."

"I'm lame?"

"Your ringtone is." She had a few good ideas of how

to fix it, too. Never let it be said that Ava Christensen identified problems without having a ready solution.

He smiled and pulled out the phone to check the display, but shoved it back into his pocket without answering.

"You're not going to answer it?" Wild curiosity had her wanting to know who it was and why Jake would ignore it.

"No."

"Why?"

"Because it isn't important."

"Why? Who is it?" He took the phone out again to show her the screen. "Rachel?"

"My sister," he clarified before she had a chance to assume that Rachel was a girlfriend or wife or something worse. Though she didn't know what could be worse. And that clarification brought her much more joy than it should have. Had she already forgotten that they were friends, colleagues and no more?

She was spending far too much time thinking about this little flirtation they had going and not enough thinking about the job. She should be thrilled by Jake's proposal. The chance to host a pilot that had potential to be so much more. Instead, she was looking at him with what she feared were moony calf eyes and wondering if he might be tempted to kiss her. She held out her hand. "Your phone, please."

He frowned. "Why?"

"I need to fix that ringtone."

"Because it's lame." He placed it in her palm.

She ignored the sizzle of connection when his gloved hand bumped against hers. Seriously, it wasn't even skin-on-skin contact and she was weak in the knees.

How sad was that? "It lumps you in with all those people who think it's the awesomest ringtone ever and show it off by never answering on the first ring."

"I always answer on the first ring."

She tucked the phone into her pocket. "You can do better." She had a few ideas already percolating, but she needed to think about it.

"Wait." He frowned. Was it wrong for her to notice how cute he looked doing it? "You're not changing it now?"

"A good ringtone requires thinking time. It can't be rushed."

"No deal." He put out his hand. "Decide on the ringtone and then you get the phone."

She sidestepped him. "I have to see which carrier you're with to see what's available." And if the address book should happen to open and if she should happen to read the names and research those of the female persuasion, well, he didn't need to know that. "I'll give it back tomorrow."

"So I won't have my phone all night?" He shook his head. "Forget it"

"What? You're so important that you need your phone every second? Do you have another career as a surgeon that I don't know about?"

"Ava." There was a warning note in his voice, but it still made her shivery.

"Having a night away from your phone isn't going to kill you."

He thought about it. "Fine. But only if you give me yours."

"No." He would see her email and texts, all those

discussions with Jilly about her feelings and what was or wasn't going on. "No way."

"Why not? It's only fair."

"Because I need my phone. I have a blog to update."

"You update using your computer," Jake reminded her.

He had a point. "Still, the answer is no."

"Then I guess you'll be giving mine back." He reached for it again.

"Wrong." She jerked back out of his hold and when he advanced on her, turned and ran.

She heard his grunt of surprise before his footsteps pounded after her. "Ava, come on."

"I'm doing you a favor," she called over her shoulder. "Saving you from being part of the bad-ringtone club. You should thank me." Her boots crunched through the formerly untouched snow. She could hear him behind her. Probably gaining ground with every step. She stepped up her pace.

The trees spread out before her, creating a clear path that she ran through. The snow was deeper here, and it was harder to get through, but she did her best. She could hear him getting closer, but then he wasn't wearing heeled boots and running with a broken wrist. She thought she was doing pretty well, all things considered.

When she realized she couldn't hear him anymore, she eased her pace slightly. Was it because the blood was pounding too loudly in her ears to hear anything or had he actually given up? She hoped it wasn't the latter. What would be the fun in leading him on a merry chase if he didn't play along?

She slowed a little more, just enough so that she could turn and peek without accidentally slamming into a tree. Before she'd even had a chance to try, his arms snaked around her waist and lifted her off the ground. She gasped. "Jake, don't you dare drop me."

He was laughing in her ear, his breath brushing her skin. "I won't drop you." When he loosened his hold, it was just enough to let her slide down the length of his body. "I would never let you get hurt."

A shiver raced through her. "You better not." Her boots touched the ground, but Jake didn't let go. Ava started to wonder what game they were really playing. Nerves reared up. "Jake, I—"

"Shh." He spun her so they were facing each other and placed a finger against her mouth. "I have something for you."

Ava didn't need to be a romantic-movie expert, even though she was, to know what was coming next. Her breath caught. She knew she'd told Jilly that one more kiss would cure her of this attraction, but the one at the restaurant had only intensified it.

He moved closer, curving his body around her like a shield, and she swore that if he didn't kiss her, she was going to die. Shrivel up into a pile of cold, untouched snow and blow away.

So when he lowered her to the ground, she went along with it. It was just like the last scene in *Serendipity* when John Cusack and Kate Beckinsale finally reunite after all those years apart. Okay, so there was no chance meeting in a department store or a lost phone number. No leading separate lives and getting engaged to other people. No reconnecting just as they were about to walk down the aisle with the wrong people. But otherwise, it was totally the same.

And while John Cusack was no Rob Lowe and wasn't

considered an official member of the Brat Pack, he was pretty close, and she'd avidly followed his career through the years.

"Close your eyes," Jake said.

Ava did and felt something cold pass across her lips. Confusion cooled some of her internal fire. "Jake?" She opened her eyes.

He was still hovering above her, but there was a very large snowball in his hand. One held only inches from her face and dripping. He grinned. "I suggest a trade. You hand over the phone and I'll drop the snow."

"No." She tried to scrabble back.

But he had her trapped. He caught her around the waist with one arm and held her firmly. "Yes. Hand it over."

"Never." She turned her head to the side, but he anticipated the move.

"Last chance."

She could feel the cold radiating from the snow to her skin. Another drip fell onto her cheek. She bet Kate Beckinsale never had to deal with anything like this. "You wouldn't."

"I would."

Which meant there was only one thing she could do.

She clutched a handful of snow with her good arm and threw it at him. He shook off the light dusting and rubbed his handful into her face. Then they were both laughing, shoving snow at each other and rolling around on the ground.

Ava was pretty pleased when she managed to jam a chunk down the back of his neck, less pleased when he got her back. But she was laughing so hard she couldn't catch her breath.

"Truce?" Jake asked.

She nodded. What was she going to say—"Actually, no. I'd prefer another face wash"? She let him help her to her feet.

"Are you giving me back my phone now?"

"I'm cold," she answered instead and brushed the snow off her jeans. It was cold standing, more so when the wind blew through the trees. "Make that freezing. My jeans are all wet, thanks to you."

"You started it."

"I know. And it's not very gentlemanly of you to remind me of that. Just for that, you are definitely not getting your phone back tonight."

They made their way back to the front of the restaurant. They were still the only ones waiting in the small alcove.

This time when he made a move to put his arm around her, she let him. She was too chilled to worry about professionalism and propriety. Plus, there was no one around to see them.

And when he put a finger under her chin and tilted it toward him, she didn't stop him. She didn't even put up any resistance when he bent his head and covered her lips with his. She could tell herself that she was just trying to chase away the need so that they could move forward into friendship, but it would be a lie.

So she let him kiss her until she was breathless, until her hands were twisted in his coat as she tried to get closer and the snow around them threatened to steam. Maybe what happened in Idaho could stay in Idaho?

Chapter 12

Jake drummed his fingers on his desk and tried to focus on work. He and Ava had arrived back in Vancouver yesterday afternoon and he hadn't stopped moving since. He'd managed to explain their extra day away by telling everyone that Ava's wrist had started bothering her and they'd decided to have it looked at by the doctor immediately instead of waiting until they got home.

The fact that everyone, even Harvey, had bought the lie without question made him feel guilty. He didn't like people who traded on their personal relationships to further their own ambitions, and he didn't like being one of them. But it had been an emergency. If Ava hadn't agreed to host the pilot, he might have lost his permits, and the money already spent would have been wasted.

But his solution had created its own set of problems. Although he hadn't slept with Ava, he was pretty sure things were heading that way.

The only reason they hadn't yet was because he didn't want their first night together to be one where she was shivering so hard that her lips turned blue. He'd dropped her off safely in her hotel room and returned to his own, where he'd stood under the shower, running the water so hot that it left his skin the color of boiled lobster. But even that hadn't eased the itching beneath it.

Though he told himself that he should have been grateful that cooler heads—or in their case, icy jeans—had prevailed, he was annoyed. Whatever was going on between him and Ava wasn't going away. That kiss in the snow had proved it.

He intended to find out what they were going to do about it tonight.

Last night, he and Alex had met with the investors. The dinner meeting had gone well. Well enough that he thought the money would soon be rolling into his account. But until that was official, he had work to do here, and there was a lot of it.

He spent an hour weeding through the mess that losing a producer had left him with. He hadn't yet decided if he should hire someone or let Hanna do that, but was leaning toward narrowing down the field with a couple of rounds of interviews and stopping there. He made a mental note to ask Harvey if he'd contacted Hanna yet.

He also had to book some space to run auditions for the travel-show host. It was great that Ava could fill in so he could get the pilot finished, but it wasn't a long-term solution. He'd lived the disaster that came from mixing personal and professional lives already, and wasn't willing to risk it again.

After making a note to look through his files for the number of the audition space they'd used last time,

Jake picked up his cell. He was the proud owner of a new ringtone featuring the chorus of Loverboy's "Everybody's Working for the Weekend," and though he still didn't think his old-fashioned ring had been lame, he could admit that Ava's choice was better.

He scrolled through the numbers until he found the one marked PITA and hit Talk. Two rings later, his little sister answered.

"To what do I owe this pleasure?"

Jake grinned. "Just good luck. That or you must have earned some good karma in another life since you've spent the majority of this one tormenting me."

There was a brief pause. "Oh, my, oh, my, my, my."

"What?"

"This is the first time in a month that you haven't snarled at me. Not only that, you actually made a joke. I feel like I should call the press."

"Hilarious. Listen, I just called to let you know that I talked to Mom last night, so you can stop accusing me of being a bad son." A bad son would never have spent the time talking to his mother when he could have been devising a way to get a late-night invitation to Ava's place after his meeting.

"I know. How was the Skype chat anyway?"

"Yeah, about that. Thanks for telling her that if she had Skype I wouldn't always be rushing to get off the phone."

"I do what I can. Did she actually get the camera to work or did you just look at a black screen the whole time?

"She got it working, but I wouldn't say it was a success. The camera got stuck when she tried to adjust it, so I spent most of the conversation looking at her forehead."

Rachel laughed. "Why didn't you tell her?"

"I was afraid she'd adjust it again and miss the other way."

"You didn't want to spend the call looking at your mother's breasts?"

Jake flinched. "Stop talking. Now. Seriously."

"Why?" He could picture the evil smile on his sister's face. "Those breasts nourished you as a baby."

"Stop it. You're sick. Sick." He wiped a hand across his forehead. "What is wrong with you?"

She was laughing too hard to answer. Jake didn't think it was a laughing matter. She was ruining breasts for him. And Skype.

"All right, I just called to let you know I talked to Mom. I'm hanging up now."

"No." The giggling finally ceased. "You aren't getting off this phone before telling me about the meeting."

Jake hadn't planned on telling anyone else in the family exactly when the investor meeting was scheduled, hoping to keep the details to himself until he had the deal all sewn up. But he knew he could trust Rachel. She was the only one in Toronto who hadn't told him he was crazy to give up everything he had there to try starting over here. "It was fine."

"Fine? How fine? Are they putting up the money?"

"I hope so." Jake kept his voice neutral. He didn't want to give Rachel any reason to go blabbing to their parents before the contract was signed.

While a secret part of him had hoped the dinner would close the deal, that the investors would feel reassured that he wouldn't waste their money on a project that looked as if it had been shot by someone's phone, he was practical. They'd need to look at the proposal more closely and work out exactly how much they were willing to put up before moving forward.

He just hoped it didn't take too long. While they hadn't shown any of their own money, they'd eaten and drunk enough to just about wipe out Jake's personal account.

"It was promising," he told her. Some people liked to sleep on a big decision. He understood.

And it wasn't as if he needed their money to survive. He had other investments that his father had made in his name before he was old enough to know what investments were. Rachel did, too, but unlike her, Jake had never touched his, preferring to make his own way. And he made a good wage working at the station.

He'd briefly considered using that money to back the show if these investors didn't pan out, but decided against it. Maybe he'd have felt differently if he hadn't followed in his father's footsteps. Even at the start of his career, when he hadn't minded being known as Chuck Durham's son, there had been a stubborn part of him that didn't want anyone saying he'd made it because of his father's money. So it sat in an account back in Toronto, untouched and unused.

"Rob and I had breakfast with Mom and Dad this morning." She paused and Jake felt his shoulders tense. "I might have made a tiny mention of your meeting."

"Rachel. I told you that in confidence. You promised you wouldn't say anything."

"I know, I know. It slipped out. I was excited for you. I didn't mean to go behind your back and I'm sorry."

"Great. So what did he say and how soon can I expect a call from him?"

"I made Dad promise not to call, so you're welcome."

"Yeah, thanks for blabbing and causing the issue in the first place."

"Caught that part, did you? Anyway, that isn't why I'm bringing it up. Dad mentioned that you should be careful with these investors. He said they've had meetings with other people, as well."

"Oh?" Jake tried to swallow the disappointment that rose on his tongue. It tasted like old coffee.

"Yeah, a month ago. Dad said those meetings didn't go anywhere. That these guys just enjoyed a lot of food and drink and moved on. He's worried about you."

"There's nothing to worry about." He could handle this. He ignored the stone that settled in his stomach. "Maybe they just haven't found the right project." Investors didn't jump on every project that caught their notice. They wouldn't have much money for long if that were the case. "Don't you think it's possible that they just hadn't found the right fit before?"

"Yes, but Dad was pretty insistent. He thinks they're just making the rounds with no intention of ever putting money forward. He doesn't want to see you waste your time and cash on them."

"Dad doesn't know everything." He was just used to being surrounded by people who thought he did. Jake sighed. He shouldn't be taking his frustration out on his sister. "Look, it's possible and I appreciate you bringing it to my attention, but it was one dinner meeting and everything went very well. Hopefully, they'll call in a few days to work out a deal."

"I hope so. I just wanted to tell you. I would never

forgive myself if something were to happen and I'd kept the information to myself."

Jake knew her heart, as always, was in the right place. Didn't make him feel any better. "I'm sure it's fine, Rache. You told me about it, so now you can rest easy, okay?"

He acted as if he wasn't concerned, but the truth was, it bothered him. These had been the only investors he'd heard from that he could be assured weren't trying to curry favor with his father. Everyone else was an old friend, a former colleague or tied to his father or his father's company in some way. And how could he prove that he was capable of doing this on his own with all those strings attached?

Jake finally got the chance to talk to Ava later that afternoon. He caught her in her office when she got back from her shoot and asked if she'd have dinner with him tonight. She'd agreed with a quick smile that had him forgetting about everything else.

He'd made reservations for eight o'clock at a restaurant renowned for its local fare. Everything on the menu featured regional, seasonal ingredients. Even the wine and beer were local. He'd spoken with the owners a few weeks ago about filming a clip there for his travel show, but hadn't yet had the chance to test it out firsthand. Seemed fitting now to do so with Ava.

She looked great. Her hair bounced around her face and her lips looked sweet and fresh. When he'd arrived at her apartment to pick her up, he hadn't been able to resist leaning forward for a taste of them and was pleased when, rather than pulling back to remind him that they needed to be professional or complain that he was going to ruin her gloss, she'd pressed forward to meet him.

"You look amazing." She was wearing a silky black dress that fluttered and dipped in secret movements that tantalized with hints of skin. But no matter how quickly he looked, he never saw anything more than a brief glimpse before the material settled back into place. He wanted to rip the dress off her. With his teeth.

He contained himself. Barely.

They were seated at a table with a view of the city, the mountains rising behind it, hulking shadows to the city's twinkling lights. But Jake only had eyes for Ava. "So."

"So," she repeated.

He wanted to pull her across the table into his lap and kiss her until she told him to take her to bed or lose her forever. "We still pretending that kiss never happened?"

A pretty flush rose to her cheeks. "Is that what you want?"

He leveled her with a stare. "What do you think?" All she had to do was look at the way his body was straining toward her to know the answer.

"I think you're avoiding the question."

They were interrupted by the waiter returning with the bottle of sparkling water they'd ordered. The man poured them each a glass.

Jake waited until he'd stepped away to answer Ava's challenge. "No, that's not what I want." The pink in her cheeks deepened, but she didn't say anything. He waited. She sipped her water. "And?" he finally prompted.

"And what?"

He reached across the table, plucked the glass out

of her fingers and set it to the side of the table. "What do you want?"

"My water."

He moved it farther out of reach. "Wrong answer."

"Jake."

"Ava." He studied her. It was obvious to him that they both wanted the same thing. "In case you're wondering, the correct answer is me."

She laughed, a bright warble that lightened his spirits.

He smiled back as the tension in his shoulders eased. "Great. So we're clear." He pushed her glass back to her.

She took a small sip. "Is that what you want?"

"I'm not against it." He saw the disappointment flash in her eyes and pushed his own glass to the side so he could lean closer to her. "Yes, that's what I want. This— whatever is happening here—isn't going away." He gave her a chance to take that in. "And I don't want it to."

Her smile was slow, sexy. "Me, neither."

Jake had to take a deep breath before he really did haul her onto his lap and see exactly how that dress tasted.

"But."

He looked at her, his mouth suddenly dry.

"But we still work together."

He smiled, reaching out to wrap his fingers around hers. "You know my contract is up in six weeks. I'm not signing an extension, so we won't be colleagues any longer."

She nodded, but didn't say anything.

"Don't tell me you're going to insist on keeping things platonic until then." He could not be held responsible for what happened afterward if she tried to insist upon that.

"No." She untangled their fingers and reached for her glass again. "But that doesn't mean I'm going to jump into bed with you right away, either." She studied him over the rim and then took a sip. "We still work together, and I'd prefer we keep things quiet at the office. I've worked really hard to get where I am. I don't want people to think I'm sleeping my way into a job."

He could respect that. "Done. We keep it quiet at the office."

Her insistence on keeping their career separate from their personal relationship struck a chord in him. She was here because she liked him. Just him. He put his hand out, palm up, waiting for her.

"And there's no one else."

Jake almost laughed that she thought he had time for anyone else, but the look on her face was so solemn that he knew she wouldn't find the idea humorous. "Definitely not."

"Then I guess we're clear," she said. She moved her hand toward his and then stopped. "Unless there's something else?"

"No." He reached up to capture her fingers again. There was nothing else. No one else.

Jake smiled and brought her palm to his lips. "I think I've got everything I want." Or pretty darn close.

Chapter 13

Ava picked Jilly up in a cab before heading over to her mother's house for their biweekly Sunday dinner. Jilly often joined them, and today Ava found herself looking forward to the dinner more than usual, if only because it would give her a break from thinking about Jake and appropriate office behavior for a few hours.

The light blue siding and white shutters of the house her mother had bought when Ava was ten looked cheerful even against the frozen grass and bare trees. It would only be a couple of months before they would both burst to life. The grass would become lush and green, the branches growing thick and heavy with the delicate pink of cherry blossoms. And the house would look pretty as a picture. Just like her mother standing in the doorway in a pale blue dress shirt and linen trousers that looked neat and stylish.

"Hi, Mom." Ava hugged her mother in greeting,

inhaling the scent of Joie. It was her mother's signature scent and always made her feel better. Tension she hadn't known she'd been carrying rolled out of her shoulders. "How are you?"

"I'm fine, dear." Her mother hugged back briefly and then let go. "You look tired." She peered into Ava's face and reached up to smooth away a line between Ava's eyes. "Don't do that, you'll get wrinkles. Not good for your career."

"I don't see why," Ava said, even as she relaxed the muscles in her forehead. She began to shrug out of her coat. "Why is it that men are allowed to get wrinkled and become distinguished-looking, but women are supposed to look twenty forever?"

"If I knew that, dear, I'd be running the world instead of just the hospital." Her mother turned to greet Jilly. "Nice to see you, Jillian. How have you been?"

"Great. How are you, Barbara? You look well."

It was true, Ava thought. Her mother had always been an attractive woman, petite and blonde with the wide blue eyes that Ava had inherited. Her hair was cut into a smooth bob that was never out of place and she wore perfectly tailored clothing that showed off the slender figure she'd maintained since she was a teenager. But there was a glow about her today. New face-cleaning regimen?

"Thank you, Jillian. I am well. I like your hair."

Ava smiled. Her mother would have a coronary if she ever dyed her hair pink, but Jilly was appraised by a different set of standards. It was fine with Ava, since she never intended to dye her hair pink. She didn't think she could pull off cotton-candy anything. Not even lipstick.

Ava hung up their coats and then joined her mom

and friend in the formal living room. It was furnished with long, overstuffed couches and a pair of high-backed chairs. Despite the cool colors of platinum and ice-blue, the room felt comfortable with her mother's homey touches. The silver frames on the walls displayed black-and-white photos of Ava growing up, the white fireplace mantel held fat, flickering candles and the pale gray rug was so cushiony and soft that Ava couldn't resist curling her toes into it.

They reconvened there after dinner. It had been a lovely evening. General chitchat about what was happening in the world—her mother was a bit of a news junkie—and an update on her uncle Dennis and aunt Yolanda, who lived in Calgary and were coming for a visit in the summer. They'd lived nearby until Ava was seventeen, her mother's brother filling in as a surrogate father since her own had died before she was born, and she was looking forward to seeing them. They hadn't made it out for Christmas this year and Ava had missed them.

She sank back into the couch. This was exactly what she'd needed after a stressful couple of weeks. No drama, no tension and no discussion of work.

"Ava." Her mother turned to her with an assessing gaze. "How's work?"

She tried not to sigh. "It's fine, Mom." Maybe if she didn't create an opening, her mother would let the subject drop.

"And what is going on with this new producer of yours—Jake?"

Or not.

"You seemed very friendly when I called last week."

Ava, in the midst of sipping her water, choked. She

covered her mouth, coughing. "Went down the wrong way," she said in response to the questioning looks turned her way.

Her mother frowned when she coughed again. "Are you all right?"

"Fine." Ava sucked in a few breaths and a few more sips of water.

"Don't drink so fast, Ava. It isn't ladylike, and it's probably why you choked."

She could see Jilly pressing her lips together so she wouldn't laugh. Some friend. "I wasn't drinking it fast. You just surprised me." Right. It had absolutely nothing to do with the fact that the mere mention of Jake made naughty fantasies fill her head. Nothing at all. "I'm probably tired." She forced her eyes to remain on her mother's, but felt her fingers tightening around the glass.

Barbara studied her and then nodded, accepting the answer. "Is it your arm? Have you not been sleeping well?"

"My wrist is fine. But the festival was busy and I'm still recovering."

"Things went well?" She waited until Ava nodded. "Did you make that list like I told you?"

"Yes, Mom," Ava lied because it was easier. "And you were right—" her mother loved to hear she was right "—it helped a lot."

"That is wonderful." Her mother's smile could have charmed Simon Cowell. "You see? When you put your mind to it and make a plan, things have a way of working out."

Ava merely nodded. Her mother would not be impressed to hear that she was letting things flow without a plan. But Barbara refused to acknowledge that Ava's life had taken a turn for the better once she'd stopped creating lists to control it. The job at the station had fallen into her lap, she'd met a nice guy and dated him for a couple of years—although it hadn't worked out, they had parted amicably—and she'd been happier. So much happier.

"How is work, Mom?" Since Barbara loved to talk about her work, the subject change was a success. Ava smiled into her glass as Jilly made a wiping motion over her brow. Phew, indeed.

Her mother told them about some new policies that had recently been implemented at the hospital and that her longtime assistant was retiring. "I'm sad to lose him. He knew the value of a job well done. Do either of you know anyone who might be a good fit?"

"Someone who wants to work twelve-hour days?" Ava joked. "No."

Her mother pinned her with a look. "Roger worked eight hours a day as scheduled. Occasionally, he was expected to take notes at evening board meetings, but that duty was shared with the other office assistants and that time was always counted as part of his forty-hour workweek."

"I know, Mom. I was only teasing." It was her mother who put in the sixty-hour weeks. Had as long as Ava could remember. In the beginning, Barbara hadn't had much choice—not if she wanted to get to the top of her profession—but she'd reached that pinnacle years ago and she still worked those hours. Ava had watched as any sort of social life slipped away and eventually determined that her mother just wasn't interested in one.

It wasn't the kind of life she wanted for herself.

"You should take your job more seriously, Ava. I know you enjoy making fun of me, but you could learn a thing or two. I was one of the first female administrators hired by the hospital and I worked very hard to earn my position."

"I wasn't making fun of you," Ava insisted, "and I know you work hard. But you don't always seem to enjoy it." Sometimes, it looked like a never-ending battle to stay on top or climb the next rung of the corporate ladder. And Ava was expected to do the same.

"I enjoy my work."

Jilly cleared her throat, breaking the stare down between mother and daughter. "I might know someone. I'll ask and get back to you."

"Thank you, Jillian. That would be very much appreciated since my daughter thinks that I'm impossible to work for."

"I don't think you're impossible to work for," Ava said. It was just that her mother was so stuck in her belief that the only way to be successful was the Barbara Christensen way that she ignored other valid viewpoints. It was a discussion they'd had many times. "I think your work/life balance is out of whack. For example, when was the last time you went on a date?"

Her mother's cheeks turned pink. "I could ask the same of you."

There was no way she was telling her mother it had been just two days ago and that it had been with her only-for-another-six-weeks boss. Barbara wouldn't understand. "Fine. We'll drop it."

By nine o'clock, Jilly had excused herself to meet her latest suitor for a drink, but Ava remained at her mother's, enjoying the company now that they weren't talking about work or dating or Jake.

They shifted into the family room off the kitchen. It was smaller and less formal than the living room and was where the two of them usually sat when they were alone.

When she'd been a teenager, Ava used to lounge on the soft suede couch and do her homework with a movie playing in the background for company. When her mother got home, they'd watch television and chat, occasionally even eat dinner there when her mother was too exhausted to argue that dinner should be eaten at a dining table. It was the room that, to Ava, felt the most like home.

She settled into the cushions and sighed. She could hear the familiar sounds of her mother making tea. The clink of her grandmother's white china pot as Barbara pulled it from the upper cabinet. The tink of the metal spoon against the mesh strainer as she put the loose leaves into it. The rattle of the china cups being added to the same tray as the teapot. And the whistle of the kettle when the water boiled.

"Here we are." Her mother carried in the mahogany tray and placed it on the long coffee table that was only a shade or two darker than the tray. There were ginger-bread cookies on a small plate along with a creamer and the sugar bowl.

Ava sat up and inhaled. The scent of Earl Grey filled her senses. "Smells great. Thanks, Mom."

"My pleasure."

Barbara sat in the high-backed, pastel blue velvet chair she always chose. It was oversize, making her look even smaller, but somehow it suited her. She'd had it recovered twice over the years, always in the same material and color. Though she'd never do so in company, Ava knew her mother liked to kick off her shoes and curl her feet beneath her when she read a book or watched television. Ava could remember finding her like that when she'd been little, and they and the chair had been crammed into a much smaller apartment, usually with a textbook in her lap and her glasses sliding down her nose.

They each doctored their tea according to preference. Ava added a splash of cream, while Barbara was content with a single lump of sugar. Her mother sipped once and then looked at her. "You're going to see Dr. Merion tomorrow?"

"At eleven," Ava confirmed. Dr. Merion had been her personal physician for the past ten years and worked at the same hospital as her mother.

"Good. I'm sure that the hospital in Idaho did a fine job, but I'll feel better knowing that Marcia has looked at it." Dr. Marcia Merion and Barbara were friends as well as colleagues, though Ava didn't think their personal relationship extended past eating lunch together. "Have you met with the physiotherapist I recommended yet?"

Ava shook her head. "I can worry about that later." Along with the black hair that was probably already sprouting beneath the cast. Sometimes Google was not her friend.

"We'll see what Marcia says."

Ava had no doubt that Barbara would mention it to Marcia before her appointment tomorrow.

Barbara sipped her tea and set the cup back into the saucer with only the tiniest of rattles. "We got off the topic of the festival earlier." Yes, because Ava had changed the subject. "But I'd like to hear about it. You and Jake seemed to be getting along. What were you able to check off the list we made?"

Since Ava was pretty sure that the truth wouldn't make her very popular, she blew on her tea and thought fast. "You know, I'm not sure I can remember everything without the list in front of me." She should have listened more closely when her mother had been jabbering at her about it on the phone.

"Were you able to talk about your future at the station with Jake?"

Ava blew on the tea again. "No, we were swamped running to events and getting the stories cut for the station."

She briefly contemplated telling her mother about Jake's pilot, but in the end chose not to. While mentioning it would definitely please her mother and get her off the lecture of career advancement, it had huge potential to backfire. Barbara would want to know everything, would demand details and would ask about it every time she saw or spoke with Ava. Barbara's examination of the facts would last long past this evening.

No, it was better for Ava to keep her mouth closed on the subject for now. She would wait until the pilot had sold.

"What did you check off the list, then?"

"Well…" Ava fumbled, trying to think of something that was likely to fit her mother's idea of an appropriate and achievable goal.

"Ava?" Her mother had put down her tea while Ava had been thinking. "Did you use the list at all?"

"Not exactly." The disappointed look on her mother's

face was worse than the annoyed one she'd expected. "Mom, we've discussed this before. I don't like making lists and planning out every detail."

Although, if she had, she would never have ended up alone on an icy street in Rockdale. But then, she and Jake wouldn't have connected, either, so the trade-off seemed fair.

Barbara shook her head, her perfect blond hair swinging back and forth before settling back into its original style. "You do know this cavalier attitude won't take you to the next level in your career."

The tea burned Ava's tongue and she put the cup and saucer down. "Do we have to talk about this right now?"

"Yes." Barbara looked at her pointedly. "If you plan ahead and position yourself properly, you get promoted. I think we should make a list for you now."

"No." Ava waved her cast. "We're having tea and relaxing. We're not making any lists."

"I don't understand why you're so resistant to this idea. You were happy to make lists when you were younger."

"I was never happy to make them," Ava pointed out.

"Regardless, you can't deny their usefulness. I started making them just after your father died."

Ava had once tried to point out that perhaps this need for lists was a way for Barbara to control her life, but her mother had refused to consider that as even the remotest possibility.

"I would never have gotten through university with a young child without them, and I certainly wouldn't have found any success in my career if I had just let things happen." Barbara looked at her sharply.

Ava felt like one of those worms that the neighborhood kids were eyeballing just before the first incision. "I'm happy, Mom. Doesn't that count for anything?"

"Of course it does. I want you to be happy. But how happy are you going to be if the station decides to downsize and you're laid off because you didn't make sure they recognized your worth?"

"That isn't going to—"

"You have to rely on yourself, dear. It was a lesson I had to learn at a young age with a small child. I don't want you to end up in the same position."

"I'm not going to, Mom." For one, she already had her education and a good job. Two things her mother hadn't had when she'd needed them.

"You don't know that. Things happen, Ava. I never expected to end up a single mom. I just think—" The sound of Beethoven's *Ode to Joy* swelled through the room.

Ava blinked. "What is that?"

"My phone. Excuse me." Her mother was already moving to the small green dish in the kitchen where she kept her keys and phone. "Hello?" Ava watched her smile, say something low into the phone. When Barbara looked up and noticed Ava watching her, she blushed and moved into the living room, out of eavesdropping range.

Odd.

Ava thought about getting up and pretending to get something from the fridge so she could hear, but decided against it. It was probably just a call from work. She didn't think anyone else called her mother. And the relief at getting off the hook about the list making made her unwilling to do anything that would incur her mother's irritation.

She bit into her second cookie and wondered if she could get away with sneaking out if she told her mother it was on a list. Probably not.

"I apologize for the interruption," Barbara said when she returned a few minutes later.

"No problem. When did you change your ringtone?" Better to introduce a new subject in the hopes that her mother would forget about the previous one.

"My what?" Barbara sank back into the chair looking young and graceful. Whoever it was obviously hadn't called with a crisis.

"Your ringtone. It's playing classical music now. I didn't set that up." What was wrong with the Black Eyed Peas?

"I am capable of learning to change the phone's settings, dear."

Ava laughed. "Since when? The only time it changes is when I do it."

"Well, it's changed now and without your help." Barbara was holding her tea, but not drinking it.

"I'm impressed. So who was it?"

"Just a friend." Her mother made an airy motion with her hand and went back to holding her cup. "Nothing important."

"Then why did they call?"

"To discuss some plans we'd made."

"You're acting skittish," Ava said. She swallowed the last bite of cookie and focused on her mother. "Why?"

"I'm not acting anything," Barbara said, and if it wasn't for the small tremor in her hand, Ava might have believed her.

"Then why are you avoiding the question?"

"You know, you're a very good reporter. However, I don't like it when you interrogate me."

"Please, this is nothing compared to what you put me through." There was a reason Ava was a good reporter. She came by her ability to suss out questions and secrets naturally.

"I don't interrogate. I merely show interest in your life, and I never push."

"You always push." Ava could think of a million instances. When she'd been fifteen and out past curfew and she'd called with a story about falling asleep on a girlfriend's couch and would it be okay if she just stayed over? Her mother had asked a few question and then said no, somehow intuiting that she hadn't been at the friend's house but with a boy instead.

Or the time Ava had said that she'd been studying for her university finals at the library when she'd really been at a party all night. Her mother had made a few noises and then written out a study schedule for her that Ava had to mark off at the end of each night. Plus, a list of how this would ensure that she kept a high grade-point average. Ava had aced her tests, but was it really any wonder that she hated those lists?

"I don't push," Barbara repeated, her pale eyebrows rising in challenge. "For instance, did you know that your tone of voice changes when you talk about your new producer, Jake?"

"It does not."

"It does." Barbara nodded sagely. "And you blush." Ava raised a hand to her cheek, which was undeniably warm. "Yet, I didn't push you tonight when it was clear that you didn't wish to speak about him."

Ava looked down at the table and tried not to fidget.

"I thought so." Barbara placed her tea on the table and crossed her arms. "Are you interested in him?"

"Mom, no. We're friends."

She could feel her mother continuing to study her. "Are you sure?"

Sure that there was only one right answer to the questions. "Yes."

"Ava, I know that it can be difficult to meet people when you work long hours, but starting a relationship with a colleague has the potential to be disastrous. You need to think about your career."

She looked up. "I am, which is why we're just friends."

Barbara shook her head. "Just see that you're careful. You don't want to throw away your career over a handsome face."

"Who said he was handsome?"

"Oh?" Her mother tilted her head. "So you are interested in discussing it?"

Touché. Ava rose from the couch. "No, I'm only interested in my bed tonight." With Jake in it.

But she kept that last part to herself.

Chapter 14

Jake was swamped Monday and Tuesday but managed to get his head above water long enough on Wednesday to insist that Ava have dinner with him. After pizza, they'd had a hot-and-heavy make-out session on her couch. Which he was still thinking about Thursday morning.

Luckily, there were a million things to do at the station, which kept him from walking into her office, locking the door and initiating another session.

He'd set up a phone interview between Harvey and Hanna. On top of that, he was juggling his day-to-day activities and trying to help Tommy improve in his new role as cohost. The kid wasn't horrible, wasn't even bad, he was just a little flat.

Not for the first time, Jake thought about how much easier it would have been to promote Ava. She would have been able to slide in seamlessly and hold her own with Danica. But Jake still felt there was gold to be mined from the Tommy and Danica pairing. Or maybe it was just that he saw a bit of himself in the young eager-to-please kid and he wanted to help Tommy achieve what he hadn't: making his family proud.

Tommy had a head start on him in one aspect. He didn't feel the need to do so by working outside the family business.

Jake spent the rest of the day working in his office, stopping only to refuel with a stale cheese Danish that was in the break room and massive amounts of coffee. The show ran smoothly though Ava wasn't in attendance. She didn't have a story on the evening program, but she often hung around anyway. He tried not to be too disappointed that she hadn't tonight.

By the time he got home that evening, he was tired and starving. There was nothing in his fridge but one sad little lime, club soda and ketchup. He found some bread in the freezer and seriously considered making a ketchup sandwich. It covered grains and vegetables. Sort of.

His culinary experiment was interrupted by the ringing of his phone and Loverboy singing about working for the weekend. He answered it before the song got to the part about going off the deep end. But by the time he hung up ten minutes later, he'd felt as if he'd fallen off it anyway.

He stared at the phone, then at the table. Then got up and stumbled to the high cabinet over the fridge where he found half a bottle of tequila and a cut-glass tumbler. Thirty seconds later he was back at the table with an empty tumbler and a slightly emptier bottle.

He started to think about it, decided he wasn't ready and poured himself another shot of tequila.

Was this really—

No. Not yet. He gritted his teeth, poured another shot, eyed it before adding a little more and then slung it back. The liquor burned a path down his throat and into his bloodstream. It didn't feel good, but it was better than he'd felt a minute ago.

A half hour into his solo party, his vision was fuzzy around the edges, his stomach was on fire and his fingers were twice their normal size. Or that's what it felt like when he tried to navigate his cell phone with them. He closed one eye, which helped considerably.

Aba? Where you at? Home?

Aba? Excuse me, but who is this?

Who was Aba? Was she trying to be funny? And why wasn't his phone playing Loverboy anymore?

Huh? My phones is playing the wrong song. What happened to the work song?

Broaden your music horizons. That is Matthew Sweet's seminal hit, "Girlfriend." I personalized my number when you were snoring on my couch last night. You're welcome.

He didn't snore, did he? Didn't matter. He wanted to see her.

What are you doin'?

In a cab on my way home. Just finished having dinner with Jilly.

Good. He squinted at the clock on the microwave. It was only a few minutes past eight. If he put his shoes on right now, he could be at her place by eight-fifteen.

Comin' over. Be there in 10.

I don't recall inviting you.

But he needed her. Didn't she know that?

Sriously. Have to see you tonight.

4 real? Do I have a say in this?

But he had already tucked his phone into his pocket and was busy putting on his shoes. If he ran, he might make it there by eight-twelve.

Jake? Hello?
 Hello? Anyone?
 Anyone? Bueller?

He stepped out into the cool night and locked his door behind him, ignoring the rest of Ava's texts. She would only try to talk him out of coming over or want to know what was so urgent and this was too big to talk about over the phone. His town house was in a mixed complex with apartments and there was a large underground lot the residents shared. Jake continued down the street, bypassing the short path that led to the lobby and the elevator for the lot. The tequila had hit him harder than expected and he thought a walk in the fresh air would do him good.

By the time he got to Ava's building—a blurry fifteen minutes later—it had started to rain. He shook off the droplets in the elevator and closed one eye to focus on the floor numbers as they climbed. Ava was waiting at her door and Jake couldn't help the stupid grin that appeared on his face when he saw her. He practically fell on top of her in his haste to give her a proper greeting.

"Whoa. Easy there, tiger." She sniffed. "Why do you smell like lime juice?"

"Tequila." He saw her rear back when he breathed liquor fumes. "Sorry." And dug in his pocket for some gum. But he only found his wallet, which promptly slipped out of his grip. "Whoops."

"Oh, God. You are loaded." But she didn't sound mad. He was pretty sure she even smiled when he looked up from trying to get his wallet, but by the time he tried his one-eye trick, the expression was gone, so he couldn't be sure.

He managed to stuff his wallet back in his pants and hugged her again. She was so soft. Her shirt felt sort of velvety. He liked running his hands over it. "I'm a diddle drunk. I mean, little."

"Diddle?" She was definitely grinning now. And laughing. He smiled, too. "Is that why you came over here?"

"I could be convinced." He wrapped his arms around her, hugged her to his chest and rested his chin on her head.

"Hey." She was wriggling. "I can't breathe here and do not use me as a resting post."

He shifted, moving his face to the side of her neck, and inhaled. She smelled like the outside, the rain and clean air. A hint of the perfume she'd sprayed on this morning clung there, too. He inhaled again. "You smell so good. I could eat you up."

"None of that, either," she said, but he noticed she'd stopped wriggling.

She pulled back to look at him and he gave her a sloppy smile. "Hi."

"Hi." She took a half step back. Jake took one with her. "Exactly how much have you had to drink?" she asked.

"'Bout half a bottle." He'd left the empty container on the table along with the glass and a bunch of drained lime wedges. He pulled Ava close again. She fit right into the curve of his body, just nestled right in there. Or would have if she'd quit trying to push him away.

"Half a bottle of tequila? You are going to be hurting tomorrow."

He shrugged. It was probably true, but he wasn't hurting right now, so his mission was a success. "Come over here."

"No." She danced away. "Why were you drinking half a bottle of tequila on your own at eight o'clock?"

"I don't want to talk about it." He danced toward her.

"Really?" She sidestepped him when he tried to twirl her back into his arms. "So you got drunk, called me and invited yourself over *not* to talk about it?"

"Yep." He tried to catch her again, but she was slippery, like an eel. He closed one eye again.

"You need coffee."

"Nope." He snagged her arm this time and yanked her into his chest. "I need this."

She snaked out of his hold. Jake looked down at his arms now holding air and then back at her.

"How did you do that?"

"Coffee. I'll make you some."

He managed to hop up on one of the stools in front

of her large breakfast bar. The kitchen was all stainless steel and white, but she'd added splashes of red. A picture of an apple, a dish towel, a vase that she'd filled with cheerful daisies. The room looked bright and clean.

Jake watched as she started opening and closing cupboard doors. "I'd rather have another drink," he told her. His buzz was finally beginning to wind down, but Jake didn't like the misery that was attempting to take its spot.

"Do you really need one?" She paused in her search to glance back. Lust washed over him. The way her blond hair curled over her shoulder, the creamy look of her skin and the light in her eyes.

"Well, I can think of something else I'd rather have, but you told me not tonight."

"I think you'd be better off with coffee."

"I think you should have a drink with me."

"I think you should tell me why you're here."

"I ran out of tequila?" He drummed his fingers on the countertop.

Ava quit searching, leaving one of the doors half-open, and crossed the room. The counter was still between them, but Jake figured he was strong enough to haul her over top of it and into his lap. He might have done it, too, if she hadn't stopped short. "Seriously." He could read the concern in her blue eyes. He didn't like it. "What happened?"

"I felt like seeing you." Maybe it would be better not to talk about any of this tonight. Tomorrow would be soon enough. Actually, tomorrow would probably still be too soon, although if he were honest, it was always going to be too soon to talk about it.

"Jake." She reached out and laid a small hand over his. He threaded their fingers together. "Tell me."

It was suddenly hard to breathe. "Coffee, and then I'll tell you."

She made the coffee, not asking him anything even once the cups were poured. She simply placed his in front of him and waited.

Jake inhaled the fragrant brew and then told her everything. "The investors called. We didn't get the money and I don't have anyone else lined up." His free hand curled into a fist. "It's done. I'm done."

He'd failed. Again. And eventually, he was going to have to tell his family about it. He closed his eyes. More proof that, unlike his father, he couldn't hack it in the real world.

He opened his eyes and looked at her, expecting to see a horrified expression. The kind that said she wanted him and his stink of disappointment out of her apartment now. Claudia would have already had him off the stool and halfway to the door while making an excuse that she had a lot of things to do before bed tonight so it was best that he left. But Ava hadn't moved and her expression hadn't changed. Probably just too polite to tell him to get lost.

He let go of her hand and pushed himself off the stool. "I should go." He needed to figure out how he was going to tell everyone the news, what he was going to do now.

She swept around the side of the counter and blocked his path. "No."

Her good hand was on his chest. Heat seeped through the thin material of his T-shirt and into his bloodstream. His heart jolted.

"No," she said again, softly this time. "I don't want you to go."

They stood like that for a minute. Her hand over his

heart. Jake felt it thump harder. "I don't know why I came over. This isn't your problem."

He didn't know why he expected her to get involved. She wasn't even getting a permanent job out of this.

"Jake." She curled her fingers into his shirt when he made a move to head for the door again. "I want to help."

He didn't feel drunk anymore. Wasn't sure if it was the coffee or staring into the face of his failure. "There's nothing to help. It's over." He looked at her. "Guess this means you have your weekend free now." There was no point in going through the filming without even the chance of obtaining financial backing.

"You're just giving up?"

He searched her face for the distaste she must be feeling. He couldn't blame her. He felt it for himself. "It's called cutting your losses," he said, still surprised that she hadn't kicked him out. Claudia, she was not. "I'm not throwing good money after bad."

"No, you're just throwing away everything that you've worked for." Her hand fisted in his tee when he tried to move around her. "Didn't you tell me that you moved here to pursue this? And that it was your dream?" There was a bite of anger to her voice now.

"Yes." But that was back when he'd thought generating interest in the show would be a snap.

"Then you can't just give up on it. Fight. They aren't the only investors in the world. They're not even the only investors in this city. And you've already set everything up for this weekend. You'd be crazy not to go ahead with the filming."

He placed his hand over hers intending to peel it

off, but instead pressed it more tightly to him. "It isn't that easy."

"Actually, it is." She leaned into him. "You've set everything up—it would be a waste not to continue."

She had a point. "Maybe."

"Definitely. Having a show you can actually screen for potential investors will make it easier to shop around. Maybe you could even go directly to the airlines. You don't need an investor for that."

"No." But he couldn't move forward very far without one, either. He had no way to film a second episode or pitch to multiple buyers. This would be a one-shot deal and if the first pitch didn't sell, he'd be broke. He told her so.

"Then we better make the show so great that it sells right away. In the meantime, you can start looking for another investor."

She made a move to untangle herself, but Jake held her tighter, not willing to let go of her or the little beacon of hope she was shining on him. "And what if I can't find another investor and the show doesn't sell?"

She looked up at him. She was so close that he didn't need to close one eye to see her clearly. She smiled. "Then we come up with another plan."

They took their coffee into the living room where Ava proceeded to bombard him with questions. "What about looking for an investor back in Toronto? You must have a lot of connections there."

"No." He bit the word out. She blinked at him from behind the rim of her bright red coffee cup. "Sorry, that was a bit harsh, but I don't want to use any of those connections."

"Why not?"

"This is something I have to prove that I can do on my own." He stopped there, not wanting to delve deeper.

Ava had other ideas. "Why does it matter where the money comes from?"

"Because." He sipped his coffee and then told her the story. "My dad is kind of a big shot in Toronto. Self-made man, all that. He started his company with nothing but a dollar and hard work."

Instead of looking impressed, Ava laughed. "A dollar? I highly doubt that."

"Maybe not a dollar," Jake conceded, "but he didn't have family money to fall back on. He had to make it on merit."

She frowned. "So, you think you have to do the same or you're some epic failure?"

"No, but I want to prove that I can." Had to prove it to rid himself of this heavy load that had followed him to Vancouver.

"You think your dad didn't use his connections to get money for his company when he was starting out?"

"But they were his connections."

"And these would be your connections."

"That's the problem." Jake exhaled loudly and put his half-finished coffee on the end table. "They *wouldn't* be my connections. They'd be his. I have no way to separate the two unless I get investors who are virtual strangers to him." Which had turned out to be much more difficult that he'd ever anticipated. "I need to know that the money is coming in because they believe in the project."

She titled her head. "Surely they'd believe in it. Do you run with a crowd that has so much money they can throw it away on a vanity project?"

Jake shot her a look.

"Must be nice."

"Actually, it sucks. You never know what people's motivations are." He thought he'd gotten pretty good at recognizing them over the years, but Claudia's betrayal had proven him wrong. "Look, I don't expect you to understand. But I moved here because I needed a fresh start. That meant leaving behind everything I had there, including those connections. So I need to find another way."

"All right." She nodded slowly and sipped her coffee. But he could tell she still had something to say. It was evident by the lift of her eyebrow and the twist of her mouth, though she was trying to play innocent.

"What?"

"Nothing." She raised her eyebrow even farther in feigned surprise, but he wasn't buying what she was selling.

"You clearly have an opinion on this. Spit it out."

She shrugged. "It's not really my business."

"So make it your business." He trusted her opinion. She was smart, and it would be good to get a different opinion on this. He reached out and put a hand on her knee. "Talk to me, Ava."

Her whole body softened, turning toward him. "I understand parental issues." She laughed softly to herself. "Believe me, I understand. But I don't want to see you throw this opportunity away over some misguided sense of pride."

"I wouldn't say it's pride. You'd feel the same way in my situation."

"I don't think I would." She shook her head. When she looked at him, her eyes were clear. "If my mom owned the television station and wanted to make me the host of our show? I wouldn't think twice before saying yes and celebrating."

"It's not quite the same."

"Yes, it is."

"No, my situation is more like your mother owning a TV station, but refusing to hire you because she doesn't think you're good enough. Instead, she pays off an old friend to let you work at his station. You think you do a pretty good job, but you make one small error in judgment—" though the mess with Claudia had felt anything but small at the time "—and suddenly all anyone can talk about is that you only have the job because your mom is friends with the boss."

She put her hand over his. "Is that what happened?"

"Close enough." He didn't share the part about overhearing his father tell his mother that he wasn't surprised Jake's situation hadn't worked out. It made Jake feel like a failure as a businessman and a son, and still hurt too much to say out loud. "Wouldn't you then want to prove that you could succeed on your own?"

She placed her cup on the coffee table and scooted across the couch so their thighs were touching. "I still don't think you should cut off all those possible sources of funding." She put her hand on his arm. "Who cares why they give you the money? That's not important. What's important is what you do with it. You believe in the show, don't you?"

"Yes." Despite the fact that nothing had fallen into place as planned, Jake still thought the show had potential.

"Then take the money. However you can get it. Make the show into a huge success and sit back and be proud of what you've accomplished. Trust me, no one will care how you got the money once the show takes off."

It was tempting, so tempting. "But I'll care," Jake said. It wasn't just the thought of taking pity money, though that was something Jake wanted no part of. But if he did, he could never say that he had managed this on his own. There would always be the question about his father's influence. "I want to do this on my own."

"Jake." She leaned closer. "You'd still be doing it on your own. Everyone needs financial support when they're starting a company. Everyone. What makes you think you're different?"

He shrugged and leaned back, hauling her with him. "I just need to do this on my own terms."

Their lips were practically touching. When she spoke, Jake could feel the whisper of her breath buffeting against his mouth. "Is that more important than making the show happen?"

He studied her. There were little flecks of gold in her eyes, just a few shades darker than her hair. "I haven't decided yet."

She leaned back. "Really?"

He tightened his hold on her. This wasn't supposed to be the point when she pulled away—this was where she should have been curved into him and they stopped talking completely. "Where do you think you're going?" he asked.

"To try to knock some sense into you."

"No." He clasped her to him so she couldn't move. "I think you should stay right here."

It had started to rain about an hour ago, and had gradually increased in intensity from a delicate drizzle to a loud downpour. It slapped against the window in an unending rhythm. But they were tucked inside where it was nice and dry.

"I'm not letting you give up," she said.

"Okay." Jake probably would have agreed to anything in that moment.

"We should probably think about making a list of potential investors."

"Sure." But the thought made him feel tired. Been there, done that. Nothing to show for it.

"Jake. Come on. Are you really going to give up that easily?"

He closed his eyes and let his hands tangle in the waves of her silky hair. "No, but can we talk about this later?" Right now he just wanted to stay here, absorb some of her warmth and try to ignore the fact that maybe he wasn't going to reach that brass ring.

"What's wrong with talking about it now?" she wanted to know.

"Right now, I have other things in mind. Like kissing you until you're convinced to show me the inside of your bedroom."

His ploy to distract her didn't work, though he did get a nice kiss out of the deal.

When she broke away from him, she simply said, "First, we get started on that list." Forcing Jake to rack his brain for anyone he and Alex might have missed the first time.

Chapter 15

They hadn't had sex.

Though she'd tried to keep them focused on the task, Ava hadn't been able to turn Jake down when he'd bargained for a kiss per name. It had made the evening much more enjoyable for both of them and had helped distract them from the fact that Jake's travel project might not ever make it out of the production stage.

They'd ended up with about ten names, all people that Jake claimed he was comfortable contacting. Ava wasn't quite sure she fully understood his reluctance to add anyone who had a closer relationship to his father—there was more going on there than Jake had mentioned—but she was willing to leave it alone. Especially when he so readily agreed never to tell her mother that she had been the one to extol the virtues of making a list. A daughter had to have some secrets.

Somehow his project had become her project, too,

and being the host, she felt as if she had a vested interest in ensuring its success.

Just thinking about traveling to all those fabulous locations was enough to make her giddy and plan to get her legs waxed. And unlike the cohost position at *Entertainment News Now,* she was confident that this time the job was hers. There was no one better qualified.

If he struck out on the new names, she could push a little more. For now, she was willing to leave it. She was sure that once the pilot was complete, finding an investor or, even better, a buyer, would pose no problem.

The weekend came quickly. They started filming early Saturday morning, beginning at Kits beach. Though it was April and not nearly warm enough for bathing suits or swimming, there were still plenty of people out walking dogs and watching the waves. Come summer, Ava explained to the camera, it would be packed with sun worshippers and volleyball players. There were even public tennis courts and a swimming pool. It was Vancouver's version of Venice Beach. Her patter flowed smoothly and she felt really relaxed. Much less tense than she did under the station's studio lights.

They visited Granville Island next, then Cambie Street and finished the day in South Granville. There were multiple restaurants in the area that were world-renowned for their ethnic cuisine and frequented by celebrities. Sunday was more of the same, but took place in the busy downtown core. Even on the weekend, the streets and shops were filled with people.

As their last bit of filming rolled to an end, Ava was feeling really good. She and Jake had already planned a small and intimate celebration. Dinner and drinks to toast the completion of filming and the start of a successful future. And maybe a little more.

No, definitely a little more. She'd used a fresh razor blade this morning.

Her phone buzzed. Ava checked the screen and pressed Ignore. It was her mother again. That woman had a sixth sense when it came to her daughter. This was the third call of the day, fifth of the weekend, but since they hadn't started arriving at half-hour intervals yet, Ava knew it wasn't an emergency. And she already had plans this evening. Ones that did not include her mother.

"Aves?" She turned at Brandon's voice. "You want to go out for drinks?"

Brandon hadn't been originally contracted to shoot the pilot, but when the cameraman Jake had hired had decided he didn't really feel like working on the weekend only a couple of days earlier, options had been limited. Brandon had been happy to step in, turning the whole experience into a Rockdale reunion, with Brandon behind the camera, Ava in front of it and Jake directing the proceedings.

"Drinks? I hadn't thought about it," she lied. Having drinks with Brandon was better than talking to her mother, but it still wasn't the evening she had in mind.

"Well, think about it." Brandon finished winding cables and slung the equipment bag over his shoulder. "Maybe something to eat, too. I'm starving."

He started toward his car—a small red hatchback—as Jake appeared from inside the store where they'd shot the last segment. Ava felt her pulse skip when his eyes found hers and he smiled.

Brandon either missed the shared look or didn't care. "What about you, Jake? You up for going out?"

Jake looked at her. "What do you think?"

She thought he should make it clear what he wanted, but his expression told her nothing. No wink. No shake of his head. Not even rubbing the side of his nose like a baseball player. "Uh, it's been a long day?"

"Don't act like a grandma," Brandon told her with a laugh. "I know underneath it all that you're a party animal."

"Don't you ever get tired?" Ava asked him.

"No. Too much fun to waste time sleeping. So we in?"

It wasn't as though Brandon could know that she and Jake had plans for a private dinner and drinks, and so what if she had to spend the next few hours refraining from kissing Jake? It would only add to the anticipation. She smiled. "We're in."

They ended up at a local lounge that was known for its pretty waitstaff and party crowd. Typical Brandon. Ava guessed they'd be lucky to get a full drink out of him before he whisked away or was whisked off by some beautiful woman.

She and Jake arrived first, settling at one of the low tables, the glossy white reflecting their drinks back at them. The couches were sleek and firm, meant for show rather than comfort, and had no armrests to lean against or balance a drink.

Ava took a sip of her club soda with lemon as she and Jake discussed the shoot, how they thought it had gone and how it should be edited together while they waited for their errant cameraman. His hand brushed against her shoulder, then her leg. She was tingly all over. Like a twelve-year-old waiting for her first kiss.

When Brandon turned up a few minutes later, Ava shifted away from Jake just slightly. They had been careful not to let their burgeoning relationship slip out in front of anyone at the office, and while he only had a month left on his contract, she had no intention of changing that now. Even Brandon, who was currently working the room like a pro, would pick up on it if she and Jake were snuggled up on the couch together.

"The kid has moves," she told Jake, taking another sip from her glass.

"You haven't seen my moves yet."

She felt her cheeks get hot and was glad the lounge kept the lighting low. "Is that what you have in mind for this evening?"

"Well, I *am* buying you dinner."

She laughed. Part of her wanted to shift closer and see what else he had in mind, but she was interrupted by Brandon's arrival. She sat back against the armless couch and reminded herself that it was only another month. Seriously, she'd been the one to insist they keep things professional in public. She wasn't going to be the one to break that deal.

Jake's hand crept over to rest on her knee, and she had a brief internal struggle about leaving it there. Then she shifted sideways, as close to the edge as she could get without tumbling to the floor, and pretended that her glass, the other lounge patrons and the material of the couch were very interesting.

As the two men turned to talking about the Canucks' chances at the Stanley Cup this year, Ava sipped her drink, hoping the chill would cool her down.

But when she snuck a look at Jake, his gray eyes alight with laughter at something Brandon had said, he caught her eye and smiled. That crooked smile that made her pulse leap and her skin tingle.

And those jeans. Her gaze drifted down to eye the perfectly washed denim more closely. She both loved and hated those jeans.

It wasn't long before a delicate brunette with soft eyes and a sweet smile made her way over to a table a couple of feet away from them. The woman was tall and willowy and clearly into Brandon. She stood there alone, until he looked up, then she made a show of running her finger around the rim of her martini glass. Five minutes later, the two were in an intense conversation, leaving Jake and Ava alone.

"Let's go," Jake said, plucking the still-half-full glass out of her hand and putting it on the table along with a bill large enough to cover the drinks and a tip.

She stumbled, surprised by the sudden rush. "Shouldn't we—"

"No." Jake steered her toward the door.

"But—"

"He won't welcome the interruption. And it's against the Man Code." Whatever that was.

"We should at least let him know that we've left," she told Jake as he bundled her out into the cold. She appreciated the cool air on her flushed cheeks. Maybe it would calm some of her thoughts, too, so she didn't jump Jake in his car.

"He won't care."

"How do you know?" The wind picked up and sent her blond hair flying around her face and into her mouth. She brushed it away.

"I'm a man. We learn it in the womb. Trust me."

Ava opened her mouth to disagree, but her phone

buzzed yet again, the sound loud in the clear night. She glanced down, recognized her mother's number and pressed Ignore. "I just think—"

"You aren't going to answer?"

"It's my mom," she told him as if that explained everything, which it did.

"And?"

"And she's trying to run my life," Ava said. "I refuse to let her."

"She's being a mother."

"No, she's being an overcontrolling mother." She checked her call list and saw that her mother was now on her every-half-hour-call plan, which would continue until Ava either answered or turned up dead. "My dad died before I was born, so it was just the two of us. She thinks that means she needs to give enough advice for two parents."

"Sorry about your dad."

Ava shrugged. "Thanks, but it was a long time ago." She'd learned, with some assistance from her mother, not to let his death define her life. "And I had an aunt and uncle who lived beside us growing up. They were pretty involved."

"So he provided the stare down with the shotgun over his shoulder when your dates showed up."

Ava laughed. "No, my mother is plenty capable of doing that on her own. But Uncle Dennis took me to hockey games, came to father-daughter events, things like that. He and Aunt Yolanda moved to Calgary about fifteen years ago."

"You miss them?"

"We see them at holidays and I often go back for the Stampede in the summer. Plus, my mother... Oh, for crying out loud." She looked down at the phone in her hand as it began to play the familiar song by Queen. "I swear she implanted a homing device in my arm when I was a kid so that she always knows how to find me."

"Wouldn't that mean she wouldn't need to call you?"

Ava considered that. "Yes, but then how would she tell me what to do?" Her phone buzzed again.

"Pick it up," Jake said. "What if it's an emergency?"

She started to tell him that it wasn't an emergency, her mother was just irked that she'd been avoiding her phone calls all weekend, but realized that wouldn't solve the issue. Her mother would just call back until she answered.

She pushed a button on the phone and put it to her ear. "Yes, Mom. How can I help you?"

"You know I don't like that, Ava."

"Sorry. Hello? Who is this? Why are you calling me?"

"I've been calling you all day, dear." Her mother did not sound amused.

"I was busy." She omitted the part about what she'd been doing.

"I was concerned when you didn't call me back last night."

Ava scanned the block as she and Jake continued walking. They were in the heart of Yaletown, an upscale neighborhood that had thrown off its warehouse beginnings years ago and was now a hot spot for the young and wealthy. People wearing pricey jeans and pricier shoes wandered in and out of bars and restaurants. Music and lights spilled from open doors and windows. The boutique shops were closed for the evening, but the attractive displays invited pedestrians to stop and study. "I was working."

There—that should shut her up.

"Did you forget that it was Sunday?" Or not.

"No." What did her mother think, she was going senile now?

"Then where are you?"

Ava peeked at Jake, who was watching her with a small smirk. Easy for him. His mother wasn't calling to find out the details of his life. "I'm out," she said.

"Did you forget about dinner?"

"We had dinner last Sunday," Ava reminded her. "With Jilly, remember? That means we don't meet until next weekend."

"No," Barbara corrected. "We missed the Sunday when you were away for work. Last week was our re-scheduled dinner, which means we're also supposed to have dinner tonight. It's on the calendar." She paused. "I did try to call you last night to confirm, but you didn't answer."

Ava's stomach sank. Her mother was right. How could she have forgotten? She took another peek at Jake. Okay, she knew how she'd forgotten. "Well, tonight isn't good for me. Can we reschedule?"

"But dinner is here. It's hot."

"I have plans. I'm sorry I forgot. Maybe I could come over tomorrow instead?"

"I have meetings tomorrow night. I really wish you would have called me back, dear. I could have canceled my order if I'd known. Now I have Thai for two."

Thai for three or more, Ava guessed, since her mother always ordered a variety of choices. "I'm sorry," she apologized again. True, her mother hadn't been slaving over a hot stove all afternoon, but that didn't make Ava feel any better about blowing her off. She was a terrible daughter. She didn't listen to advice, she didn't answer her phone and now she was going to make her mother eat dinner alone. "What about another night this week?"

"I'll have to check my schedule, but I'm not sure this week works. I have meetings at the hospital Tuesday and Thursday, my book club is Wednesday and tomorrow is my Union Gospel meeting." Her mother had volunteered with the local charity for years, donating time, money and charity to helping the homeless with shelter, food and recovery.

Which just made Ava feel even worse. Her mother couldn't get together because she was helping people. She couldn't do it because she wanted to flirt with a handsome man. "Maybe I can stop by for a little while." She mouthed an apology to Jake.

"If it wouldn't be too much trouble."

"No," Ava said, thinking that it would be more trouble to put her mother off for another week. "It isn't too much trouble." She covered the mouthpiece of the phone with her hand. "I need to go visit my mother."

"Meeting the parent already? You must be getting serious about me."

She grinned. "I didn't say you were invited, and believe me, I'm doing you a favor. She's kind of a lot to take."

A tinny voice came out of the phone she'd thought she was muting. "I can hear you, Ava. Who is there with you?"

Ava scrabbled to get the phone back to her ear. "It's

nothing," she lied. "Just some people talking on the street."

Her mother was not fooled. "You were talking to someone. I recognize your voice." She paused just long enough to tease Ava into thinking she was off the hook. "I take it you're with Jake. I'd like to meet him and I have more than enough for three."

Of course she did. "Mom, I—"

"It would be rude not to invite him, Ava. I'll expect you shortly." And with that directive, she hung up.

Ava stared at the phone for a second and wondered if she could fake an attack of some kind. Her wrist was bothering her, she felt as if she was coming down with the flu, something, anything.

"Am I invited for dinner?"

She looked up at Jake. "You don't have to come." She wouldn't expect him to undergo the questioning that was sure to ensue once her mother got him in her sights. She loved her mother, but Barbara could be difficult. It was why, on the rare occasion that she was seeing someone, she didn't bring him home.

"Are you disinviting me?"

"No."

"Then I'd love to have dinner with you and your mother."

Ava sighed. "That's because you haven't met her yet."

Chapter 16

Jake didn't know what Ava had gotten herself so worked up about. Her mother was an intelligent and charming woman. Okay, so she wasn't helping with the romance portion of the evening, but he figured there was still time for that.

A nice dinner with her mother, followed by a nightcap at his place. He'd even changed his sheets.

"Would you like something more to eat?" Barbara interrupted his fantasy about ravishing her daughter. Her smile belied the fact that she was brandishing a pair of silver spoons capable of being used as lethal weapons.

"Please." He thanked her after she loaded his plate with a third serving.

The Thai food, which Ava had informed him was ordered in, was served from expensive-looking dishes that went with the crisp white tablecloth, silver candlesticks and elegant place settings. A crystal chandelier bathed the room in a shimmery light. Jake was impressed with the trick of putting the takeout into proper serving dishes. He was going to have to add that to his repertoire.

Barbara placed more shrimp and noodles on Ava's plate and then her own.

"Mom, I said I was finished." Ava scowled at the plate and then her mother.

"You need to keep your strength up," Barbara said. "You're healing." She sat down at the head of the table and cut the shrimp into a bite-size piece. "What did Dr. Merion say about your wrist when you saw her?"

"Like you haven't already talked to her yourself."

"Doctor-patient privilege," Barbara said. "She wouldn't tell me."

Ava smiled. "Have I told you how much I adore Dr. Merion?"

Barbara had another bite of shrimp and stared at her daughter. Clearly, this was a familiar battle and reminded Jake a little of his own family. His mother and sister generally got along well—too well when it came to discussing his life—but their closeness occasionally gave way to meaningless bickering. He'd learned to stay out of it, as they were fiercely loyal to one another and didn't value any input. He'd lay money on the fact that Ava and her mother were the same.

The staring contest continued for another moment until Ava blinked. "I'm fine. The wrist is fine. Dr. Merion said that everything is fine. Happy?"

"Quite." Barbara nodded. "I want only the best for you, dear."

"Lucky me."

Jake hid his grin. He didn't think Ava would appreciate it. "Would either of you care for some more wine?" he asked.

He'd insisted on stopping at the liquor store on their way to her mother's house. Ava had told him that her mother would have already selected something to match the meal, but he wouldn't be deterred. Especially not after she mumbled something about how her mom would probably fall in love with him.

Never a bad thing to get the mother onside.

He would have stopped for flowers, too, but Ava had told him if he did, she was catching a cab and he could just go hungry. He relented. No point in getting on the mother's good side if it meant getting on the daughter's bad one.

The wine now sat in a metal ice bucket on a stand beside the table. He pulled it out and offered it around.

"Thank you, Jake," Barbara said. "A little more would be lovely."

"I would like a lot," Ava said, holding out her empty glass.

"Ava," her mother chided, "do you really think that's a good idea?"

"I do." They stared at one another.

Jake could see where Ava had gotten her petite figure and coloring. As well as her attitude. Their chins jutted toward each other in mirror images.

He poured a small glass for Barbara, a larger one for Ava.

"Fine—" Barbara waved a delicate hand "—but don't complain if you don't feel well tomorrow."

"I never complain," Ava said.

Jake felt the corners of his lips start to rise. Ava kicked him lightly when he sat back down. He rubbed his shin and sent her a look. Did she really think he'd say otherwise? Did he look stupid?

"Tell me about your job, Jake." Barbara sat upright, her posture perfect as she sipped. "Ava says that you're an executive producer."

"I am." Jake went on to explain the details that came with his position.

"You're rather young to have the position, aren't you?"

It set his teeth on edge. Too close to the comments he'd heard about his career for the past ten years. But he trusted that Ava hadn't said anything about his background to her mother. A belief borne out by the horrified look on her face. He kept his tone light. "Not particularly. The entertainment industry is a young field. It's important that the decision makers are in touch with the youth demographic."

Barbara nodded. "But still, you must have worked hard to reach your position at such a young age. You must be thirty? Thirty-one?"

"Thirty-five."

"Mom, enough with the third degree."

"I was merely making conversation," Barbara told her daughter before sending Jake a pleasant smile. "However, I apologize if I've offended you."

"Not at all." He wouldn't say it had offended him, just brought up some emotions he'd rather not deal with at the moment. "I'm actually looking to make a change in my career."

Barbara raised one pale eyebrow at her daughter. "Really? Ava didn't mention that."

"Mom, you're making it sound like I spend my days

and nights talking about Jake. Which I don't. And besides I only found out recently."

"Interesting." Barbara dabbed her lips with a cloth napkin before she turned back to Jake. "What sort of change?"

"You don't have to tell her," Ava said. "She's being nosy."

"I'm showing interest," Barbara corrected.

Jake figured he knew where Ava got that part of her personality, too. "I don't mind," he said. "I'm starting my own production company." He briefly explained the plan. "Ava was actually helping me shoot a pilot today."

"Was she?" This time both of Barbara's eyebrows went up.

"I was." Ava lifted her chin. "For a travel show Jake is producing."

"I imagine that will be good for your career, dear," Barbara said. "You can use it on your, what is it you call that, B-roll?"

"Demo reel," Ava corrected. "B-roll is the extra footage we shoot to intercut with the story during editing."

"Demo reel." Barbara turned to look at him, assessing. "Or perhaps something with this new production company you're starting?"

"Mom. Enough. I didn't ask Jake to come over here so you could grill him about my career prospects." She glanced at him, embarrassment and irritation warring on her face.

Jake made his lips turn up in a smile. He couldn't assume that Barbara was acting as Ava's mouthpiece. That was twice now that she'd looked less than happy with her mother's questions. But it niggled at him.

"We've only shot the pilot so far. Now that I have an

actual show I'll start pitching it to possible buyers. The airlines. And looking for investors."

"Shouldn't you have looked for funding before shooting the pilot?" A delicate frown marred Barbara's features.

"Mom," Ava moaned.

"That's true." Jake's fingers tightened around his fork. "I have been meeting with people, but sometimes it takes a while to find the right backer."

"So you'll be working at the television station and doing this on the side?"

He felt as if he was sitting in front of his father, answering as best he could and not meeting expectations. "No, I've decided to give my full attention to the production company. My contract with the station ends next month."

A short pause, but one that was rich in meaning. "Oh. Well, that sounds very exciting. Don't you agree, Ava?"

Ava mumbled something around the noodles she'd stuffed in her mouth and refused to look him in the eye. Jake tried not to let it eat at him. But he wasn't very successful.

He'd been clear that Ava was only working on the pilot, hadn't he?

"You were a nightmare," Ava said to her mother. She'd called as soon as Jake had dropped her off that night.

After being forced to endure pie and coffee and more of her mother's interference disguised as polite conversation, the idea of continuing the date with Jake had been kind of shot. When the dinner was over, he'd just driven her to her apartment and walked her to the lobby door. That had hurt and there was no question at whose feet she should lay the blame.

"Asking all those questions about his job, hinting around that you didn't approve. Why did you do that?"

"I didn't do anything, dear. I merely asked what his plans were."

"You said they sounded *interesting*. You might as well have said they were doomed to fail." Jake hadn't even hung around long enough to kiss her good-night. Not even a peck. Mood Killer Barbara Christensen strikes again.

"Stop exaggerating. I do think his plans sound interesting. But, Ava, dear, I hope you weren't planning to follow in his footsteps. It's all well and good to quit your job for a guaranteed position somewhere else, but it didn't sound like Jake was offering that."

"That isn't any of your business." And she could quit if she wanted. "How many times do I have to tell you that it's my career and my life? I know you love me and you're only trying to help, but enough."

"If you would just—"

"Mom—" Ava was losing hold of her rapidly fraying patience "—I'm not you. I tried it your way and it sucked."

"Language, dear."

"It was awful," Ava repeated. "I studied economics in school because you thought accounting was a stable career and worked in an accounting firm after graduation. I hated it and I was miserable."

"You didn't give that job a fair chance. You'd made up your mind before you even started."

"Because I hated my four years at university, too." Really, if it hadn't been for Jilly dragging her out to parties and showing her there was more to Friday nights than whatever two-decades-old movie happened to be on TV, she'd probably still be hunched over a desk, crunching numbers. "My job at the station is the best thing that ever happened to my career."

"I don't know if I'd go that far."

"I would." And it had just fallen into her lap.

She'd been complaining about her day to Jilly and wishing her life was more like the celebrities' she read about in the magazines when Jilly had mentioned there was a reporting position open at the TV station she worked at. She'd encouraged Ava to put together a fake story and had delivered it to Harvey herself. Three weeks later, Ava had a new job. It was the first time in years that she'd gone off list, and she promised herself she'd never go back on. A promise she'd managed to mostly keep.

"I have my own way of doing things, Mom, and just because it's not the way you would do it doesn't make it wrong."

"I never said you were wrong, dear."

"No, you just acted like it. Why can't you trust me?"

"I do trust you. I simply don't want to see you make a mistake."

Ava rolled her eyes even though her mother wasn't there to see the effect. "I'm not making a mistake. I helped Jake with his pilot. That's it."

"Is that really all?"

Her heart thumped and her whole body felt hot. She pushed open the window in her living room. "Of course that's all." It was still dry outside, but the scent of rain hung heavy. She sucked in some of the thick air. "What else would there be?"

"I saw the way he looked at you."

"He didn't look at me any way." A tickle of pleasure joined the cool breeze coming in through the window. Maybe she'd misunderstood Jake's platonic good-night. Maybe he'd just been really tired.

"He looked at you. And you looked back."

Ava dragged her attention back to her mother. "There wasn't any looking. At least, not the kind you're implying."

"Are you sure?"

"Of course I'm sure." She shoved away any feelings of guilt about lying. It would be a billion times worse to talk about her sex life—not that she had one to speak of yet—with her mother. "We're friends."

"Ava, I'm not a fool and I don't appreciate you treating me like one."

"No one is treating you like a fool."

"I know what that look means, and I'm concerned. Do you have plans to quit the station and join his show?"

"I'm not quitting the station." She wasn't just telling her mother what she wanted to hear, either. For the time being, she planned to work at the station during the week and fly off to be with Jake on weekends. Once the show took off, it would be a different story. And then she was asking for shares.

"Well, I'm glad to hear you haven't let your hormones take over entirely. Have you slept with him?"

"Mom. I wouldn't answer that even if it were your business."

The relief in her mother's voice was evident. "Then you haven't. Good. Keep it that way."

"You know, it's bad enough that you insist on deluging me with professional advice, now you think you have the right to run my personal life, too?"

"You work with him," her mother said as if that answered everything.

"Only for a few more weeks."

"A few more weeks isn't very long to wait."

No, it wasn't. But it was her choice. "Mom, I can make my own decisions." The low wind from outside did its best to cool her cheeks, but Ava still felt hot. Very hot. She stripped off her sweater. "What I choose to do with or about Jake is my own business."

"Don't be rash, dear. I didn't mean to hurt your feelings. I'm just telling you what I've learned over the years."

"About having a relationship with someone in the office?" Ava pushed the window open wider. "When have you ever done that? When have you had a relationship with anyone besides my father?"

"I didn't have a lot of free time."

"Then," Ava pointed out. "But what's your excuse now?"

"An office romance is doomed to fail."

Ava avoided bringing up the example of Meredith and Derek on *Grey's Anatomy*. Her mother would be less swayed by the hospital drama than she had been. "So it's a good thing I'm not having one." Yet. "Rest easy."

"Are you sure?"

"I'm pretty sure that's something I would know."

"A romance doesn't have to just mean sex."

"There is nothing going on." Well, except for that amazing kissing. And touching. She lowered her forehead against the glass.

"You should probably refrain from seeing him socially for the time being."

"Are you serious?" Even the whip of cool air couldn't prevent her temper from rising now. "Now I can't even be friends with him? What else, Mom? Should I cut him off and go into hiding?"

"Now you're just being ridiculous."

"I come by it honestly." She couldn't believe her mother. Well, no, she could. This was typical Barbara Christensen. And it always brought out her defiant side. "What would be so bad about me having a relationship with Jake anyway? He's a great guy."

"He seems very nice, but—"

Ava cut her off. "He has a lot going for him. He's not some jobless vagrant looking for a sugar mama. He's polite and kind. I like him." Saying it out loud felt good. Really good. "And if I want to do something about it, it's my decision." Why was she waiting anyway? Because her mother thought it was best? What did her mother know about it? "You can't stop me."

"You're being childish."

She probably was. She also didn't care. A few weeks, schmoo weeks. Why was she sitting around in her apartment alone, when there was a great guy waiting for her? Why was she still letting her mother's beliefs dictate her life? Hadn't she been letting that happen long enough? "I have to go."

"Ava."

"I love you, Mom." But it was time she started making the decisions that she wanted. "I have to go."

She hung up on her mother midsentence and turned off the phone.

Chapter 17

Jake looked surprised to find her at his door. Ava couldn't blame him. She hadn't bothered to call or text, hadn't bothered to do anything except put on a coat and shoes before she headed out of her apartment and up to Granville Street, where she flagged a taxi.

"I apologize for my mother," she said. "I don't know why she acts that way. But that's not why I'm here. Just so you know, this isn't about anything except us."

"Okay."

"Okay." She put a finger to his lips and shushed him. "No talking." If he started talking, she'd feel obligated to respond and all she wanted to do right now was feel. She stepped into the entryway of his town house and closed the door behind her.

She hadn't been to his place before, but he'd pointed it out one night on their way home from dinner. She saw now that he still hadn't unpacked. There were moving boxes still piled in the living room and against the wall of the entryway. A couch sat in the living room, but there was no coffee table and the walls were empty.

Ava didn't care. She wasn't here to chat about moving and packing or decorating and furniture. She wasn't here to chat about anything.

"Ava."

She silenced him with a kiss. The long, hot one that she should have received when he'd taken her home. He was breathing hard when she pulled back.

"You sure about this?" he asked.

She nodded. She was beyond sure. She slipped off her ballet flats and followed him up the stairs. He led her to his bedroom, his hands working at the buttons of her coat, stopping only to kiss her every few seconds. This was so much better than talking.

Ava got a sense of a large bedroom, but maybe it only seemed that way was because there was nothing but a bed in it. A king-size bed with a fluffy comforter and puffy pillows. Ava gasped when Jake scooped her up and lifted her onto it.

"I've got you," he said as he lowered her. He was careful, as always, not to jar her broken wrist.

"I know," she whispered, but she didn't have time to analyze what that might mean before he climbed on the bed, too. A sigh glided from her lips. She was on Jake's bed. In his room. And she was about to get naked.

He undid the few buttons on her coat that hadn't yet been attacked and spread the material behind her. The way he watched her made her feel sexy and desirable. Even her cast seemed erotic, which was pretty remarkable for an inanimate object made of fiberglass.

"I've wanted you from the first time I saw you," he said.

"Really?" Then she realized how needy that sounded and distracted him by telling him that she wasn't wearing a bra.

His eyes lit up and he stripped her out of the coat and thin silk T-shirt in record time. She shivered and didn't stop until he wrapped his arms around her. "You okay?"

"Just a little cold, I guess."

He smiled. "I'll warm you up." Then he reached down to undo her jeans. The zipper made a soft sound, which was drowned out by the low growl in his throat.

Ava could feel the hunger rolling off him and reveled in it. She lifted her hips so he could slide her jeans off, and then lay before him in just her underwear, which—because she didn't want to be pulling a Bridget Jones with her granny panties in stretchy nylon—were small and lacy and the palest of pinks. Only La Perla would do on a night like this.

"Wow." Jake sucked the word in through his teeth.

Ava felt her own need surge. "You like them?"

"Oh, yeah."

And from the speed with which he shucked off his own clothes, she guessed he did. She rolled to her side to watch the show, shamelessly checking out his butt. It really was a great butt. Her heart jittered when he finished and stood before her for a moment, proud and naked.

She wanted to be naked with him.

He lowered his body over hers, running his tongue along her neck. She clutched at his shoulder, her body beginning to ache. She was going to burst out of her skin pretty soon. She rubbed against him, wanting more and wanting it now.

But Jake seemed to have his own plan for how things were going to unfold and he was relentless in his pursuit of it. Using his mouth, his fingers, his teeth, he tempted and tormented her until Ava was sure she would die from the exquisite pain of it all. But the whole time he never went past teasing. Forget bursting, she was talking volcanic eruption here.

"Please," she gasped. She couldn't say anything more. She was too busy concentrating on breathing.

He brushed a knuckle between her thighs. "Is this what you want?" When she closed her eyes on a sigh, he laughed, low and long. "Yeah?"

Oh, yeah.

He leaned down, so his mouth was beside her ear. His hand still hovered, deliciously close without actually touching. He was driving her right to the edge, and she was sure it wasn't going to take much to push her straight over. "Tell me."

She opened her eyes and stared at him. "What?"

His smile was slow. "Tell me what you want."

"What I…" She stumbled over the words. She was usually the silent type in bed, preferring to let her fingers do the talking, but it was impossible to deny the fact that his request had made her entire body pulse.

"Talk to me," he said, his fingers hovering just out of range.

Ava swallowed. All right, then, so that's how they were going to play this. She marshaled her reserves. "Touch me."

"Where?"

He wanted her to spell it all out? She stared at him, not so sure about this little game.

But then he leaned down, nuzzled her ear and whispered, "Trust me. Tell me what you want."

Intrigue joined uncertainty and the knowledge that

in some surprising way, all this chatter was turning her on. She reached out and grasped his hand, then put it exactly where she meant. There. Much better.

But as soon as she let go, Jake lifted his palm.

"No," she told him, feeling the cry of the lost contact. "Right there."

He bent his head again and licked the side of her neck. "Tell me."

Fire skidded through her body when she realized that he wasn't going to let her half-ass her way out of it. If she wanted him to touch her, she was going to have to tell him. Fine. She would.

"Put your hand between my legs." She was silent until he did as she asked. "Now touch me."

"How?"

She shot him a look, but he only looked back, waiting. So it was going to be like that, was it? Well, she was up to the task. "Stroke your fingers up and down," she told him. He complied, sending a shower of pleasure reverberating through her. So good. So, so good.

His thumb ran along the edge of her panties, then slowly began to worm its way under. Ava clamped her legs together even though it practically killed her. "I didn't say you could touch me there." Two could play at this game.

He lifted an eyebrow in acknowledgment and stopped. Longing radiated from his eyes, but he didn't move, awaiting her next command.

She smiled. "Slide your fingers up and down, just like before. Over the top of the panties." Her body itched to go further, but she wasn't giving in that easily. She rode the delicate pleasure as it wafted through her, feeling the material between her legs grow hot and wet. "Now kiss my breasts. Slowly."

She ran her fingers through his hair as he lowered his head. His lips were amazing and Ava didn't know how much longer she could keep this up, but she planned to enjoy it while she could.

"Good." Very good. He moaned against her skin and the vibration added to the sensations swarming her. She closed her eyes and exhaled. Jake might have started this little game, but she was going to finish it.

"No more hands," she told him, guessing just how close he was to losing control and wanting to see if she could push him to do it. "Just your mouth."

Another moan, but she could hear the pleasure behind it. He liked this just fine.

He kissed his way down her stomach, leaving a trail of shivers behind. But her temperature soared when he caught the waistband of her underwear with his teeth. He paused there, eyebrows raised.

She raised an eyebrow back. "I said no hands."

Lace scraped over her thighs as he wriggled them off and then he was back. Lust sparked through her, making her back arch and her legs shake.

Oh, my God.

She didn't notice when his hands rejoined the party, didn't care. She felt good, so good that all she wanted was more. More of this. More of him.

Lust and need twined together, creating a desire so overwhelming that she didn't know if her body could contain it. It shuddered through her, growing bigger before finally crashing through her like waves on the shore.

It was a while before either of them moved.

"Wow," she finally said.

Jake lifted his head from the crook of her neck where he'd buried it after collapsing on top of her, and grinned down at her. "Good?"

"Way better than good." Like never-before-in-this-lifetime good. Sell-your-firstborn-child good. Give-up-your-Louboutin-shoes good.

"I'm glad." He shifted off her and laid his head on her stomach. She ran her fingers through his thick dark hair, enjoying the way it spilled through her fingers like silk. He turned to face her. "How's your wrist?"

Wrist? What wrist? She glanced down at her cast as though it belonged to someone else. "It's fine. Doesn't hurt at all." But seeing as her body was still pulsing with hormonal release, that didn't really come as a surprise.

He nodded. Then kissed his way up her body and nipped the side of her neck.

"Hey, stop that." She pushed at him. "I work on camera. I can't show up with a big hickey."

He caught her hands and pressed them back into the mattress. "You can wear a turtleneck."

"I don't have any," she said, angling her neck to make it more difficult for him. "And I don't recall telling you that hands were allowed yet."

Jake laughed and let go, but kept his face pressed between the smooth curve of her shoulder and neck. "Okay, no hands." She felt his teeth flash against her skin.

"No hickeys, either."

"I like the idea of marking you. How about a little one?"

"No." She twisted sideways, but he merely moved to her other side, where his tongue began tracing delicate patterns that were making her forget what she was supposed to be saying. Ava fought for sanity. "I'm not kidding. No hickeys. Makeup will not cover them and then everyone will know what I've been doing."

"Was it so bad that you want to forget?" Another lick.

She shivered. "Looking for an ego stroke?"

"It's not my ego that needs stroking." When he shifted his hips, she felt the length of him harden. Her body flamed in response.

All at once, his hands were everywhere, hard and soft, cool and warm. She'd have rather cut out her own tongue than remind him of the no-hands rule now. He played across her body, leaving tiny rivers of need in his wake. Her breathing increased. Her eyes slipped shut.

And as quickly as he'd started, he stopped.

What now? He was using his hands, but she wasn't complaining. What was the problem? Her eyes popped open to find out.

"Much better." He was smiling down at her. "I want you to look at me this time." His voice caressed her body and made her all melty inside.

Their eyes met and held. "Why?"

"Because I want you to watch me when I make you come again."

Little shocks of pleasure began to rain through her when he slipped back inside her. But she didn't look away, didn't even blink. Just watched the way his eyes never left hers. Never looked anywhere but at her as he drove himself deep inside her.

Cohost Amazingness!

Filling in for Miss Danica for the next two weeks.
I tried to talk her into staying away permanently,
but she told me no, that it's just a vacation.

I'll do my best to live up to her most excellent
standards.

Also (I know I told you that I'd spilled everything about Rockdale…I lied…get over it), there
are just a few more celebrity secrets to share. I'll
be unveiling them all week. Unless you don't care
if George is a briefs or boxers man?
Kiss kiss,
Ava

Chapter 18

Jake booked an editing suite for Thursday evening, feeling pretty good about life. After Ava's apology, he was sure that she understood that her role with the pilot was only temporary. As for what had happened after? That would put a smile on anyone's face.

He returned his attention to editing the travel-show pilot, which was why he'd booked the suite in the first place, watching the tape through a couple of times, noting spots that showcased the city or Ava particularly well. Normally, he wouldn't use company resources for a personal project, but he'd spoken to Harvey and they'd agreed that as long as it was after hours and didn't create extra work for anyone else, it was fine. Jake had even offered to pay for the time, but Harvey had refused the money, telling Jake to think of it as repayment for stepping in to help out the station.

Ava still refused to arrive with him in the morning,

but she was helping out tonight with the editing of the pilot. He told himself that he needed her for voice-overs as well as her keen eye for how to improve the flow of the show, but it was more than that.

He needed her.

He'd been in the editing suite for about thirty minutes when he heard the door open.

"Sorry I'm late," Ava said. She was still wearing full studio makeup though she'd pulled her hair into a ponytail. "Tommy was feeling a little insecure about his stumble." Harvey's nephew had flubbed one of his lines earlier this evening and since they shot live, there was no way to cover it. "I had to find that YouTube clip of the time I freaked out when that spider crawled up my leg to show him that it really wasn't a big deal."

"There's a YouTube clip of you with a spider?"

"I wouldn't say 'with.' It's mostly me running around screaming, 'Get it off. Get if off.' While the crew laughs hysterically in the background. Not one of my finer moments."

Jake laughed and reached for her. They'd kept their promise to maintain a professional distance when colleagues were around, but it wasn't easy. Not when Jake wanted to kiss and touch her every chance he got. He'd taken to watching the show from the booth this week rather than being on the floor, which he usually preferred, because it gave him a larger buffer. Even then, he felt his fingers itch with desire. He lowered his face to her hair and inhaled the orange scent of her shampoo, but didn't say anything.

After a few minutes, she tilted her head to look at him, but stayed within the circle of his arms. "Hey, you okay?"

"Not really. I talked to Harvey about investing."

And though Harvey had given him the courtesy of listening, he hadn't been interested. Harvey was looking to ease his workload, not increase it. He wanted to use his free time to groom Tommy. "Succession planning," he'd told Jake, which made Jake feel worse.

Back in the day, upon graduation from Ryerson University with his degree in radio and television, his father hadn't been able to shunt him off on someone else quick enough. There had never been any mention of Jake taking over the family business.

"You did?" Ava's eyebrows jumped into the middle of her forehead.

"He said no," Jake told her before she could get too excited. "But we have the meeting with the airline scheduled for next week. If that goes well, we might not need an investor."

"Or you'll have your choice of them once they hear there's a buyer on board."

When the possibility of meeting a group of executives from an airline had first come up, Jake had wanted to hold off. He'd wanted the money situation in hand first, but when that showed no signs of happening, he'd revisited the idea.

At the rate things were moving, if he waited for an investor to get on board, he'd still be waiting to pitch the show on his deathbed. So Alex had called in a favor with an old contact and scheduled an appointment for next Friday, which meant Jake had just over a week to make the pilot perfect, practice his pitch and get himself out to Toronto.

Ava gave him one more squeeze and then lowered herself into one of the rolling chairs, kicking off her heels at the same time. "Does that mean you're leaving the list alone until after the meeting?"

"No." Jake pulled out the piece of paper from his back pocket. He wasn't sure why he was keeping it on him, as there was no hope left on it. "There's nothing to leave alone. Crossed them all off." He handed it over so she could see each line. "Every name."

She scanned it and then raised her eyebrows at him. "You called them all?"

"I called them all," he confirmed. "And then I called people they'd recommended."

"And you're telling me no one was interested?" She shook her head. "I can't believe that."

Her words soothed some of those old aches. "Believe it. If I didn't know better, I'd think someone was working against me."

"Really? Do you think that's possible? Who would want to do that to you?"

"No, I don't think that." He laughed. "You watch too many movies. It's a difficult economy right now. People want to hang on to their money. I think they're nervous that travel will drop and this project won't find a home."

"Are they right?"

"No. There's always a market for travel and most analysts confirm that travel is just as strong, if not stronger, than it was before the recession."

Jake had even considered cashing in the stocks and bonds that his father had purchased for him over the past three decades. He rationalized the move by telling himself that his father had not earmarked the money for anything specific and this would be an investment in his future.

But according to his financial planner, that wasn't an

option. It seemed during his annual sit-down last year, Jake had told his adviser that he had no plans to use the money in the short term, and signed off on the majority being funneled into a variety of long-range ventures. The money that was readily available was limited— barely enough to keep a rubber ducky afloat—and if he liquidated anything else, he faced stiff penalties.

Ava glanced at the list again. "There are a lot of names on here. Are you sure that's everyone?"

"Everyone except my father." He smoothed her raised eyebrow with his thumb. "No, I'm not asking him."

"Why not? You asked Harvey. You would have accepted his investment."

"Harvey is not my father." He didn't need to prove anything to Harvey. But he couldn't help remembering that proud Papa Bear look Harvey had gotten in his eye when he'd been talking about Tommy's future at the station. And thinking, even though it was probably impossible and definitely foolish, that if he pulled this off his father might get that same look in his eye.

"But what about if you just treated your father like any other investor?"

He shot her a look. "No."

To her credit, she dropped that line of questioning, though he wasn't convinced that it was permanent. He kissed her hard just to make sure. Then did it again. She sighed against his lips and he would have done it a third time, but he knew where that would take them and it wasn't a finished pilot.

Groaning, he placed his hands on her shoulders and gently rolled her chair away, spinning it to face the television console. "We need to work on the show."

His meeting with the airline wasn't going to wait,

which meant making out with Ava in the editing suite would have to.

They settled down to work, getting in a few hours before calling in for sustenance in the form of Chinese takeout from a local restaurant and sodas from the vending machine. Then they worked another couple hours.

It took longer than Jake had anticipated, but it was getting there. Full of light and charm with Ava's cheerful smile welcoming them to her city. Surely the executives would bite on this.

"Okay, I need a break." Ava had put her feet on his lap about an hour ago, claiming that they were sore, and since she was here helping him, it was his duty to massage them. "I don't know if I have anything else left in me tonight."

"Nothing at all?" Jake smirked at her. "Because I thought we'd go back to your place." He ran a hand up her calf. "I have a few ideas in mind of how to thank you for all your hard work."

"You don't have to thank me." She wriggled her toes and looked at him. "I want to help you."

Reason number 842 for why he was crazy about her. He tugged on her leg until she was on his lap then pulled her tight, feeling the beat of their hearts sync up.

"But maybe I could be convinced."

And though Jake was tired, too, he felt his body stand up and tell him that they could put off sleep for a few hours.

Chapter 19

A week later, Ava was bustling around her apartment, trying to keep busy while she waited for Jake's flight to arrive. He was due back from his meeting with the airline executives and she couldn't wait to hear the news.

She'd managed to keep her mind off it most of the day. It had been her last day of covering for Danica, which had kept her in almost constant motion. It had been a lot of work filling in as well as managing her regular reporting duties, but Ava found it enormously rewarding and was sorry to see the end.

There was just something about hosting, about helping stitch the pieces into a united whole, that satisfied her soul. She liked providing the pieces, ensuring that her bit blended with the others, but it didn't give her the same charge that standing in front of the camera and linking those pieces together did. Or maybe it was knowing that by keeping things running at the station, she was helping Jake.

She hadn't anticipated the rush she would get from helping him, but there was no denying it. It wasn't just about the job and what it meant for her career. She loved the fact that she was doing something to help him achieve his goals.

Unable to sit still, she puttered around her apartment, killing time. Every couple of minutes she'd end up in front of her laptop to refresh the airport's website so that she'd know the exact moment Jake's plane landed.

He'd called only once, early this morning before the meeting, but Ava knew his appointment was set for the afternoon and if things went well, he'd be pressed to make his flight back home.

She wasn't even going to consider that the airline wouldn't buy the show. It was lively and fresh and different. What more could they want?

By the time nine o'clock rolled around, she'd given up pacing and was filing her nails and drinking coffee—not that she needed the caffeine. Jake's flight had landed thirty minutes ago and he'd assured her that he would come here first. Still, she jumped when her buzzer sounded and she felt jittery as she waited for him to take the elevator to her floor.

But those jitters disappeared the moment he stepped into her apartment wearing a grin wide enough to split his face, and picked her up to swing her around. Definitely good news.

"Hey." She wrapped her arms around his neck. "You seem happy."

"I'm pumped." He slid her down to the floor but didn't let go. She reveled in his nearness. He'd only been away for one night, but she'd missed him. It startled her to realize it. When had he become such a part of her life that she missed him being around?

"So it's good news?" She could think about this whole missing-him thing later, when she wasn't plastered to him with other, more pressing things to consider.

"Very good." He bent his head to kiss her, then did it again. "You taste good."

"It's the coffee." She was trying to catch her breath after the kissing.

"It's not the coffee," he said and dipped his head for another kiss. "I missed you."

She opened her eyes and looked at him. "You were only gone a day." But her heart stuttered. He'd missed her, too.

His fingers closed over her hips, held her steady and pressed more deeply against her. Ava felt the delicious shivers of pleasure begin to radiate from her core. "I still missed you."

She looked into his eyes, felt the swirl of emotion in the dark gray surrounding her. "I missed you, too."

When they eventually made it to the bed, Ava was too sated from their interlude in the entryway to care about things like creature comforts. But when she felt the suppleness of the mattress beneath her, the pillows plump and soft, she decided that maybe she cared a little.

She tugged Jake back down when he made a move to stand. "Stay."

"I'm coming back," he told her, bracing his arms

on either side of her head and pressing another kiss to her lips.

"I know." She cupped his face in her hands. "But I want you here now." The sheets needed him because although they weren't nearly as cold as the tile by the door, they weren't exactly warm, either.

"I might need a little time to recharge. I'm not sixteen anymore."

She laughed. "I'll settle for you warming up the bed."

"I will." He lowered his head to kiss her and then disappeared. She watched him go, his fine butt waving at her as he walked. Seriously, it might actually look better out of his jeans, though she wouldn't have thought it was possible.

When he returned he was carrying two cups of coffee. She knew without asking that hers would be just the way she liked it: a splash of cream and one sugar. He carefully sat on the bed, then handed a cup to her.

"Tell me about the meeting. Exactly how well did it go?"

They hadn't managed to get to that part of the conversation, too busy giving each other a proper greeting at the door.

"My celebration didn't make that clear? I guess I'll have to practice some more." He slid into bed beside her and ran his hand along her leg, pausing when he reached her hip. "You ready for that?"

For him? "Always." She tapped her mug against his. It didn't have the same chime as champagne flutes, but it served her purpose. They sipped companionably, comfortable in the moment and each other. His hand stroked her skin, but he made no further move.

She stole a peek at him. He was watching her, his crooked smile playing over his lips. "The meeting?"

He nodded. "It was good." His smile widened. "Really good." There had been two men and one woman. One short, one young and one quiet, respectively. It started with a hard handshake from the short one. Overcompensating, obviously. A volley of questions from the junior one. And contemplation from the quiet one, who was clearly the decision maker.

"And did they sign on the dotted line?"

"Not yet." But he didn't appear bothered, not like before. "They'll need to discuss how they would roll it out, time line, that sort of thing, before they'll offer a contract."

"So it's just a matter of time." Pride washed over her and she couldn't stop grinning at him. Only a matter of time until the show was a reality. She ran a hand through his hair, playing with the length of it.

"I'm thinking Toronto for the next show." He turned his head to kiss the inside of her arm. "My city, so I know it. Makes it easy." He turned those liquid eyes on her. "And you can come and meet my family."

Any words she might have said got stuck in her throat. Just for a second, but long enough that he started talking again.

"Seeing as I've already met yours, it only seems fair. And I want to show you the city. Share it with you. We'll fit some fun in with the work. Assuming you can get away from the station for the weekend, of course."

"Of course." Pleased relief made her tongue shrink back to its normal size. "Of course." She put her coffee cup down on the nightstand and threw her arms around him.

"I wouldn't get that excited." He laughed into her hair. "My sister will want to know everything about you and she isn't easily put off."

Ava didn't care. They were going to Toronto. She was going to host. She was going to meet his family, which was a clear sign that he was getting serious. Her nerves were tingling again, but that didn't bother her. She was ready for this. She hugged him again.

"But if you really want to show me how grateful you are…" He trailed off as he yanked her on top of him, pressed his hard body against hers. "I could be talked into it."

Chapter 20

They went out on Saturday evening to celebrate again, this time with Jilly and Alex. A popular nightclub that was less glitz and more grunge yet was somehow the most popular in the city. Jilly, who knew everyone, had gotten them on the guest list, so they were able to bypass the larger and continually growing lineup. She even managed to reserve a booth along the floor-to-ceiling brick wall that faced the stage where a live band played cover tunes.

The bass echoed through the red velvet bench seats as the band rolled into an eighties montage. Ava grinned when Jilly grabbed her hand and dragged her to the dance floor as they waited for the men to arrive.

"So?" Jilly asked as they got down on it. "You and McHot Stuff getting serious?"

"I like him."

"Oh, please. I know that look in your eye." Jilly executed a move that had half the guys on the floor drooling. She flipped her pink hair at them and refocused on Ava. "You are in love."

"I'm not in love. I like him." But her heart fluttered at the thought.

"Uh-huh." Jilly didn't look convinced. "Well, I guess you'll be the last to know, then. Let me know when you catch up to the rest of us."

"Jilly." Ava laughed, but she let the subject drop. While she wasn't ready to say the *L* word, she wasn't comfortable denying it, either. Did that mean she was in love? Or just getting there? She concentrated on the music instead, feeling the sudden butterflies in her stomach settle when she spotted Jake watching her from across the room.

Whether she was or wasn't in love with him, she didn't need to worry about it right now. All she needed to do was have a good time tonight and maybe tomorrow start researching some other cities they might film.

Jake had said that Toronto was next on the list, which made perfect sense since he'd lived there, but she wanted to help with the others. Did he have a mind to hit all the large Canadian metropolises next? Or was he going to branch into the U.S. right away? She'd been to Montreal a few times and knew where to find the best smoked-meat sandwich, and she'd spent lots of time in various American cities for work and pleasure.

She was trying not to think too far ahead—after all, nothing was official yet—but Jake had seemed so certain that the airline would buy in and she believed him. Once they knew what was expected, they could make some decisions. She wondered if she'd be able to stay on at the station or if she'd need to focus full-time on the travel show.

It was hard to recall that only a few weeks ago, she'd been sitting in Jake's office while he told her that she wasn't going to be the station's next cohost and her career had seemed as if it might be over. And now she felt as if it had never been on a bigger upswing.

She laughed when Jilly grabbed her hand and twirled her around the dance floor. Life was grand.

"She is smokin'." Alex emitted a low whistle as he dropped into the booth beside Jake.

He glanced over for about a nanosecond before returning his attention to Ava. "She's mine. Hands off."

"Come on, man. You think I'd say that about your girl? Not that she isn't a very attractive woman." Jake took his eyes off the dance floor long enough to glare at his soon-to-be-former best friend, but Alex only laughed. "I meant her friend. What's her name?"

"Jilly, but don't."

Alex feigned a wounded look. "You're blocking me? Harsh."

Jake was not swayed. "She's Ava's best friend."

"Great, so you can introduce me."

"No."

"Why not?" Alex leaned against the booth. "She married?"

"No."

"Then what's the problem?"

The problem was that Jake didn't trust Alex not to pull his usual moves on Jilly, which inevitably ended in a breakup. And while Alex was never cruel and made an effort to remain friendly with everyone, Jake knew that hurt feelings were still a strong possibility. He wasn't going to risk Alex's playboy behavior reflecting poorly on him. "There are plenty of other women here tonight. Choose one of them."

Alex looked around disinterestedly and shrugged. "Nah."

"Why not?"

"Because I like her."

"Get over it," Jake told him. "Because I'm not letting you do anything to piss off Ava. Especially not dumping her best friend."

"I haven't even met her and you've already got us breaking up." Alex put a hand on his chest. "I'm crushed, man."

Jake was not moved by this display of obsequiousness. "I know you." He looked at his friend just long enough to see that the message got through.

Alex leaned back, his blue eyes alight. "I didn't know you were serious about her."

"I am."

It was something that had snuck up on him. In the past few weeks, she'd somehow become a part of his life, creeping past those barriers he'd thought he'd erected to protect himself. He liked it. Liked the way she'd looked at him when he'd arrived at her place last night. Liked how she felt plastered up against him. Liked how hard she worked for her career, and that she put forth the same determination for his project.

"Cheers to that." Alex raised his bottle and they toasted.

Jake was still feeling good when Ava returned from her swing around the dance floor. Jilly was still spinning near the stage, leaving a trail of dizzy men in her wake.

"Hey, you." She moved to sit beside him, but Jake caught her hand and pulled her into his lap instead. She responded by kissing him.

"Wow. Must be love." Alex stuck out his hand. "Alex Harrington." Jake growled in warning, but Alex ignored him, capturing Ava's hand and bringing it to his lips. "I've heard a lot about you."

Ava smiled at him. "Nice to meet you."

"You, too." Alex ignored Jake's glare. "Tell me what a pretty girl like you is doing with this guy."

"Alex is going to hit on Jilly," Jake said and flashed his teeth when Alex gave an annoyed "hey."

But to his surprise, Ava didn't appear to be concerned. "Jilly can take care of herself."

"Now, that's a challenge I can't pass up." Alex didn't waste any time beating it out of the booth and heading straight for Jilly. They both watched as she turned to look at him, a cool been-there-done-that expression on her face. Then Alex said something that made her throw back her head and laugh.

Jake locked his arm around Ava's waist just in case she had any ideas about climbing off his lap. "He's a bit of a lady-killer," he whispered into her ear.

She leaned back into him, the silky strands of her hair tickling his skin. "He's never met anyone like Jilly."

"So if things blow up it isn't my fault."

"Yes, it is." She swiveled to face him, her expression one of complete seriousness. "I plan to hold you responsible for all your friends' behavior. Maybe even your acquaintances'." She pondered that. "To be on the safe side, maybe we should just say everyone you've ever met."

"Ha-ha."

She snickered and kissed him again. Jake was content to let her. Once the travel show was settled, he foresaw a lot more nights like this one, where he and his team would film during the week, leaving his weekend free for Ava to visit. He hoped that she'd be willing to fly in to whichever city he was working in. If she came as soon as she got off work on Friday, they could have the entire weekend before she'd have to return to the station.

And he wouldn't be traveling all the time. Those weeks when he wasn't on location somewhere, he pictured being very similar to the past few weeks they'd spent together. Maybe a few more dates because, while they hadn't exactly hidden away, tonight had been the first time she'd been so overt in public.

"Want to go home and leave our friends to handle themselves?" he asked.

"No, but only because my butt is still frozen from last night on the tile."

"I didn't hear you complaining at the time." No, there had only been kissing and touching and asking for more. "And you did steal my shirt to use as a barrier."

"A gentleman would have offered it."

"I took the tile the second time." It had been cold. Fortunately, he hadn't cared.

"I know. I think my knees are bruised, too."

"Do you need me to kiss them better?"

"Not here, but yes." She smiled.

"Then let's go."

Chapter 21

Jake's good mood lasted until Wednesday, when everything started to suck.

He'd held interviews on Monday and Tuesday, looking for Lena's replacement, which had resulted in three mediocre and one outstanding candidate. The outstanding candidate had sent an email Wednesday morning thanking him for his time, but saying that he'd accepted an offer at another company. Jake wasn't sure if he should bring back the other candidates for a second round of interviews—were they really mediocre or did they just not interview well?—or repost the position and see if he got any new bites.

While he mulled over this new snag, he'd managed to spill coffee on his pant leg. And when he took a sip from his cup, the coffee was cold. Now there was a splotch over his right knee and he still hadn't had his caffeine fix.

Hanna Compton, a friend and the person he'd convinced Harvey to hire to fill the executive producer role, had called around noon to let him know that she was still taking the job, but had been unable to dissolve her current contract early, which meant she couldn't get to Vancouver for another month. Jake's contract was scheduled to end in two weeks, but he didn't want to leave Harvey high and dry. He was debating whether one of the senior segment producers could fill in for the interim or if he should stick around until Hanna arrived. Neither option was good.

Finance had asked him to cut his budget by ten percent, one of his segment producers had arrived to the morning meeting, wiping away tears because her boyfriend had just dumped her, and Ava was out of the office on an all-day shoot, so he couldn't even pop in to see her smiling face for a quick pick-me-up.

But nothing really hit the fan until late that afternoon when the phone rang and everything he'd been planning and working on came crashing down.

He wasn't able to get to Ava's apartment until the show wrapped, and by that time he was tired, hungry and angry.

"It's over," he said as soon as she opened the front door.

She frowned at him, that cute little line appearing between her eyebrows. "What? What are you talking about?"

"My show. The travel show. It's over." He stepped in, closing the door behind him and pulling Ava in tight against him. If he could just hold her, maybe he would feel better.

"What do you mean 'over'?"

He let his eyes slide shut, closing out everything but her for one blissful moment. The she poked him in the ribs.

"Jake? What do you mean *'over'?*"

He exhaled, but it didn't help. "The airline called me today just as I was heading down to the studio." He'd been ready for the day to end and had already promised himself a cold beer once the show had finished filming. But when he'd seen the Toronto area code on his phone, his exhaustion had ebbed, replaced by a pulse as a fast as a cheetah. "They've passed on the show."

"Oh." Ava exhaled softly, sympathy shimmering in the sound.

Jake sighed and let his face fall into her hair. It curled over his cheek, tickling his nose, but he didn't move. He didn't have the energy. He'd put everything he had into the show and he was left with nothing. No investors, no buyers, nothing but a DVD of his pilot episode, which wasn't enough to make a career out of.

"Now what?"

He tightened his hold around her waist. At least he had her. It wasn't what he'd come to Vancouver for, but he was happy he'd found it. "Now it's time for me to face the fact that this show isn't a go and never will be."

"Oh, Jake." She rubbed his back. "Don't say that. I know you're disappointed. I'm disappointed for you. But it's not over."

Actually, it was. He'd crunched some numbers after the phone call from the airline. He could qualify for a bank loan that would give him enough funds to film a few more shows, and liquidate some assets to make a couple more. But at the end of that, he'd be tapped out. And what was the point if he didn't have a buyer?

"There are other airlines," Ava said. "Other investors. You just haven't found the right one yet."

"I don't think time is going to change anything." His business plan hadn't counted on zero interest from anyone. He thought he'd be splitting shares or in a bidding war. He ran a hand through his hair. "I think it's time for me to recognize that this show isn't happening." Christ, he couldn't even stay at the station, since he'd forced Harvey to hire Hanna. He was going to have to start job hunting.

"But the show is so good."

He shrugged. "If no one buys it, it doesn't matter if it's the best show in the world. No distribution, no viewers, no money."

The quality of the show didn't appear to be the problem. That airline certainly seemed to like it, but they were nervous about the timing. Worried that the travel market was going to slow down and they'd be forced to make cutbacks to keep planes in the air. His show was a nice-to-have but not a necessity.

And there was no way to convince them that the previous drop in travel had been a knee-jerk reaction and the current stronger forecast was the correct one. In a depressed market, no one wanted to get caught out with their funds tied up.

She leaned her head against his chest for a moment. "Can I do anything?"

Really, he just wanted to forget about it all for the night. Soon enough he'd have to tell everyone, figure out what he was going to do with his life, but right now he wasn't up to it.

They moved into the living room and sat on the couch, less than a millimeter of space between them.

"I can't believe they passed on it. There's nothing like it out there. Don't people have any imagination? Can't they see that you're at the forefront of a new type of show?"

"Guess the airline didn't see it that way. I'll have to start looking for another job. Know anyone who's hiring?"

"Only my mother, but I wouldn't wish that on my worst enemy. Anyway, what do you mean you need to find a job? What's wrong with the one you have?"

"Harvey's already hired my replacement. She starts in a month."

"Couldn't she unstart?" She swiveled so she could look at him. "Couldn't you explain to Harvey? I'm sure he'd want you to stay."

Jake let his head droop against the back of the couch. "I wouldn't do that to Hanna. She's a friend. You'll like working with her."

"I like working with you." She crawled into his lap.

"You've got a couple more weeks of it." He settled her more comfortably on his legs.

"What are you going to do?"

"I'll figure something out." He knew he'd be able to find a job somewhere. His father's contacts, who would once again be hiring him as a favor. Maybe Alex knew someone.

"Will you stay here? In Vancouver?" She watched him with those big, blue eyes. "Maybe you could try starting the show again in a few months, when the market improves."

It was sweet that she thought so, but Jake knew better. "I don't think there's any point. If no one's willing to invest now, a few months won't change that."

He touched a finger to the side of her mouth. "Don't frown. It'll be fine."

"But it's your dream."

"I have other dreams." One of which was sitting in his lap right now. He wrapped both his arms around her. She rested her head on his shoulder. "Once I tie off the loose ends, it'll be just like leaving any job."

"What can I do?"

"Nothing. There's not much. I only need to close down the business account and cancel the audition space."

She raised her head to look at him. "Audition space for what?"

"The host." He smiled at her. "Not that any of them would have compared to you."

But she wasn't smiling back. "I thought I was the host."

"You were." He pressed a kiss to her forehead. "For the pilot. But I needed someone permanent." And now he didn't. His stomach clenched. It was just so damn disappointing.

"But I thought I *was* the permanent host." She was frowning now.

"No." He was confused. "We talked about that when I asked. You were just filling in so I could shoot the pilot." He ignored the icy feeling trickling through his veins. It was a simple misunderstanding. Nothing more.

"Then what have I been doing for the last month?" She pulled out of his arms, lines bracketing her mouth. "I thought I was your choice to host." Her voice broke on the last word.

"You have a job," he reminded her. "I wasn't going to ask you to give that up."

Her eyes got that wet look that meant tears were on their way. "You didn't think I was good enough." Her voice was bitter, and the table shook when she slapped her glass on it. "Just like the cohost position."

"That's not fair, Ava. These are two totally different things."

"I don't think they are." She glared at him. "So what, you were using me?"

"Using you?" The icy feeling went from a trickle to a gush. He hadn't used anyone. "I needed your help. I paid you fair market value."

"And what about everything else? Editing the show, trying to help you find investors? What was that for if I wasn't going to be the host?"

Anger melted the ice and made his heart pound. "I thought you were helping because you cared about me."

"And what about all that stuff about taking me to Toronto when you filmed there? Why would I be going if I wasn't the host?" Her eyes could have pierced steel. "Exactly what was I supposed to think, Jake?"

He couldn't believe this was happening. Couldn't believe he'd fallen for this again. He supposed he should be grateful that he was finding out now before he fell any deeper, but he didn't. And he wasn't sure there was any farther to fall.

"You said you didn't want to be involved with someone that you work with," he reminded her. "How could you do the show and date me? Or was that part of the plan?" He heard the resentment in his tone, was helpless to stop it. "To sleep with me and ensure that this time you wouldn't get passed over?"

"What?" Her blue eyes looked shocked for a second, and then filled with a white fury. "You think I...

You're insane. God, I should have trusted my instincts with you. You're cruel."

That hurt. He wanted to hurt back. "As I recall, your first instinct was to shove your tongue down my throat at that anti–Valentine's Day party."

"I was drunk and lonely. I didn't even like you, so don't get a swollen head." She flipped her hair. "You know what? I wouldn't want to host your show anymore anyway."

"Don't worry. That won't be a problem." He pushed himself up from the couch, which had been so soft and welcoming only moments earlier. "I'm leaving."

"Of course you are." Her voice followed him as he strode to the door. "Just like you ran away from Toronto, you're running away here."

He whirled. "That was a low blow and this isn't the same thing."

She tilted her head in a challenging glare. "Isn't it?"

No, it wasn't. He ignored the questions that rattled through his head. "It's different." He shut the questions down before he had to answer them. It was better this way. "And let's not forget, you were using me to further your career."

"I would never do that."

Right, because no woman on the face of the planet had ever been known to do such a thing. "I thought you were different." But she wasn't and apparently neither was he. Still stupidly getting conned by game players. He was disgusted with her, with himself, with the world in general. "I'll show myself out."

He let the door slam shut behind him and wished he could take a little more comfort in getting the last word.

Chapter 22

Jake stomped home, sure that steam was coming out his ears the whole way. He'd left his car parked near Ava's building, but he didn't care. He could get it later and in this state of mind, he shouldn't be driving.

Where had he gone so wrong? What was wrong with him?

"Nothing," Rachel said when he called her. "You're fine, perfect."

"Okay, now I know you're lying."

"I'm not lying. Look, you're overwhelmed. Understandably. Just don't do anything rash tonight."

"What would I do?" His entire life had crumbled. No job, no relationship. There was nothing left for him to damage.

"I don't know. But don't do it anyway. Why don't you go to bed?"

"It's barely eight o'clock here."

"Well, it's eleven here and I have an early class in the morning. I'll call you as soon as I can tomorrow and we'll figure something out. Okay?"

Jake doubted it, but he let her go. And when his phone rang ten minutes later, he couldn't help the small sick part of him that hoped it was Ava calling to tell him that he'd misinterpreted everything. That she hadn't been acting the girlfriend to guarantee herself the hosting job. That she cared about him.

It wasn't. He cursed when he recognized his parents' number. He should have known Rachel would call to tip them off—they were both night owls—and now he was going to have to spend the next few minutes reassuring his mother that he wasn't having a mental breakdown and he didn't need her to fly out and take care of him.

"Yes?" He knew he sounded highly irritated, but it was better than ignoring the call. If he let it go to voice mail, she would worry. And then she'd call Rachel, who would start worrying, too, and then he'd be tag-teamed by the two of them for the rest of the night.

"Jake?" Not his mother's voice. "It's Dad."

Surprise had Jake sinking into one of the kitchen chairs Ava had helped him pick out last week. His father never called him. That was his mom's job. Occasionally during his weekly Mom Calls, his dad would pipe in from the background. Once they'd spoken for two minutes about the use of freelance versus salaried employees. But in general all parental contact went through and came from his mom.

Jake exhaled and he was suddenly glad he'd had the walk home to clear his head. He was going to need all his wits about him for this conversation. "What's going on, Dad?"

"I heard about the show. You okay?"

Jake's hope that he could have one night to grieve, to figure out his next step before admitting to his failure, died a hurried death. He was going to kill Rachel. She knew how he felt about this and she'd gone and tattled to Dad anyway. "Fine. You?"

Jake couldn't imagine being any less fine, but he wasn't about to show his dad that weakness.

There was a pause while his dad cleared his throat. Jake could picture him tugging the silver hair at his temples. "I thought we could talk. I could help."

"I've got it handled." His dad was so quick to jump to the rescue, so sure that Jake was incapable of rescuing himself. "Don't worry. I won't be leaning on you for anything."

His father didn't respond, just exhaled softly and said, "Your mother misses you, you know."

"So she tells me." Jake drummed his fingers on his knee and wished he hadn't answered the phone after all. Dealing with the tag-team worry twins would have been better than this. "Did she put you up to this?"

"Oh. Well." There was a bit of blustering on the other end of the phone. "Yes, she did."

"Tell her I'm fine. There's nothing to be concerned about." If he didn't count the small fact that his travel-show dream was over and he'd been fooled by someone he'd started to fall for. "I should go, Dad."

"You know I'm here if you need advice or help."

"Mom put you up to saying that, too?"

"No, but she would have if she'd thought of it." Chuck laughed. "But I'd like to help, if you'll let me."

"I'm good, Dad." Because he sure as hell didn't need advice from his father. "It's been a long day. I should go."

"Why won't you talk to me?"

Jake didn't want to get into this now. Maybe not ever. Couldn't they just go on living with this uncomfortable distance between them? "Nothing. I told you. I'm just tired."

"It's not nothing. I'm not stupid, Jake." He exhaled loudly. "What happened? I know we haven't been close, but what did I do to turn you away from me? From us? You moved halfway across the country."

"I needed a change."

"It was more than that. You were barely speaking to me before you left."

That was true. Jake hadn't been able to. Every time he'd looked at his father, his throat had clogged up, filled with those old fears that waited until he was at his most vulnerable to get him.

It might have been different if they'd been close. But they weren't. They hadn't been since Jake was a teenager and had completed his first and only internship at his dad's production company. That Jake had been a sixteen-year-old more interested in convincing his father to hold a staff summer barbecue bash and hitting on the other interns had been a grave disappointment to his father. Jake had continued the trend ever since.

"I was busy packing," he lied.

"You had time for your mother and your sister."

"They supported my move," Jake pointed out.

"Just because I mentioned that you could have started up your travel show more easily from Toronto doesn't mean I didn't support you."

If it had only been that. But it wasn't. It never was. And Jake was tired of it. He didn't want to dance around the truth anymore. "It wasn't just that, Dad. You've never supported me. You told me to study engineering. You didn't hire me for your company. And you acted like my life blowing up in Toronto was expected."

"Nothing in Toronto blew up. You had a relationship that didn't work out and you decided you needed to throw away everything you had."

Jake couldn't believe his dad was ignoring the crux of the matter. "You didn't want me to join the industry."

"I never said that."

"You didn't have to." It had been clear in every action. Jake stood and grabbed a bottle of water from the fridge. He twisted off the cap and took a long chug, but the burning feeling in his stomach remained. "But don't worry about it. I'll figure something out." Eventually.

"You think I don't support you?"

Hadn't he just said that? He tipped the water into his mouth again, draining half the bottle.

"Of course I support you. I wanted you to go into engineering because I thought you'd like it. You certainly showed no interest in working at my company after that internship. Your mother made me promise I wouldn't try to force you into it, so I didn't."

"What about after I got my degree? You didn't even hint that there would be a position available at your company."

"I didn't think you wanted it. You'd been pretty clear that you were looking to make your own way."

"I thought that's what you wanted me to do." There was no way this animosity was just some miscommunication. "You always talked about making it on your own. Not having anyone's help. What was I supposed to think?"

"I didn't know you felt that way."

"Well, now you do." Not that it mattered. Jake had tried to keep his career separate from his father's to prove to everyone that he was capable regardless of his surname. In the end, all his hard work hadn't mattered. "As it turns out, you were right to keep me away from your precious company. I would have just messed it up."

"You wouldn't have messed it up." Silence and probably some hair pulling. Finally, "Is it so bad to be my son?"

"No, Dad, it's not. That's not it. I needed to prove that I could do it on my own."

"You didn't need to move to Vancouver to do that."

"Actually, I did. You're a well-known guy in Toronto, Dad. There were a lot of people who felt that I got where I was because of your name."

"That's ridiculous. I never asked anyone to do you or me any favors. Everything you had here, you earned."

"Did I?" He'd always been so careful to keep his distance, not to use those connections, but he'd still heard the whispers. There was no way to prove it to himself if he stayed in Toronto in the industry where his father was a giant. At least in Vancouver, when people heard his name, they didn't immediately follow up with, "Any relation to Chuck?"

"Absolutely. And anyone who thinks otherwise is a fool."

Jake shrugged. It didn't really matter any longer.

All he'd wanted was to carve out a little bit of success. It didn't have to be as grandiose as his father's or even Harvey's, but it would be something that was his, that no one could say he'd been handed because he'd been born with a silver spoon in his mouth. "What about the cushy job you set up for me with your old buddy

Frank Forgione." Jake paused. "And don't tell me you didn't. I know you asked him to hire me as a favor."

"Sure I did. You graduated top of your class. You think I asked him as a favor to me? No, I told him as a favor to him. He was lucky to get you."

The words eased some of Jake's hurt. Chuck Durham didn't do flattery or any of that faux charm that permeated the industry. If he said something, he meant it.

"I know this probably isn't the right time, but you've got me fired up here. I'm sorry for the way things have worked out, but I'm glad, too."

Jake laughed quietly. "Gee, thanks, Dad." Trust his father to finally be on his side and to insult him while getting there.

"Hear me out. I hadn't dared to think about this before, but now I am. What would you think about coming to work for me?"

A pity job? Jake would rather starve. But he didn't get the chance to tell his father that. The old man was already talking again.

"I don't want you to answer right now. I know there are some things going on over there besides the travel show. You've got to finish your contract with Harvey, and Rachel thinks you've got a girlfriend. I should warn you, your mother is going to want to know all about that."

Jake had skipped the whole Ava portion of the evening in his account to his father. It was bad enough that they'd all seen the Claudia debacle play out. He didn't know if he could tell them that it had happened again. "There's no one," he said. Because as of an hour ago, it was true.

"No matter. It's still a big decision to move back." A

small pause. "I didn't say much when you told us you were moving out there because I wouldn't have liked my old man getting his nose in my business, and I hope you appreciate that I tried not to do that to you. But I'm doing it now. Come back home."

Chapter 23

Ava couldn't believe Jake had left town without saying anything to her. And this wasn't just a short jaunt
to clear his head, either—he'd gone all the way back to
Toronto. Permanently.

She sniffed in an effort to hold back the hurt. She was
in Jilly's "office" getting her makeup done for tonight's
show and Jilly would kill her if she ruined it. Jilly had
already chewed her out for having red eyes and made
Ava put on an ice mask for ten minutes before admin-
istering eye drops. It made her eyes look better, but did
nothing to heal the ache in her heart.

It wasn't as though Jake had up and left without a
word to anyone. She could have handled that. Instead,
he'd finished out his contract, and on his last day—from
what she'd heard around the break room—made time
to visit the rest of the staff to personally introduce his
replacement, a pretty brunette named Hanna Compton.

But for her? The woman he'd actually been involved with? Not even a whisper.

Granted, she'd done her best to avoid him at every turn. Including calling in sick on that last day. But there had been plenty of days before that, and if he'd really wanted to see her, he'd have found a way. He knew where she lived, he knew her favorite coffee spots and he knew her work schedule. It wouldn't have been that hard.

She sniffed again. If he'd had any feelings for her at all, he'd have tried. He'd have made some sort of effort instead of sneaking off as though they'd had nothing more than a one-night stand that he forgot.

She exhaled slowly, carefully, trying to get that smooth, even flow that was supposed to center your chi and calm your nerves. Not that Ava had ever been one for yoga. She wasn't bendy enough and too competitive. The one time she'd tried, she'd hated not being able to slide into the poses like the other people in the class. Also, the overheated room and smell of sweat had made her feel nauseated.

But she blew out another breath anyway. Fine. She was fine. If Jake wasn't going to show even the slightest concern for her, she would happily return the favor. She would never think about him again. Unless it was to imagine him crawling on his knees toward her, begging for forgiveness. After which, she would pretend to give it some thought before putting one gorgeous high-heeled shoe on his forehead—because a moment like that called for a gorgeous shoe—and kicking him away. Then she would strut off, while he watched with tears in his eyes, and she would go on to succeed in every aspect of life. The end.

"Are you thinking about him?"

"What?" Ava blinked. Jilly was no longer sweeping powder across Ava's face in long, wide strokes but was pointing the bronzing brush at her.

"Him. McJerk Face. I thought we agreed you weren't to give him the time of day."

"I'm not." But even she could hear the lame, slightly whiny note in her voice. "I'm not," she repeated more firmly. She was not about to have this conversation. She was due on set in twenty minutes, as Danica had been out sick the past few days, and she wasn't going out there with a sad-clown face, which was how thinking about Jake made her feel.

"Oh, Ava…" Jilly sighed and returned to powdering. "You so are."

Since there was zero point in denying it, Ava didn't. It had been a month since the fight in her apartment, three weeks since her cast had come off and two weeks since Jake had officially left the station. She was doing her best to move past him. It was just hard when every corner she turned, every camera she saw, reminded him of her.

Why had he overlooked her again? And so easily? Didn't he think she was good enough? She was a good host. No, she was a great host. So what was the problem? Was she too cheerful? Too blonde? Too old?

"This isn't healthy, you know," Jilly said, frowning as she dusted an extra layer across Ava's forehead and nose. "You haven't been out in weeks."

"I haven't felt like it," Ava said. She just didn't have the energy to gear herself up for a night out on the town. Instead, her evenings consisted of putting on her favorite pair of soft sweatpants and curling up in the front of the television. Or doing the exercises her sadistic physiotherapist insisted were necessary to make sure she regained a full range of motion in her wrist.

Everything else was a bother that she just couldn't deal with.

She'd even managed to avoid dinner with her mother during her time of mourning, which only proved the depth of her exhaustion. Never before had she put up with a long-winded lecture about family and priorities just so that she didn't have to leave her apartment.

"Want to come out tonight?"

"No," Ava said. It was the same answer she'd given Jilly every Friday for the past month. She caught her friend's worried expression. "I'm just tired," she explained. "It's been a lot of work covering for Danica and filming my stories, too."

Jilly made a rude snorting sound. "You keep telling yourself that." She finished with the powder and eyed Ava's face. Seeing something she obviously didn't like, she grabbed a different brush and the blusher. "When's the last time you left the apartment for something other than work? I swear, if you tell me you're thinking of getting a cat, I'm staging an intervention."

"I'm not getting a cat." Even if she had been checking out the adoption page of the local SPCA recently. They were so sweet with their cuddly little faces and she had a good home—she could save a life.

If she was going to be a caricature, sitting home alone with a TV dinner and no one to share it with, she might as well play up the spinster stereotype for all it was worth. Plus, a cat could be a boon companion. A cat wouldn't tell her that she wasn't good enough to host or believe that she'd only been with Jake so she could get the job on his travel show.

She was glad when Jilly finished with her makeup and she could escape to the bright lights of the studio. Even if it was only for a half hour, it was time during which she was so focused on the job that no thoughts of Jake could sneak through her defenses.

She was just buttoning up her coat to make her get-away for another weekend of burning excitement, when Hanna Compton, the new executive producer, stuck her head in Ava's office. "Got a minute?"

Ava's fingers stilled on the buttons, but she nodded. "Of course."

Jake had mentioned that Hanna was a friend, and she'd heard from other sources that they'd actually known each other for years. Made it sort of hard to like the leggy brunette, but Ava was trying. She knew she shouldn't take out her feelings about the old producer on the new producer.

She took her coat off, but brought it and her purse with her to Hanna's office with hopes this wouldn't take long.

Although Hanna had only been at the station a couple of weeks, she'd already made her presence felt both in and out of the studio. Ava saw that her office was no exception. The awful plastic brown couch was gone, replaced by a pair of art deco chairs in gray suede. The color reminded Ava of Jake's eyes, so she looked instead at the tasteful prints adorning the newly painted walls.

Hanna sat in one of the chairs and motioned for Ava to do the same. "There's something I'd like to discuss with you."

Suddenly, Ava wasn't noticing how much more comfortable Hanna's chairs were than Jake's monstrosity of a couch. She gripped the handle of her purse and felt a trickle of sweat begin to work its way down her spine. Exactly what was this meeting about?

She tried not to think about the fact that it was Friday, the classic time to fire someone. Surely they weren't going to let her go. With Danica out, they needed her. Even without Danica, they needed her.

But it was foolish to think that Jake and Hanna wouldn't have talked. Of course they had. They would have discussed the staff Hanna was inheriting in-depth. Which made her wonder exactly what Jake had told his old friend.

Ava cleared her throat. "I hope this isn't because you're displeased with my performance." Because that would be totally unfair. No one else at the station was juggling two full-time jobs, and Ava planned to point that out if necessary. Also, she was willing to consider Botox.

"Not at all." Hanna's easy posture didn't change. "I think you've done a fine job, given the situation."

"Thank you." Ava wasn't sure she felt any less tense, but at least there was no new trickle of sweat to dampen the back of her shirt.

"How do you like working here?"

Ava looked into Hanna's calm expression, hoping for a hint about what she was getting at, but the cool, competent expression didn't change. And even if it had, there wasn't really any answer she could give other than the one she decided on. "It's a good company to work for. I've been here for the past three years and in that time, I've been promoted from junior to senior re-

porter. I attend the majority of film festivals and fill in
as the show's cohost when required. I'm a team player
and I've been mentoring some of the junior reporters
the past year." She debated whether or not to add anything about her desire to become a permanent cohost.

"You don't need to give me your résumé, Ava. I'm
well aware of your accomplishments."

The comment could have been insulting, but even
with Ava's hypersensitive feeling that Jake might have
said something to color Hanna's opinion, she couldn't
find anything but kindness in the executive producer's
voice.

"But how do you like working here? Is it a positive
environment? Does the staff get along?" Hanna shifted,
tenting her hands in front of her.

Was this a test? And if Ava failed, was she going to
find herself marginalized until she either quit on her
own or her job was declared redundant?

She considered the best way to answer. If she was
too bubbly and gushing, she would come off as a kiss
ass. If she was coy and avoided the question, that would
give the impression that this was a toxic place to work.
Plus, she was tired of games, tired of playing and being
played. So she was honest.

"I like it. It can be a high-stress environment. I know
we don't report news in the traditional sense, but we
deal with the same issues about time and being the first
to break information to our audience. And I think we've
got a good team. For the most part, we work well together and get along."

Hanna absorbed the information without moving and
for a moment Ava wondered if she'd failed the test. Then
Hanna smiled again. It was a friendly smile. "I wouldn't

normally ask this without giving you some preparation time, but I'd like to know what your five-year plan is."

Ava's pulse kicked up. Had Jake said something? That she'd thought she was going to host his show and so obviously was planning to leave? The sweat was back along with its friend, dry mouth.

She pretended to smooth the length of her skirt, but was really wiping the wetness from her palms. Then she met Hanna's calm, assessing gaze. "I'd like to continue to work my way up through the company." Age notwithstanding.

"And where do you see yourself at the end of that?"

"I want to be cohost." Ava didn't see any point in hiding the truth. Hanna would be aware that hosting was the ultimate job for on-air personalities and to pretend otherwise would just be insulting.

"Good." If Ava had thought Hanna's smile was friendly before, it was nothing compared to the glow she had now. Seriously, if Ava could smile and get a glow like that on command she'd give up her Louboutins. Maybe even wine and chocolate. "Because I'd like to offer you the cohost position permanently."

"You...what?" There was a pop of surprise followed by a rush of excitement. "Really?" Cohost? On this show?

"Yes, really. I've been watching you closely this week and you're good. Very good."

Ava couldn't help but preen a little. And picture herself giving Jake a well-placed, well-deserved kick in the butt. She knew there was a reason she'd liked Hanna in spite of her Jake connection.

Danica was going to have a cow. An elegant, haughty cow, but a cow all the same. Ava wondered if she should invest in a series of scarves for her on-air wardrobe to ward off the chill she was sure to face. "So, there will be three of us?"

"No, there will only be two of you. Danica telephoned me this afternoon before the show. She's accepted a job offer in L.A. and has tendered her resignation. I'd like you to replace her."

This hadn't even crossed Ava's mind when Hanna asked to talk to her—the idea that Danica hadn't really been ill but off interviewing somewhere else was almost inconceivable. But now? She let the images overwhelm her. Standing in front of the camera introducing stories and off-site reporters, seeing her name flash across the screen at the start of every show, updating her résumé to read Cohost.

She wanted to jump up and down, do a Snoopy dance or let out a rebel yell, but that wouldn't be professional. She nodded at Hanna as though she was calmly considering the situation. "If I were to take the promotion, I assume there would be a raise?"

"Of course." And though Ava wouldn't have thought it possible, Hanna's expression brightened another degree. "So does that mean yes?"

"Yes." Yes, yes, a thousand times yes. And for the first time in weeks, Ava felt like going out to celebrate.

She called her mom instead.

Chapter 24

Jake put the finishing touches on the meal by straightening the place mats he'd found in his sister's linen closet and then stood back to take a critical look. The water goblets gleamed in the chandelier's light and the pristine white plates shone against the golden mats and orange napkins. He'd discovered some serving dishes that seemed to match the plates in the back of one of the cupboards, and after putting them through the dishwasher, deemed them clean enough to eat off.

He'd loaded them full of Chinese takeout, honey-garlic chicken balls, broccoli in black bean sauce, barbecued pork chow mein and egg rolls—all his sister's favorite dishes. A small way to say thank-you for letting him crash here until he found a place of his own.

When he heard her key in the door, he hung a white dish towel over one arm and greeted her in the entry. "Dinner is served."

Rachel blinked at him, looking a little confused through her glasses. "What the...?"

"This way, please." He led her down the hall and into the perfectly dressed dining room. Rob was working late tonight and since Rachel's lecture didn't end until after six, Jake had thought she'd appreciate coming home to a hot meal that she didn't have to prepare or clean up after.

Rachel's eyes widened. She turned to gape at him. "You did this?"

"Yes." And he was pretty pleased with himself. He'd borrowed the idea of fancying up the takeout from Ava's mother and thought it had turned out brilliantly. Also, preparing dinner kept him busy between getting home from his father's office and waiting for Rachel to turn up. He didn't like to have a lot of free time on his hands these days. There were too many thoughts he'd rather not have floating around in his head.

"Why?" She let her bag slide off her shoulder and land with a thump on the wood floor. "I mean, not that I'm unhappy." She plucked one of the chicken balls out of the bowl and popped it in her mouth. "But why all this? It's kind of romantic."

"It's not romantic, you weirdo," Jake said, flicking her with the dish towel and turning up the dimmer switch just to make sure. "I thought it would be nice for us to act like a couple of civilized adults for a change."

In the month since he'd been back in Toronto, dinners at Rachel's had consisted of pizza out of the box, hamburgers in wrappers and Thai out of foam containers.

Rachel ate another chicken ball. "Okay. So what do you want?"

"A guy can't make his little sister dinner just because?"

"Some brothers can. You are not one of those brothers. What's up?"

"Nothing. I swear." He sat at the table without waiting for her. "Just saying thanks for letting me stay here."

She snorted and sat down across from him. "You planning on leaving soon?"

Rachel and Rob lived in a large, rambling Victorian near the heart of downtown that had plenty of room and was convenient to his father's office building. Jake didn't plan to stay there indefinitely, but it was a good fit for now.

"You planning on kicking me out?"

Rachel loaded her plate until the food reached the edges. "You can stay here as long as you want. You know that."

He did know that and felt a surge of gratitude. Rachel had accepted his return with an easy shrug and treated him the way she always had, with none of the wariness he'd been afraid of.

In fact, no one had treated him with wariness. Not his mother or father. None of his old friends and colleagues. Even at his father's company, where he'd been slotted in as VP of production, no one had seemed put out in the least. There had been no snide comments about him taking on a pivotal role in the company, no questions about why he'd left and returned just as quickly, or about the fact that his very public ex was now an anchor on the number-two station's nightly news, wearing a huge diamond engagement ring.

Jake had watched Claudia a couple of nights ago. She'd looked as sexy and sultry as he remembered, but he'd felt nothing. Not even when the light caught the enormous rock on her left hand.

"Everything okay?" Rachel stopped eating and studied him.

"Of course." Or close enough to okay that he wouldn't complain. Being back was better than he ever could have thought. And if some nights it felt a little empty, he could learn to deal with it. He scooped up a forkful of chow mein.

"How are you settling in?"

"Fine."

She twirled up some noodles. "And it's working out okay with Dad?"

"Surprisingly, yes." After realizing that there was nothing keeping him in Vancouver and that most of the issues he had with his father were self-made, Jake had accepted the job he'd offered. But he hadn't come without reservations.

He'd been pleased to discover that instead of acting like the autocrat he remembered from his teen years, his father had welcomed any ideas that Jake cared to offer.

"Then you're glad you came back?"

He nodded. "Yeah." Or, if not glad exactly, then not unhappy, either.

He'd been doing his best not to think of Vancouver and what had happened there. But excising Ava from his thoughts wasn't as easy as he'd hoped. He didn't understand it. He'd been able to cut Claudia out pretty succinctly and there was no reason he couldn't do the same with Ava. Maybe it was just that it stung more the second time around.

Rachel sipped her water. "I sense that you're not really here. Thinking about Vancouver?"

"No." But he should probably call a real-estate agent there tomorrow to talk about putting his place on the market. It wasn't as though there was any reason to keep it.

"Ever going to be ready to talk about what actually happened?"

Jake felt the tension close a tight fist around his lungs and forced himself to take a slow breath. "I already told you," he said and then took a sip from his own glass. He'd decided on the flight home that he wasn't going to discuss Ava. His family had forgiven his naiveté the first time; it was too embarrassing to tell them that it had happened again. Too painful. "I made the pilot, but was unable to get financing. I'd already hired someone for my position at Harvey's station, so I decided to take Dad up on his job offer. That's it."

"Right."

"It is."

Rachel tilted her head, her gray eyes clear and questioning. "Who was she?"

Jake ignored the thump of his heart. "What are you talking about?"

"Are we still playing this game?" She eyeballed him until he looked away. But even winning the staring contest didn't appease her. "I'm talking about the woman who has you looking tired and worn-out. Probably crying yourself to sleep at night in your pillow." She met his disgusted look with one of her own. "What? The walls are thin."

"I have never cried myself to sleep at night." And even if he had, he would never admit it.

Rachel was undeterred. "Who was she? You know Mom thinks there was someone in Vancouver, too." She grinned when he glared at her, clearly not bothered that the heat of his stare should have set her hair on fire. "What? I can't control what Mom thinks."

"I wonder who put that thought into her head," Jake grumbled. "Do you two talk about everything I do?"

"Of course. We love you and part of that means doing our best to keep you on the straight and narrow."

"I'm not a charity case."

"No, but your intuition about women sucks. Don't feel bad. Dad and Rob both have limited resources in that area, too. But they have Mom and me to help."

"Lucky them."

"Lucky you, too." She sent him a Cheshire-cat smile. "We're willing to lend you a hand until you find someone lovely to settle down with. Back to my point, who was she? What happened? And is she the reason you came back?"

Jake ate another mouthful of food without tasting it and decided not to answer. There was no point. He'd learned over the years that the best way to get Rachel off a topic was to let her ramble on without interruption until she felt she'd exhausted it.

"You're not fooling me with that whole 'there wasn't anyone' thing anyway. As soon as you started calling Mom without getting a reminder from me, I knew."

"I didn't need your reminder—"

Rachel simply talked over him. "Then when you actually talked to her for a half hour instead of grunting and getting off the phone after about five minutes, I could only conclude that someone who knows a little something about the female psyche was advising you."

Jake stuffed a chicken ball in his mouth, feeling his molars grind against each other as he chewed, but reminding himself that it would all be over much sooner if he could just keep his mouth shut.

"And you were chipper," she told him. "Like 'singing from the mountaintops, little birdies flying around your head with hearts' chipper."

Okay, that was too much. "I did not have hearts flying around my head and I don't sing from mountaintops or anywhere. It wasn't like we were in love. I'd only known her a couple of months."

As soon as he said it, he realized his error. Hell.

But Rachel was already crowing, doing her best to deafen him. "I knew it! Why do you try to deny the power of my intuition? It never fails. I never fail."

"I'm not sure I would go that far. Or have you forgotten about Daryl Simcox?" It was a desperate attempt to distract her, but it worked.

"I was fifteen."

Daryl, with his oily hair and greasy Camaro, had been a source of family contention for the six months Rachel had claimed he was her one true love. She'd gotten over that the night she caught him making out with another girl at a party. She'd poured a drink over his head, Jake remembered fondly. And he'd been able to give Daryl a good sock in the gut when he'd spread a rumor at school the breakup was because Rachel was a frigid bitch. No one was allowed to call his baby sister names except him. "My point stands. Your intuition? Not infallible."

She snorted, loudly and with gusto. "Quit trying to change the subject. You know it isn't going to work, so there's no point in wasting both our time. The fact is, I knew you were hiding something—or should I say someone—and now you've admitted it. Spill your guts before I'm forced to sic Mom on you. She's not as nice as me."

Jake frowned as the little pocket of good humor that had eased the ache in his heart for a minute disappeared. For Rachel, this was just a story, an anecdote she wouldn't remember in a month. But it wasn't so easy for him. "I don't want to talk about it, Rache."

"Come on. You'll feel better if you get it all out."

"I don't want to talk about it," he repeated. And why would he? It was over. He and Ava were over. What was the point in belaboring it? The tines of his fork screeched across his plate as he frowned at his sister. Why had he let her goad him into mentioning it?

She did not look threatened. "So it didn't end well."

"No."

"And?" There was no sound in the room. Rachel cleared her throat. "You know you won't be able to out-wait me. I'll just keep asking. I'll get Mom in on it, too. Think of it like a Band-Aid—just rip it off and spill."

He looked at his little sister, embarrassment crawling up the back of his neck. "She used me, Rache. She made me think she cared and then when she found out the show was a no-go, she suddenly discovered she wasn't that interested." Not exactly the truth, but close enough.

"What?"

"Yeah."

"That bitch."

"She's not a bitch." Jake looked back at his plate.

"She is. Just like Claudia."

"No." He pinned his sister with a stare. "She's not like Claudia." Ava was nothing like Claudia.

He waited until his sister nodded. "Okay."

She didn't say anything for the rest of the meal. But Jake knew it was only a matter of time.

Chapter 25

Lydia Durham laid the roast in the middle of the dining table and took her seat. "This is nice, isn't it? The whole family together under one roof again for Sunday dinner."

Jake didn't respond that he didn't see what was so nice about it. His mom looked so happy, smiling at all of them, and her cheerful demeanor wasn't what was bothering him anyway. He'd been irritable ever since his conversation with Rachel last week.

Getting a phone call from Hanna to talk about how much she was enjoying the job and in particular her new cohost, one Ava Christensen, didn't help his mood.

That Ava had gotten the job wasn't a surprise to Jake. Hanna had asked him for his opinion when Danica had up and quit on her and he hadn't hesitated to recommend Ava. She was the best choice, and putting aside his own feelings about her behavior with him in her attempt to get ahead, he knew she'd do a great job.

But he hadn't expected that the two of them would become friends. They'd gone out to celebrate the night Hanna had offered her the cohost position and had made a habit of it since. It irked him and in some odd way felt like a betrayal. Like the two of them shouldn't have gotten along because Hanna was his friend and Ava had done him wrong, which sounded like a bad country-and-western song.

But he was not mentioning it to his family. Aside from that one night last week with Rachel, he'd managed to avoid talking about Ava entirely, and he wasn't about to change that now.

He forced a tight smile for his mother, who was watching him expectantly, and then tucked into the food. She'd made all his favorites—not a zucchini in sight—and she'd be disappointed if he didn't eat at least two plates. He only needed to keep up appearances for a couple of hours and then he could make his escape.

He'd driven himself over, since Rachel and Rob had been visiting friends earlier in the day on the opposite side of town, and it was silly for them to come all the way back for him, so he didn't have to wait for them. Rachel and his mother could sit over coffee for hours gabbing about nothing.

Dinner was a leisurely affair, lasting longer than Jake had anticipated, but since he didn't have anywhere to be and no one asked probing questions, he didn't mind. He even agreed to stay for coffee. He figured another half hour or so and then he could excuse himself. It would make his mother happy.

They'd shifted into the great room at the back of the house with the two-story fireplace and large sectional couch when he got pinned. Like a bug on a fourth-grade science project.

His father, seated in a leather chair that faced the arm of the sectional Jake had sunk into, cleared his throat. "We need to talk about Vancouver." His tone was gruff and brought back childhood memories of getting caught with his hand in the cookie jar.

Jake closed his eyes for a half second. He should have excused himself after helping his mother clear the table and made up an excuse to leave before coffee. Maybe not about work, since his father was aware of his projects there, but he could have come up with something.

But no. Instead, he'd allowed himself to be lulled by the peaceful conversation about opening the family cottage for the summer. And now he was surrounded. He opened his eyes and looked at them. His father directly across from him, Rob and Rachel on his left and the empty space beside them that would be filled by his mother when she returned.

"What about it?" There was still a chance he could handle this, but only if he went on the offensive. "You planning on filming something there?"

"No." His father leaned forward. "We need to talk about whatever's been eating at you."

Jake stared his father down, knowing it was best not to show signs of weakness. "Nothing's eating at me." But seriously, he was going to kill his sister.

Rachel snorted. "When is the last time you were out somewhere that wasn't for work?"

Jake turned his attention on her. "I didn't realize my personal life had become your business."

"Well, it is." She frowned at him. "You aren't yourself. Haven't been since you came back."

He knew he shouldn't have told her about Ava. She'd probably blabbed to Mom as soon as he'd gone upstairs.

"Sweetheart." His mother stood behind his father's chair, her hand on his shoulder. "We're just worried about you."

His father's hand came up to cover his mother's. A small protective gesture that linked them as a team as clearly as if they'd shown up wearing matching uniforms. "Your mother and I are aware that you aren't happy." The gray eyes identical to his own were concerned. "We want to help."

"I'm fine," Jake insisted.

"You aren't," his father insisted back. "Look, I had a chance to see your pilot. It was good—really good." Jake's irritation that his father had somehow dug that up was only slightly tempered by the news that he'd liked it. "I want to send it to a friend of mine who works for an airline in Europe. See what he thinks."

"No." Jake shook his head. "That's in the past. I'm moving forward."

"Are you?" Rachel piping in again, her eyes bright behind her glasses. The square red frames gave her a scholarly hipster vibe. "Because that's not what it sounded like when we talked last week."

When she'd blindsided him with her barrage of questions about Ava. He scowled at her. "Yes, I am."

"Jake." Even his mother's calm tone didn't soothe him. "It's okay if you don't want to talk about whatever happened there. We don't want to intrude on your personal life." Jake couldn't resist shooting a glance at his sister. He was sure as hell going to repeat that verbatim the next time she tried to butt in. "But I want you to be honest with yourself about what you want. Whatever you choose, we won't be mad. We just want you to be happy."

"Exactly." His father closed his hand more tightly over his mother's fingers. The familiar gesture made Jake's heart ache. He'd thought that he'd find that kind of intimacy for himself one day, but was beginning to believe that maybe he was meant to go through life alone. "And if working at the family company isn't for you, then it isn't for you."

"It's fine," Jake interrupted before they could convince him to try again. He didn't want to try again. Been there, done that. Got slapped down by the gods of karma. "It's been a big change and I'm just adjusting, okay?"

There was a short pause and then his father cleared his throat. "It's been five weeks."

"So give me six."

Their eyes met again, held, and his father nodded. "All right. Six weeks. Then we talk."

Ava was finding her new career in the spotlight less satisfying than she'd anticipated. And it was all Jake's fault.

Hanna had let it slip last week that it had been Jake who suggested she be promoted. That he'd said she was a hard worker with a ton of charm that drew an audience in. Ava had almost snorted out loud.

Charm, her ass. She'd like to show him where she wanted to stick that charm.

If that were true, not only would he have given her the cohost job the first time through, he definitely would have hired her to host his travel show. Since he'd done neither, she could only assume that he'd encouraged Hanna out of a sense of guilt. Ava didn't need his guilt. She could do this on her own. Had done it on her own.

Though she'd called her mother to tell her the good news, she hadn't seen her. Barbara, shocker of shockers, had been busy that weekend. Jilly had wanted to take her out Saturday night and celebrate in style, but Ava had convinced her that a quiet dinner was a better option and had been back in her apartment by nine o'clock.

What was so wrong with wanting a little time to herself anyway? She could lounge in the tub with a book, maybe play some Tori Amos on repeat and slowly wash away the marks that Jake had left. And finally forget about him.

But she shoved all that aside at the office. There she was the consummate professional. She doubted anyone had any idea about the war her emotions were waging inside.

She met Hanna for what was becoming a regular lunch date at a small café about a block from the station. It was one of those bright May days that promised summer was coming soon. Vancouverites were out in droves, walking their dogs, riding their bikes and just generally soaking up the sun. Ava lifted her face to the light as they sat at one of the small wrought-iron tables set out on the sidewalk.

She was halfway through her veggie sandwich—selected for the cream cheese rather than the alfalfa sprouts—when Hanna asked, "Did something happen between you and Jake?"

So much for her consummate professionalism. Ava choked, as if it wasn't hard enough to eat those sprouts without being asked invasive questions. She finished coughing and guzzled some water. Hanna watched her, a sympathetic expression on her normally cheerful face.

"I don't mean to intrude, but I just thought maybe…"

"No," Ava managed to say between swallows of water. "Nothing happened." Unless she counted dream-smashing. Since her appetite was suddenly gone and she was pretty sure she'd heave if she even tried to bite into the sandwich again, she clutched her water instead.

"Because I saw your face when I mentioned that he recommended you. You were surprised."

"No," Ava lied. "I don't remember that."

"We were having drinks at that bar on Thursday after work. Almost as soon as I said it, you left."

Yes, because when the surprise had worn off, she'd realized she was furious. She'd been so proud of her accomplishment, of achieving cohost status on her own. Take that, Mr. Big-Shot Producer. And then he'd gone and taken that away from her.

"I had things to do."

"And you canceled on Saturday night."

"I wasn't feeling well."

Hanna eyed her steadily. "You seem fine now."

"It was a twenty-four-hour cold." Ava noticed that she'd shredded most of the label off her water bottle.

"And when I talked to Jake on the weekend, he acted funny, too."

Funny? Funny how? Funny like he'd realized he was a horse's ass? Or funny like he was so unmoved by what had happened that he was cracking jokes? Ava couldn't bring herself to ask.

Fortunately, Hanna answered. "It was sort of odd, actually. Like he was jealous." She nibbled at her ham-and-cheese croissant, leaving perfect little bite marks.

"Jealous of what?" The question popped out before Ava remembered that she no longer cared about Jake and wasn't going to waste any more of her brain power thinking about him. Her face flamed and she wondered if she could blame it on her skin being exposed to the sun for the first time in months.

"I think that we were hanging out." Hanna shook her head. "Like I said, it was weird. Anyway, coupled with your reaction, I just thought maybe something had happened."

Ava forced a cheery smile. "No." Nothing to see here. Don't pay attention to the man behind the curtain.

"Too bad. Jake is a great guy."

Ava went back to shredding her label.

Hanna kept talking. "He was really happy when he first moved here." Ava steeled her heart, which tried to soften. Treacherous, weak thing. "I was pretty surprised when he decided to go back to Toronto."

"Guess things just didn't work out."

"No, I guess not." Hanna shook her head as though shooing the thought away. "Anyway, I guess I shouldn't be surprised that he didn't meet someone. Not after what happened in Toronto."

Ava couldn't prevent her heart from speeding up. "Oh?" She wasn't being nosy; she was merely showing interest in Hanna's conversation. It was only polite.

"Yeah, it was pretty ugly. But maybe it's good for him to go back. Face all that down."

Now Ava was dying to know, but she couldn't ask without indicating that there was more going on between her and Jake than she'd admitted. Bah. She was down to plastic on the bottle.

Of course, Hanna changed the subject and started talking about the station then, some ideas she had and some changes she'd like to make so that the show stood out a little more from the competition. Ava was still stuck on the ugly something that had involved Jake. Finally, she couldn't take it anymore.

"Okay. I have to know. What happened with Jake in Toronto?"

Hanna couldn't quite hide her little smile that Ava had broken so easily. "I thought there was nothing going on between you two."

"There isn't. Not anymore."

"What happened?"

"It was ugly here, too." She told Hanna the PG-rated version. "And then he walked out and I haven't spoken to him since."

But Hanna was more astute than Jilly. That, or Jilly had put her up to this and warned her not to let Ava get away with anything. "That doesn't sound like enough for you two to never speak to each other again."

Ava swallowed the rest of her water and rolled the empty bottle between her palms. A fly buzzed around her sandwich and she swatted it away before continuing. "He said that he thought I'd gotten involved with him to advance my career." Her face was burning again.

"He said what?"

Ava couldn't meet her eyes. "He said that I used him, implied that I'd traded…sex, for the job."

"That idiot," Hanna said.

Ava let out the breath she'd been holding. She hadn't realized that she'd been afraid Hanna would take Jake's side until now. "I know. It was so insulting I kicked him out."

"I'd have kicked his ass."

"I thought about it." Still thought about it, in fact. "After that, he went back home and never made any attempt to contact me, so I returned the favor. That's it."

Hanna took another bite of her sandwich, chewed thoughtfully. "I don't want to make excuses for him."

Ava held up a hand. "Please don't."

"But," Hanna continued, "did he ever tell you about Claudia?"

"No, he didn't." Who was Claudia? Some long-lost love he'd left behind and had now run back to? The part of the sandwich Ava had eaten rose up her throat.

"She is not a nice person." Which made Ava feel a little better or at least able to keep her meal down. "Ambitious, driven, but cutthroat about it. She wouldn't think twice about backstabbing someone to get ahead. She dated Jake for a while."

Ava began to shred the lettuce from her sandwich.

"He wouldn't tell me exactly what happened, but I got the impression that she was up for a big job at Jake's station."

"Which he gave her, no doubt." When he wouldn't even consider Ava.

"No. Actually, he hired someone else, and when she found out, she started dating someone at a different station. That guy did promote her and that's when she broke it off with Jake."

"Oh." Ava began working on making a pile of bread and sprouts.

"That might have something to do with what he said to you."

Ava shrugged. "Doesn't matter. He's still a jerk."

"Completely. And I plan to tell him that the next time he calls. Come on." Hanna stood up, waited for Ava to join her. "I'm treating you to ice cream."

But the ice cream, though delicious, did nothing to ease the pain in her heart.

Chapter 26

"You're fired."

"Excuse me?" Jake looked up from the file folder sitting on his lap. He'd only just settled down in the chair across from his father's desk intending to discuss a project he'd like to head and some concerns he had with it.

"You're fired."

For a fraction of a moment, his old insecurities swelled, whispering in his ear that he'd known this would all come to an end, that he really wasn't good enough to carry the family name. Then he spotted the smile on his father's face and they slithered away. "Since when are you Donald Trump? Since you had to get a rug?"

"This is all natural." His father tugged on his silver hair to prove it. "And you're still fired."

Jake considered that. He'd only been at the office for a short time, but he felt confident that he'd done an average job. Actually, better than average. Which meant this was about something else. "Look, I told you last week that I was fine. I even went out the other night."

Granted, the date with one of Rachel's colleagues had been an utter disaster. The woman was a professor of French literature and had not been impressed when Jake joked that his only experience with her area of expertise was watching *Les Misérables* on Broadway and being elbowed by his date when he fell asleep. Ava would have laughed and told him he deserved it for being so uncultured.

He missed her.

But he did his best to brush away the hurt that still lingered. Rachel had been digging at him about Ava all week, somehow inferring that his blind date hadn't gone well because he wasn't over her. Nothing Jake had said could convince her otherwise.

And then, as if it wasn't insulting enough to have his dating skills questioned by his baby sister, just this morning she'd hinted that perhaps he might be partly responsible for what had happened in Vancouver. That he'd overreacted or said things he shouldn't have. When he'd asked why she would think that, she'd conveniently remembered that she had a class to teach and had left the house.

However, he'd flicked through the calls that had come into the house in the past few days and seen one from Hanna that he hadn't answered and that no one had mentioned. Possibly, no one had been home to pick up and Hanna hadn't left a message. But more likely, since Hanna hadn't called again, she'd said something to Rachel and let her do the dirty work.

"I'll give you a month's severance," his father said. "But I should tell you, if you push, I can go up to two."

"No." Jake shook his head, brought himself back to the present. "Why are you firing me exactly?"

"You aren't happy." His father shrugged and placed his big hands on the desk.

"I'm happy," Jake said. Happy as he could be.

"You're pretending. Don't think we can't see through it. Your mother has been on me about this, so you're fired."

"Yeah, I'm sure Mom's going to be thrilled that you're leaving me unemployed."

His father's smile widened. "Now, see, that's where you're wrong. I sent a copy of your show to that friend of mine. The one who works for the European airline." Jake didn't even have a chance to feel resentful or annoyed at the interference before his father went charging ahead. "He loved it and he wants to meet with you about it. He's in town tonight."

"Dad, I told you that's in the past. I'm not throwing good money after bad."

"You're not throwing any money. If he likes it, he'll pay. You can tell him I said that."

Jake smiled in spite of himself. "I appreciate where this is coming from, but I'm okay. I like working here with you." He told himself that he didn't need to prove himself anymore. But still, hope was building. He could get the travel show off the ground this time. Run his own show, be his own boss.

"You could do the show from Toronto this time," his father said. "Stay close to family."

Jake thought about it. There would be some benefits. He wouldn't have to Skype with his mother, popular European travel destinations would be a much shorter flight away and he'd be closer to Rachel.

On the flip side, he'd probably never see Ava again, he'd miss Hanna and Alex, and he'd be closer to Rachel.

"Your mother wants you to be happy," his father said.

"I had Liz book you a dinner reservation at Canoe for tonight. You can meet with my friend at the restaurant, pitch him your show. Liz will have the details. I thought something a little more casual was the way to go since he's already interested. It'll be less about convincing him and more showing him that you two can work well together. Now, he likes his reds, so order a good one."

"Dad."

"You can put it on my tab."

Jake sat back, insulted. "I can pay my own tab."

"Good." His father cleared his throat. "There's something else."

"What? Mom thinks I'm too skinny and you've been tasked with getting me to eat more?"

His father laughed. "That does sound like your mother, but no. This came from Rachel."

Jake started to rise. "I'm out of here."

"Wait. It's about the woman you were seeing in Vancouver. Ava."

Jake's stomach spasmed and his shoulders tightened. He didn't want to talk about this or about the fact that he'd been looking forward to showing her off when they came to Toronto to film. "As I told Rachel, there's nothing to discuss. That's over." She'd gotten what she wanted from him.

"Your sister seems to think otherwise and she's convinced your mother."

"Then I guess you'll have to unconvince her." He was not spending the next family dinner explaining the relationship to his mother.

His father simply watched him. "I'm not asking for the private details." He cleared his throat and shifted in his seat. "If your mother wants those she can ask you herself, but I'd like to know if it was serious."

Jake closed his eyes and wondered who he'd pissed off to deserve this. Was it not bad enough that he had lived it, now he had to talk about it? He exhaled slowly, and opened his eyes, doing his best to look indifferent. "We only dated a couple months."

"I knew I wanted to marry your mother after our first date." Chuck waited. "So? Was it serious?"

Jake's stomach had moved past spasming and right into knot-making. "It doesn't matter," he finally said. "We broke up and we've gone our separate ways."

"It matters." His father's mouth was grim. "What happened?"

Jake gazed at the file folder on his lap, the blue cover looking like the summer sky, all bright and shiny and full of hope. He wanted to rip it into a thousand pieces and light it on fire. "It was Claudia all over again."

Because Rachel was wrong. The only thing he'd misunderstood was how Ava actually felt about him.

"What does that mean? That she took up with Harvey? Because I think his wife might have something to say about that."

"No, not that way. I meant that she was looking for a way to get ahead in her career and saw me as an avenue." He shrugged as though it was no big deal, simply one of the land mines that a man who had the ability to make or break a career had to navigate.

His father was silent for a moment, no doubt wondering how he could have raised a son so foolish as to fall for the same ploy twice.

"Well." His father leaned back in the old captain's chair his mother had found in an antique shop. She'd had it refurbished, covered in a deep red leather, but the base still squeaked when Chuck rocked in it, as he was doing now. "Rachel didn't think she was like Claudia."

"Rachel doesn't know everything."

"True. Don't tell her that, though. Listen, son. I know that Claudia threw you for a loop." His mouth tightened. "But that's no reason to doubt yourself. You trusted her and she used that to her own advantage. Now, I know Rachel doesn't know everything, but she does have good instincts."

"She's never even met Ava," Jake burst out.

"I think you owe Ava and yourself a phone call. Or better yet, a visit."

"I'm not going to see her," Jake said, even as his heart jumped at the thought. Watching her bright eyes, feeling her silky hair, touching her soft skin.

"No? Then how do you propose that you convince her to host your travel show?"

"What?" Jake frowned. "She's not the host."

"I wouldn't be so sure about that. The airline loved her. *Loved* her. I don't have to tell you what that means."

No, he didn't. It meant if Jake was going to move forward and try to make a go of his travel show, he was going to have to do it with Ava as host.

"Okay, I don't know why you're all mopey and hang-doggy."

It had been four days since he'd been officially canned. As Jake had expected, his mother had not been pleased to hear it. But to his surprise she'd come around in full support of the idea when his father had explained. And, of course, Rachel was no help. She was probably the one who'd put the idea in their father's head in the first place.

"Hangdoggy?" Jake looked over at his sister, who'd

said she wanted to help him pack but had done nothing other than lie on the bed and blather at him.

"Yes, like this." She pulled her face into a mournful expression and sighed loudly. "Like Eeyore. This is your chance—you should be pumped." She pumped a fist to show him how.

The meeting with the airline executive had gone exceedingly well. So well that Jake now had a letter of intent from the airline. They'd ordered twelve episodes, cities to be selected from the airline's top fifteen travel destinations, delivered by the end of the year, and were offering an advance considerably larger than Jake had expected. He just had to convince Ava to host. If she refused, the deal was off.

"Come on. You're going to head back there the conquering hero." Jake figured Rachel must be teaching a class on heroic themes in art. "It's your chance to win her back. To get everything."

Jake ignored her and kept packing. Next, she was probably going to show him how he should pose when he saw Ava again.

It was nothing she hadn't already said a thousand times already, starting the minute she'd heard he was heading back to Vancouver. Though Jake had given some thought to moving his base to Toronto, he'd decided to go back instead. Ava was in Vancouver and without her there was no show. The airline had been very clear about that.

"You'll have the show, the relationship." Rachel rose and raised her arm in victory. Yep, there it was. "And you can thank me in your wedding speech."

A wedding? His sister was certifiably insane. He'd be lucky if Ava would even agree to see him, never mind marry him. And he wasn't thinking past how he was going to convince her to join the show anyway.

"And don't play the martyr," Rachel advised. Yeah, definitely doing heroic elements in art right now. She dropped back on the bed. "You need to be strong. Women like a man who's strong."

"I'm not trying to win her back, Rache. Okay?"

"Yeah, you are." She smiled at him, all smugness and challenge. "You just don't know it yet."

"Fine." He dug his socks out of the dresser.

"I know that I haven't met her, but Hanna said she's great. And I trust Hanna."

As he'd suspected, Hanna was the guilty party who had told Rachel all the details of what had occurred between him and Ava. Jake wondered why he'd ever introduced the two of them, since all they did was gang up on him. He jammed the socks into his suitcase.

"Speaking of Hanna, you didn't tell her about my arrival, did you?" He planned to go straight from the airport to Ava's apartment, before anyone else knew that he was back. He needed the element of surprise on his side. If he called to let her know he was coming, or told anyone else, she was very likely to avoid him. She was good at that.

"No, of course not." But Rachel suddenly got very busy polishing her glasses.

"Rachel. It was the one thing I asked you not to do." He ran a hand through his hair and wondered if strangling his well-meaning sister was a viable option.

She put her glasses back on and looked at him with the gray eyes they'd both inherited from their dad. "Hanna isn't going to say anything to Ava. We discussed it and as it happens, we agree with you."

Since she seemed to be expecting his thanks, as if

he was supposed to be grateful that she was letting him decide his own life, Jake didn't say anything. He'd thank her to keep out of his business.

"Jake." She sat up and put a hand on his arm when he turned to get the rest of his clothing out of the dresser. "I want you to be happy. I think Ava made you happy."

He shored up the part of him that wanted to soften and tell her everything, to get that woman's perspective she so loved to share. "I'll be fine, Rachel."

"I want you to be better than fine." She peered up at him, the lenses making her eyes seem bigger. "I know you think that whatever happened there was the be-all and end-all of your relationship with Ava, but I think you're wrong. Hanna thinks so, too."

"You talk about my love life?"

She looked surprised that he asked. "Of course we do. Anyway, she said she doesn't think Ava's so much angry as hurt."

Jake didn't see the difference. "Does it really matter?"

"Yes. You have to tell her how you feel."

Since Jake didn't like the sound of that, he shrugged her hand off and returned to grab his T-shirts.

"You know I'm right."

"No, you're not." He folded the T-shirts very carefully and placed them in the suitcase.

"Yes, I am. I'm always right. Ask Rob. Ask my students."

"Not about this." Because while he might have told his sister that he was only going back for the show, he knew it was much more than that. From the moment Ava had agreed to help him that weekend at Rockdale, it had been about more.

He just wasn't sure he was ready to tell her that.

Chapter 27

"What are you doing here?" It was the end of the week and Ava was exhausted. She almost hadn't answered the knock at her door. Now she wished she hadn't.

"I want to talk," Jake said.

She did her best to stare him down, narrowing her eyes and not moving from the doorway of her apartment, barring him entrance. She crossed her arms over her chest for extra emphasis. But he looked good. So good. And he wasn't even wearing the jeans.

"There's nothing to talk about." She sniffed.

"Ava."

She steeled herself against the whisper of yearning that crept across her skin. She wasn't going to be the kind of woman who let herself be so easily swayed. He'd cut her deeply, and she didn't know there was anything he could say to repair it. "Look, Jake. I don't know what you think you have to say, but I don't want to hear it, okay?"

She just wanted him to go. Get out of her life and out of her sight and never, ever come back. She inhaled slowly, hoping to ease the sudden thumping of her heart.

"I'd like to come in," he said.

She sniffed again. And she'd like a closet full of Blahniks to rival Carrie Bradshaw's, but neither of those things were happening. "No. How did you get in the building anyway?"

He flashed her that crooked smile she loved. "I helped a sweet old lady cross the street. Turns out she lives on the fourth floor. When she found out I was coming to see you, she happily let me in."

Ava scowled. "Well, she might have, but I'm not. I'd like you to leave."

"I've been traveling all day." He ran a hand through his hair, and even the movement was tired. She could see the circles under his eyes, but reminded herself that how he'd spent his day didn't matter. He could have lain in bed with a pair of naked twins for all she cared. Her stomach twisted. Okay, maybe not naked twins, but still. "Can I please come in and sit down?"

"No." She crossed her arms more tightly. "You're lucky I don't call security to bounce you out right now." Which was an empty threat as the building didn't have on-site security, but she was pretty sure he didn't know that.

"So you want to do this right here?"

"I don't want to do this at all."

"Harsh."

It was, but she needed to be strong. "What do you want, Jake?" She leaned into the edge of the door for support.

"A chance to explain."

He gave her those puppy-dog eyes that had so often been her downfall, but not anymore. "There's nothing to explain," she said. "I think we made things pretty clear the last time we saw each other."

"Did we?" He cocked an eyebrow at her.

Ava felt her resolve waver, and reminded herself that she didn't care if he had a bitchy ex-girlfriend who'd messed with his head. That wasn't her problem. She'd done her time holed up in her apartment like a crazy cat lady and she was never doing it again.

She was back on the proverbial horse. Not yet ready to date, but going out a few nights a week with Jilly and Hanna and other friends and acquaintances. She'd even promised her mother dinner this weekend and she wasn't about to cancel it again.

It was a miracle her mother had let her get away with it for this long.

"We did," she told him. "But if you don't remember, maybe you could go do your reminiscing somewhere else."

"I just need a minute." He took a step forward.

Ava held her ground even as her pulse shot up. "This isn't a good time. I'm busy."

His quick glance took in her comfy sweatpants and oversize T-shirt, and a glimmer of that smug grin reappeared. "Busy doing what?"

"Not that it's any of your business, but I have company." In the form of a movie and a bowl of popcorn as big as her head. She'd been too wiped to go out tonight, but now she wished she'd dragged her butt to whatever club Jilly had pinpointed as the place to be.

He kept smirking. She wanted to wipe it off his face with a smack, but that would mean she still cared. And she didn't. Or at least she was working on it. "Oh. So I should come back later?"

"No, you shouldn't." She was about to tell him that there would be no later. Not here. Not anywhere, and he could take his explanation back on the plane to Toronto, when one of her neighbors poked his head out into the hallway and looked at her.

"Everything okay?"

"Fine." She pasted on a fake smile.

This particular neighbor was known around the building for being a bit paranoid, calling the police for the least incident, but he was quiet and always made a point of holding the elevator for Ava if they were leaving at the same time. She didn't need him jumping to the wrong conclusion now. The only thing worse than letting Jake into her apartment would be having the cops show up and having to explain that he wasn't a threat and letting him into her apartment anyway.

"Sorry about the noise," she said, since she knew that would be the neighbor's next concern.

He humphed and shut his door. Ava knew he'd be standing behind it, ear pressed to the metal to listen. If he didn't approve of how things went, he'd either be making that phone call or poking out his head for a second time.

Jake raised one eyebrow when she looked back at him. "Can I come in now?"

Seeing as she couldn't force him to leave and remaining in the hall would only raise her neighbor's ire, Ava stepped back to allow him entrance, but she didn't hold the door. Jake had to catch it before it hit him in the nose. It was a small victory, but she'd take it.

When Jake flipped the lock closed behind him, she

reached over and flicked it back open. She didn't know what he thought was going to happen tonight, but she wasn't letting him hang around long enough to find out.

He followed her down the short hall that led to the living room and looked around. "I thought you said you had company?"

"I lied," she told him. "Now, what do you want?"

She didn't sit, didn't offer him a seat, either, but stood at the edge of the room, making it clear that she didn't expect this to take long.

Jake ignored the memo and plopped himself down on the couch in the same spot he always sat. He patted the space beside him. "Come on. I promise I won't bite."

"I'd rather stand." Which wasn't true. Her legs were wobbly, but she locked her knees and stayed where she was. She was not sitting on the couch beside him. Or even the chair across from him.

He stared at her for a second and then nodded. "I think there are some things you need to know. About why I reacted the way I did."

He told her about Claudia, about what had happened and how it had driven him to go to work on his own, about how he'd decided it was best to keep his professional relationships separate from his personal ones. His recitation didn't move Ava in the least; she'd managed to figure all of that out based on what Hanna had told her. "So?"

"So then I met you." His eyes were all soft and melty.

She looked away. "Yeah, and then you said I used my body to get ahead. Like I was a prostitute."

"I didn't say that."

"You did." She stared at him, daring him to deny it. He was smart enough not to. "That hurt, Jake. It hurt a lot." So much that it still made her heart ache every day. "For the record, I didn't use you."

"I know." His voice was quiet.

"I cared about you and you threw it all away because you didn't trust me. Didn't believe in me." She felt the catch in her chest and didn't say anything else, afraid that he'd hear just how deeply affected she still was by what had happened. By him.

"I was an idiot."

"Something we can finally agree on."

"I want to make it up to you."

She shook her head. "There's nothing to make up. You were honest about how you felt. Now I know."

"No, I wasn't honest. I was scared and I panicked."

"Let me guess—you're all better now?"

His eyes caught hers and held. The gray was that dark stormy color of the Pacific Ocean in winter. He rose, moved across the living room like a hunter. She felt caught in his snare, forced herself not to blink or flinch or show any sign of weakness. She raised her chin and kept looking into his eyes.

His voice was soft. "You said I didn't believe in you. That's not true. I thought you were an amazing host. I just didn't want to get my personal and professional lives twisted together."

Ava swallowed but maintained eye contact. "So instead you decided to dump us both."

"No." He sat on the arm of the couch, just close enough that if Ava reached out her hand she could touch him. She managed to control herself.

"Yes." Her nerves were buzzing. She was surprised it didn't sound like an attack of African killer bees.

"I made a mistake. And you were right when you

said I ran. That's not easy to admit." The half smile he gave her almost did what the puppy-dog eyes couldn't. "I ran home to my family, who proceeded to give me a very necessary kick in the ass." He smiled again.

She didn't smile back.

"I had a meeting with a foreign airline last week. They offered me a contract to produce thirteen episodes."

"Really?" That shocked her, and for a moment she smiled. Really smiled. "That's great."

"Yes." He leaned forward but remained sitting. "I want you to host."

"Jake."

"Ava, hear me out." She wanted to turn away, to remind herself why she shouldn't trust him, but she didn't. "I made a mistake when I gave up on the show." She noticed he didn't include her in the mix. "I'm here to fix that."

"Why now?" She wanted him to say that he cared for her, that he'd realized these past few weeks he'd been miserable and lonely without her.

Instead, he just cocked his head and looked at her. "Because I've realized those issues were mine."

She swallowed her disappointment. That wasn't true. Not anymore.

"Maybe, but now you've made them mine." She couldn't stand here any longer, with so little space between them. She stepped sideways into the living room and turned to face him, gesturing toward the door. "I think you should go."

"Ava."

His voice snuck under her defenses, tried to warm the cold shield around her heart. But she wasn't the

Grinch and her heart was not going to grow three sizes that day. "You've said what you came here to say. I'd like you to leave."

"I want you to host. The show is a huge opportunity for your career."

"I don't think it's a good idea." From the way her heart was trying to talk her arms into opening up for him, Ava knew she wouldn't be able to hold back if he asked for more. She didn't think she could handle the heartbreak again.

"Don't decide now. Think about it."

"Jake." She forced herself to meet his eyes. "I've already had weeks to think about things."

But he refused to be deterred by her logic. "Not about this. Take a few days."

"Seventy-two hours won't change my mind." Or ease her emotional aches.

"Then I'll give you a week. I'll be in town until Friday."

Ava simply herded him to the door without responding and waited until he was gone, watching through the peephole to make sure he wasn't coming back before she let out the breath trapped in her lungs.

Chapter 28

"Well, what did she say?"

Hanna had shown up on Jake's doorstep only twenty minutes after he'd returned from Ava's apartment—thanks to Rachel's big mouth, no doubt—and demanded that he come out for dinner with her. He'd tried to defer for another night, but she'd ignored him and dragged him to some noisy lounge that served child-size scraps and called them fine dining. He'd already eaten four plates.

"Who said I asked her anything." He speared a chunk of fish off Hanna's plate.

She rolled her eyes at him. "Isn't that why you came back?"

"I'm not sure I can trust you with that information. What was with tattling to my sister anyway?"

Hanna laughed, her dark hair swinging. "You and Ava were clearly still hung up on each other but too stubborn to do anything about it. I simply helped move things along."

Since that happened to be true, Jake wasn't actually mad. But still. His life, his business. "Don't do it again."

"I won't have to as long as you quit screwing things up." She grinned.

The lounge was one large warehouse-size room lit by neon glass, the colors swirling and shifting in time with the music. Exposed air ducts were overhead and the concrete floor had been polished to a high gleam. Jake hated it.

He ate the last of Hanna's fish and then sighed.

"She said she'd think about it." That wasn't entirely true, but close enough. When he'd offered her the week, she definitely hadn't said no. "She's going to get back to me Friday."

"Does this mean I need to start looking for another cohost?"

He shrugged. "I guess we'll both know on Friday." It was going to be a long seven days. Not that Jake didn't have a ton of things to keep him busy, but he knew he wouldn't be able to stop thinking about Ava, about what she was thinking, what she was deciding. "I told her about Claudia," he said to Hanna.

"I did, too."

He frowned at her. "Oh?"

She shrugged, unconcerned by his angry glare. "Someone needed to. You were acting all hurt when she hadn't actually done anything wrong, and it was clear you were both unhappy."

"Maybe I was fine."

"Maybe you were." She shrugged. "But you sure didn't waste any time before going to see her."

Jake let that one go. He saw no point in fighting a losing battle. Instead, they chatted about other things. How Hanna was finding the city and fitting in at the station.

"What about your travel show? Will you still be based here?"

"Assuming the show is a go, yes. I'm planning to stay."

"What do you mean, assuming?" Hanna stared at him. "I thought this was a done deal, contracts signed and all that. Jake, if this isn't a sure thing I don't think you should be asking Ava to quit her job here."

Obviously, Hanna had heard that little snippet from Rachel.

"I'm not asking her to quit anything, okay?" He nodded when the server strolled by to ask if they'd like a second round.

"Good." Hanna sat back in her seat. "Because if Ava didn't kill you over that, I would have."

"Nice to see where your loyalties lie." But she was trying to help him, and he did appreciate the intel she'd shared with Rachel, even if it meant his sister was more involved in his personal life than he'd like. "Here's the thing—the airline executives are crazy about her. She's the only host they want."

Hanna thought about that for a moment. "And what if she says no?"

"Then she says no." Jake tried to look unconcerned, but it was the thought that had been gnawing at him since he signed the temporary contract with the airline. If Ava said no, it was very possible that they would cancel the project entirely.

"Did you tell her that the whole thing hinges on her participation?" Hanna asked.

"No." He'd debated the whole plane flight over, but ultimately decided against it.

Hanna's eyes widened. "Why not?"

"Because." He ran a hand through his hair. "I didn't want that to influence her decision." The server reappeared with fresh drinks and Jake took a long draw from his. He was going to need a lot more of them if Hanna insisted on talking about Ava all night. "I want her to choose based on what she wants." Not on what he needed.

"Even if it means you don't get a show?"

"Yeah. Even if."

"I do not agree with that. How is tossing your dream career away a good plan?"

"Hanna, it's not your decision." It was his. And he'd decided that putting that kind of pressure on Ava wasn't fair. If she didn't want to host his show, she didn't have to, and she shouldn't feel obligated to agree just because some executives wanted her. "You aren't going to change my mind about this, either."

"But—"

"If it isn't the feminist." They both turned to see Alex walking toward them. Alex had never forgiven Hanna for trying to ruin his dating life in university after his three-dates-in-one-night mistake. But then, she'd never forgiven him for doing it in the first place. It was the main reason Jake tried not to go out with them at the same time.

Alex plopped down beside Hanna, picked up her water glass and drained half of it.

"Hey." She swatted at him and grabbed it back.

He grinned and looked at Jake. "My man."

Jake inclined his head. "Alex."

"So?" Alex leaned back and slung his arm around Hanna's shoulder. She immediately dislodged it with a jerk of her shoulder. He put it back. "What's the good news? When can we start officially moving ahead with the show?" When no one answered, he frowned. "She is coming back, right?"

"She's deciding," Jake said and then turned a steely look at Hanna. "And you can't say anything to her."

Hanna sniffed and curled a protective hand around her glass as she slid down the length of the couch to put as much space between her and Alex as possible. "You should tell her."

"I'm not doing that."

She tried to stare him down and failed. "Fine."

"Not fine," Alex said. "How long are we waiting on this decision?" He put the last word in air quotes.

"You are so lame," Hanna told him.

Jake ignored their bickering. "One week." One long week that was going to seem like a decade.

"A week? No." Alex shook his head. "I can't wait that long. Jilly has been avoiding my phone calls ever since you left town. You need to get me back in the good books."

As if Alex's dating life meant anything to Jake. "I don't know what you think I'm supposed to do about that."

"Put in a good word for me."

"I never put in a bad word."

"Someone did. We went out a few times after that night at the club. I thought things were pretty good and then all of a sudden, she's ignoring me." He said this as though he was stunned. As though people didn't ignore Alex Harrington.

"It wasn't me."

"It was me," Hanna said and took a slow sip of her water while they both stared at her. "What? I like Jilly and I felt it was my duty to warn her about your philandering ways." She poked Alex in the chest.

"Thanks for that."

"You're welcome." Her smile could have sweetened sugar as she turned back to Jake. "So what are you going to do to convince Ava that she wants to host the show?"

"Nothing. I laid it all out. Now she just needs to decide." He realized the pair of them were looking at him as if he'd lost his mind. "What?"

"Bad move," Hanna said.

"Totally," Alex agreed. "You need to do something or this whole project is dead."

Jake tried to discount their opinions, but way deep down in his gut, he was afraid they were right.

The week went more slowly than Jake had anticipated, crawling like an injured snail toward Friday. He'd kept to his promise and given Ava the time to consider his proposal with no pressure, though it had been hard not to call her up just to ask how she was doing. Particularly the night *Die Hard* was on TV. He'd almost texted her to ask if she was watching, but put the phone down without pressing a button.

Every night he'd tuned in to the show to watch her. Unlike Claudia, seeing Ava on screen felt like a physical yank. As if his body was telling him to get over to the station and tell her how he felt. But he rebelled against the urge.

He'd wanted to give her the space to make her decision without his influence. But it was now Friday night, and he needed to know her decision.

She answered her buzzer on the second ring, which eased the tightness in his lungs a touch. He hadn't been sure she wouldn't let him stand outside all night. "It's Jake," he said, though he suspected she already knew.

"Hello." Measured, guarded.

"I thought I could come up so we could talk about the show."

There was a long pause as though she was considering telling him to leave, then a sigh. "All right." And the loud hum as the building door unlocked.

She was waiting in the doorway to her apartment. Probably didn't want to catch any flak from her crabby neighbor tonight. Since it got him inside, Jake wasn't going to complain.

"I was going to call you," she said, pointedly not locking the door.

"I thought this was something we should discuss in person." He had a full list of reasons she should say yes. He'd considered emailing them to her during the week, but thought he might have more success face-to-face. He headed into the living room and made himself comfortable on the couch, just as he had last time.

"Jake." She hovered between the hall and living room. "I appreciate the offer, but I have to say no."

Since he'd been prepared for this, Jake wasn't taken aback. "Can I ask why?"

She came in from the hall and sat on the chair on the opposite side of the room. He'd have to cross the table and rug, not to mention her cool veneer, to even reach her. "I just don't think it's a good idea. I'm a cohost now. I can't just give that up to go racing around the world."

He nodded. "You wouldn't have to give it up. We can work around your schedule. I'm confident the airline would be amenable to that. And we can shoot on weekends."

She blinked at him. "Really?"

"Really." He'd even gone so far as to bounce the idea off the airline and Hanna to make sure they were flexible enough to accommodate such a schedule. "Is that your only concern?"

"No." But she didn't elaborate. She picked at the knee of her jeans. She was wearing one of those silky shirts that clung to her body and made him get all hot and bothered. He was glad he hadn't worn a jacket.

"What else then?"

"You."

"Meaning?"

"Meaning, things didn't go so well the last time we worked together." She still wasn't looking at him.

"I know, but this time it can be different." He was willing to let her set the tone. Friends, lovers, enemies, colleagues, whatever she wanted. "We can be different."

"Can we?"

He nodded and pulled out a sheaf of papers from the folder he'd carried in. "This is a contract I had drawn up for you. Of course, you can have a lawyer look it over, make suggestions or changes, but I think you'll see it offers fair compensation."

He slid the papers across the table toward her. She scooted forward far enough to pick them up, then moved. The cute little wrinkle between her brows appeared and he knew she'd gotten to the salary line. "This much?"

"That much." A pittance to ensure success. "Unless you want to ask for more."

"No." She shook her head. Her hair was longer now, and he imagined running his fingers down the length of it. "It's more than fair, but—"

"You'll get to stay at the station." He started talking before she could finish that thought. "You'll get to host your own show on the side and you'll make good money. I know it sounds like a lot of work and it will be. But it's also seasonal. We might have to film every weekend for the first month, but then we could slow to every other." And probably even further after they had a solid base of shows completed. "I know you were looking for an opportunity to prove what you're capable of. This is it."

"That's a hard pitch," she said.

"Just pointing out the benefits." He didn't mention the one that would have them in close proximity at least forty-eight hours a week. She was wavering; he could tell by the softening of her shoulders. He wasn't about to scare her off now.

She looked at the contract in her lap, then back at him. "And this is only for the first six months? After that we would either renegotiate or walk away?"

"Only the first six months." He tried not to think about what would happen if she said no, but his stomach muscles tightened. "If it helps, I'm willing to beg."

A surprised smile flickered across her lips and disappeared. "I won't say I haven't thought of that, but…" She looked at the contract then back at him. Her shoulders dipped. "I can't turn this down. You've got yourself a deal, Jake."

His tension melted away in a rush of pleasure.

"Great." This would just be the start. Spending all that time together, surely they'd find their way back to each other again. He smiled.

She didn't smile back. "I'm only agreeing to do the show. I'm not agreeing that we should—" she gestured between them "—whatever this is."

Disappointment was curtailed by the fact that no matter what she was saying, she clearly still felt the same way he did. It was almost more than he could stand. He forced himself not to rush over and swoop her into a long hug. "Absolutely." They could work back into it gradually. "Can I at least get a handshake?"

She stood and stuck her hand out. The moment he wrapped his fingers around hers, the "whatever" sizzled and threatened to ignite into a hot burn. He saw the flash mirrored in her eyes. She yanked her hand away. "Okay, well, thanks for coming by."

He left, managing a friendly smile and goodbye while every part of him wanted to turn around, grab her until she was pressed so close to him that there would be no beginning or end and hold her until she agreed that they should be together. In all ways.

He could wait.

Chapter 29

"So, are you going to tell me what's wrong or am I going to have to resort to badgering it out of you?"

Ava was so surprised by her mother's question, she nearly choked on her tea. She was pleased to recover with relative grace, which in this case meant not flinging herself around on her mother's couch as she attempted to cough liquid from her lungs. Flailing averted, she turned what she hoped was an innocent look her mother's way. "Pardon?"

"What's bothering you?" Never one to shy away from the question that would punch a hole in Ava's heart, Barbara got right to it. She sipped from her delicate china cup. "I didn't say anything during dinner because you're looking thin and I thought it was important that you eat, but there's clearly something wrong. I'd like to help."

Ava bought some time by sipping her own tea. If she'd known she had this to look forward to, she might have tried to pull off another scheduling conflict. "It's nothing, Mom. Just some work stuff."

Barbara merely raised a platinum eyebrow, the same even shade as her hair, and waited.

It was a game Ava was used to losing. "I'm going to be hosting Jake's travel show," she said in a rush. There—it was out. "And I'm not leaving the station, so you don't have to worry about career stability, okay?"

"Ava, that's fantastic."

It was the response she'd expected, but she wasn't feeling so fantastic inside. She was nervous, but she couldn't say that to her mother. For one thing, Barbara didn't get nervous. And for another, Ava had never come clean about her relationship with Jake.

"So why don't you look happy? Ava?" The gentleness of her mother's voice and the kind light in her eye made the thin veneer Ava had been clinging to start to crumble.

"I'm just worried, that's all." She could feel the shuddering in her chest. She didn't want to cry, but her eyes had other ideas. "I think I might be in over my head."

"Oh, darling." The second Ava started crying, Barbara was off the chair and onto the couch, opening her arms wide and hugging her close. "You're fine. It's okay." She made soothing shushing noises while Ava wept. The feel of her mother's steady hands stroking up and down her back, being surrounded by her familiar scent, only made Ava cry harder. "It's all right. Don't cry. What's bothering you?"

"I don't know," she sobbed.

"Then we'll figure it out together."

It took Ava another minute to gather her composure, but when she saw the look in her mother's eye she felt like crying all over again. "No." She raised a hand in warning. "If you say we're going to write a list, I cannot be held accountable for what might happen."

"Don't be silly, dear." Her mother patted her on the shoulder. "Everything makes more sense when you get it down on paper." Barbara rubbed her back a few more times before getting up to retrieve a pen and some paper from the antique writing desk that stood in the corner of the room. Ava used to do her homework at that desk, flipping down the front and pulling up a kitchen chair. Her mother had insisted when she'd learned that Ava's idea of homework while in her bedroom consisted of hurrying through her assignments and spending the rest of her time reading *Tiger Beat*.

Her mother sat back down, laying the creamy monogrammed stationery on the table and uncapping the felt-tipped pen she'd received from the hospital for twenty years of service. "Let's start from the beginning."

Since there was no good place to start, Ava just spilled everything out. Her belief that she was going to be the host of Jake's travel show, the effort she'd put into it, getting the cohost promotion, the fight with Jake, that she was spending most nights alone on her couch, and she was thinking of getting a cat. "They just look so sad online. Their furry little faces with no one to love them."

Her mother blinked at her. "I'm confused. You're upset about a cat?"

"No. I don't want to be a crazy cat lady."

Her mother shook her head and kept writing, then read the list over. "So the gist is that you and Jake broke up, but you've agreed to work with him on this project anyway and you're concerned that you might get your heart broken again?"

"How did you know that? I didn't tell you that."

"Really, dear? It's all here." She tapped the list with her pen. But when Ava started to tear up again, Barbara gathered her into a loving embrace. "Oh, Ava. Now do you see why I warned you about getting involved with a colleague?"

"I didn't expect it to turn out like this." She cried into her mother's shoulder until her eyes felt puffy. "And I still care about him."

"Does he feel the same way?"

"We didn't really talk about it." Well, Ava had told him that nothing was going to happen, but that had only been to protect her heart. He hadn't had to agree so readily. She sniffled. "I should probably just move on and forget about him." Except that was going to be tricky, given that they'd be spending a lot of time together.

"Do you think you can do that? Because you haven't been very successful this past month and a half." Ava would have been annoyed if it weren't so embarrassingly true. Her mother's fingers were cool as she brushed the hair off her face. "I think you need to talk to him face-to-face."

"No."

"Yes." Her mother nodded. "Call him and make an appointment to discuss this."

"It's not a business transaction, Mom. And no, that is not happening." She threw herself against the back of the couch and crossed her arms over her chest in a smooth motion that would have made her teenage self proud.

"Ava, you're being ridiculous."

"This coming from the woman who's avoided all romantic contact for twentysomething years."

A light flush colored her mother's cheeks. "We aren't

talking about my life, but for the record, I am seeing someone."

"What?" Ava's arms dropped to her sides and for the first time in weeks all thoughts of her own life vanished. "You? You're dating? A man?"

"Yes, a man."

"Who? Do I know him? Where did you meet him? How could you keep this a secret from me?"

"I met him on one of those computer sites."

Now Ava was really gobsmacked. "You met him online?" Who was this woman and what had she done with her mother? "How did you manage that? You can barely work email."

"I am perfectly adept at the email," Barbara said. "And one of the women at the office helped me. She often invites me to join her and her husband for evenings and said she was tired of me turning her down because I didn't have a date. So she set up, what is it called, a profile?"

Ava shook her head, still processing this chunk of information. She could only imagine what her mother's profile would read. Urban professional seeks same. Must like: eating out, antiquing and having someone up in your business at all times. "I can't believe you're online dating."

"That's not technically true anymore." A small smile flitted across her lips. "Or is it still dating when you're only seeing one person?

Not only was her mother dipping her toes into the dating pool, but she'd actually met someone that had tempted her enough to dive in? "Give me a minute." Ava put a hand to her heart. "This is kind of a shock."

Barbara waited a grand total of about thirty seconds

and then said, "Enough about me. Will you call Jake tonight or wait until morning?"

But Ava was still stuck on the fact that her mother had a better and busier love life than she did. "Is that how you changed your cell ringtone?" The color in Barbara's cheeks darkened. "I knew you couldn't have done that on your own."

"As it turns out, I did do it on my own. With a little help from Gary."

"Gary. Now we're getting somewhere. And what does Gary do for a living?"

"He's a psychiatrist."

"Of course he is." Since Barbara couldn't get Ava into medical school, this was obviously the next best thing. Ava shook her head. "I cannot believe that my mother is dating a shrink."

"That is a derogatory term for someone who helps people in great need." Barbara brushed at the knees of her pants. "And he would say that you are showing classic signs of avoidance."

"How is this avoidance? I'm showing interest in your life."

"Yes, but only because you'd rather not deal with your own." Barbara reached out and tucked a lock of Ava's hair into place. "Gary says you can't live your life being afraid to try. Well, actually you can, but it isn't really living."

Ava pondered that, considered how things might play out if she were to phone Jake and tell him that she needed to see him. Fear closed her throat. She took a shaky sip of tea to ease it. "So you think I should what—try again? Tell Jake that I need more time? Or say that pigs will fly first?"

"It isn't my decision."

"That's never stopped you from telling me what to do before." Ava could think of a thousand examples. From what kind of degree she should get to what kind of cereal she should eat for breakfast, Barbara Christensen always had an opinion that she wasn't afraid to share.

"Gary told me that my need to advise comes from a need to control things. I've decided that's something I should work on."

"Did he?" Ava grinned. "I think I might like this guy."

"You will," Barbara said. "I want you to do what makes you happy. Go see Jake. You'll know what to say."

But that's where her mother was wrong. Ava didn't have a clue and she wasn't sure she was ready to find out.

"You haven't talked to him since you agreed to do the show?"

Ava was out for dinner with Jilly at a Japanese restaurant after work on Wednesday. Ava was still wearing her heavy eye makeup from the show, but Jilly swore it looked good. Like Cleopatra and not a Goth.

"I don't know what to say to him." A spread of small plates sat on the table in front of them as they waited for Hanna, but where Jilly was digging in, Ava could only pick.

"Yeah, no. That's not going to work."

"Why not?" Ava had figured it all out. She'd even, much to her chagrin, written a list. And while it didn't expose all the deep secrets she was hoping for, it had helped her to decide that the only approach she was comfortable with was of the wait-and-see nature. But she still wasn't telling her mother she was right.

"It won't work," Jilly said, "because you still love him."

"Who loves him?" Hanna dropped onto the low couch beside Jilly and crossed her legs. "I love a good love story."

"No one loves anyone," Ava said quickly. "I don't know what Jilly's talking about." And she shot her best friend a look that told her to zip her lips. Hanna had become a friend, but she was also friends with Jake, and Ava couldn't risk anything getting back to him.

"Ava and Jake," Jilly answered as though Ava had never even glanced in her direction.

"Jilly."

"What?" She shrugged and tossed her hair, which was still Hello Kitty pink. "I don't know why you're fighting it. You're clearly still cuckoo for him."

"I'm not," Ava said, feeling embarrassment crawl up her neck and onto her cheeks.

"So you just decided to do the travel show out of the goodness of your heart?"

"It was a good opportunity." But she could hear how weak she sounded. Because, of course, the truth was more than that.

The travel show was his dream. A chance to make his own reputation. And he'd asked for her help. She wouldn't have been able to live with herself if she'd turned him down.

"It was the right decision," she told Jilly.

Hanna nodded. "Not to mention it wouldn't have happened without you."

Ava's heart skipped a beat then resumed its rhythm double time. "Pardon?"

"You know." Hanna popped a sushi roll into her mouth and chewed slowly before answering. "The airline people wanted you. They weren't going to green-light the show otherwise. I told Jake to just tell you that, but he had this weird idea that you had to agree to do the show without his influence."

"He did?" Her voice was faint, which made sense because she didn't feel a if she could breathe.

"Yes, even if it meant there would be no show." She shrugged and ate another roll. "I told him he was crazy, but he was insistent." Hanna smiled. "Anyway, I'm glad it all worked out."

Ava swallowed some tea, but it did nothing to ease the sudden buzzing in her ears. What did Hanna mean, exactly, that Jake had been willing to let the show go?

She watched Hanna's lips move. Apparently, she said something funny, because Jilly laughed. Ava forced her lips into a grin as though she, too, was highly amused by Hanna's witticism. But she was still thinking about the bomb Hanna had just dropped.

Would Jake really have let his dream go? Or was that just something he'd said to Hanna? And why would he say it if he didn't mean it?

Her mind swirled, thoughts colliding and crashing. She pushed herself up from the couch. Both Hanna and Jilly turned to look at her.

"Everything okay?"

"No." But it would be. "I have to go. There's something I have to do." Someone to see. She grabbed her bag and headed for the door, dodging through the after-work crowd in her high-heeled boots without slowing down.

Chapter 30

"Why didn't you tell me about the airline?"

A light rain had begun to fall by the time Ava hopped out of the cab in front of Jake's town house. She could feel it soaking into her hair. She didn't care. She tucked her hands into the pockets of her coat and waited, watching his expression morph from surprise to confusion.

He blinked at her. "What?"

"The airline," she repeated, and shouldered her way inside, ignoring the spark of attraction that ran through her at the minor contact. "Why didn't you tell me that they made the deal depend on me being host?"

He stared at her, looked her slowly up and down as though she were an ice-cream cone he wanted to lick, and then chugged from the beer bottle he was holding.

"Jake." She pushed the door closed behind her, reminding herself that she was not dessert. "Why didn't you tell me?"

"You're here."

"And waiting for an answer." Her nerves were on high alert, jangling against each other. She clamped her arms to her sides and tried to think calming thoughts.

He exhaled and rubbed his thumb around the rim of the bottle. "Hanna told you."

"She mentioned it in passing." Ava brushed the water from her hair. "Why didn't you?"

"I considered it." He took another sip from the bottle, his eyes never leaving hers. "Decided that it wasn't fair to you."

"Fair how?" Her arms dropped, making the beads of water on her jacket drip to the floor.

"I didn't want you to feel obligated."

"So instead you just offered me a contract that most people would kill for?" He'd practically given her the stars and moon.

He shrugged. "I wanted you to take the job."

"You should have told me."

"Maybe." He leaned a shoulder against the wall. "But then I wouldn't have known if you were taking the job because you wanted it."

There was silence for a moment, broken only by the patter of rain as it hit the window. Ava stared at him. He stared back, those clear gray eyes that saw everything. Her throat went dry and, without thinking, she plucked the beer from his hand and took a drink.

"What if I'd said no?"

"Then you'd have said no." Jake shrugged again.

"That doesn't make sense." She frowned. He'd worked so hard, she couldn't understand why he'd risk losing it all now. "If all you needed was my participation, you would have told me that. So why the big secret?"

She studied him, thinking how good he looked even with messy hair and a ketchup spot on his T-shirt.

"It wasn't a secret."

Ava dragged her eyes from his torso. Right. His eyes were up there. "But you didn't mention it. God, Jake. What if I'd said no? Were you willing to just let the show die?"

"Actually, I was."

"What?" It wasn't the answer she'd expected. She'd thought about it on her cab ride over and come to the conclusion that Hanna had been misinformed.

"This isn't just about the show, Ava. You know that." He took the beer from her suddenly numb fingers and smiled that slow crooked smile that made her stomach flip. "If it meant I could have a chance with you, I was more than willing to let the show go."

"But." She reminded herself that she still hadn't forgiven him yet, but it was hard when his eyes were crinkling at the corners and he was sipping from the bottle, putting his lips where hers had just been.

She felt the sizzle that always marked their interactions flare up, threatening to make her walk into his arms, close her eyes and forget about everything that had left her feeling broken these past few weeks. She fought back. "Why didn't you say anything?"

"I didn't want to scare you off."

She flipped her hair and wished her knees didn't feel quite so wobbly. "I think I might need to sit down for this."

She followed him into the living room, leaving her coat and boots on. It was the first time she'd been to his house since the night she'd shown up after dinner at her mother's. Though he'd only been back in town a week, it looked much more lived-in than before. There was a long beige sectional in the living room, along with a side chair and coffee table. There was even a print on the wall and she could see the kitchen chairs she'd helped him pick out around the dining table.

"Your place looks nice," she told him, needing a minute to compose herself. "Settled."

"Yeah." He waited until she took a seat—the chair to ensure he couldn't get too close to her—and then sat on the left side of the couch nearest to her. "That's because I'm staying this time."

Ava could feel a rogue trickle of sweat moving down her back. She should have taken off her coat, but just as she'd been about to shrug out of it she'd had this panicked thought that if things didn't go well, she'd need to make a quick getaway, and dealing with her boots would already be too much. Why hadn't she thought to wear flats today of all days? Seriously, she was going to break an ankle streaking down the sidewalk and then Jake would probably have to rescue her again.

"You okay?" he asked.

"Fine," she lied, wondering if her cheeks were as red as they felt. She pressed her fingers to them, first one side then the other. He'd been willing to let the show go for her. She swallowed. "I don't understand what made you change your mind."

When he'd moved back to Toronto and started working for his father, she hadn't thought she'd ever see him again.

"Us."

She raised an eyebrow at him. "There's an us now?"

"There was always an us, Ava."

He was right. Even as far back as that anti–Valentine's Day party they'd been circling each other, their orbits always colliding. They'd only managed to avoid it through sheer stubbornness and stupidity. "I know."

She reminded herself to breathe slowly. In and out. And not to hyperventilate. "Why did you leave without saying anything?"

"I was angry and you were avoiding me." So her little ruse hadn't gone undetected.

"You knew where to find me."

"I thought you wanted it that way."

She had. Though it was hard to believe now when all she wanted to do was reach out and run her hand over his cheek, feel the familiar line of his jaw, the stubble on his chin. "What happens now?"

"I'm staying," he repeated, and leaned a little closer to her. "Because leaving the first time was a huge mistake and one that my family has chewed me out about. If it helps."

"It does." She felt a smile tickle the edges of her mouth.

He reached out and wrapped his hand over hers. She felt the heat seep into her skin, wanted to wallow in it. "I want to do this together, Ava."

She ignored the quaking in her belly and was glad she was already sitting down. She desperately wanted things to go back to the way they were, wanted to trust him, but she was scared. What if it didn't work out? She wouldn't just be risking her heart, but her career, too. And she'd be left with nothing.

"Ava." His voice whispered through her, making her shiver. "You don't have to decide this second. I'll wait."

"No." She shook her head. She didn't want to wait.

She needed to know now. "Would you have still come back even if there was no show?"

He nodded. "I have some connections. I could probably talk my father into opening a West Coast branch of his company that I could run."

That was unexpected. He'd been so adamant about not working with his father. "Really? With your dad?" He nodded, and she smiled. "What brought on this change of heart?"

"I did some growing up. Realized what's important." He squeezed her hand. "And what isn't. I want to do the show, Ava. But I want to be with you more. It's an easy decision, if you're asking me to choose."

"No." That thought had never crossed her mind. "I wouldn't want that."

He tilted his head toward her. "What do you want?"

Him. Always him. "I want you to do the show and I want to be a part of it." Her heart beat faster, like a drum solo in her chest. "Also, you are not allowed to fire me ever."

It took less than 2.2 seconds for him to haul her onto his lap, holding her so tightly that for a moment she couldn't breathe. Or maybe that was just the thrill of being so near him again when she'd been sure that would never happen.

"Christ, Ava." His lips were all over her face, her neck, his hands grasping and stroking every inch of her. "I missed you so much. When I thought I'd lost you..."

"You almost did," she told him. "You're lucky I'm so forgiving."

He laughed, sending a puff of air brushing over her neck. "I am lucky." He hugged her closer. "I'm not going to let you change your mind, either. You're stuck with me now, and I don't plan to let you forget it."

Since that sounded pretty good to her, Ava wasn't complaining. She lay her head on his chest, listening to the steady thump of his heart. It felt right.

"I want to hear you say it."

"Hmm?" She lifted her head to look at him.

Her clothes felt too tight. It was so warm in here. He ran his hand up the back of her coat, which was much too heavy to be wearing anyway, and cupped the back of her head, turning it until she was facing him. "Look at me and tell me that you want the job."

She raised one hand and placed it over her heart. "I solemnly swear that I want the job."

"And me?"

She knew that look in his eyes and shivered in delicious anticipation. "And you."

"Is that all?"

"Isn't that enough?" She kissed him once, then again, until they were both breathing harder. Her heart was so full that she was sure it would burst and it would be wonderful.

He cupped her face and looked at her. "No, you have to promise that the next time I act like an idiot, you'll stick around."

"I'm not the one who left," she pointed out, watching as he unbuttoned her coat, spreading the heavy fabric wide.

"I'm not leaving again." He spanned her stomach with his hands, slipped them around her back and beneath her silky tee. She ached at his touch. "I was going crazy without you."

She shivered from his words and his hands. Her skin

grew tight with need. She closed her eyes and let her head droop. "I was going crazy, too." His fingers were doing the most delightful things, making her insides feel all fuzzy. She missed this, missed him so badly. She wanted more—more of this, more of him. She gasped when his fingers hit a particularly sweet spot and felt a shudder of pleasure melt her brain. And slipped right off the edge of the cliff.

He was murmuring in her ear, the combination of hands and words drowning her in need. And that's when those three little words she hadn't dared to say, to even think, just slipped out as if they'd been lying in wait.

"I love you, Jake."

She felt him still and her eyes popped open immediately. Oh, no. No, no, no. It wasn't supposed to come out like that. He was studying her, but she couldn't read his gaze. Oh, God.

This was all wrong. He was supposed to say it first and she was supposed to look up at him with large, coy eyes and smile sweetly before telling him that she loved him, too. Now he was going to get all panicky and weird and tell her that things were moving too fast.

"I mean *that*. I love that." But it was too late. They both knew it. Ava closed her eyes and ducked her head. She was not looking at him. No way. No how. She wanted to die, wanted a big hole to open up in the floor that she could jump into and never return.

He caught her chin, forced it up. "Say it again."

His eyes burned into her. She swallowed, lifted her chin without his help. "I love that."

"No." His eyes were dark. "The other thing." She squeezed her eyes shut. "And look at me when you do."

Fear clawed at her throat, and her skin itched. She

tensed, preparing to jump off his lap, stumble out the door and away from him. And if she broke an ankle in her escape? Small price to pay.

But his hands were locked around her hips, holding her firmly in place. And she knew she wasn't going to get away quite so easily.

"Ava."

Why did he have to say her name? Why now? When she was so near to breaking?

"Tell me."

She opened her eyes slowly, telling herself that it was best to meet this kind of challenge head-on. Her heart accelerated, but her voice was clear. "I think we both know what I said."

"We do, but I'd like to hear it just to be sure."

She glared at him.

"Don't be shy." He slipped a hand up her back, the feel of his palm on her skin making her shiver. Her fear slipped and then drifted away. He wasn't pushing her to say it again just so he could tell her he wasn't interested.

"You first," she said.

He laughed. "Too late for that. Say it." His eyes softened and he pressed a tender kiss to her jawline. "Please." His lips trailed up to her ear.

Ava's toes curled. "I hate you for making me do this." She gasped when he ran his tongue across her neck. "But I love you."

"That's what I thought." She got a flash of that smug smirk of his before he kissed her hard and hot and so perfectly that Ava almost forgot he hadn't returned the sentiment.

Almost.

"Hey." She pulled back and frowned at him. "I'm not

the only one who should be saying something here."
Where was his declaration of undying love? His claim
that she completed him? She'd even settle for a little
kissing of her feet. "Don't you want to say something?"

"Yes, you're hired." His hand cupped her head,
pulled her toward him for one of those brain-washing
kisses. She could feel the smile on his lips when they
touched hers.

"I already had the job, remember?" She turned her
head to the side, shivered when he trailed his mouth
down her neck instead. "But that's not what I'm waiting
to hear. And just in case you're wondering, you aren't
getting any of this—" she gestured to herself "—until
you do say it."

He laughed, head thrown back, the tension that had
been bracketing his eyes gone. "You say the sweetest
things."

"Still waiting."

He captured her hands when she rested them against
his chest. She could feel the thump of his heart echo
through her. "I love you, Ava."

She pulled one hand free, ran it through his hair and
tugged him forward so their lips were touching. "Was
that so hard?"

EntNewsNow.com/avasblog

So Long, Farewell

Big news. Along with my current gig as cohost of *Entertainment News Now,* I will be hosting a travel show, as well. (Look for me on airplanes soon!)

But all this extra work means I won't have time to update this blog with any regularity. This will be the last official post. I've loved every minute of it, but it's time to move on. Wishing you all much love and excellent gossip.

Kiss kiss,

Ava

* * * * *

THE WORLD IS BETTER WITH

Romance

Harlequin has everything from contemporary, passionate and heartwarming to suspenseful and inspirational stories.

Whatever your mood, we have a romance just for you!

Connect with us to find your next great read, special offers and more.

f /HarlequinBooks

🐦 @HarlequinBooks

www.HarlequinBlog.com

www.Harlequin.com/Newsletters

HARLEQUIN®

A *Romance* FOR EVERY MOOD™

www.Harlequin.com

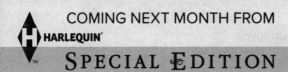
#2395 THE TAMING OF DELANEY FORTUNE
The Fortunes of Texas: Cowboy Country • by Michelle Major
Francisco Mendoza is having a bout of bad Fortune. Though he's been hired to help with the new Cowboy Country theme park, Cisco is told to lasso a member of the famous Fortune clan to help him out. So he courts spunky rancher Delaney Fortune Jones under the guise of helping him with his project...but falls for her instead! Can Delaney and Cisco find love in their very own pastures?

#2396 A DECENT PROPOSAL
The Bachelors of Blackwater Lake • by Teresa Southwick
When billionaire Burke Holden enters McKnight Automotive, he gets more than just an oil change. When beautiful mechanic Sydney McKnight asks him to be her pretend boyfriend, the sexy single dad happily accepts. But no-strings-attached can't last forever, especially since Burke's vowed to stay commitment-free. It might just take a true Montana miracle to give the Big Sky bachelor and the brunette beauty their very own happily-ever-after.

#2397 MEANT-TO-BE MOM
Jersey Boys • by Karen Templeton
Cole Rayburn's back home in Maple River, New Jersey...but he's definitely not a kid anymore. For one, he's got sole custody of his *own* two children; second, his boyhood best friend, Sabrina Noble, is all grown-up and easy on the eyes. Sabrina has just called off a disastrous engagement, so she's not looking to get buddy-buddy with any man...but it's soon clear that her bond with Cole is still very much alive. And he's not planning on letting her go—ever!

#2398 THE CEO'S BABY SURPRISE
The Prestons of Crystal Point • by Helen Lacey
Daniel Anderson is the richest and most arrogant man in town. He's also the most charming, and Mary-Jayne Preston falls under his spell—for one night. But that's all it takes for Mary-Jayne to fall pregnant with twins! The devastatingly handsome Daniel isn't daddy material, or so she thinks. As the mogul and the mom-to-be grow closer, can Daniel overcome his own tragic past to create a bright future with Mary-Jayne and their twins?

#2399 HIS SECRET SON
The Pirelli Brothers • by Stacy Connelly
Ten years ago, one night changed Lindsay Brookes's life forever, giving her a beloved son. But it didn't seem to mean as much to Ryder Kincaid, who went back to his cheerleader girlfriend. Now Lindsay is back home in Clearville, California, to tell her long-ago fling that he's a father. Already brokenhearted from a bitter divorce, Ryder is flabbergasted at this change of fortune...but little Trevor could bring together the family he's always dreamed of.

#2400 OH, BABY
The Crandall Lake Chronicles • by Patricia Kay
Sophie Marlowe and Dillon Burke parted ways long ago, but Fate has reunited the long-lost lovers. Sophie's young half sister and Dillon's nephew are expecting a baby, and it's up to these exes to help the youngsters create a happy family. Though the rakish former football player and the responsible guidance counselor seem to be complete opposites, there's no denying the irresistible attraction between them... and where there's smoke, there are flames of true love!

YOU CAN FIND MORE INFORMATION ON UPCOMING HARLEQUIN® TITLES, FREE EXCERPTS AND MORE AT WWW.HARLEQUIN.COM.

HSECNM0315

*To placate her father, Sydney McKnight convinced
Burke Holden to be her temporary boyfriend. But could
a temporary relationship of convenience turn into a
forever love?*

*Read on for a sneak preview of
A DECENT PROPOSAL,
the latest volume in
Teresa Southwick's miniseries
THE BACHELORS OF BLACKWATER LAKE.*

"I don't know why you're willing to go along with this but
I'm grateful. Seriously, thanks."

"You're welcome."

Oddly enough it had been an easy decision. The simple
answer was that he'd agreed because she had asked and he
wanted to see her again. Granted, he could have asked her
out, but he'd already have had a black mark against him
because of turning down her request. Now she owed him.

Sydney leaned against the bar, a thoughtful look on her
face. "I've never done anything like this before, but I know
my father. He'll ask questions. In fact he already did. We're
going to need a cover story. How we met. How long we've
been dating. That sort of thing."

"It makes sense to be prepared."

"So we should get together soon and discuss it."

"What about right now?" Burke suggested.

Her eyes widened. "You don't waste time, do you?"

"No time like the present. Have you already had dinner?"

She shook her head. "Why?"

"Do you have a date?" If not, there was a very real possibility that she'd changed into the red blazer, skinny jeans and heels just for him. Probably wanted to look her best while making her case. Still, he really hoped she wasn't meeting another guy.

She gave him an ironic look. "Seriously? If I was going out with someone, I wouldn't have asked you to participate in this crazy scheme."

"Crazy? I don't know, it's a decent proposal." He shrugged. "So you're free. Have dinner with me. What about the restaurant here at the lodge? It's pretty good."

"The best in town." But she shook her head. "Too intimate."

So she didn't want to be alone with him. "Oh?"

"Something more public. People should see us together." She snapped her fingers. "The Grizzly Bear Diner would be perfect."

"I know the place. Both charming. And romantic."

"You're either being a smart-ass or a snob."

"Heaven forbid."

"You haven't been there yet?" she asked.

"No, I have."

He signaled the bartender, and when she handed the bill to him, he took care of it. Then he settled his hand at the small of her back and said, "Let the adventure begin."

Don't miss
A DECENT PROPOSAL
by Teresa Southwick,
available April 2015 wherever
Harlequin® Special Edition books and ebooks are sold.

www.Harlequin.com

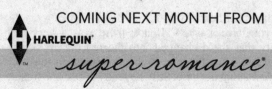

COMING NEXT MONTH FROM

HARLEQUIN

super romance

Available April 7, 2015